ROSIE
in the garden

BOOK ONE

A NOVEL

DIANE C. SHORE

DCShore Publishing
dcshorepublishing.com

ISBN: 0-9905231-8-7
ISBN-13: 978-0-9905231-8-5

2.3

DEDICATION

To my Lord and Savior, Jesus Christ.
May Your Name be honored above all.

Mentorship

1

It started in a garden...doesn't everything? The soil is tilled. The seed is planted. And out grows something in our lives, good or bad, that changes the path we are on.

* _ * _ * _ * _ *

Spring 2017

Rebecca's life just took an unexpected turn down a path she knew very little about. She walked into a church searching for something...anything, to help how lost and alone she felt each day. She made a surprising decision that morning. She said "yes" when asked if she wanted to have a relationship with Jesus. She raised her hand when the invitation was given. What was she thinking? What was she doing? And who were those people surrounding her in that new setting?

After some prayers that sounded strange, and a Bible being placed in her hand that she knew she wouldn't understand, Rebecca walked out of church thinking she would never return. Why should she? Oh, she was moved for a moment. The music was good. The coffee was okay, And the message she heard made some sense at the time; at least parts of it did. But now she was barely able to remember it. Tomorrow she would go back to work—back to her life, and probably forget all about today. Something inside of her hoped she wouldn't. But she knew herself. She had reached out for help before and it didn't last long, even with the best therapists. This world didn't seem to offer what she needed. Why were others able to cope? Why were they happy? She wondered where the emptiness started?

But even more, she wanted to know where it would end?

As Rebecca left the building, the sun seemed a little more comforting. At first, she didn't notice it. But when she got in her car, the warmth inside settled a little deeper into her bones...maybe even her soul. As she pushed the button to start her car, nothing happened. Why didn't it start? The battery? The starter? Seriously? "Didn't I just go to church?" she muttered to herself. "Didn't I just say yes to You God? And now You've let me down already? I knew this was all hocus pocus. I should have just slept in this morning instead of coming here. Now I'm stuck."

Rebecca recalled she had let her road service lapse a few months ago. Now she regretted neglecting it because she knew no one here. Everyone was walking to their cars with their families, smiling and laughing. She grumbled, "Oh, you're all so happy! But I'm here all alone in this stinking hot car that won't start. Arghhhhh!!!!!"

The sweat on Rebecca's brow was beginning to roll down the sides of her face. She didn't want to leave the privacy of her car until the after-church crowd was gone—some lingered and visited nearby. She didn't want to seem helpless, although wasn't that why she came to church this morning? But that was between her and a God who may or may not exist. Checking her phone, it read 9:48. Her friend started work soon, so she couldn't call her for help. She might as well get out and start walking. It wasn't that far home, and home would bring her the solitude she craved. Rebecca lived alone, and that's the way she liked it after her divorce—no one to argue with. Then again, there was no one to help her right now either. Don probably wouldn't even answer his phone if she tried it. There had been too many unkind words said, and feelings hurt, to even try going down that path.

Suddenly, Rebecca's phone rang. It startled her! It was an unfamiliar number, so she ignored it. Probably another sales call. But it made her think...Nelson lives nearby. Why didn't she think of him before? He always has time for people, and he wouldn't mind helping her at all. She met Nelson about a year ago in the pouring rain. Dropping some groceries out of her bag in the grocery store parking lot, they started up a conversation that soon turned into a cup of coffee. That conversation didn't lead to anything, but she got a new friend to talk to from time to time. Nelson always offered his help should she ever need it. She looked for his number, and hit the button...Nelson answered almost immediately.

"Hi there, Becca!" He was the only one to ever call her that.

"Hi, Nelson. What's up? Are you busy?" Even this call was hard for Rebecca. Would he think she was weak?

"For you? Never? What can I help you with?" Nelson said warmly.

"I'm just down the street from you at that church called Forever His.

For some reason, my car won't start. Could you come to my rescue?"

"Sure, Becca. I'll be right there. Hang tight."

As the minutes passed, it gave Rebecca some time to ponder Nelson. What set him apart from other men she knew? And why didn't they ever take it past the friendship stage? It was hard to figure. Nelson was a nice enough looking man, just a head taller than her, light brown hair, and a strong but not too rugged face. Nelson had never initiated anything. He was always such a gentleman, with no hint of romance even being on his mind. Rebecca appreciated that after her divorce. She didn't need another complicated set of feelings to sort through. She and Nelson seemed content to just relax in each other's company.

The lingering churchgoers were almost gone now, and Rebecca stepped outside her car for fresh air. She walked around a bit, noticing the beautiful freshly planted flowers and the mulch that covered the ground surrounding them. She wished for a green thumb, but it was never her strong suit. It was spring in the Bay Area, and a warmer day than usual for this time of the year. Off in the distance she could hear the freeway traffic. But mostly, it was quiet and peaceful. She found a bench under a tree, and waited for Nelson. It wasn't long, and his truck pulled into the parking lot. As usual, he jumped out with a big smile on his face, and greeted her with a generous hug and, "It's always good to see you Becca." The two of them made their way back over to the car. Nelson tried to give it a start. It was dead. Hooking some jumper cables to the batteries, it started without hesitation, Rebecca felt relief. Perhaps her lights were left on. With a few miles of driving to recharge the battery, the problem would be solved. Oh, if only all her problems in life could be solved that quickly. Nelson popped off the cables, and lowered the hood of her car. It clanked when it shut, as if to say, "The job is finished."

Nelson glanced over at Rebecca standing there, a bit of a distance from the car. Her dress accentuated her blue eyes. Even in flats, she appeared tall at about 5'8". Did her slender build come from exercise or healthy eating? He wondered about this woman who always seemed so stressed, but also kind. What was it that bothered her so? Why so standoffish? Who wounded her soul to create such a wall of resistance to those around her? It took him months to see that wall come down a bit and welcome a conversation that wasn't so strained. When less guarded, he found Becca to be very interesting. Nelson knew taking his time with her was best. He would be patient.

"Thank you so much, Nelson. You saved my morning, and my day!"

"Becca, it's not a problem at all. I needed to run to the store anyway, and you just got me up and out a bit earlier. Is there anything else I can do for you?" Nelson inquired.

"Nope, that's it! I appreciate your quick response and help."

"Call me anytime. Bye now!" Nelson said cheerfully.

"See ya!" Rebecca said, as she quickly got into her car and drove away, barely looking back.

2

Monday came much too early as Rebecca woke up and got ready for work. The weekend was okay, even with the car trouble. It's odd that it allowed her to see Nelson again. She was wondering about him the past few weeks. She was also curious about the church thing. Why had she really gone? It didn't seem to make much difference. Although she wouldn't have seen Nelson if she hadn't. Would her car still have had problems, even though now it seemed to be doing fine? What was that all about anyway? Was it part of God's plan to put them together again? Does God really work in ways like that? Rebecca didn't think so, but she was entertaining the thought. And they were just friends anyway, so what would be the point? Nelson seemed a bit surprised when she told him she was in a church parking lot. Did he think it was odd? Should she ask him? She really did want to know more about Nelson. But she liked that it seemed he was more interested in her than she was in him. For now, she was fine with that. Not many had taken an interest in her life since the divorce. It was nice to find someone who would sit and listen. She would need to call him soon.

Preparing her coffee, Rebecca noticed she was about out. A run to the grocery store was on her "to do" list for the day. She was glad she could trust her car again after driving into the foothills after church and recharging the battery. After a very rainy year, everything was so green. It reminded her of her time in Ireland. The sky was blue, with a few puffy clouds that blocked the sun from time to time. Rising out of the congestion Sunday afternoon made it seem not just like another country, but another world. Such busy-ness below, such beauty above. The drive not only recharged her car battery, but also her soul. She wondered about God on the drive...could He really be true? Did He really create the world she was looking at? Did that bird that just soared by really get its flight from a big old Father in Heaven who looked down on all of us? Could He hear all our prayers at once?

Rebecca prayed more than usual recently. Her hurting heart needed it. A good friend had just lost her battle with cancer, and it seemed so hard to believe she was really gone. After arriving home from the hospital that day, and doing something as simple as washing the dishes, Rebecca thought how Bonnie would no longer have to do dishes. It seemed unfair. Bonnie's problems were finished. Her worries were over. She got to leave this all behind, and be free of the stresses of this world. And yet, Rebecca really had no idea where Bonnie went. Did Heaven exist? And if it did, is that where Bonnie was now? How would Rebecca ever know? Maybe that's what caused her to finally go to church on Sunday. She pondered...did somebody there have the answer? The pastor talked about Heaven, just a bit, but he didn't really describe what it would be like. He talked more about how to get there...something about Jesus' death. How could a man's death make a way to Heaven for anyone? She would have to go back and listen more. Maybe she could find the answer. For now, it just seemed confusing, and wrong. It seemed like just more sadness. A man had died, and Bonnie had died. How were they linked together? Maybe that's why she raised her hand when the invitation to know Jesus was given at the end...maybe all she was saying was, "I have a question. Can you answer it for me?"

Rebecca's mind wandered throughout the day. She thought about Bonnie not even having to go to work anymore. She was sad, as waves of grief washed over her and brought tears to her eyes. She and Bonnie had been friends for over 30 years. She missed her. Bonnie knew her like no one else did, and now she felt unknown in the world. Without a sibling to share life with, and with her parents being elderly and suffering with their own health issues, Rebecca didn't have many friends or family to turn to. The divorce actually caused divisions in past friendships. Most sided with her ex, Don, for some reason. Maybe it was her pushing them away in her discomfort of all that had transpired. Don was always the more outgoing one anyway, so he might as well enjoy their friends. Rebecca could move on. But doing so was turning out to be so much harder than she expected. Making new friends was complicated. Rebecca mostly buried herself in work, and acted like everything was okay in her sensible little world.

Rebecca sat in the shade outside her office for lunch, enjoying the warm spring day. The food seemed to fill a bit of her emptiness. Some squirrels were having their own fun on the lawn, and the birds seemed to be particularly enjoying the new leaves coming out on the trees. Allergy season was on the way. Rebecca could feel an itchiness in her eyes and nose, but she resisted taking anything just yet. Maybe she could get by another day without suffering from it too much. She caught sight of a couple walking by arm in arm. It made her miss being two instead of one. But then, not. That involved so much she wasn't willing to give anymore. In the beginning, she and Don were a good match. He was nice, and she laughed a lot with him. It seemed a happy time. But marriage took its toll on them when kids weren't possible. They started drifting apart. Don so wanted children. She didn't care as much one way or the other. After years of trying, she stopped wanting to try. That broke Don's heart. It took two to make a marriage, and a baby, so Don lost interest in her as a wife. It wasn't his fault, really. She had already withdrawn most of her love from him, leaving Don lonely even when they were together. Don tried to hang in there, until the day when he couldn't anymore. Then he quietly and tearfully asked her for a divorce. She knew it was coming, long before the sad words were spoken. By the time Don voiced the inevitable, she was already separated in her heart. She agreed without hesitation. She wanted Don to have someone who could satisfy his longings, and she knew she was not that person. At the end, she actually didn't want to be. She desired her own happiness more. Rebecca admitted that she was selfish. But just unselfish enough to let him go and find the love he was so deserving of. Their marriage was over.

With lunch finished, Rebecca reentered the office and finished out her work day, almost without thinking about it. Her job wasn't complicated. She managed the front desk, doing a bit of administrative work, handling phone calls, and making sure the office flowed easily so her boss, Ben, didn't have to think about anything but his own job. As long as Ben was not hassled, Rebecca was not hassled, and she liked it that way. They were a good team. She worked with Ben for about fifteen years, so he had seen her marriage come and go. He had probably seen Rebecca age 10 years in the last five, also. Sadly, that can happen. The very life can be sucked right out of a person. Ben, on the other hand, had been married many years. He was a good man, and his wife, Lucy, was joyful to the core. She always came into the office laughing and happy to see Ben. Sometimes Lucy would just come in to drop off his lunch, and be on her way. Other times they would go out for a bite together. With one grown son and an old dog, they seemed well suited. It was heartwarming to watch them, knowing that sometimes marriage can be a very good thing.

At the grocery store on the way home, Rebecca found herself lost in the bakery section. She always loved getting the piece of cake made for one, although she usually split it up to last her three days. That's what living alone can be like, with no one else there sharing your food. She knew it was time to move out of the bakery section after putting the cake and other goodies into her basket—this was not the way to stay healthy. But so far, this junk food hadn't harmed her too much. She had always had a good metabolism. Maybe one day, she would regret these decisions. The lines up front were longer than Rebecca had hoped for, but she found the one with her favorite quick checker. She overheard the checker talking about his back pain one day, and interestingly enough, the woman he was telling it to actually prayed for him on the spot. Rebecca never saw anything like that. She thought that was a very bold thing to do. The checker seemed okay with it. Rebecca watched as the two of them acted like this was just a normal everyday occurrence. She wondered how she would respond if someone offered to pray that way for her. She didn't believe it would help anything. How could it, when it was a physical problem? Rebecca didn't really understand it all. But she did find it amazing that others believed in it so much. Sometimes she would switch the channels on the TV and find pastors talking and praying about healing. Several seemed fake, others real enough. How was she to tell the truth from the lies? She didn't know.

At last it was her turn, and Ronnie, as it said on his nametag, got her speedily through. Rebecca could tell his back still hurt him, and she wondered how he could work every day in such pain. She guessed he probably had no choice. As Rebecca made her way to her car and opened the door to set her groceries on the front seat, she noticed the Bible that had been left there from Sunday. It looked scary to her. It seemed too thick, and too wordy to be of any use. She quickly piled her grocery bags on top of it, and tried not to think about it. But think about it, she did…maybe she would just take the Bible home and put it on the coffee table? Or maybe she would just leave it in the car…she really didn't know what to do with it. Rebecca wished they had never given it to her. It's not like she could throw it out with the day's junk mail. She knew enough to know that would be totally disrespectful. This aggravated her…she didn't need one more thing to be worried about.

Suddenly, "BECCA!... BECCA!" interrupted her thoughts from across the parking lot.

Rebecca turned to see Nelson. She didn't know if seeing him so soon after yesterday was good. She would have preferred to give it some time. She didn't want Nelson to have the wrong impression of what she felt about him, because she really didn't know what she felt. But here he was, and it would be hard to ignore him at this point. Putting on a fake smile, she called back to him, "Hi Nelson!"

Nelson was walking toward her. She hoped there was a way to make this quick. She had gotten ice cream to go with the cake. That would help.

"Hi Becca, so good to see you again!"

"Hi," was about all Rebecca could muster.

"Out getting some groceries after work, huh?" questioned Nelson.

"Yes."

"What's on the menu for dinner?"

She didn't want to reply. One, because the answer wasn't a good one. And two, because she was only giving him one-word answers so far, hoping to make this as quick as possible. Nelson wasn't the type to be put off by her curtness, so the conversation continued.

Rebecca lied, and said, "I'm not sure yet."

"How about we grab something to eat together?" Nelson was hopeful she was going to warm up to him.

"Not possible tonight," Rebecca answered quickly.

"Oh?" Nelson's face showed a bit of disappointment.

"I've got ice cream in the car." She could see this was stinging a bit for Nelson.

"Oh, okay, I understand. Good to see you. Let's not wait too long to have some dinner though, okay? Don't let the ice cream melt!"

"Okay. Bye." Rebecca was relieved. That went easier than she expected.

"See ya, Becca."

Rebecca got in her car and shut the door to the world, and to Nelson. She drove off with him still standing there. At the same time, she wondered how many times he would still be standing there with how rude she could be to him. Why was she so mean to such a nice man who only wanted to be her friend? She didn't know. And truthfully, she didn't want to think about it anymore. She just wanted to go home, put on her pajamas, and eat some cake and ice cream.

As Rebecca thought about her dinner, she said, "Happy Birthday to somebody in the world tonight."

3

The week went by very fast. Rebecca was back to Saturday night before she knew it, and wondering if church was on the "menu" for tomorrow. She made her way into the kitchen to find something to eat. It always seemed easier to figure out alone; just a bit of cheese and crackers seemed to satisfy most times. Don would have wanted to barbecue steaks, and make some pasta to go with it. Rebecca liked that, too. She had to admit, she missed it at times.

There wasn't much on TV, so she decided to sit on the front porch and eat. The sun was setting, but it was still high enough in the sky to bring the needed warmth. She could see cars passing by on the busier road up the block. Her street was usually fairly quiet. At the big house across the street, Rosie was out tending to her garden. Rebecca didn't know Rosie well...she knew that was her own fault. Rosie was always gentle and inviting. It was her own walls that stood between them. Rosie loved her garden. Sitting on her front porch, Rebecca would watch as Rosie knew just how to trim each bush to maximize its beauty. Rosie reminded her of her own sweet grandma. How many times had Rebecca been playing in the yard with her Grandma Bella pulling weeds, and yet acting like there was nothing she would rather be doing. Grandma, too, had been gentle and approachable...never harsh, never cruel, never mean. Being with her grandma was always comforting. Sometimes in her younger years she had attended church with Grandma Bella, but not often. She did remember the prayer, "Now I lay me down to sleep..." that her grandma taught her. She often wondered what, "I pray the Lord my soul to keep" meant exactly? As a child, Rebecca had no idea. What is a soul? Where would He keep it? Would it be safe? They prayed, "If I should die before I wake, I pray the Lord my soul to take." Would she die before she woke up? Do people do that? It wasn't long though, and Rebecca would drift off to sleep, no longer concerned with the unknowns of the prayer. If her grandma prayed it with her, all should be fine. One thing she knew, her Grandma Bella would never steer her wrong.

Rosie looked up from her rose bushes and saw Rebecca sitting there watching her. Rosie waved first, and then Rebecca waved back. They rarely ventured to each other's homes. It was like they knew they would always be there for each other if anything happened, but they didn't sit and have coffee together like friends do. It might have been their age difference. With Rebecca just turning 44, and Rosie probably in her 60's, Rebecca wondered what they could really have in common? Distance was probably best, thought Rebecca. Although she felt that way about most people these days. When people got up close and personal, it just didn't feel comfortable. Other than a few close friends that she retained after the divorce, she rarely got into conversations with anyone. Isolation felt better. Don was always the big talker. People found him to be entertaining. Don would always have a good story to tell. Every couple needs a quiet one, and she seemed to fill that role just fine.

The sun started to set behind the hills, and a slight breeze came up. Rebecca knew it was time to go in and have a cup of tea. She looked over to see if she needed to wave to Rosie, but Rosie had her back to her snipping at a rose bush, so Rebecca went inside. Turning on the burner, the teakettle was already in place. She sorted through the mail, waiting for it to whistle at her. But it didn't. It seemed to be taking much longer than normal. Lifting the lid, the kettle was empty. She took it to the sink and added some water, which was a big mistake! With the tea kettle being so hot already, the steam from the water shot right out of it onto her fingers, scalding them as she gripped the handle. Rebecca immediately dropped it into the sink! The damage to her fingers was instant—almost immediate pain! If Don had been there, he would have helped her, getting whatever she might need. Being alone, it was up to her. She grabbed a glass out of the cupboard for ice water, took some ibuprofen, and sat down. At first, it didn't seem too bad. But when she got a better look at it, blisters were already forming on three of her fingers. One was quite large. Then the pain that began to shoot through her fingers made her want to cry. She thought she might as well. Who was going to hear her, as a tear rolled down her cheek. Rebecca had been scalded once before as a child when she tipped an iron backwards, pouring the steamy water over her hand. Her mother had tended to her wounds then… It felt good to be taken care of. Now, she felt alone in her pain, both physically and emotionally.

The house started to grow dark. Rebecca got up, fingers soaking in ice water, and made her way through the house turning on some lights. She thought she heard a knock at the door—but maybe it was just her moving around that caused it. It had been so long since anyone had visited, it wasn't a familiar sound. But there it was again, just a faint little knock. It wasn't suspicious, but she surely wondered who it could be. Looking through the peephole, she could barely see the top of a head that looked like it could belong to Rosie. Hmmm, I wonder if it is Rosie, and what would have brought her over right now? Rebecca called through the door, "Who is it?" and sure enough, Rosie answered, "Your neighbor, Rosie, from across the street."

Lifting her hand out of the glass with water dripping onto the floor, she turned the doorknob. The pain was so great, she winced as she opened the door. Rosie was startled by the look on Rebecca's face. It was so filled with discomfort. She saw Rebecca quickly dip her fingers back into the glass of ice water. "Ouch!!" Rebecca called out. And then quickly said, "I'm sorry. It's just that I burned my fingers a bit ago with the steam while making tea, and it really hurts!" Rebecca felt too uncomfortable to be bothered by company right now. But she restrained her agitation as best she could while also noticing that Rosie had come with a plate of cookies.

Rosie was the one who now felt uncomfortable, understanding that this wasn't a good time to visit…or was it? Rosie stood silent, waiting for Rebecca to say something. Rosie didn't want to invite herself in. But she didn't want to leave Rebecca alone in her pain either. The silence seemed to go on longer than the four or so seconds it took Rebecca to speak.

"Would you like to come in?" Rebecca finally asked.

"Oh, thank you. I made cookies today, and I wanted to give you some before you left your porch. But when I turned around to see if you were still there, you'd already gone in."

It was a detailed answer to Rebecca's simple invitation, and she wondered how long this visit was going to take? Rebecca was in no mood for conversation. She needed the ibuprofen to take effect, and rest. But she knew she needed to be nice to Rosie.

Rosie walked in and made her way to the kitchen with the cookies. Rebecca followed her, and watched as Rosie placed the cookies on the counter. Rebecca thought to herself, she really is a sweet woman. It's just that her timing is off. Of all nights, this is not good. But Rosie didn't seem to be in a hurry, so Rebecca would have to be patient.

"I'd get you a cup of tea, but that's how I burned my hand," Rebecca said, a bit agitated.

"That's quite all right. Is there anything I can do for you?" Rosie's concern was apparent in her voice. "May I take a look at your burn?"

Rebecca didn't really want to let Rosie see what happened. She was a bit embarrassed for some reason. Pulling her hand out of the water, she hesitantly showed Rosie.

"Oh my! You did burn yourself quite well. Do you know how to care for a steam burn?"

"No, not really." Rebecca replied.

"I'm not sure either. Let's look it up," Rosie said, while at the same time getting out her phone.

Rebecca was surprised at this since Rosie didn't look like the type to be using a cell phone for research.

"It says here that honey is good for it." Rosie continued to read, "It has anti-inflammatory and antibacterial properties that promote healing…it draws out fluids and cleans wounds. Should we give that a try?"

Rebecca said, "I have some honey in the house."

"Let's do it!" Rosie replied. "And do you have gauze?"

"No gauze," said Rebecca.

Rosie wasn't put off by that. "We can just use some tissue and tape then. That should work."

Rebecca was a bit leery about having Rosie bandage her up. It had been so long since anyone had taken care of her. She had grown fiercely independent. Rebecca had to admit to herself, it would be hard one-handed to bandage her other fingers…so she complied.

Rosie worked swiftly, and efficiently, dripping honey onto the blisters, and then wrapping some toilet tissue around them. It took a few tries to get it right, as she folded it into a strip, but soon, the fingers were wrapped. With the ibuprofen now starting to take effect, Rebecca was feeling some relief.

Rosie could feel Rebecca's uneasiness, and she didn't want to outstay her welcome…if she had been welcomed at all. She was glad to have been able to help with the bandage. Rosie also prayed silently for healing—it became clear why God impressed it upon her heart to make cookies that morning. Rosie hadn't known who they were for. When she saw Rebecca sitting out front, God whispered to her, "Rebecca needs some of your cookies." Rosie was hesitant. Rebecca usually kept to herself. But Rosie heard God's whisper before, and ignoring God only brought about regret. Obedience contained such joy. Rosie knew even if Rebecca didn't answer the door, it's always better to give it a try. Rosie often saw Rebecca sitting alone on the porch, and turning the lights out early for bed. To Rosie, Rebecca's life seemed lonely since Don had moved out, although Rebecca never talked with Rosie about any of it. Rosie wondered if in time she would…

"I need to get on home now, Rebecca. I'll check back with you in a few days and see how you're doing; and also get my plate. No need for you to make a trip over with it."

"Thank you, Rosie. I really appreciate your help, and the cookies. I do have a sweet tooth."

"You're quite welcome. Hope you get some sleep tonight."

Rebecca walked Rosie to the front door, watching as she crossed the street toward home. Once Rosie was safely inside, Rebecca shut the door, and locked it. Turning off the lights, she made her way upstairs to bed. Rebecca thought about Rosie as she drifted off to sleep that night. She is so thoughtful. Maybe I should stop in from time to time and visit with her? She might be as lonely as I am, and we might be good company for each other—even with the age difference.

4

Rebecca didn't sleep very well at all, and woke up with a headache. Her fingers did feel better—so that was good. Maybe that honey really helped? She rolled over and looked at the clock. It said 7:14. Rebecca got up, started the coffee pot, took a couple pills for her headache, and went back to bed. Quickly falling asleep, she slept for another hour. When she woke the second time, her headache was gone.

Rebecca always liked to open her bedroom blinds first thing. It gave her a view of the mountains, the street below, and most importantly, she could see if the sun was shining. A foggy day could mean a "dark cloud" over her day. This morning was sunny, so she got her "picker-upper." Rebecca could smell the coffee from downstairs now. She was thinking of how she really should learn to set the timer on the coffee pot. Why was that a "mountain" she didn't want to climb? Maybe because Don was more the techie, and she always left those details up to him. It's not like she couldn't figure it out...

With the coffee tasting good, the sun shining, and a cookie off Rosie's plate, Rebecca started to think about church, although she really didn't want to go. There were so many people, and she felt uncomfortable not yet knowing how it all worked. When it came time to greet those around her, as she found out last week she had to do shortly into the service, that was the worst time of all...standing up, and shaking someone's hand, and letting them know your name, or not. Couldn't she just sit, be quiet, stay to herself, and listen to what the pastor had to say? It would have been so much easier. She began to think maybe it would be best if she forced herself to go this morning. What to wear became her next challenge. Back upstairs, into the closet...

As Rebecca left the house, she noticed the same familiar car at Rosie's that she usually watched through her living room window. The white car was Rosie's ride to a small church she attended somewhere nearby. That's about all Rebecca knew. Rosie never pushed her religion on her, but she could tell Rosie loved God. To Rebecca it seemed Rosie wore God like a robe…He flowed around Rosie, and came out as love. That was how best Rebecca could describe it. Rebecca thought of most Christians as being judgmental, but Rosie never came across that way. Even yesterday, when bringing over the cookies, Rosie seemed so accepting. She never looked at Rebecca any different before or after the divorce. Most people, she could tell in their eyes were judging her, and wondering whose fault it was? Rosie always remained the same. Could it be that God can do that for a person? Or had Rosie always been that way? Maybe if she did start spending a little more time with Rosie, she could better understand these things. Rebecca knew she would really have to put some effort into that since she mostly felt resistant.

Arriving at church, it was a little more crowded than it had been the week before. When announcements were made, there was some talk about this being a special Sunday. Rebecca thought Easter, the next Sunday, would be important. But why today? The pastor talked about Jesus riding on a donkey. She was having trouble picturing that, since Jesus seemed to be such a great man. When the pastor said palm branches and coats were put on the road in front of Jesus, palm branches were handed out to the entire church. She wasn't sure what to do with hers, so she just watched everyone around her. They seemed to just be holding onto it, so she did the same. At one point in the service, they lifted the palm branches into the air saying, "Hosanna in the highest!" She listened, watched, and was impressed with the whole group cooperating in this. She wondered if everyone here believed in Jesus?

Rebecca got a few things out of the sermon. It seemed good. But what she was really looking for was how it applied to her life…today…in her pain. The pastor said that Jesus was on a journey to Jerusalem, and what was coming that week was going to be very painful for Jesus. He was going to be abandoned, and handed over to die on a Cross. Rebecca knew enough to know that's what preceded Easter, the Cross. But she was more fascinated by Jesus' willingness to ride right into that scenario. Why didn't He run in the opposite direction? Why was He willing to head into disaster? Did it have to be this way? Everyone around her seemed to understand more than she did. But then again, they had no idea what she was thinking either as she lifted her palm branch into the air along with them. Maybe she could find this mysterious story in the Bible that she had yet to even get out of her car? Maybe there was something more there for her? Something she needed desperately? Why was her life heading in this direction? What was it in her that was bringing her to church, and even thinking about getting to know Rosie a bit better? Rebecca's mind was swirling with so many different thoughts as she walked out of church. It left her hungry and just looking forward to getting home and making something to eat. She'd had enough "God" for one day, and it was still before noon.

On the drive home, something in Rebecca seemed to change. She wasn't really ready to be alone. But what was she supposed to do with that? Anita was out of town—she left for the whole week since her kids were on Spring Break, otherwise she could swing by her house and hang out for a bit. Susan was working at the beauty shop, as usual on any given morning. And other than that, Rebecca's friend list sort of petered out...leaving one friend, who she didn't see all that often, Jennifer. She was a bit younger than Rebecca. Jennifer was 32, and single. They met through Nelson. They'd both been at his 40th birthday party in October, and really enjoyed talking with each other. They got together for coffee a couple of times since, but it had been a while since they'd seen each other. Rebecca pulled into a parking lot, deciding to text Jennifer. Texting seemed easier and less intrusive. That way, if Jennifer wasn't interested she could just not answer, or text back that she was busy.

Hi Jennifer, this is Rebecca. How are u? Have some time today?

It wasn't but thirty seconds or so later that Rebecca got a reply.

Hi Rebecca. Good to hear from u! I'd love to see u. Come on by my house for lunch. Oh, and Nelson is here. Hope that's ok with u?

That made Rebecca rethink her decision. If it had only been Jennifer, she would have jumped on the invitation. But with Nelson in the mix, she just didn't know. Rebecca waited what was probably too long before replying. She was sure Jennifer and Nelson were probably wondering about her...that made her more uncomfortable. Looking ahead at a lonely afternoon, Rebecca decided to go for it.

Rebecca texted, That sounds fine. See u soon.

It wasn't but a couple of miles to Jennifer's condo. Rebecca drove slowly, wanting to gather her thoughts before she got there. She was trying to remember just how Jennifer and Nelson knew one another. If she remembered right, Nelson had a friend in Phoenix, and Jennifer was his sister. She had moved to California from Arizona, and was all alone. Nelson had befriended her, helping her get settled and find her way around the area. Once again, Nelson being the perfect gentleman. Rebecca admired Nelson, and his ability to be there for people. As her thoughts rambled on, Rebecca realized she was starting to welcome some time with Nelson, too. That was good, because she was just pulling onto the street where Jennifer lived. It was best to arrive with a smile knowing they would be sensitive to what she might be feeling. It was too pretty of a day to be grumpy. She wanted to relax and enjoy this time with them.

Ringing Jennifer's doorbell, she could hear voices from inside and footsteps quickly approaching the door. It opened wide to Jennifer's grin from ear to ear. Her dark hair bounced on her shoulders as she eagerly ushered Rebecca in, gave her a warm hug, and told her how good it was to see her again.

How does a 32-year-old bubble with such life, Rebecca wondered. She wanted that...that confidence and joy that she saw in Jennifer. Perhaps that's why she gravitated to her at the birthday party for Nelson? The rest of the room almost seemed dull in comparison to where Jennifer stood. Happiness appeared to be captured where she was, and it was alluring.

"Hi Jennifer, thanks for having me over," Rebecca said, putting in her best effort to be up. "Sorry it's been so long."

"Oh, Rebecca, it was perfect timing, and I'm sorry I haven't gotten ahold of you, either. Nelson and I were having something to eat, and we have too much for just the two of us. We just said, 'Wouldn't it be nice to share this with someone.' And then you texted me. Doesn't God know just how to orchestrate things?"

Rebecca's ears perked up. She never remembered Jennifer making a reference to God before. Why did it seem that lately she was meeting people who knew of God? Maybe she was just more aware of it? Even Nelson, having never said anything about God, now reminded her of the same warmth that Rosie had. There was a peace in them that the world, and all its stressful situations, couldn't seem to penetrate. Rosie and Nelson rolled with the punches, so to speak, better than most. Could Jennifer be in this same "club"? The Christian Club, if you wanted to call it that? Rebecca was suddenly very happy she attended church that morning. If that's how you join this "club," then she was wanting in. She wasn't sure how, where, or what, but she hoped to find out one day.

When they walked into the kitchen, Nelson was busy skewering meat out of a marinating bag. He was adding peppers and onions. Rebecca wasn't much of a cook, but she appreciated those who were. Nelson looked up as she entered, and gave her a wink and a smile. "Hey there, Becca. What a perfect day! Sharing a meal with two of my favorite people. I like to cook, but cooking for myself isn't much fun. Thanks for coming over to help us eat all of this."

"That already smells good. What did you marinate it in?" asked Rebecca, trying to make conversation...not that she would remember or even try it herself.

Without hesitation, Nelson answered, "Teriyaki sauce, honey, garlic, and ginger. I started it yesterday at my place, and knew I was going to have way too much for one. Jennifer was happy to let me use her grill today to finish them off, and help me eat them. And then you texted, and it was perfect. Our own little Sunday afternoon party."

Rebecca liked the ease with which Nelson talked. He expressed himself well, but his ego didn't take over, like with a lot of guys she'd known. Rebecca watched his hands as he put each piece on the skewer and she could see that he was practiced at it. Maybe this was because of his job, too? He handled small tools and machinery well. She learned that Nelson worked on ATM's. She didn't even know those broke down but, obviously, they did. Nelson told her he drove a lot, taking calls, fixing the machines. His hours were kind of crazy, not having the normal weekends off, but he said it was good to have days free during the week—not so busy when he needed to do things. Now that she thought about it, it was good he'd been available when her car wouldn't start. He worked a lot of Sundays—just not that one, she guessed.

"Are you hungry, Becca?" Nelson asked, like he truly cared.

"Yes. Yes, I am. I had some coffee this morning, but that was about it. (Rebecca didn't really want to mention the cookie.) I was headed home to make myself something to eat for lunch when I thought about giving Jennifer a call. That's how I ended up here. She was nice enough to invite me over."

"Well, I'm sure glad she did. I hope you don't mind that I'm here with you gals. I know sometimes it's nice to have girl talk without a guy around."

"No, it's fine. I know that I'm overdue on getting back to you Nelson. Sorry about that, and having to rush home the other night with the ice cream. Time just seems to go by so fast." Rebecca watched his face as she said this, wondering if she could read his expression. But it didn't change. He just kept skewering meat and veggies, happy as a lark.

"I work crazy hours, Becca. I'm not the easiest guy to get hold of, or to meet up with. I appreciate your patience in that. I always enjoy when we get some time together, but I know it can be long times in between. I hope you never think I'm avoiding you." He glanced up at Rebecca when he said that. She just smiled slightly, and nodded. She really didn't know what to say in response. Rebecca didn't think Nelson was avoiding her. But if he was, that was okay, too. She was the one who seemed to be avoiding most people these days.

Rebecca didn't know where Jennifer had gone. Then she suddenly appeared carrying a bowl of potato salad. Rebecca wondered where it came from since she hadn't seen Jennifer get into the fridge. That question was soon answered when a man she never met walked in behind Jennifer. She hadn't heard the doorbell, so she wondered when he arrived.

"Rebecca, this is Justin. Justin, Rebecca."

"Hi."

"Hi."

Jennifer began to explain, "Justin decided to surprise me today! His plans got canceled. And look! He brought some of his mom's potato salad. I've had it before, and it's delicious! This is perfect!"

Justin looked to be about 35, blonde hair, wavy, about six feet tall, with a thin build. Nice enough looking. He gave Jennifer a look that said they were more than friends. Could Jennifer have already found someone to date since she moved here? When Jennifer looked back at Justin, and then gave him a small hug, laying her head on his shoulder, the question was answered. That's probably why it had been a while since Jennifer had gotten hold of her. Rebecca knew that when a guy enters the picture, most attention is given there. She understood that. And she was happy for Jennifer. A strange new city, a new job, and no family nearby...how sweet that she had found someone to spend her time with outside of work.

The afternoon flew by, and it seemed to Rebecca that it had been a success. She did her best to be sociable, and it appeared to have gone well. Justin was a nice guy, a little immature, but Jennifer seemed to like his quirkiness. She found out they had been seeing each other for a few months. Rebecca and Nelson got to talk some, catching up on life. Nelson said his job was going well, although they worked him too many hours.

Jennifer was a sweet hostess. She made everyone feel at home. All in all, Rebecca was glad she had gone. It felt good to have friends, enjoy some laughter, and start to live a little again outside of just going to work. Rebecca was thinking about the prayer before their meal that had been offered up by Jennifer. Nelson had given a resonating "Amen," when it was finished. That surprised Rebecca a bit. Was he making fun, or agreeing? Rebecca wasn't quite sure yet. Sometimes he was hard to read because he was always so jovial.

Rebecca arrived home about eight that evening. Grabbing her purse off the front seat, she noticed the Bible still sitting there. It ran through her mind, it's time I bring that into the house. Can't just leave it in the car forever. After unlocking the front door and setting her purse down, she carried the Bible carefully over to the coffee table and laid it down. It seemed a good enough place to put it. She had to admit it looked strange to her—to have a Bible on display for anyone to see. Would they think she was overly religious? But then again, that wasn't much of a worry...there weren't a lot of people coming over to visit these days.

As Rebecca turned out the lights and made her way to bed, she knew she had lots to be thankful for. She wasn't sure if the "Man upstairs" in Heaven could hear her thanks, or not, but she hoped so. If this day had been planned by God, He had done a good job of helping her feel loved and accepted. Rebecca was more peaceful than she had been in a long time. Maybe her life was turning in a good direction? Noticing that her fingers were already healing nicely...she wondered if maybe her heart was starting to also.

5

Rebecca's cell phone started ringing soon after she had fallen asleep. It was loud, and obtrusive, after such a peaceful slumber that didn't seem to last near long enough. In her grogginess, she looked at the clock, 10:15. It was later than she thought, since it seemed like she only slept for a few minutes. She reached for the phone to at least see who it was. She didn't plan on talking to them, but with elderly parents, you just never know…

When Rebecca saw Nelson's name, she pondered it for just a moment and then it hit her…she forgot to take the leftovers home with her that they set aside. Of course, Nelson would call to remind her. That's who he was. Mr. Thoughtful. He probably didn't realize that she went to bed quite so early. For most people, ten o'clock was still early. Rebecca decided to let it go to voicemail. She would listen to it in the morning. Even if Nelson was telling her he would drop them off on his way home, she didn't want to deal with that tonight. She would have to get up and get dressed, and that wasn't about to happen.

Rebecca set the phone back on the nightstand, and quickly dozed off again. It didn't seem but a few minutes later and the phone was ringing again. Really? What's going on? I've got work tomorrow, and I keep getting woken up. Who could it be now? She grabbed the phone and took a look, thinking this time it might really be about her parents. Who else would call her at this hour? Her phone didn't ring that much.

When she saw that it was Nelson again, it startled her for a second. Why would he be so persistent about some leftovers? That didn't seem in line with his character. He was always so careful not to be intrusive. Rebecca decided she'd better answer it.

"Hi Nelson," she said, still very groggy.

"Rebecca…. I'm sorry to wake you…. really I am."

Nelson's voice sounded very different. And, he called her Rebecca, not Becca, in his usual friendly way. Rebecca started to wonder if she had done something wrong that she hadn't noticed that day? It all seemed to have gone well from her perspective. Had she made Nelson, or someone else angry? These thoughts flashed through her mind in a matter of milliseconds before she heard Nelson speak again.

"I...I don't know quite how to say this...it's bad, Becca, bad."

"What is Nelson? I don't understand." Her voice was starting to get shaky. She had never known this side of Nelson.

"Uhhh, it wasn't long after you left, that I left, too, leaving Jennifer and Justin there to have a little time together before the night ended. I had been home about two hours, when...well, when I got a frantic call from Jennifer. Justin... uhhhh... Justin... he.... ummm..."

"Justin what!?" Rebecca was really getting scared now.

"Justin was in an accident on his motorcycle after he left Jennifer's, and...he was killed, Becca. He died on the scene. His neck was broken."

Rebecca let out a gasp like she only heard once before come out of her, and that was when she found out Bonnie had stage four cancer. Rebecca was shocked and speechless, and then she felt the tears roll down her face. The phone was silent on Nelson's end, but she was sure he could now hear her starting to cry. It started softly, and then increased into sobbing. Her heart was pounding, and she wanted to drop the phone, but she didn't. She just sat there on the edge of her bed, crying into the phone, into Nelson's ear...not knowing what, if anything she could say.

After what seemed like much too long of a time, they were able to speak to one another again. Rebecca began to ask questions. Nelson gave her the answers he did have. It wasn't complicated. No alcohol had been involved. Justin was a good rider. It's just that he took a different way home, riding through Crow Canyon, and the road was curvy. It was late, with little traffic, so he must have thought it was okay to pass a slow car in front of him. It was a very tight curve when he did. The speed he must have accelerated to, caused him to veer off the side of the road into a field. One eye-witness said he tumbled like a rag doll before coming to a stop. It probably could have been a soft landing, causing little damage, but in all the twisting and turning, he broke his neck. By the time help arrived, he was gone. He wasn't even all that scraped up. He must have just tumbled the wrong way at the wrong time. God only knows...

Rebecca started to quiet down as she listened to Nelson, and was actually a little surprised at the emotions she felt. It had just welled up in her before she could get a handle on it. She only met Justin once. She barely knew him. Maybe it was just having been with someone, and then having him gone from this earth so quickly that scared her. We think we have years before death comes, especially when we are young, but our life can be taken so quickly. And poor Jennifer...she looked so happy and content with Justin. That broke her heart, too. They made a cute couple. Who knows what their future could have held? Rebecca sighed deeply, "Oh poor Jennifer. I'm so, so sorry..."

Nelson listened and then spoke softly to Rebecca, letting her feel what she needed, wanting to be kind and patient. He let her know that Jennifer asked him to call her. Jennifer was at the hospital. The police called Jennifer from the accident with Justin's phone. He had her in as his ICE number, probably since he had no family nearby. Jennifer met them at the hospital, not knowing yet of Justin's condition. They kept it from her until she arrived. That was smart. She had enough trouble driving herself there, not knowing. Jennifer was barely able to talk to Nelson when she called him. Getting the words out in spurts between sobs. She said the hospital staff was helping her as much as they could, but she needed someone to be there with her. Jennifer asked him to please come, and to bring Rebecca if he could.

Jennifer told Nelson she was trying to help them reach Justin's family in Florida. But with the time difference, they were having trouble getting through to them on the phone. They probably weren't answering so late at night. Nelson said he was going to the hospital soon.

Rebecca wasn't sure about going...she felt so uncomfortable in times like these. What would she say to Jennifer? There were no words...but then again, Jennifer asked Nelson to call her, specifically. Jennifer didn't have a lot of friends here, and no family. Going to see her would probably be the most loving thing to do. Nelson would be there for Jennifer, of course, and he would know how to be of help. But Jennifer might need a female friend there, too.

"Oh...this is so hard. LIFE is so hard, Nelson! I hate this! I hate that this had to happen!" Rebecca could feel anger rising up inside of her now. "This is unfair! He was so young! They were just falling in love! Could the timing be any worse for a young couple?! I don't know what to say when I see Jennifer, but I will go with you. Help me be strong for her, Nelson. She doesn't need me to be a basket case when she is the one we are there to help."

"We will be helping each other." Nelson didn't say much after that. He just listened and let Rebecca vent her feelings for a few minutes more, because he understood. Many of those same thoughts were going through his head. He hated this, too. He loved God with all his heart. But it was hard for him to understand why God allowed such pain and suffering in the world, too. He knew this was going to test Jennifer's faith. It was testing his own again. He and Jennifer talked about their love of Jesus.

That was something they shared. They had some discussions about how life works, and how the Bible is helpful in times of hardship. But he never expected that Jennifer's faith would be tested in this way, right now, as she was just starting a life here in California. Everything seemed to have been falling into place for her. This was definitely going to be a struggle, and one that she would need prayer and support through. He would be there as much as he could, but he knew he wouldn't be nearly enough help. Nelson knew, personally, that Jesus was needed to heal a broken heart. Maybe in time, he would share his story with Jennifer. For now, he would pray for her, and love her as God would have him do. It was her time to cry on his shoulder and share her pain with him.

Nelson ended their conversation by saying, "Rebecca, this is the hard stuff of life. It doesn't get much worse... I'm going to be leaving for the hospital here in a minute. I'll swing by and get you." Rebecca could tell by Nelson's voice that he was ready to do battle, as she put it. He would face this tragedy with calm and reason, and do what needed to be done for Jennifer. She so admired a man who could take charge, without being forceful. Nelson was that man.

As Rebecca got dressed, for what could be a very long night, she thought about Nelson. She was so glad he would be with her when she saw Jennifer tonight. Rebecca didn't know what the future held for their friendship, but the longer she knew Nelson, the more she wanted to get to know him. Tonight, things would be tough. But she and Nelson would be there together, and she knew that was what was needed right now.

6

Nelson gathered a few things, including his small travel Bible, and locked the door on his way out. The evening was cooling down after such a warm spring day. The Bay Area was like that, the evenings usually brought on a chill. Climbing into his truck, Nelson paused for a few moments. He knew what was ahead would be extremely difficult. He continued to learn how, apart from God, he could do nothing. That was taking him a while to incorporate into his faith, even though he had been a Christian since his early twenties. Nelson realized he still tried for so many years to do things in his own strength. He recently read a good book on the Holy Spirit. It had helped him understand that Jesus didn't even expect us to do this life without His help. That is why the Holy Spirit is such a Gift. Jesus told the disciples to not even leave Jerusalem until they received the Gift from the Father. And yet Nelson knew he lived too much of his life without depending on this Gift. He didn't want to do that anymore. He whispered, "Living in our own strength is probably why so many people feel the Christian life doesn't work...because we aren't 'working' it right." As he gathered his thoughts, he boldly said, "If there was ever a time to work it 'right,' this is it. Tonight. This is where the rubber meets the road."

Nelson paused and prayed, asking for help, for strength, and for guidance. Taking in a deep breath, his emotions seemed to settle a bit. God's ways were so subtle most times. But usually when looking back at the whole of what God was doing, Nelson noticed a pattern of Jesus being there in difficult times. The enemy's ways were not so subtle. Why did evil always sound louder than good, more forceful, and easier to follow? God is a Gentleman. The enemy is not, Nelson reminded himself. He needed to remember that, and to listen closely tonight. Jennifer would have questions, and doubts, and she would be fearful. He would need to be standing firmly on the Rock of Jesus, and do what he had just been reading in his quiet time with God this morning. When Nelson opened his Bible, and turned there...the enemy began to scream at him, "YOU NEED TO GET GOING! YOU DON'T HAVE TIME FOR THIS!" Nelson fought the urge to hurry, and looking at 1 John 4:12, he read out loud, *"No one has ever seen God. But if we love each other, God lives in us, and his love has been brought to full expression through us."*

That was the desire of Nelson's heart as he pulled out of the driveway and drove toward Rebecca's house...he wanted to love Jennifer tonight as Jesus would. He wanted her to see the full expression of God's love through kindness and gentleness. Nelson continued to talk with God as he drove, and by the time he pulled in at Rebecca's he may not have felt totally ready, but he trusted in God that he didn't need to be, because the Holy Spirit who lived in him is always ready.

Rebecca saw him pull up. She had been standing at the window waiting. Nelson took a little longer to get there than she expected. She had her coat and a bottle of water for both of them. Nelson greeted her with a nod and a squeeze of her hand as she buckled in. For the rest of the drive to the hospital, they mostly sat in silence—both lost in their own thoughts. Tragic times like this are never easy for anyone; they both knew that. Jennifer should not be alone with only strangers, and they were her closest friends here. Her family would probably be flying in, or someone, eventually. But for now, they were who she had, and they were not going to let her down.

It was fairly quiet around the hospital. They decided to park by the emergency room. The ER had a few people waiting in it, but it, too, was quiet for the most part. One lady sat in a chair, slumped down, with what seemed to be her husband holding her hand. She looked feverish, and since a bad flu was going around, they didn't want to get anywhere near where they sat. Another little boy cried in his mother's arms. His dad sat next to them looking worried. It seemed too late at night for a childhood injury. But the boy was holding his arm as the mother tried to keep him still.

Nelson texted Jennifer to see where she was. Jennifer answered back quickly, and Nelson wasn't surprised that she said she was in the hospital Chapel. Nelson knew where it was...down a long hallway from the ER, and then taking a left, it was in a small wing of the hospital close to the front door. Rebecca didn't say much as they walked along, but her mind was going a thousand miles a minute—this was so out of her comfort zone. Nelson was quiet, too...this was a difficult "walk" for him. The door to the Chapel was closed when they got there. Nelson opened it slowly, not wanting to disturb the stillness from within. As they walked in, Jennifer stood up and turned in their direction heaving a sigh of relief. Jennifer practically collapsed in Nelson's arms as a wave of grief overtook her. Nelson steadied her, and led her back to a place where she could sit down. Her head was bowed, and then she bent at the waist, her head falling into her lap, as large sobs escaped her. Rebecca took a seat with them, not knowing what to do. There had been a Chaplain with Jennifer, but she nodded to them when they entered, said a few things, and then left them to be alone. Nelson recognized the Chaplain. She seemed a bit surprised to see Nelson there, but he was not surprised to see her.

As Rebecca sat on one side of Jennifer, and Nelson on the other, Rebecca reached her hand out and placed it on Jennifer's back. She was not good with a lot of physical contact, but words did not seem appropriate just then. She wanted to let Jennifer know she was supporting her. Rebecca's eyes filled with tears as she fearfully watched Jennifer in such pain. She was again so glad that she was not here alone with Jennifer. Both of them needed the strength that Nelson had to see them through these initial moments together. Slowly Jennifer regained some composure and she sat back in the pew. It was a small chapel, with about four rows on each side of a narrow aisle. There was a stained-glass window up front depicting a rainbow set among dark clouds with the rays of sun pouring in from the side. It was lit from behind with a light. It seemed to offer hope in the midst of a storm. Obviously, someone had put thought into what should be in this place of prayer…no matter what religious affiliation they were connected with…or none at all. Rebecca wondered how many broken hearts sat here seeking comfort in this Chapel? All too many, she was sure.

Nelson waited for Jennifer to speak. He knew better than to force anything out of her until she was ready to share. Slowly, Jennifer began, telling them about how she arrived at the hospital, and asked for Justin. The look on the nurse's face behind the counter in the ER told her what she didn't want to know…it was bad. The nurse asked her to take a seat for a few moments until she could get a doctor to talk with her. Her stomach was churning as she waited the five minutes that seemed like an eternity. A tall man in a white coat came walking toward her. His name badge read *Rick Jensen, M.D.* He looked concerned, but calm, and that had given Jennifer some hope that Justin was going to be okay. Dr. Jensen stood in front of her, offering his hand, and asking her if she could come with him. Jennifer rose in silence, almost frozen in time now…where were they going? To see Justin? Was he in a room somewhere, or still here in the ER? She just wanted to see him. Even though their relationship was only a few months old, they had grown very close. She listened, as they walked through the hall, trying to catch the sound of Justin's voice somewhere in the distance.

Dr. Jensen took her to a small room just past the ER. It had a leather couch, a couple of chairs, and a few pictures on the wall. It seemed like it had been decorated to be comforting, but it felt to Jennifer like it had a definite chill in the air. As they sat down, Dr. Jensen, told her the news... Justin had been brought in from his accident, and he was so sorry, but there was nothing they could do. His neck had been broken in the accident. Dr. Jensen continued to tell her that although they tried to administer some aid to him on the journey to the hospital in faint hopes of reviving him, and did all they could when he arrived, he was gone. Jennifer said it felt like all the air in her lungs had been sucked out, and she was sick to her stomach. When she looked around to see if there was a bathroom attached to the room, her eyes locked on a picture on the wall. It was a field full of flowers. It suddenly brought her a sense of peace. To her it was God speaking to her heart of His beauty, in all the craziness of the moment.

Jennifer was then able to ask where Justin was...and could she see him? Dr. Jensen recommended that she wait until she had someone there with her, if she were to see him. Then he asked her if she would like to talk with the hospital Chaplain? Jennifer said she would, and she waited there after Dr. Jensen left, to meet with the Chaplain. Then the two of them walked to the hospital Chapel. It all went by so fast, and yet not...it seemed to be foggy in her mind, and she just wanted to wake up from this nightmare and have none of it be real.

Jennifer was staring straight ahead as she related all this to Nelson and Rebecca, sometimes glancing up at the stained-glass window, sometimes staring off into nothingness. Eventually she drew quiet and turned to look at Nelson on her right, and then Rebecca on her left. Nelson asked if he could pray, and Jennifer nodded yes. Rebecca was relieved that Nelson spoke first. She knew she would have said something wrong, and that was the last thing she wanted to do at a time like this.

Nelson began... "Father in Heaven, this is too much for any of us to comprehend right now. Justin was such a nice guy. Even though I didn't know him well, it is good to know that You do. You saw the day he was born, and You knew the day he would leave this earth. Even though it is shocking to us, it isn't to You. Help us to trust You with this. Help Jennifer to have the strength she needs from You to get through one of the most difficult things in life, going on now without someone she cared very deeply about. She needs You now, Lord Jesus. She needs the Hope Your death and resurrection give us. She needs to know You will always be with her as she walks through this trial. There will be so much we don't understand, but we will cling tightly to You along the way, and to each other. Please help Jennifer, and us, as the days unfold. In Jesus' name. Amen."

Rebecca listened as Nelson prayed. She hadn't been around many people who prayed, and certainly nothing like this. She had heard the Lord's Prayer at times in the past, but she couldn't recite it. Even simple prayers before meals, and bedtimes prayers from her grandma were familiar, but this seemed so much more personal. It was like Nelson was actually talking to someone who understood their situation. Could God be that real? Was He really listening as Nelson talked with Him about their situation?...about Jennifer's situation? And if God could hear them, and He was helping them, how would they know? It seemed Nelson and Jennifer shared something that she didn't really understand yet, but she wanted to. If God was really that willing to be a part of the things they went through, she knew she needed His help, too. This was all so foreign to her, but maybe a door was opening to something that she longed for all her life, yet felt was so far out of reach. Maybe Bonnie's death helped her walk through that first door, into the church, and raise her hand, seeking answers to so many questions. And obviously Justin's death led her here tonight. What if Nelson could help her know God? Or she could probably also have a talk with Rosie...yes...it was time to find some answers. If she surrounded herself with people who seemed to know if God is real, she might get to know if He is, too.

The evening was long. But once all the things were taken care of, and Justin's family finally had been reached, the three of them made their way out of the hospital. Jennifer decided it was best to not see Justin. She wanted to picture him the way he was the last time she saw him...smiling, as he put his helmet on, and waving a "see ya later" as he rode off. That was the happy, free-spirited Justin she had come to know, and would remember for the rest of her life.

Jennifer seemed composed enough as they walked to their cars. But by the way she talked, they could tell her mind was not clear enough to really be driving. Rebecca offered to drive her home, and she agreed. Nelson followed them in his truck, and then drove Rebecca back to her place. They all got to bed in the wee morning hours, exhausted from the tragedy. Nelson and Rebecca were concerned about leaving Jennifer alone in her condo, but she assured them she would be ok. They agreed that they would all be in contact the next day, and be there for each other. It was an evening that stretched Rebecca beyond what she was used to. But in the end, she was glad to have been a part of it. As she laid down in her bed that night, she knew there was a lot to process. She wanted to know more about a faith that could possibly see Jennifer through something so hard, as she also grieved Bonnie. She was beginning to think there might be a way to live this life in a way that she never experienced before. She surely hoped so.

7

At such a late hour, sleep came easily but not without much tossing and turning until the sun came up. Rebecca decided she was not in any shape to go to work that morning so she sent her boss an email from her phone, and tried to go back to sleep. Knowing Ben was always up early, he would see the email long before he got to the office. It would be fine. She worked for Ben long enough and built a strong work relationship with him. Whenever Rebecca needed personal time, Ben never hesitated to give it to her.

The phone rang about eight. It was Nelson. He wasn't going to work either. The night really took a toll on them, let alone what it had done to Jennifer. Nelson said he was going to get some coffee and take it to Jennifer about nine. She had texted him at 7 saying she couldn't sleep. He wanted to know if Rebecca wanted to go with him, but she declined. Rebecca thought if they had some time just the two of them, they could talk about things in a different way. She and Jennifer had been able to talk the night before when Nelson walked off to discuss some things with the hospital personnel. Rebecca was surprised at how she consoled Jennifer on her own. It wasn't as hard as she thought it would be. She mostly listened as Jennifer repeated parts of her story of what happened again, adding in a few new details that she left out the first time. It seems that Jennifer and Justin experienced an interesting conversation before he left that night. Almost like he knew something was about to happen…but how could he have? Would God give a head's up before an accident? Rebecca didn't know. Jennifer shared with her how Justin told her he felt he wouldn't live to an old age. Jennifer didn't know why he was telling her that, but it didn't freak her out. Jennifer, too, had a strange thought that she would die when she was 28, and now she was 32. Since it didn't happen, she just figured a lot of people don't really see themselves as growing old. Justin seemed to be one of them. Justin also wanted her to know that his parents divorced when he was about ten, and he feared marriage because he never wanted to get divorced. He didn't want to do that to his kids. Jennifer reassured him that the pattern didn't have to repeat itself—but he wasn't buying it. She told Justin she was enjoying their relationship for what it was, and not to worry. She wasn't going to pressure him into anything more.

Rebecca remembered Jennifer being quiet for a bit then—and with a far-off look, Jennifer told her when Justin went out the door, after giving her an especially long hug, he looked deeply into her eyes saying, "Jennifer, I want you to know how happy you make me." It caught Jennifer by surprise because Justin didn't speak much about his feelings. Jennifer gave him an extra little squeeze. Then Justin walked out to his motorcycle, smiled at her as he put on his helmet, and waved as he rode off.

The crisis made it hard to get up the next morning. Rebecca took a long hot shower. Sometimes in the shower, her head would clear and things would make more sense. Not this morning, there was too much to sort through. And she was tired. But the shower did feel good. Rebecca had already started the coffee, so after dressing, she got a cup, grabbed the last cookie off the plate from Rosie, and sat down to rest a bit more. While flipping through Facebook on her phone, Rebecca heard a knock at the door. It sounded familiar...Rosie's knock. It felt good to recognize it, like they were friends. Rebecca wasn't sure she was up for a visit, but she would at least need to answer it and see what Rosie had come over for. She wanted Rosie to know she was welcome, especially now that she was hoping to spend some time with her. As Rebecca opened the door, Rosie spoke up quickly.

"Good morning, Rebecca. I'm sorry if I'm bothering you. But I saw your car in the driveway this morning. I was a bit concerned, wondering if your fingers were causing you some problems?"

Rebecca was touched. It felt good to know that someone was watching out for her.

"Thank you, Rosie. It's so nice of you to worry about me. My fingers are doing fine. They hurt a bit, and the blisters are still there, but they seem to be healing. Can you come in for a minute? I have something I need to talk to you about."

Rosie didn't know what to make of this. She saw Rebecca drive off to work every Monday morning like clockwork. Rosie's morning quiet-time chair was positioned by the front window. She noticed that Rebecca was never late, and never in a hurry. She must have been very good at time management. And to be home and inviting her in now...that was a change.

It's not that Rebecca was ever mean...she always gave her a cordial wave, and usually a smile. But other than that, Rosie felt the need to let Rebecca have her privacy. Rosie knew, when the time was right for more, God would show her. He would be the One to open the door...could it be He was doing that this morning?

Rosie respectfully, yet without delay, accepted Rebecca's invitation. After letting Rebecca pour her a cup of coffee, they took a seat in the living room together. What came next, surprised even Rosie...

"Rosie, I don't quite know how to start, so I hope you'll bear with me..." Rebecca sounded tentative, and sad. Rosie hadn't seen her this way before. Even with going through the divorce, Rosie had witnessed Rebecca seemingly confident. Sad, at times, but sure of herself.

"Of course, Rebecca, just take your time. I'm not in any hurry." Rosie watched as Rebecca shifted her weight back and forth a couple of times in her chair, and seemed to be searching for words that were hard to find.

"I was up very, very late last night," Rebecca started in. "After a good day, something very tragic happened. I was with friends for dinner last night, and one of them was killed in a motorcycle accident on his way home. He was my friend's boyfriend. When I got home after the barbeque, I heard the news. Needless to say, I was very shocked...very much at a loss in many ways. I don't even know quite where I'm going with this..." Rebecca stopped talking, and Rosie waited in silence, sensing Rebecca had something more she wanted to say. Rebecca pondered her next words... "Rosie, I'm scared. I'm scared about death. I'm scared for my friend, Jennifer, and the sadness she will be feeling. I'm confused...I...I don't know what to think or what to do."

Rosie nodded sympathetically, wondering if Rebecca was finished. Rosie learned that it was best to listen a lot, before speaking. People who are hurting are filled with so much pain That pain needs to be emptied out before anything can be poured in and be of any help. As Rebecca's silence continued, Rosie spoke softly...

"Rebecca, what can I do for you? Is there a way I can help either you, or your friend?"

Rebecca almost cried out, "I don't know, Rosie! I just don't know. My heart hurts for Jennifer today. I didn't know Justin very well. We just met. I won't be the one missing him, but Jennifer will. She doesn't have a lot of friends in the area, since she is new here. We have a mutual friend, Nelson, and he is a wonderful man with a good heart. And he will be there for her. He believes in God. He reminds me a bit of you, Rosie."

Rebecca looked at Rosie now, after having spoken much of this while looking out the window, or at the floor. She didn't know what to expect from Rosie, or even if Rosie would understand what she was getting at.

"Have you been through something like this before, Rebecca? I mean, has anyone close to you died? I ask this because of the kind of support Jennifer will need now."

"Funny you should ask that…although, funny is not the right word. My best friend of many years recently died. In fact, that is why I went to church a week ago. I need some answers, Rosie. I get scared, and I don't understand why things have to be the way they are." Rebecca had so much on her heart she wanted to ask Rosie, but even just sharing this made her feel so vulnerable. She didn't know how much she should really say. She didn't want to bother Rosie with her problems. Rebecca knew she should be able to handle these things on her own. She was an adult, after all!

"Oh, Rebecca, I'm so sorry about your friend. I didn't know. I know you have been through some tough things in the last few years, but I didn't know about your friend. What's her name?"

"Bonnie. Bonnie Simpkins. She and I went to Jr. High together, and we were in each other's weddings. We shared so much of life together. Even though there were years when we didn't see each other, we talked often. When we were together, it was always the same. Friends to the end—I just didn't expect the end to come so soon. She was diagnosed with stage four cancer, and given about a year. Seven months later, she was gone." Rebecca could have gone on and on about Bonnie, but once again she felt like she was talking too much. Rosie gave her no indication that she was, or that she was even bothered by it. Rosie just sat quietly, and listened.

"You obviously had a very special friendship. I'm sure you miss her a lot. How long has she been gone?"

"Only a month." To Rebecca it seemed like a year. She missed talking to Bonnie.

"Do you have other friends in the area?" Rosie seemed genuinely concerned about what Rebecca's life looked like. She knew that Rosie probably saw changes since Don moved out. They used to have people over, do barbeques, and go out often with others. The house was mostly quiet now.

"I do, but not many. Maybe you know, Rosie, that in a divorce, friends will sometimes take sides. Don was always more outgoing than me, and many of our friends, mainly the couples, spend time with him. Some of the gals and I do things. It's been hard. I'm trying to get a new life going, but it's a slow process." Rebecca felt she was saying way too much about herself.

Rosie continued to respond with kindness. "Oh, I know. And it's good to hear that you are moving forward through the pain. Give yourself a lot of grace. Changes always take longer than we want them to."

Rebecca's phone dinged with a text, and she excused herself for a moment to check it, letting Rosie know it could be about her friend. Rosie sat quietly, glad to have a moment to reflect on what was happening. Rosie could sense that the Holy Spirit was asking her to take things very slowly with Rebecca. Rebecca had a lot of hurt and questions. It was best not to rush, not to push…not to seem overly zealous. It was hard, because Rosie knew where healing would come from, and she wanted to turn it on like a water hose at full force! But she learned that when the faith door is cracked open, as it seemed to be now with Rebecca, Jesus was best shared gently, and with as much love as possible. Too many times through the years Rosie knew she'd gotten so excited to share all that Jesus was to her, she made some mistakes and turned people off to His great love. Rosie recognized now that she had been operating in her own strength. She didn't want to do that with Rebecca. Rosie learned that offering more than "milk" in the early stages of searching for what Jesus has, can choke a person— the "steak" we're wanting to serve up has to wait until later. Easy does it…all in God's timing, all in His way. Rosie knew she had to put her flesh aside, and be still, knowing He was God, and she was not. God was calling to Rebecca, Rosie sensed that. And Rebecca was hearing Him, faintly, gingerly, wooing her to Him. Rosie prayed for many years from across the street for Rebecca. And now Rosie had been invited in…to talk…and talk they would, as God directed.

Rosie's thoughts were turned back to Rebecca as she reentered the room saying, "It was from Nelson—he has been with Jennifer a while, and he needs to go do some things. He wants to know if I can go by to see her." Rebecca heaved a sigh, and looked straight at Rosie. Tucking in her lips, and nodding her head, she reluctantly said, "I gotta do, what I gotta do. It went okay last night when it was just the two of us; I can do this again."

Rosie knew that Rebecca was yet to understand these hard "assignments" are best done in the power of the Holy Spirit. Even trying to explain all of that to her now would overwhelm her. The best thing Rosie could do for her now was pray, if Rebecca was alright with that…

"Rebecca, I won't keep you any longer then. I'm glad we've had a bit of time together this morning. I would love to talk with you more any time you are able. I'll check back with you soon, if that's okay?"

"I'd like that, Rosie. Thank you."

"Would it be okay with you if I pray for you before I go?" Rosie didn't want to seem overly "religious," but she knew sending Rebecca out today in her own strength would not be smart.

"Of course that's fine! I'd really appreciate that."

Rosie reached out and took hold of Rebecca's hand. "Father God, thank You for this time with Rebecca. She has a challenging day ahead with Jennifer, and her heart is still hurting about her own friend, Bonnie. Help

Rebecca know that You are with her—that she can call on You any time of the day, and You are willing to help her. I lift Rebecca up to You. Help her to rest in Your loving embrace. Thank You, Lord Jesus, for the Hope we have in You. Amen."

They both sat motionless when the prayer ended, as a peace settled in. Rosie then slowly stood up, followed by Rebecca. They walked to the door, where Rosie gave Rebecca a hug. She could tell that Rebecca needed more than just human love...she needed love from Heaven above. Rosie was hoping this was the beginning of a new season for them as neighbors. What she didn't know at the time was that Rebecca was feeling the same way. After all the years of practically avoiding Rosie, now Rebecca didn't want to see Rosie leave. Rebecca closed the door with care, and stood there asking God to please help her, repeating parts of what Rosie had prayed. Rebecca didn't know if anyone could really hear her. But it seemed to Nelson, and to Rosie, Someone was listening. Maybe God would listen to her, too.

As Rebecca got ready to go see Jennifer, she wanted to be able to bring her friend some comfort...maybe even some of the same comfort that Rosie had brought to her this morning. Rebecca longed for the wisdom and insight that Rosie had. Rebecca thought, if there is a God, what a treasure He has given me...to have Rosie so near at a time like this.

8

Rosie wasn't gone but about ten minutes or so when Rebecca heard another knock on the door. She looked around to see if Rosie forgot something, and then remembered, oh yes, the plate. I forgot to give it back to Rosie. Rebecca went to the kitchen to get it, and answered the door holding out the plate…only it wasn't Rosie. Rebecca took a quick breath in, her eyes widened, as she looked straight into the face of Don. He looked at the plate in her hand, and said, "Oh…looks like you were expecting someone else?"

"Uhhh, yes. Yes I was."

They stood in awkward silence for a few moments. Rebecca wasn't quite sure what she was supposed to do. And it didn't seem like Don knew either…although he was the one who had shown up at her front door.

"Is something wrong, Don? It's a work day, and neither one of us should be here right now. How did you know I was home? And why aren't you at work?" Rebecca was sounding annoyed, and she knew it. She tried to hold her tongue, not wanting him to have control of her emotions. It's not that the divorce ended so terribly that she hated Don. But it was still uncomfortable. She was hoping one day she'd get past that. Don had been a good husband, better than she had been a wife. He never treated her harshly, and even was very generous in the divorce proceedings. It's just that with an ex, there is probably always tension.

"I was in the area, Bec, and…."

Rebecca didn't really hear what he said after that. When "Bec" came out of his mouth it rubbed her the wrong way. He always called her that. It just didn't seem right to her now. They weren't really friends, and the intimate sound of her name made her feel uneasy.

"I'm sorry. What did you say, Don?"

"I said, I was in the area, on a call, and I was thinking about you."

"Thinking about me?" This really puzzled Rebecca. She didn't think Don thought much about her at all. His life seemed to have gone on, full, happy, and with barely a ripple from the divorce.

Don continued, "I didn't figure you would be home. But I hadn't been by the house in a while, so I thought I'd drive by. When I saw your car here, I decided to stop. I really hadn't planned this...I'm sorry, to just drop in like this. Are you sick today? Is there something I can get for you?"

"No, no, I'm not sick. And I don't need anything." Rebecca knew she was being short with him. She didn't seem to be able to help it. She wondered how often he just "happened to be in the area," and drove by what used to be their home? Rebecca didn't like the idea that Don might have been doing that. She was trying to move on with her life. The divorce had been final for almost two years now, and she didn't want much if any contact with Don. A lot of the anger had subsided. Rebecca just needed to keep Don out of her thought process—so seeing him, or thinking he might be driving by, was not helpful.

"Bec, I...was wondering if I might be able to come in for a moment. I won't stay long, really." Don asked her in a way that made it hard for her to resist. She knew him well enough to know that he didn't do things for no reason. And Don wasn't being forceful, although he never really was. He stood, and waited for her reply...

"If it's not a good time, I understand," Don said. He waited for Rebecca to say something, anything...although he could see by the look on her face she was considering allowing him in. He knew when she was "not having it"...so to speak, and this was not one of those times.

"Don, it's not a good morning. I have a lot going on, and I need to leave soon...but I guess you can come in for a minute."

Rebecca stepped aside, and let Don into the front entryway. He didn't attempt to go past there, although he would have liked to sit with her in the living room to talk. But, she didn't invite him to sit down, so they remained standing.

"What's going on, Don?"

"I...uhhh, have been thinking about a lot of things, and I have been meaning to call you. But I thought maybe being with you in person would be better. I know you don't have time for a lengthy conversation right now, so it's probably best that I keep this short, and save the rest for a later time..."

"Yeah..." was all Rebecca could muster. She had no idea what was on his mind, and she really didn't care all that much. She needed him to get on with it.

"What I wanted to talk with you about was 'us,' Bec." He got it out fast, not sure at all how she was going to react. And now he couldn't tell what the look on her face meant. He didn't have to wonder long...

Rebecca quickly responded, "Us?! What do you mean, 'Us'? Us, as in you and me? I thought we finished that discussion a long time ago. I really don't have time to talk about 'us' this morning!"

Don knew this was crazy, and he should have waited. He knew with Rebecca's response that it wasn't wise to continue. What was he thinking? But it seemed he couldn't stop himself once he got this ball rolling. Maybe because it took almost everything he had to stop in today, and he knew this might be a *now or never* opportunity.

"Bec, you seem to be in a hurry, and I know my timing is probably all off, but I wanted to tell you, I just needed to tell you... I... ummm... I... miss talking with you." The last part was said almost under his breath.

Rebecca reacted almost before the words were finished. "Miss talking with me?!! You gotta be kidding me! We barely talked when we were married. This was not at all what I thought my day would hold, and I'm not liking it much... Look Don, this is a loaded discussion that I'm not sure I want to be having, let alone right now. I appreciate that you felt it was better done face-to-face. I get that. But I've got so much on my mind right now... I'm totally on overload. You don't even know what's going on in my life. I think it's best that you leave." Rebecca was shaking her head like she was trying to get some cognitive thought through her brain. Don knew he surprised Rebecca, and he probably shouldn't have stopped by. He also knew how Rebecca worked. She would usually react out of emotion, flinging out a string of words, and then after a couple of days, they would be able to talk things through. At least that's how it was when they were together. But it seemed now he had little if any hope that this "seed" of thought would sprout. It was probably best if he made a quick exit.

"Bec, thanks. Thanks for letting me in. Sorry. It is unfair of me to do this to you. I don't know what I was thinking. I'm sorry...really sorry."

Rebecca could tell Don was regretting following his impulse today to stop in, and then say this out of the blue. She sort of felt bad for him. Don exposed his heart to her, and she was trampling on it, and that's not really what she wanted to be like. It was just the easiest thing to do in the moment. Rebecca knew that "easiest" had gotten her into trouble before. She found that following an "easy" path is usually not the best path. Rebecca wanted her life to be different now, and maybe she could start with Don right here, right now. She felt like she was groaning inside, and she didn't want him to hear it. Rebecca was fighting with herself...her old self, and the new self she wanted to be. She loved how Nelson and Rosie handled things, and she wanted to be like that, but she was finding it SO difficult. Maybe she could just fake it until she could make it real in her own life…whatever that looked like…whatever that took.

Swallowing her anger and a bucket load of other emotions, Rebecca said, "I have some places to be right now. Maybe we can discuss this another day." Rebecca tried to sound sincere, but she was having a hard time. She was struggling with her words. Her thinking was, "Hold on, he will be gone soon. You can shut the door and scream if you want to then!!"

"Thank you," was all Don could say. He turned to go. The door hadn't even been completely shut when he came in, so it wasn't but a moment and he was out the door. Rebecca closed it quickly, not even saying, "Good-bye." Standing there inside the door, Rebecca took in a deep breath. For some reason, she felt like crying. Then she noticed she was still holding the plate she was going to give back to Rosie. She took it into the kitchen, set it down, and then leaned on the counter for support. Rebecca didn't know how much more she could take in 24 hours. Needing to get her head back into a place of thinking about helping Jennifer, Rebecca wondered why life had to be so full of confusion? Rosie's timing seemed so perfect this morning. Don's timing seemed horrible! Rebecca walked into the living room and flopped down onto the couch. She would give herself a few moments to gather her emotions before leaving. She couldn't arrive at Jennifer's upset about Don. That was the last thing Jennifer would need.

Slumped on the couch, Rebecca breathed out almost without thinking, "Lord, give me strength!" Just then, the sun moved from behind a cloud outside her window, shining on the silver pages of the Bible she had placed on her coffee table. She gasped! "Really, God? Did You just do that? That seems too coincidental…" Rebecca stayed very still, and stared at the Bible. She feared it. What if she opened it, and it confused her more? Or what if she opened it and read something that made her feel completely uncomfortable about herself? It seemed so threatening. She wouldn't even know where to turn if she did open it up. Then again, she prayed just then, hadn't she? And if God really heard her talking to Him, and He really was making the sun shine on the pages of the Bible to get her attention, it didn't seem right to just ignore it. Isn't this what she was looking for? She heard in church the week before about having a "personal" relationship with Jesus. Rebecca never thought about God in that way. How could it be personal when He was so far away, if He was even there at all? Rebecca really didn't even know where to start. But she thought to herself, maybe it's time. I shouldn't miss this opportunity.

Rebecca pulled herself up to a sitting position—seemingly out of respect for what she was about to do. She stared at the Bible, and then picked it up. All it said on the cover was "Holy Bible." Being at a loss, she prayed as best she could, "God, help me know where to read in here. I have no idea, and I don't know if I will understand it when I do." Rebecca waited, and nothing happened. She prayed again, "God, can You make this simple for me? It seems too hard. Something inside of me is resisting opening this book, Your Book. Help me please." Still nothing. Rebecca wanted to be persistent. She didn't want to give up too easily…there was that word again. *Easy.* She didn't want the easy way out this time. Rebecca didn't want to quit before even getting started. She began to flip through the pages. She liked the way the silver edges felt as she thumbed through them. Should she start at the beginning, like with most books? Rebecca stopped where she was and opened the page fully. It said, "James 3" at the top. And then she saw a heading that talked about "Controlling the Tongue." She read in a paragraph with a number "7" by it, *"People can tame all kinds of animals and birds and reptiles and fish, but no one can tame the tongue. It is an uncontrollable evil, full of deadly poison."*

Whoa! How did that just happen? I was trying my hardest to control my tongue with Don, and then I open to this page…somewhere in the back of the entire book? Out of all the pages I could have turned to, I turn to this one? This is too crazy! This is freaky! Next to the large number 4 on the opposite page she read, *"What is causing the quarrels and fights among you?"* She closed the Bible and leaned back into the couch, trying to take this in.

"Really? I didn't know the Bible even talked about such things!" Rebecca knew she was talking to herself at this point, or to God, or whoever might be listening. But she didn't care. She just experienced something new in her life, and she wanted more of it. She wanted to know a God who could hear her prayer, shine His sun, get her attention, and then speak to her present situation with such accuracy. Did this happen to everyone? Rebecca couldn't wait to talk about this with Rosie the next time she saw her. Maybe Rosie could explain this. She would take Rosie's plate back to her soon…very soon.

Rebecca put the Bible back on the coffee table with a new respect. She made sure to place it so the silver part was facing the window, just in case God wanted to get her attention with the sun again. She really needed to get over to Jennifer's now. As Rebecca got up, she felt so different from when she flopped down onto the couch in desperation. She couldn't quite explain it, but it felt good. Maybe she felt hopeful.

9

Finally on her way to Jennifer's, the drive seemed easy compared to what Rebecca's morning had been like. She had seen the highs and lows already, and was much preferring the highs. By now, it was almost 1:00. Rebecca texted Jennifer to see if she'd like some lunch. Jennifer said she wasn't hungry, but maybe a drink from the juice place would be good. She gave Rebecca her order. It felt good to be doing something for Jennifer. Rebecca didn't feel like she could be the help that Nelson always seemed to be, but she would do her best.

Some light music was playing when she rang the bell. Jennifer called out, "Come in!" Jennifer was sitting in the front room under a blanket. Rebecca wasn't sure where best to sit. She decided it might make it easier to sit next to Jennifer so they didn't have to make as much eye contact when they talked. Jennifer slowly sipped on her drink, crying off and on. She reminisced about her times with Justin; how they met, how they felt about each other. It seemed Jennifer needed to share her memories, keeping Justin alive in that room, however long it would last. The phone rang many times—friends and family were calling to let her know they heard the news, asking what, if anything, they could do. Jennifer let most of the calls go to voicemail, listening to them, and talking about who called with Rebecca. It was the first time Rebecca really had a full scope of Jennifer's family and friends in Phoenix. There were some local calls, but mostly, they were people she knew from back home. Jennifer would take a call if it was someone particularly close to her. But it was so hard for her to talk—the calls didn't last long. As the afternoon wore on, Jennifer dozed a bit and Rebecca did the same. It felt good to be together even if Rebecca didn't have all the wise words she might need. At least Jennifer wasn't alone. Nelson called a couple of times. He was taking care of some business for Jennifer, so he had questions that needed answering. They found out later in the day that Justin's family would be doing a service for him in Florida. Jennifer would have liked it to be here, but she understood. She and Rebecca talked about maybe doing something for Justin in town, even if it were just a small gathering. That seemed to help Jennifer feel better.

Eventually, it was getting close to dinnertime and neither of them had eaten. Rebecca gave Nelson a call, and he said he would bring some Chinese food about five. Jennifer didn't think she could eat much, but she appreciated his thoughtfulness. When the food came, they sat around the table, and as friends do, laughed and cried together. Nelson was gentle as he guided the conversation in a way that was so heart-warming to Rebecca. She watched as he would listen to Jennifer, and then he would nod, or say something simple, and she would continue sharing what was on her heart. Rarely would Nelson interject too much. He would just add something when it seemed the right time. Rebecca wondered how he had learned to be so good at this? She knew she would have mostly talked about unnecessary things to fill the empty space at dinner. Rebecca saw that the empty space didn't distract Nelson from listening. He didn't seem uncomfortable with silence. He used those opportunities for some peaceful reflection, and then for a question or two that helped Jennifer process her thoughts about Justin. Nelson was skilled, like he had once been in her shoes. He seemed to know what would hurt, and what would be of help. Nelson would talk about God from time to time. He talked about eternal life, and how thankful he was for what Jesus provided. Nelson said without Jesus' death and resurrection, they would not have the Hope that they do. Rebecca didn't really get the whole *death on the cross to give us life* thing, but that was okay. Nelson was mostly speaking to Jennifer at that point, and she seemed to be agreeing with all that he was saying. It seemed a comfort to her. Jennifer added in that she was thankful she and Justin had some time to talk about their faith with one another. Justin, too, believed in the "Hope of Jesus." That's how Jennifer put it. She said Justin had been raised mostly by his mom, and they attended a small Baptist church in Florida when he was growing up. He hadn't found a church here that he liked yet. But Justin told Jennifer he tried to read his Bible as much as possible. That was one of the things that Jennifer really liked about Justin, their common faith. Jennifer invited him to her church a couple of times, but he seemed to be looking for something a little different, maybe more conservative. Jennifer said her church was on the charismatic side. These words were not very familiar to Rebecca, but she was learning. Jennifer told them it really helped her to know where Justin was. Rebecca wondered what that place was like?

Rebecca enjoyed listening to the conversation between Jennifer and Nelson. There was such a calmness about it—a common thread that seemed to weave back and forth between the two of them. She guessed it was in times of tragedy that that thread was so important. Rebecca appreciated them letting her be a "fly on the wall." They didn't pressure her to join in, or leave her out, particularly...they just let the conversation be what it was, and she felt a part of it without having to say much.

With dinner finished, and the leftovers stored in Jennifer's fridge, everyone decided it was time to get some rest. Nelson and Rebecca would need to go back to work in the morning. Jennifer said she was taking some time off. She worked at a tech company about twenty minutes from where she lived. They were being very good about giving her the time to heal. Jennifer told them her heart felt very heavy, and she knew it was going to take a while to come through this. She would go back to work when the time was right. Jennifer said she knew too many people who buried their grief in busyness. She saw the results of that, even in her own family. It was not good—many years later they were still stuck in the sadness. Jennifer said that she wanted to grieve, but as one who has Hope, like the Bible talks about. Rebecca was hearing so many new things tonight. The Bible talks about grieving? She had never surrounded herself with people who knew these things. When Rebecca had been out at dinner parties, or social functions of any kind, the talk rarely went to the spiritual side. It always seemed to be about world events, sports, politics, or the weather, if nothing else was working. She liked the depth of Nelson and Jennifer...they talked about things that seemed to really help us in this life. These new friendships were expanding Rebecca's world, and she was excited about that.

Saying goodnight to Jennifer, Nelson and Rebecca walked out together. They stood by their cars gazing up at the beauty of the night sky.

"I should really do this more often," Rebecca commented. "Even in the Bay Area, there are places to go where the lights are not so bright, and the stars can be seen well. I love looking at them."

"I know. I feel the same way," Nelson said. "It's not as cool out here tonight. It's quite comfortable."

"Yes, it is."

Rebecca and Nelson spent some time talking over all that happened, out of earshot of Jennifer. They were concerned about her, of course, but they both agreed that Jennifer was going to be able to come through this. They would not rush her. And they would tag-team in helping her so that the load would not be too heavy on either one of them. Jennifer told them her mom was coming sometime next week. They wondered if they should wait to have a little service for Justin when she got there, and decided that would be a good idea. Especially since it was Easter week, and most people were busy with their families. They would get together soon and work out some details with Jennifer. The one thing they all agreed upon was having it outside somewhere, maybe in a garden, to keep it light and hope-filled. Nelson said since they all went to different churches, that would make it easier also. To Rebecca, it felt good the way Nelson said that… "they all went to different churches." He remembered that she had been at church when her car wouldn't start. He didn't think that was odd, but more normal than not. Nelson told Rebecca that when he could, he attended church. But his job made it hard to be there on Sunday mornings. It helped that they had a Saturday night service he could sometimes attend.

Even though it felt good to talk this through, it had been draining. They needed to get to bed. With a friendly hug, they parted ways, and drove off toward home. They hadn't known that Jennifer was glancing out of her bedroom window from time to time wondering if they would be a good match. Jennifer liked them both a lot. But so far, Jennifer saw no indication that Nelson and Rebecca were interested in each other beyond friendship. Jennifer was thankful to have them in her life, especially right now. She knew that Nelson would be there, he was just that kind of a guy. But with Rebecca, she didn't know her all that well. There were times when Rebecca was very warm and friendly, and other times when she was standoffish. Jennifer was very thankful that Rebecca had come to the hospital with Nelson, knowing it was probably hard for her. Jennifer hoped their friendship would grow. She wanted to get to know Rebecca better. Jennifer knew Rebecca had been through a divorce, but they hadn't talked about it all that much. And as far as what Rebecca believed? That was sort of an unknown, too. Rebecca seemed to respond as though she, too, believed in Jesus. She certainly wasn't arguing against what they both had to say about their Hope in Him. Death can wake people up from the stupor of thinking life on this earth is forever. It was surely making Jennifer focus on things besides this world. The night Justin died, Jennifer kept thinking about what he might be experiencing in Heaven. Jennifer knew something about Heaven, but not nearly enough. Maybe she would use this time off to read up on it. Jennifer could ask her mom about a good book that might explain more about Heaven. Jennifer's mom was a strong Christian, and she read a lot. Even though they didn't talk about these things as much as she would have liked, Jennifer's mom was always open to her questions. It would be good to have her here next week. Jennifer needed her mom's comfort and wisdom at a time like this.

There seemed to be something more Jennifer should be doing. But then again, what? She was so tired, and this was all so shocking…it just didn't seem possible that Justin was gone. His last smile to her was so imprinted on her mind. Jennifer was glad she hadn't seen him at the hospital. Justin would want to be remembered in a good way. He was a happy guy, kind of nerdy, but she liked that about him. Most guys she dated thought they were way too cool. Justin didn't. He just relaxed, laughed, joked, and acted like there was plenty of time to grow up, saying he wasn't quite ready yet. He brought the kid out of Jennifer when she got too serious. She would miss him so... Wiping away many tears, Jennifer's eyes finally closed and she was able to get some sleep.

10

Nelson woke the next morning not really ready to return to work. The sadness from Jennifer intermingled with his own loss from years ago. In times like this, so many memories would come flooding back. Nelson really didn't want to relive them again, but maybe it was necessary. Maybe there were things that he missed. There was no need to fear it. It caused his faith to grow in ways that he never imagined, and he was thankful for that. What the enemy had meant for harm, God had truly used for good. It helped him to understand how what hurts most, sometimes helps most. Nelson didn't share this part of his life with many people. He was torn— not wanting it to be wasted, but also keeping it private. He also knew he wanted to be careful to not make this all about him when Jennifer was the one who needed support. There had been so many wonderful people surrounding him when he needed it. Nelson wanted to pay it back in any way he could. As tragic as this was for Jennifer, it was giving him that opportunity. From what he understood, that's the way God's economy works.

Nelson rolled over and stared at the painting on the wall. He loved that it was one of the first things he saw each day. Nelson didn't know when Jill gave him that piece out of her collection that it would become so precious to him. In fact, he didn't really care for it much at first. But because she loved it, he grew to love it. Now it was priceless to him. The artist simply signed his work, "B.H.". Nelson never heard of him before. He was a little-known painter who worked out of his home in Napa. Once when Jill toured the winery, she came upon his studio. She immediately fell in love with the color combinations, and the shadowing in his art work. Jill painted a bit herself, and she said when she spent a great deal of time painting, she would notice the shadows everywhere. She didn't like it when the busyness of life got in the way of her painting. She talked about a quieter time in life, maybe in her later years, when she could paint to her heart's content. Sadly, Jill would never see those later years. Just as Jennifer had been called to walk through grief with Justin's accident, Nelson had done the same. Jill had been on her bike, riding outside the city on a mostly deserted country road. A car that had just passed by her said she had been wearing her headset. Nelson knew how much she loved music. Jill knew she shouldn't be listening to it while riding, but it was hard not to. It added so much to her ride. Jill told Nelson that the music seemed to fit the beauty of her surroundings. The driver of the car saw her turn to cross over the tracks. She must not have heard the train. She was killed instantly. It eased Nelson's heart a bit, knowing she died listening to the music that gave her such great joy. They were going to be married in just a few months...they were both 24.

Nelson continued to stare at the painting, and he could not help tearing up. The missing he felt in the past was similar to what Jennifer would be going through now. Although Jennifer and Justin had not dated as long, or as seriously, Nelson knew it would leave a hole in Jennifer that only God could fill...and questions that only a trust in God would bring peace to. Nelson remembered so many questions in his grief, and so many doubts...they wore him out until he came to a place where God was God, and he was not, and he would learn to live in that knowing. Sixteen years without Jill, and he still thought about her every day. The pain in his heart subsided, but the missing was still there. He wondered if they had been able to marry, would they have had children together? Would marriage and all that it entailed be enjoyable? Or maybe God saw it as Jill lived her whole life by age 24. Was that God's plan, although hard to understand?

The phone dinged with a text, and Nelson's thoughts about Jill were interrupted. It was work...he would let it go. They could wait a few more minutes before absorbing his daylight hours. Nelson wanted to spend this time "with" Jill, getting lost in the painting with all its wonderful colors and brush strokes. Jill taught him how to appreciate details that he never noticed before. He loved to listen to the excitement in her voice when she talked about it, and watch the expression on her face change as she pointed out different aspects of the paintings. It didn't matter that he wouldn't be able to repeat it...they were together, and she was happy. The "B.H." paintings were a bit pricey, but she would save up to buy each one. Jill collected five—her parents kept two, one was given to her best friend, Stacy, and then he was given one other one that he eventually donated to the hospital. They placed it in a small conference room where families would gather to be told news of their loved ones' condition. He hoped that a part of Jill in that room would bring peace to someone's heart. It was a beautiful painting of a field of flowers.

Nelson and Jill met in the young adults' group at church. It didn't take Nelson long to know she was the girl for him. It took Jill a while longer to know he was her guy, but when she did, there was no turning back. Jill gave him her whole heart, and he handled it with great care because she had his whole heart, too. Nelson had never met anyone who touched his life like Jill had, although he wasn't really searching. They had been so young—just finishing college, looking forward to a bright future. Jill was raised in a strong Christian home. Nelson just the opposite. He was new to the whole church thing when they met at 20. Nelson didn't even want to go the first time, but a friend of his invited him. Nelson's curiosity got the better of him. Nelson always wondered about life in general. We are born, we live, we die...all for what? It wasn't making much sense to him at 20. It's not that he had a bad life, or a hard life. It's not that he was looking to change much about anything in his life...he just had this sinking feeling that without a God, life didn't mean anything.

Nelson asked his mom when he was about eight if she believed in God. She had flat out told him, "No." That settled it for him. He didn't believe either, until...he met Jesus one night at the young adult group. The pieces seemed to all fall into place as the youth pastor told the story of Jesus. He said that all had sinned, that all fall short of the mark, just as an archer's arrow would not just miss the bull's-eye, it wouldn't even make it to the target. Nelson could relate to that. He had done a bit of archery in high school, and he was terrible at it. He totally missed the target many times. It didn't feel good. He wanted to know more about this "Man" who could help him hit the target every time. But now it wasn't about archery, it was about life, and being able to stand before God some day and be accepted by Him. The pastor said because of Jesus, the Father in Heaven sees us like He's looking at the Champion Archer, the One who not only hits the target every time, He *is* the Target. Jesus is the One we are to focus on, and He is perfect. His perfection is what makes us perfect. It's not what we do, or how we do it, it's because Jesus has already done it for us. When we get to the medal platform, Jesus will say, "Stand here with Me." The pastor explained that Jesus accomplished all this by dying on the Cross for us, because it was His blood that washed us clean from all the mistakes we have ever made...every time we missed the mark. Nelson knew there was so much more he needed to learn. But one thing he did know, if Jesus was the way for this life to make some sense, then Nelson wanted in. He wanted to be a part of what the pastor was calling the Family of God. And so, Nelson said, "Yes." Some in the group that night gathered around him afterward, welcoming him to the family. Jill being one of them. She had been with him from his first day of walking with God, and she had been a big part of helping him find his way through those early learning steps. Jill taught him how to stand strong in what you believe, but be gentle with those new to the faith.

Nelson and Jill mostly spent time together with the group, studying the Bible each Tuesday night. On Fridays, they would all go to the local dance studio and take swing-dance lessons. At first Nelson felt like he literally had two-left feet, but he started to get the hang of it. They would rotate partners through the hour-long lesson, and every time he was able to dance with Jill, it felt right. Not only was she a good dancer, it was the way she looked at him, and supported him in his ineptness until he caught on. She was always so patient, and kind, never laughing at him, but always with him, as he learned the different steps. Sunday, they would attend church together, still as a group, sitting in the front left side of the church. It felt good to be a part of them, and to be learning more about God with people his own age. It seemed the longer he spent getting to know God, the more some of his other friends drifted away. They weren't as interested in the same things anymore. Nelson would see them to watch football once in a while, or attend a baseball game, but mostly, he would spend time with Jill and the group.

One Friday night after their dance lesson, the whole group went out for pizza. Jill and Nelson were sitting next to each other when Jill spilled her whole soda on the table, with most of it dripping off into Nelson's lap. He jumped up as quickly as possible, but not before his pants were soaked in cola. Jill was SO apologetic. But she told him weeks later that when he helped her clean up the mess, and made sure she was okay, even getting her a new glass of soda, she was seeing in him the type of man she would someday want to marry. He never once got angry at her for the mess she made all over him. He later told her that he had been happy to sit in the sticky mess, as long as she was at his side. After that night, their relationship changed. They started spending more and more time together, in church and out.

Nelson's phone went off again, pulling him back into the present day. He knew this time to get up and get going. He also knew the time was coming when he would share his story with Rebecca and Jennifer. There were things he wanted to tell them; how his grief strengthened his faith, and also how hard it was. If he didn't tell them soon, when it did come out, they would wonder why he kept it from them...considering the circumstances. It was a touchy thing, and he wanted to make sure that he was listening to the Holy Spirit guide him through this time. Both Jennifer and Rebecca were special people in his life, and they deserved his honesty. He wanted to tell them many times before about Jill, but it hadn't seemed the time, until now. He would be praying about it throughout his day, and the days to come. He wondered how it would all unfold. But one thing he knew for sure, God would help them all through this time as they depended on Him.

Nelson took one last look at the "B.H." painting, blew a kiss at Jill's picture on his nightstand, and got up to shower and dress. When his mornings started like this, he could be a bit melancholy throughout the day. Jill seemed so far away from him. But she wasn't. He knew that he was merely a heartbeat away from seeing her again. Some days, he wished he could make the journey Home sooner rather than later. But most days, he was content to live each day in the abundant life that Jesus was giving him. God taught him that death comes to us all…it's what we do with our earthly life while walking with Jesus that matters most.

Before he left for work, Nelson sat in his favorite chair for a bit, and opened his Bible to Psalm 46. He read, "God is our refuge and strength, always ready to help in times of trouble. So we will not fear, even if earthquakes come and the mountains crumble into the sea." Nelson ignored his phone vibrating again and again. The world just didn't understand, without this time with God, he would be going through the day in his own strength, and that was not a pretty sight. With God as his refuge and strength, with God as his help in this time of trouble, Nelson would not fear what was to come, or what had been. The Bay Area, even being known for earthquakes, was not to be feared. God is in control. Nelson would continue on in his own healing, and in helping Jennifer begin hers. Nelson would not give up having known Jill for anything, even though it meant living without her now. Nelson knew he had not just loved and lost, he had loved and gained so very much with Jill.

Out the door, into his work vehicle, and on his way…Nelson went out like a warrior, even if it was merely ATM's that he was fighting. "They break'em, we fix'em," he said to himself. Nelson knew his job like the back of his hand after ten years, and he enjoyed it. He was thankful to be able to go into his day confident in not only what he was doing, but in the great Hope he lived with…knowing his eternity was secure in Heaven, and he WOULD see Jill again. Nelson realized he needed to be more open about all of this with Jennifer. She needed to know that it *would* get better one day.

11

Rebecca and Nelson kept true to their word, and stayed close by Jennifer throughout the week. Nelson would stop in if he was in the area, to see how she was getting along. Jennifer was reading the book her mom recommended on Heaven. She would share parts of it with Nelson as they would visit, and it was helping both of them understand that Heaven is not just some mystical place in the sky. Heaven is very real. Very beautiful. And they would know their loved ones when they saw them again. Jennifer was reading the book slowly, along with her Bible, not having much energy to do much else. Jennifer told Nelson she was wanting to stay focused on what was true, right and honorable because she was tempted in her thoughts to go to very dark places. When she did that, it took such a toll on her emotionally. It didn't help her to think about Justin's accident, what he might have felt, or even what she may have done differently in their relationship to make it better. None of that changed anything. She had to think about how happy Justin was in Heaven, and *believe* nothing on earth bothered him anymore. Jennifer had to remember that Justin would want her to work through her grief in a healthy way. She knew Justin would be happy that she was reading a book about Heaven. Jennifer wished she understood how much the Bible talks about Heaven—but she knew it was never too late to learn. Most, like her, didn't have much of a need to focus on what is beyond this world. Now she did. And she would. Jennifer no longer wanted to just keep busy in her day-to-day things, thinking that this world was her home…she needed to remember that she was only passing through on her way to a much better place—one that Jesus was preparing for her, and for everyone who believes in Him. She shared with Nelson that she just read in Acts 4, *There is salvation in no one else! There is no other name in all of heaven for people to call on to save them.* She told Nelson her heart longed for Heaven like never before.

One night, Rebecca and Nelson were able to talk more with Jennifer about having a service for Justin. They ironed out some details. They all agreed a garden setting would be nice. It wouldn't be a large service, but maybe include some music, and a little food. Since the three of them attended different churches, and Justin hadn't settled on a church yet, Jennifer asked Nelson if he would mind handling the service. At first, Nelson felt unable to fulfill such a request. He couldn't give her an answer right away. When he did, he told Rebecca and Jennifer that God reminded him that all things were possible through Christ, and that apart from the Holy Spirit he wasn't able to do this—but with God's help, he could do it. Nelson said he would be honored to do the service, and Jennifer gave him a long, loving hug, as her tears rolled freely. They decided they would wait for Jennifer's mom to be there, and also, they would be on the lookout for a nice garden setting. They knew of a few parks, but they were concerned about the privacy, so they would see if they could find something quieter.

Good Friday was coming, and then Easter. Rebecca wanted to attend Good Friday service at her new church. She'd never been before, and didn't know much about it, but she was willing to learn. When Friday came, she was at work and Ben started talking to her about Justin. She mentioned to him that she was supporting Jennifer, and that if she seemed a bit distracted, that was why. Ben was a kind man, a good boss, and he was fatherly figure to her. But Rebecca could tell he was not comfortable with the subject of death, and some of things he said didn't sit very well with her. She tried to be forgiving, but sometimes Rebecca just wanted him to leave her be in her thoughts. When she asked Ben if she could leave a bit early on Friday to go to church, he seemed genuinely happy for her, and readily agreed. Not that Ben was going, or even believed, but Rebecca could tell he wanted her to have something that would help her right now. She was glad about that.

When Rebecca arrived at church on Friday night, she was surprised at the number of cars in the parking lot. Rebecca wished she could be walking in with someone, anyone, rather than being alone. She and Don never went to church together, but she even thought about how it might be nice to have Don accompany her...maybe like back in the days when they were happy in their marriage. She and Don started out so well, and seemed so perfectly matched. Maybe if they had been able to have children, it would have worked out differently. But now, it was too late. They would have to let bygones be bygones, and go on with their lives. Rebecca knew she would probably be walking into many places alone for years...maybe always. She wasn't sure she had the energy to invest in another relationship anyway. If she was supposed to have a "relationship" with

Jesus, maybe that is all she could handle at the moment. Once she got that figured out, then she would see.

Rebecca took a seat over in a corner, wanting to observe more than participate. She watched as so many knew each other, and were giving hugs and handshakes. She didn't recognize anyone, not even from the two Sundays she had been there. When the music started, and the talking stopped, Rebecca was able to focus on what the service was all about, rather than how she was alone and everyone else seemed to be with someone. She didn't want to be sad. But between the divorce, Bonnie, and now Justin, she was having a hard time not crying her way through the service. The songs they sang didn't make a lot of sense to her. There was a lot of talk about the blood of Jesus. The Cross. And forgiveness of sins. She didn't feel like a big sinner, or in great need of a Savior. But she decided she was going to have patience with all of this, and get what she could out of it.

The pastor spoke about Jesus' suffering, the betrayal He felt, and that this was so hard for Jesus that He actually sweat blood. Rebecca again wondered why Jesus didn't run away from it all? But it sounded like Jesus went willingly when He was arrested, and put on trial. Jesus didn't say much in His defense. That puzzled Rebecca. Didn't Jesus have a group of people that supported Him? And then one of His closest friends, Peter, denied even knowing Jesus. It made Rebecca think of her own life, and the disappointments she'd gone through with people. Could Jesus really understand the hurt and pain she felt? Maybe that's how it got personal with Jesus? Jesus wasn't just a God up in the sky somewhere...He has been here with all of us, having gone through what we go through. And He died, too, like Justin. Jesus' death was SO painful. There was so much Rebecca was learning, and she wanted to grasp it, to comprehend it; but after a while, Rebecca's mind started to drift off. Her brain felt on overload. Once again, Rebecca thought about Rosie. If only she could sit with Rosie and ask her some questions...maybe Rosie could explain it in a way that Rebecca could better understand. This weekend, maybe she could take Rosie's plate back to her, and if Rosie had some time, they could talk. Rebecca surely hoped so... Suddenly the music was playing again and people were getting up. Rebecca realized she really had been off in her own world. She felt kind of bad. It seemed disrespectful to God, so Rebecca said a quiet, "Sorry God," when getting up to leave.

It was dark when Rebecca walked out of the church. But with so many people leaving at the same time, she felt safe getting to her car. Rebecca was hungry, and decided she would call Jennifer to see if she needed something to eat. She dialed her phone, realizing that Jennifer probably was at church, too, but then Jennifer answered.

"Hi. Sorry, I forgot you were probably at church," Rebecca said a bit hesitantly.

"Hi. No. I just couldn't go, Rebecca. I knew my tears might cause a flood, so I stayed home. I'm kind of sorry I didn't go. But it's too late now." Jennifer sounded so sad.

"I was thinking of getting something to eat, and I was wondering if you were hungry? Can I stop and get us a couple of burgers or something?" Rebecca was hoping she could cheer her up some. Rebecca was starting to feel less surprised at how she was caring for another person. She liked the new way she was thinking about others and not just her own misery.

Jennifer said, "That's so nice of you. I'd love to have you come over. It doesn't feel much like Good Friday sitting here alone. A burger would be great. Would you mind getting me a chocolate shake with that?"

"Sure. And do you like fries, too?" Rebecca could hear a small lift in her voice.

"Yes. Or we could share an order of fries. I don't need all that many." Jennifer knew her appetite still wasn't back to normal.

"Okay, dokey. I'll go to the drive through down the street from you, and be right over. Anything else you might need while I'm out?" Rebecca felt like she was on a roll with this new way of being. Maybe God really was changing her attitude about things.

"Nope, that's fine. I appreciate you and Nelson taking such good care of me. I know you both have a lot of your own things going on. I hope I'm not too much of a bother."

"Not in any way, Jennifer. We are here for you. This is a very tough time in your life, and we are happy to help...see you soon."

"Okay. Bye."

"Bye."

Jennifer had been watching for Rebecca, and when Rebecca walked up to the door, Jennifer opened it without her knocking. She greeted Rebecca with a small smile, the first one Rebecca had seen from Jennifer in the week since Justin's passing. They sat together on the couch, ate their burgers, and talked about little things. Jennifer was really looking forward to her mom arriving on Monday. She had been washing some sheets for the guest room bed. Rebecca offered to help her put it together, so they did that after they ate. She said her mom, Erika, would be staying a week. Erika wanted it to be longer, but family obligations in Phoenix made it so she couldn't. Jennifer let her mom know about having a service for Justin while she was there, and Erika was glad she would be able to attend. Her mom had never met Justin. They chatted through facetime, and she liked him. Erika had been happy that Jennifer had met a nice young man to keep her company in California. Jennifer's mom mentioned her moving back to

Phoenix for a while, and living with her mom and dad, but Jennifer didn't think she wanted to do that. She was just getting her life going in California, and didn't want to delay moving forward with her career. Jennifer was thankful though, and told her mom she would keep it in mind, if things got too hard for her.

About 8:30, Nelson arrived, and it gave all them time to talk about Justin's service a bit more. Nelson asked Jennifer a few questions about what she thought Justin would like. What kind of music he preferred, and if he had any favorite scripture? Jennifer went and got her Bible, and she was thumbing through it when she suddenly remembered a conversation she had with Justin about a month ago. He was talking about a friend of his who had an addiction, and even though Justin didn't battle the same addiction, Justin really liked the scripture that his friend pointed out to him. She tried to find it, but was having difficulty. Nelson got his phone, and brought up a website that he said could be useful when you can't find something in the Bible you are looking for. He asked Jennifer a few key words in the passage.

Jennifer said, "It talked about being doomed for our sins. And God's mercy. It also said something about being seated with Christ in Heaven. I don't know, it was long when Justin read it to me, but it was packed full of good stuff. I don't know if it would be something you can use or not, but if you can find it, we can decide." Jennifer seemed to drift off in her thoughts at that point...her eyes filling with tears. She said, "This is so hard..."

No one spoke for a while, letting Jennifer take some time to process all that was going on. Nelson kept at it with his phone, and Rebecca sat looking mostly at the floor, not knowing really what to do or say. Finally, the silence was broken when Nelson started to read what he found.

"I may have found it, or something close to it. This is in Ephesians 2. See what you think... 'But God is so rich in mercy, and he loved us so very much, that even while we were dead because of our sins, he gave us life when he raised Christ from the dead. (It is only by God's special favor that you have been saved!) For he raised us from the dead along with Christ, and we are seated with him in the heavenly realms—all because we are one with Christ Jesus.'"

"I don't know, that sounds close. Justin could have been reading it from a different translation, but I like it. I like that it talks about God's mercy, and how we have been given life through Christ. And it makes me think about Justin now in the heavenly realms." Jennifer took in a deep breath, letting it out slowly...it seemed hearing this read gave Jennifer a bit of life back.

"If it's what you want, then it's what I'll do, Jennifer." Nelson was gentle, and encouraging as he worked with her in talking about Justin's service. Rebecca so marveled at the ease in which he handled life's most difficult situations. "We can use that, and I'll see what else. It will all be fine. Let me know of any songs you might want to use, and I'll also check into some that I know. I don't want you to stress about any of this."

The evening was getting late, and they could tell Jennifer needed sleep, so they said good night and told her they would be seeing her soon. As they walked out the door, giving each other hugs, it felt good to be friends. Rebecca had never known relationships like these...there was something more here than what could be seen. Rebecca didn't quite know how to explain it, but she was grateful. Rebecca did know that this Easter she *would be* going to church. The pastor said at the Good Friday service, "Sunday's a comin'!" She wanted to know all that *Sunday* meant. Not just merely Easter eggs, and bunnies this year. From all that Rebecca was hearing, Justin had traveled to a place called Heaven that was more than clouds and harps like the cartoons depicted it. It had to do with sins being forgiven, and the dead being raised to life. Rebecca hoped one day it would start to make sense to her. For now, she would just remain close to those who knew this stuff, and listen, keeping her heart open. Rebecca knew her heart had been cold and hard for much too long. She was tired of who she had been. If Jesus offered her peace in the pain, and a new way of living, she welcomed it.

12

Rebecca was so glad it was Saturday. After a long week, she wanted to lounge a bit, enjoy her coffee, and maybe try to read a little in her Bible; although now it seemed to be looming large again. She wished she hadn't waited so long to get back to it. Why the fear, she wondered. Rebecca knew she would need to break through that, and do it anyway. But first she would put some laundry in. It was piling up. As she walked through the kitchen, she was reminded that she also wanted to go see Rosie today. The plate was still there. It seemed God had it at her house to give Rebecca the incentive to make a trip across the street. Rebecca wondered what it was in her that kept her from doing what she needed, and actually wanted, to do? It was like this tug o' war inside to find God, and run from Him, all at the same time. Sometimes Rebecca was glad she lived alone so she could process her thoughts without interruption. When she lived with Don, he would usually have the TV on. Many times, she needed it quiet. She could always go to her room, but sometimes that wasn't even enough. Living alone had its advantages. It also had its disadvantages...she was living *alone.* There again, the tug o' war. Most of life seemed to be that way— Rebecca loved her job, but she also wanted to stay home. It seemed all of life was about give and take, and mostly in life, up to this point, she had been a taker. Rebecca had to admit, she liked taking. She liked things to be all about *her.* She liked things to go *her* way. But that seemed to be slowly changing, and it was puzzling at times. Rebecca was finding that delivering a burger to Jennifer felt good. And sitting with Jennifer for hours on her couch, so Jennifer wasn't alone, seemed right, even though there were other things she could have been doing. God has a strange way of satisfying our souls, she thought, while putting her first load in the washer...it seems we would be happiest satisfying ourselves. But when truth be told, it feels better to help another in their time of need.

Rebecca was getting lost in her thoughts again as she picked up things around the house, sorted through the mail, and ironed her shirt for the day. Before she knew it, it was noon, and when she plopped back down on the couch she noticed her Bible still sitting there, unopened. Hmmmm, she thought, where has the morning gone? And then continued to eat her sandwich as she got lost in her thoughts again. When she was done, Rebecca took her plate into the kitchen, and there it was again, Rosie's empty plate. "That's it...I'm going to run to the bathroom and then take this plate back to her!" Rebecca said it out loud, almost lecturing herself in the process. She had seen Rosie out front earlier in the morning, working in the garden. She hoped Rosie was still home. Rosie didn't drive, but there were many people who would come by and pick her up. Rebecca didn't know if Rosie ever drove. They spent so little time together, she didn't even know if Rosie had ever been married, had children...or much about her life. Rebecca suddenly felt regret having been such an unfriendly neighbor. She knew that Rosie always welcomed her, but Rebecca was never very interested. Keeping to herself seemed the safest route to take, so she kept their relationship mostly to a wave and a smile. It was time to step out, even though it made her a bit nervous. What if Rosie got too nosey? What if she asked too many questions, or talked about things that were boring?...like all her stories from the past...Rebecca then realized she was talking herself out of going again, and she needed to just GO!

Plate in hand, she headed over, and rang Rosie's doorbell. She could hear music from inside, and it sounded beautiful. She must have a nice stereo system because it sounded so real. It wasn't but a moment, and the music stopped as Rosie opened the door.

"Rebecca! How are you? How are your fingers doing?" Rosie was so upbeat, Rebecca was almost speechless. But she was determined to see this through.

"Hi Rosie. I brought your plate back. Thank you so much for the cookies. They were delicious." Rebecca felt and sounded mechanical and stiff as she handed Rosie her plate. But she told herself, at least she was here. That was a start.

Rosie could tell almost immediately that Rebecca was nervous and stepping out of her comfort zone. She knew she was going to have to go easy. Rosie turned her enthusiasm down a bit, gently asking, "Would you like to come in? I was just finishing my lunch, and was bringing my dishes in the house when you rang. I'm glad I didn't miss you. Sometimes I can't hear the bell from the back."

Taking in a deep breath, and trying not to let Rosie see her discomfort, Rebecca answered, "Yes. Yes. That would be nice, if I'm not bothering you."

"Not at all. Please come in. Would you like to sit in the garden for a bit? It's such a lovely day."

"Okay." That was about all Rebecca could muster in the moment.

Rosie fully expected Rebecca to refuse her offer, as Rebecca had never been beyond the front entryway of Rosie's house. Rebecca always refused staying any longer than a few minutes. Rosie tried to not act surprised, taking the plate into the kitchen as Rebecca followed her through the house. Rebecca couldn't help but notice that the house didn't seem as old and cluttered as she expected it to be. Many people have so much stuff everywhere. Pictures. Nick-knacks. Books. Rosie's house was sparse, but not in a bad way. It had an air of lightness about it with just enough things around to make it feel very homey, and enough pictures on the walls to keep it interesting—but not so many as to seem overwhelming. There were fresh flowers in a few vases, one in the kitchen, two in the fireplace room. Rebecca could see the fireplace from where they were in the kitchen, and she noticed a large photo above it of a young couple in a very old frame. Rebecca wanted to get a better look at it, but she didn't want to be rude, so she kept silent. From where they stood, she could see that there was a black man and a white woman in the photo. It didn't look like a wedding photo, but it was some special occasion. The man was in military clothing, while the woman wore a fancy dress. Maybe it was a military ball? Could they possibly be Rosie's parents? She wondered about Rosie's heritage because of her warm brown complexion and soft wavy hair. Rebecca guessed her original hair color had been a beautiful brown, but at this point, it was pure white. When Rosie worked in the garden, her hair glowed angelically when the sun would hit it. It appeared almost like a halo, and Rebecca would often wonder if there were angels on this earth who appeared as human beings? Maybe Rosie was one? But since they lived across the street from each other for so long, she doubted that. Angels probably came and went, they didn't live as your neighbor. It was fun to imagine it sometimes, though.

Rosie was talking, but Rebecca missed the first part of what she was saying because she was focusing on the picture. Rosie noticed where Rebecca's gaze landed, and she sweetly said, "Those are my parents. They were wonderful people, although their marriage was difficult. Not because of their relationship, but because of people's prejudice against mixed marriages at that time."

Rosie knew she needed to not talk so much, and it was not time to go into that. She gingerly led Rebecca toward the back sliding-glass door off the fireplace room, letting Rebecca go out first. Rebecca gasped when her eyes caught sight of Rosie's large back yard. And it wasn't just any yard, it was a garden of pure delight! To Rebecca, it looked like something right out of a magazine. The colors were spectacular, and the arrangement of plants and trees were amazing. There were fountains trickling, and a green lawn that looked almost like lush carpeting. Large rocks were distributed just so, making it seem like their natural environment—they looked inviting to sit on, or for a small child to imagine a great adventure while crawling on and through them. A sweet white bench sat off in one corner of the yard. Many bird feeders hung in the trees nearby. The birds were devouring their contents, and singing to their hearts' content. Rosie's garden oozed of love, care, and time spent crafting it in such a way that it became a peaceful place of retreat. It was unlike anything that Rebecca had ever experienced at someone's home. As Rebecca stood and took all this in, Rosie remained quiet and watched Rebecca's eyes wander throughout the garden. Rosie was pleased to see that Rebecca was enjoying it. Rosie didn't have children, but to her, as she planted each seedling, and watched it grow and blossom, they sort of felt like her babies. Rosie's mom once told her that when raising children, "You can raise weeds, or you can raise flowers." Since Rosie didn't have her own children, she raised flowers. Her garden was such a joy to her, and sharing it with others was a great part of that joy.

"Oh Rosie…this is simply beautiful! Did you do this all on your own?" Rosie could hear the awe at God's beauty in Rebecca's voice, although she was giving Rosie the credit.

"Well, let's just say I tend to it. It's God's garden. I plant. I water. And God is the One that makes things grow." Rosie always loved how Scripture talked of seeds being planted in God's Kingdom work. It reminded her each day that God is the One working all things out for His glory. Whenever Rosie looked at the unique design of each flower, she marveled at the Lord's artistry. When Rosie would smell each different scent, it seemed that she was breathing in the Lord's fragrance. Spending time in this garden in God's presence were wonderful times of refreshment for Rosie—God's promises would become so real to her. Rosie had seen so much in all her years, and she knew the world was hard, and could be very cruel. She knew it was important to get alone with her Father here, and be reminded of His goodness.

Rosie led Rebecca to an arrangement of chairs with soft cushions that were under a canopy off to the right. It was almost like having a living room outside. It felt so warm and comfortable. Rosie said she would be right back. It wasn't long and Rosie returned with a tray of cookies and lemonade. It reminded Rebecca of a story from her childhood called, "Lemonade and Cookies." It had always been one of her favorites that her mom would read. The family in the story went off on a long, hot hike, and when they returned home, the reward was going to be ice-cold lemonade and cookies. But it was locked in the house, and they lost the key. They could only see it through the window...Rebecca couldn't remember the story exactly. She searched for it through the years, but never come upon it again.

Rosie offered Rebecca a cookie, and she gladly took one. The cookie tasted yummy as usual...another one of Rosie's homemade delicacies. With lemonade in hand, Rebecca turned her attention on Rosie. Rebecca wasn't quite sure how to start, but it seemed in the moment, she should wait a bit. Rosie was sipping her lemonade, and letting her eyes take in all the colors in their midst. She saw a smile on Rosie's face...maybe it felt good for Rosie to just sit and enjoy it all instead of pulling weeds, clipping, and watering. Then again, probably to Rosie, it all held a certain amount of pleasure. Rosie started humming a tune that Rebecca wasn't familiar with, and then Rosie started to sing some of the most beautiful words Rebecca heard about God so far. When Rebecca listened to the songs on Sunday morning at church, it was different. This seemed so personal to Rosie as she sang:

"I come to the garden alone, while the dew is still on the roses. And the voice I hear, falling on my ear, the Son of God discloses. And, He walks with me and He talks with me, and He tells me I am his own. And the joy we share as we tarry there, none other has ever known."

Rosie started humming again as she turned to Rebecca saying, "I'm sorry. Sometimes, I just get lost in this place. It's where God feels most real to me."

"Oh... That was beautiful! Thank you for sharing that song with me." Rebecca loved the sound of Rosie's voice. It was probably in the alto range, although not being any sort of an expert with music, she really didn't know. It was so calm and soothing, and seemed to make the garden feel alive. (Rebecca now knew where the music was coming from when she came to Rosie's door.)

Rebecca couldn't help but ask, "Rosie, which is your favorite flower in the garden?" Rosie didn't even hesitate with her answer. Rebecca was surprised, she would have thought there were lots of special ones.

"Oh, I really love the daffodils—their beautiful yellow color. But they don't last long, Rebecca. Maybe that's a good lesson in life. Those we love can be gone quickly, so we should cherish every moment we have with them."

"It's interesting that you should say that...I hope you don't mind...I wanted to talk with you about some things. About...well...God, really...especially with going through this time with Jennifer that I told you about. And also my friend, Bonnie." Rebecca was tentative, but she knew this was important, and she had to keep going.

Rosie peacefully said, "We have all afternoon if you want. I'm in no hurry." Rosie glanced at a Bible that was sitting next to her. Rebecca hadn't noticed it when they first sat down. "I sit here for hours having my quiet time, listening to the birds sing, and longing to hear God's voice through His Word."

Rebecca didn't quite know where to go with that. Sometimes when she was with those who read their Bibles, they talked in a way that she wasn't used to hearing. She tried to listen, and really hear what Rosie was saying.

"Rosie, what's a *quiet time*? I have heard others talk about that, like Nelson, and Jennifer, and even the pastor at the new church I have started attending. Does that mean you just sit and be quiet for a length of time? Or is there something special that you do?"

Rosie loved Rebecca's interest, and thought a few moments before answering. "Really, it can be a lot of different things, and look a lot of different ways. For me, sometimes I come out here, and enjoy God's creation and soaking in God's Word. By soaking, I mean I will turn to a place in the Bible and read it over a few times. I will stop on certain words that seem to jump out at me, and I will ask God if He has something there for me to learn. Then I sit and listen, and see if I can hear God's gentle whisper. Sometimes I do, many times I don't. But that doesn't matter. I know God is listening. His silence might just mean that He wants me to read on. Quiet time is a time of being with Jesus, like He is our friend. We can tell Him what's on our mind, what's troubling us, or ask Him any questions we have about anything. We can just be still with Him, or thank Him. It's sort of like you and me sitting here together talking. But it's with God."

"You talk about God, and you talk about Jesus. Are they the same person? Is Jesus God?"

"Jesus is God. God is in three persons, the Father, the Son, Jesus, and the Holy Spirit. They are called the Trinity. This can seem confusing. But we can think of it, maybe, like an apple. There is the core, the skin, and the white flesh of the apple. They are all different, yet all apple. The Father, Son, and Holy Spirit have different roles in our lives. All are God."

"What roles?" Rebecca asked.

"Well, Father God created everything there is, and He is seated on His Throne in Heaven. But because we sin, we can't go to the Father. Jesus had to come to earth and die. His blood, that was shed on the Cross, washes away our sins so we can be clean enough to enter into Heaven. There is no other way to the Father except through the Son, Jesus. After rising from the dead, Jesus took His place beside the Father to intercede for us. The Holy Spirit then came to live in everyone who believes in Jesus. The Holy Spirit gives us counsel, strength, comfort, and so many other things that help us in this life. Am I making sense?" Rosie knew it was a lot to take in all at once.

"Yes, that seems to make sense. And when I said 'yes' to Jesus, you're saying the Holy Spirit came to live in me?" This astounded Rebecca.

Rosie responded, "Yes. *He* does. And I say 'He' because the Holy Spirit is the third *Person* of the Trinity." Rosie wanted Rebecca to know the basics that she knew a lot of long-time Christians didn't even realize.

"Okay. Well, on another note, how do you know where to read in the Bible? Do you read from front to back? Or can you just turn to any page you want?" Rebecca was starting to feel safe in asking these things of Rosie. Rosie seemed patient, and didn't act like this was something everyone should know.

"There are different ways you can do it, Rebecca. Some read through the Bible in a year. They get a special Bible that's set up to help them do that. Others, like myself, will read through different books of the Bible, slowly, and prayerfully. Like this..." Rosie picked up the well-worn Bible sitting next to her, and went to the place where she placed a bookmark toward the back. "I'm reading through the book of Acts right now. I chose Acts because I wanted to read about when the Holy Spirit came upon the new believers. I will usually turn to where I left off, which is Acts 4 today, and I start to read about Peter and John, and how they were ordinary men who had no special training but they were very bold when talking about Jesus, and all He came to do. This encourages me in what I believe, and how I want to be bold in this world. Then I might stop and pray about what I just read, and I ask God for His help in doing this and understanding it. This really becomes a dialogue between God and me. A lot of people say they never hear God speak to them. The best place to hear God speak to us is by reading the Word of God, which was written by Him to help us live each day in the best way possible."

"But how can the Bible have been written by God? Wasn't it written by people?" Rebecca didn't quite buy this whole, "Written by God" thing.

"Of course, ordinary people penned the words. You are right. And it does take faith to believe that they are God's words. The Bible says in 2 Timothy 3:16, *All scripture is inspired by God.* Many will debate this, Rebecca. I had a time in my life when I had trouble believing it also. But here's what I have found; the more I read it, the more I believe it, and the more I see how amazing and miraculous this Book is. I see God's fingerprint on everything in here. To me it seems only God could have written such an amazing book. I can't see man being so all-wise and wonderful as this. I find it to be not only inspiring, but so practical as well. I mean like in Romans 12 where it talks about not just pretending to love others, but to really love them. And also hating what is wrong and standing on the side of the good. It also talks about when God's children are in need, be the one to help them out. Who can argue with such practicality?"

"That part does seem pretty clear. But other things I have read, I have some trouble understanding it. And honestly, sometimes I just have trouble *wanting* to read it."

Rosie half chuckled. "Oh, I understand that. Even after years of being a Christian, the enemy always pulls so hard at me to not pick up my Bible."

"You mean, Satan?" Rebecca asked.

"Yes. Satan is the enemy. And the last thing he wants us to do is get any sort of encouragement from what God has in this Book."

"Wow. Well, I'm very new at this and I don't know quite what to think about it all yet. I raised my hand in church two weeks ago, and I'm not really sure what I was doing. They asked those who wanted to invite Jesus into their life to look at the pastor and raise their hand. I did. But it doesn't seem like anything is different, even though you're telling me the Holy Spirit lives in me now. I do have a desire to know more, I guess." Rebecca didn't want to sound like she was whining. But Rosie was paying special attention to all that she was saying, and that was helping Rebecca to open up and talk about it.

"What you're doing is good, Rebecca. A relationship with God has to start somewhere, and you have done that. You admitted that you're interested, just by going to church. And you listened, and you responded when the pastor made that invitation. Some people expect thunder and lightning to accompany those moments. It's not usually like that. It's simply acknowledging that we want to know God, and that we want to believe that Jesus is His Son when we hear that He came to save us. That is how we are born into the family of God. And just like a newborn baby, it takes time to grow up and learn how to live out this new life. I have been walking with God for almost half a century, and I'm still learning and growing." Rosie knew she needed to be careful and not pour so much Living Water into Rebecca that she would drown in it, and just as she was thinking that, Rebecca seemed to have had enough for one day.

"I really appreciate you explaining some of this to me, Rosie. I do have some things I need to get done at home. But I hope we can spend more time in your garden in the future. Would it be okay if I brought my Bible over sometime, and maybe you could help me understand it better?"

"That would be wonderful. We can surely do that." Rosie smiled, and nodded to Rebecca. "Anytime, my friend." Rosie felt better after Rebecca asked to come back. She was concerned it had been too much for Rebecca.

As Rebecca walked back across the street toward home, she was happy…Rosie called her friend, and she liked the sound of that. The time they were together went by so quickly that Rebecca could scarcely believe it. She really enjoyed being with Rosie. It seemed they had only scratched the surface of so many things. But it would have to wait. Rebecca had things to do, and she didn't want to wear Rosie out.

Rebecca's heart felt better with this new knowledge about God, but she also thirsted for more. It was a strange mixture of emotions she wasn't sure what to do with.

13

It was Sunday morning, and Rebecca was fast asleep. Her phone went off with an app announcement that she got each morning. She figured it was better than an alarm clock—she remembered as a teenager having to get up for school to that annoying sound.

Rebecca grabbed her phone to read what the word of encouragement would be for her today.

"Our doubts are traitors and make us lose the
good that we might win, by fearing to attempt."

Hmmm…that's interesting, she thought. As the fog began to clear out of Rebecca's head, she let those words sink in. It was Easter morning. Although she really didn't feel like getting up, Rebecca knew she needed to. With all that happened, God was becoming more real to her. She didn't want to miss what He might have for her today. This was a big day in the church, and she wanted to learn more about it. Jesus supposedly died on Friday. She didn't know what happened on Saturday, but Sunday was the day they say He was alive again. Rebecca heard this for years, in movies, TV shows, and other ways, but this was getting personal now. She wanted to know what this meant for her own life. She doubted that there even was a God for so many years, questioning what so-called Christians believed. But as the quote for the day said, she didn't want to "lose the good" she might win, "by fearing to attempt" to discover what this Christian faith was all about. Rebecca wondered if God orchestrated that quote, knowing she would need an extra push to walk into church today. Does God really care that much? She just didn't know…

Rebecca's long hot shower felt good. She thought back on so many

Easter mornings as a child. There was excitement in getting up and finding their baskets filled with all kinds of goodies. And of course, the hollow chocolate Easter bunny it always contained. She loved the ears most because it was the only solid piece of chocolate. Rebecca knew there would be no basket for her this morning...living alone didn't come with that benefit. When she and Don were together, they would try to do little things for each other, even though they never had the children that would fill a home with that kind of fun. Don knew her favorite chocolates, and he would make sure Rebecca received a box full of them. She would do the same for him. They always shared what they gave each other, which was an added bonus. But holidays were harder now. They were so filled with emotions. Rebecca wished these days could just be ignored, or treated like any other. Sadly, the world continued on after divorce, after death, after all kinds of hurt and pain. People put on their smiles and made their way into the day, just like she was about to do.

Rebecca picked out a springy looking outfit, hoping the pastel colors would mask any darkness she felt inside. She laughed when she thought of Easter bonnets, almost wishing she had some sort of hat to wear just for the fun of it. Church would probably be crowded. She better get an earlier start today. Putting her breakfast dishes in the dishwasher, grabbing her purse, and heading out the door, Rebecca stopped after taking one step onto the porch. Her eyes widened as she was suddenly gazing at the most beautiful basket of flowers she had ever seen. Every color of flower imaginable was perfectly placed in a white wicker basket, and draping over each side was greenery that offset the flowers perfectly. She took hold of the tall handle on the basket and as she picked it up, the fragrant scent of all the flowers combined smelled so fresh and alive. She looked up from the basket, for just a moment, wondering...and then she knew...it had to be Rosie. Her new friend. Rosie must have picked these for her. Rebecca's eyes filled with tears at the tenderness of such thoughtfulness. She took the basket into the house and placed it in the middle of her dining room table. She checked to see if the flowers needed water, but Rosie had even taken care of that. Rosie really cared, not only for others, but for her "babies," too. What a wonderful person she was.

As Rebecca pulled into the church lot, she could tell it was going to be hard to find a spot to park. It frustrated her a bit. Then she the thought of Rosie's flowers, and she decided it wasn't worth it to get mad. She wanted to think about what made her happy...like her friend's kindness. Rebecca eventually found a good place on the far side of the lot, and entered into church with her best smile, along with all the other Easter attenders. The church had a celebratory feel to it this morning. Rebecca took a seat more toward the center. She didn't want to sit in the back and feel sorry for herself today. She wanted to be fully present—otherwise, what was she doing here?

When the music started, Rebecca sang as cheerfully and joyfully as she could. It felt good to participate more fully than the previous two Sundays. She really tried to focus on the words, and when they got to the part where it was exuberantly sung, "He is alive!" many times over, she sang that energetically, too. Rebecca noticed a big difference between the Friday service and this one. She was looking forward to what the pastor would say about Sunday with Jesus. She was surprised how dressed up he was when he walked on stage. She could tell his hair was freshly cut, too. It was appropriate though, being Easter. Everything seemed special today.

The pastor began by welcoming everyone, and then quickly got into a message that kept Rebecca's attention from start to finish. He reminded everyone of Friday's message, talking about the darkness of that day, of how Jesus suffered and died. But Jesus did it with great purpose and focus on the joy that was set before Him. What struck Rebecca was the answer to the question she had...why didn't Jesus get away when He had the chance? Why did He go willingly to be hung on the Cross? He hadn't done anything wrong, from what the pastor said. She realized in that moment, that morning, that Jesus had done what He did for *her,* and it was because of *love.* Not the kind of love she had been used to all her life. This was a new kind of love. This "Love" was a noun, and not just a verb. The pastor explained that God doesn't just love us, He *is* Love. Love is Who God **is,** not just what He does. And the fact that God loves her that much, with a "noun" kind of love, a love that will never change, astounded Rebecca. It seemed to sink into her, piercing her heart. No one ever loved her like that, not even Don. Don loved her with all he had to give. But he failed her in so many ways. He disappointed her. He hurt her, even if it was unintentional. Her parents loved her, as best they could, but they disappointed her also. Rebecca's friends and family loved her, those that stuck by her side. But no one ever loved her in the way that the pastor was describing this morning...with a love that had no limits, no conditions, and no reservations. It was a love that said if she were the only one in the world, Jesus would have still died just for her. Jesus wanted her with Him always.

And this part really blew Rebecca away....Jesus *knew,* beyond a shadow of any doubt, that the grave would NOT hold Him. Jesus knew when they killed Him, He would rise in three days, and the enemy would be defeated. That was the goal, and He knew it WOULD BE accomplished. The pastor said that Jesus told people what would happen before it happened, so when it happened, they would believe. The tomb was empty on Sunday morning. The stone was rolled aside, and when the women looked in, there were two angels inside of it. The angels asked them why they were looking for the living among the dead? Jesus was not there. And then Jesus was standing there with Mary. She thought He was the gardener. But when He said her name, "Mary," she knew it was Jesus.

Rebecca never experienced an Easter like this...one that moved her so deeply. Maybe when she raised her hand two weeks ago, something really had taken place? Maybe her heart had been softening since then, making her more able to hear what the pastor was explaining to her today. Rebecca left church excited, and wanting to know more. She was so glad to have an open door to Rosie and her garden so she could talk to Rosie about what she learned today. Rebecca still had many questions. But one thing was sinking into her heart...she was *loved* by God, and that meant the world to her. She was finding out that she didn't need to change before God would love her. He already loved her, and changes would happen gradually—in the way she thought about things, the way she felt about things, and the way she would live out the rest of her life. That thrilled her! She was tired of the same old Rebecca. She was broken, and she needed some repairs. Life beat her up pretty badly, and if some things in her past could start to heal with Jesus' help, maybe she could actually find joy in her life. That would be very good news to her, indeed.

The drive home was so different than her drive to church. Love can do that to a person. She remembered when she first fell in love with Don. It was an exciting time. They had such fun together. He treated her tenderly, and she always appreciated that about him. Maybe she should give him a call and just say, "Hi," and "Happy Easter." She never got back to him since he stopped in that day, unexpectedly. She didn't appreciate seeing him then, but maybe they could at least be friends. She was starting to think she would like that. Rebecca went to press the button on her steering wheel to dial up Don, when her phone rang. It was Nelson calling. How sweet of him to remember her today!

"Hi Nelson. Happy Easter!" Rebecca surprised herself by the cheerful tone of her voice.

"Why hello, Becca. Happy Easter! How's everything with you?" Nelson was pleased to hear the light heartedness in Becca's voice.

"I'm doing very well, thanks. Just driving home from church. It was a good service. Lots of people. I really liked it." Rebecca didn't know if she wanted to share with Nelson just yet all that she had gotten out of what the pastor said.

"Oh. That's awesome! Good to hear it. I have to work today, so I wasn't able to go to church. I'm on the road, out in Fremont, and I had a few minutes. I wanted to see how you were, and wish you a Happy Easter. I talked to Jennifer earlier today, and she said she was going to church. She said it would be good for her to go, even though very hard. It will be somewhat easier for her when her mom arrives. I think that will lift her spirits." Nelson was just pulling into his next call, and he wouldn't be able to stay on the phone long.

"I do, too, Nelson. As much as we try to help, she has spent a lot of time alone this week. It's hard with both of us having to work. Her mom will be able to be more available this coming week."

"Jennifer told me she thought Thursday would be a good day for remembering Justin...maybe an after-work time, like at 6:30 or so. What do you think of that?" Nelson was getting out of his car, and walking over to the ATM that he had been called to repair.

"I think Thursday will be fine, and that's a good time. Does Jennifer need any help contacting people?" Rebecca was concerned about her energy level.

"No, I asked her about that. She said when her mom gets here, she would help her." Nelson then started to talk just a bit with Rebecca about still searching for a garden setting. He said he was on the lookout for one as he drove around on his job, but hadn't found anything he thought would be private enough.

"Nelson!! I think I have the perfect spot! I didn't think of it before just this moment! But yesterday, I spent time across the street with my neighbor, Rosie. Her backyard is absolutely gorgeous! It is big enough, too. Oh, I'm so happy about this, Nelson! It could be a wonderful place for a service. I could talk with her about it. What do you think?" Rebecca couldn't believe that it hadn't even crossed her mind when she was visiting with Rosie.

"That sounds awesome, Becca. I'm so glad, because I was getting a little concerned. And the weather is supposed to be nice this week. Let me know what Rosie says, ok? I need to get to work now. The ATM's are waitin' on me."

"Ok, thanks for checking in, Nelson. Hope you aren't working too hard on Easter." Rebecca felt bad for him, but she figured he was pretty used to working on holidays by now.

Nelson quickly finished with, "Bye! Talk with you soon."

"Bye."

Rebecca heard the phone go dead just as she pulled into her driveway. She was so thankful for the type of guy Nelson was. He just made things easy, no matter what it was. Rebecca gave Jennifer a call when she got into the house, and Jennifer said that she was over at a friend's home. They met up at church, and the family invited her to spend the afternoon with them. Jennifer said they have children, and watching them enjoy the day was helping to lift her spirits. Rebecca didn't say anything about Justin's service during that conversation. She didn't want to bring Jennifer down if she was feeling good. She would give Jennifer a call on Monday after talking with Rosie. During their visit, Rosie told Rebecca that she loved to share her garden...it made Rebecca smile to think about the joy this would probably bring to Rosie.

Later that afternoon, while relaxing and watching a movie, Rebecca saw the familiar white car pull up in front of Rosie's house. Rosie was getting home from church much later than normal, but it was Easter, and she probably spent some time with friends or family. She watched as Rosie exited the car and walked up to her front door. Rebecca figured she would give Rosie some time to get settled, and then go over and talk with her. Then it came to her, Rosie is probably tired, and may try to take a nap. Maybe I should go over right now while I know she is still awake. I don't want to disturb her later. This was out of Rebecca's comfort zone, to be this forward, but she knew it was something she needed to do. Rebecca got up and quickly crossed over to Rosie's, ringing the bell. While she was still standing there deciding she wouldn't go in today, Rosie opened the door.

"Hi Rebecca. Happy Easter!" Rosie was her cheerful self, and this put Rebecca at ease, immediately.

"Hi Rosie. Happy Easter!"

"Please come in...I was just making a cup of tea." Rebecca wasn't surprised at the invitation, but she stuck to her plan.

"Oh, thank you, but not today. I am actually in the middle of a movie at home. But I needed to ask a favor of you, and I just saw you arrive home." Rebecca didn't want Rosie to think she was always spying on her... "Sometimes I see you getting dropped off after church."

"Yes, a good friend from church usually gives me a ride. Today she was sweet enough to invite me over to spend time with her family for Easter. It was lovely." Rosie always seemed to smile as she talked.

"How nice." Rebecca pictured Rosie with this family, and thought how wonderful it must be for them to have her as company.

"What's the favor, Rebecca? What can I do for you?"

"Well, as you know...Oh, I first want to thank you so very, very much for the beautiful basket of flowers. There was no note on them, but they looked reminiscent of your garden, so I figured they were from you." Suddenly, Rebecca questioned whether they were or not. She didn't want to look like a fool...

"You are welcome. I thought you might enjoy a little springtime surprise filled with the goodness of our Lord since this is HIS day. Sometimes flowers are better than chocolates! Although I do love chocolates, and I had plenty of those today!" Rosie gave a small chuckle as she said that.

"I am enjoying the flowers, greatly. That was so sweet of you to think of me." Rebecca felt better, not having thanked the wrong person, although she didn't know of anyone who would have done that besides Rosie.

"Oh good...Now, what can I do for you? You said you have a favor to ask?"

"Yes...ummmm...well, uh, this week, on Thursday, to be exact, we are putting together a small memorial for the young man I told you about, Justin. It won't be many people because his service was really in Florida where his family lives. They had it a couple days ago. His girlfriend, my friend, Jennifer, was not able to be there for that. It was just too much for her to travel there right now. But she would like to do something for him here. Jennifer's mom arrives tomorrow to help her with this. We all thought, Jennifer, our friend Nelson, and myself, about finding a beautiful outdoor setting to have it in. Then I saw your amazing backyard. And I hope it's not too much to ask, but do you think it would be possible to gather here this Thursday night, at 6:30? You wouldn't need to do anything, we would do it all, and..."

"Oh, Rebecca," Rosie was so quick to answer, Rebecca didn't even need to finish her sentence, "...nothing would please me more than to share God's beauty in remembering Justin. I would love to have you all come and do whatever you need to do. I will be here. But I don't even need to attend if that is not appropriate. I can stay in the house."

"Oh, no. Of course, you're welcome to join us. Your presence would be wonderful. The way you love God, Justin would be happy to know you were there. He loved God, too."

"Well, you can count on my garden to be available to all of you. Just let me know if there is anything I can do to help you."

"Rosie, you are so kind. Thank you. I look forward to telling Jennifer that we have the perfect place to remember Justin. I hope it will ease some of her sadness... Now, I hate to rush off, but I just wanted to catch you before you settled in. I'm going to get back home and relax some myself. I'll be in touch." Rebecca gave Rosie a gentle yet loving hug, and said good-bye. It felt strange to be hugging a neighbor she ignored for so long, but now felt was a friend. Things were changing inside of Rebecca. She welcomed it, yet feared it in some unknown way.

Rebecca returned home, satisfied with how things were going. Easter had been good, in fact much better than she expected. And when Rebecca turned in that night, she did something she was not accustomed to doing. She talked with God about her day. She thanked Him for loving her, and for sending Jesus to die for her. She asked God to help her understand more about all of this, and to help her get to know Him. And in honor of her grandma, Rebecca said a prayer she hadn't said in a long time... "Now

I lay me down to sleep. I pray the Lord my soul to keep. If I should die before I wake, I pray the Lord my soul to take."

"Good night grandma. Thank you for loving me, too."

14

Monday morning came, and it wasn't good. Rebecca woke up feeling like she had been duped—that Jesus was a fraud and she had been lied to. Rebecca didn't want anything to do with anyone...not Nelson, not Jennifer, and especially not Rosie. Rebecca felt sick in the pit of her stomach, and she knew it wasn't the flu. It was lies! God was not true! And she didn't want to hear any more about Him. It was time to get her head screwed back on straight, go to work, and get back to the life she knew best. This whole God thing was for wimps. It was for those who needed something, and couldn't make it on their own. Rebecca was done.

Downstairs, getting her breakfast, Rebecca was running late. She never hurried in her mornings, she was always methodical, and right on time. This morning she lingered too long, thinking over everything that was spinning in her head. Nothing seemed to make sense anymore. Rebecca took her breakfast to the living room and paced as she ate it. Back and forth she walked, scooping bites of scrambled eggs into her mouth while a voice inside her head coaxed her to shout, "I'm done! This is not what I want! I want to be free to be me!" Rebecca was getting more upset by the minute.

In her pacing, Rebecca again saw her Bible on the coffee table. When she got home, she was going to put it on a shelf somewhere. It didn't make sense anyway. And she hoped that Rosie didn't see her leaving this morning, because she didn't feel much like waving. What was she going to do about Justin's service on Thursday? She sure didn't feel like going...maybe she could fake an illness, and just bow out. That would probably be best. Right now...she had to get to work!

Rebecca grabbed her purse, a light jacket for the cool morning mist, and headed out the door. Her car was always in the driveway. But this morning it wasn't! "WHAT?! Where in the world is my car?!" Rebecca practically screamed. She couldn't believe it. It was gone! Had someone really stolen her car in the middle of the night? What else could have happened to it? She would have to call the police. Rebecca didn't know what else to do. Back into the house she went. She also called Ben to let him know that she wouldn't be in right away, or at all that day. Rebecca was in shock. She thought, this is a good neighborhood. I don't have that great of a car. It's four years old, and not super fancy. Why would they even want it?

It wasn't long until the police showed up. Rebecca explained to them that she left her car in the driveway, like she normally does. It was there when she went to bed, as far as she knew. But this morning when she was leaving for work, it was gone. The police were very understanding, and kind. Rebecca was not. She was ticked! This was a total inconvenience, and she didn't appreciate it at all. Someone was driving around in her car, and she was stuck here figuring out what to do next. Now she would have to get ahold of her insurance company, and work through this. Arghhh! And she thought the morning had been bad before! Now this on top of it! This surely showed her that God was not in charge of ANYTHING! Why would He let someone steal her car? What is the point in that?

Rebecca went back into the house once the police were done. They said they would be on the lookout for it, of course, but chances are it had been stripped and sold for parts. Even if she did get it back, there wouldn't be much left. Rebecca's heart sank at those words, and she wondered what to do next. She didn't want to call Nelson. He would try to soothe it over with kind words. Rebecca wanted him to be mad along with her. Who could she call? How about Susan? Yes, she would call Susan. She wouldn't be at work yet. Sue didn't go in until about 10:00. She would have a sympathetic ear for her. She dialed her number.

"Hi Rebecca. How are things? It's been a while." Susan sounded a bit sleepy, but not annoyed.

"Hey Sue, I'm ticked! My car was stolen right out of my driveway last night."

"WHAT? That's crazy! Who in the world would do that?" Susan woke up quickly. She knew Rebecca lived in a good neighborhood.

Rebecca said angrily, "I don't know. I have no idea. And the police said it was probably being stripped and sold for parts. And even if I get it back, it won't be worth anything. This totally makes my week. NOT! You know, Sue, things seemed to be turning around for me...or at least I thought so. Now this! How much more junk do I need to go through in life?"

"I don't know Rebecca, this is so not right. I'm *mad* with you! Whoever took your car...I hope they smash it into a tree, instead of even getting the chance to strip it. Maybe they are in the hospital as we speak, getting what they deserve!" Susan thought that harsh revenge was totally deserved here.

"I'm with you!" Rebecca screeched. "They need to pay for what they have done! And if I ever get my hands on them...I'll take them to court and sue them for all of this and more!" Rebecca was getting more fired up the longer she talked to Sue, and it felt good! The anger was growing into a rage, and she felt entitled. "I don't know what I'm going to do now. I guess I'll figure it out. What else can I do?" Rebecca let out a growl, and then a big sigh.

"What can I do for you, Rebecca? Anything? Want me to come over and hang out with you this morning before I go to work? I can, ya know." Susan didn't really want to. She would rather stay in bed until it was time to get up for work, but she didn't want to let on to Rebecca. She had to try to do the right thing.

"Nah, that's okay. I'll be fine. I know you've got my back. I'll get this figured out. Sorry if I woke you this morning." Rebecca was realizing that she called pretty early and shocked Susan into the start of her day...she probably shouldn't have done that. Rebecca reacted, and that was probably not so smart. Now Susan would have something to go to work and tell her colleagues, and they would all join in together complaining about how life never works out the way we expect it to. Rebecca really didn't want her business to be all of their business. She could feel herself calming down just a bit, having let out some of her rage. She was glad to have Sue to reach out to, someone who would jump on her band wagon and ride it with her! But now she just wanted to sulk alone.

Rebecca sat down on the couch. She knew Ben wasn't expecting her at work any time soon, so she wasn't going to hurry. She was trying to decide what to do next. Rebecca called her insurance company. They were very nice on the phone, and said that these things happen. There was a protocol to handle it, and she was not to worry. They talked about her getting a rental car until the car could be found. Or, if it wasn't found, how they would cover the cost of replacing her vehicle since she had replacement coverage. It seemed the worst of the storm was starting to ease. Rebecca realized these things do happen, and this time, it was just her turn. She would come through this.

After phone calls were made, Rebecca laid down on the couch and took a nap. The sun was shining through the front window, and it felt warm and comforting to just lay there and soak it in. When Rebecca woke up, she didn't move right away. She began to look around the room, and take in where she lived, realizing what a nice home she had. She never really took a lot of time to consider the good things in her life. Rebecca was a bit surprised at even doing it now. She started to think about her health, and how so many people are fighting cancer, or arthritis, and many other things that limit their mobility. She didn't have those struggles. Rebecca was in very good health at 44. She was thankful, realizing her eyesight was good, too. What if she were blind? Life would be so different. And then she heard the birds singing outside her window... There are people who can't hear that, she thought to herself. What was this that was happening to her thoughts? Rebecca had never done this before. Usually when she got mad, she stayed mad, and upset, for days. Why was her thinking changing after she woke from her nap? She must have really gotten up on the wrong side of the bed earlier.

Rebecca went into the kitchen. As she opened her fridge looking for something to eat, she thought about the starving people in China she always heard about as a kid. She thought, I'm not one of them...look how much I have in here. I could feed the whole neighborhood, and still have food left. And I'm upset about a car? Seriously? How many people don't have a car, or have insurance to replace it when it does get stolen? Rebecca sort of shook her head, like shaking out cobwebs...not because she wasn't thinking clearly, but just because she didn't know where her new thinking was coming from. Rebecca knew she was starting to be appreciative, instead of being angry...when *she thought* she should be angry.

Rebecca walked out onto her back deck, and stood there, breathing in deep. And then she heard it...

"I am the air you breathe."

What was that? It almost seemed to be an audible voice, and yet Rebecca didn't hear it with her ears, she heard it from deep inside of her. "Wow! That seemed so real," Rebecca said out loud. Once again, she shook her head to clear her thoughts. She didn't know what was happening, and these thoughts from deep inside started to speak even more, like things being revealed. She was soaking in all that she had in life, instead of what she had lost. This was a way of thinking she hadn't experienced much in the past, if at all.

Rebecca thought back to how she started her day, feeling empty and lost. Feeling like all she learned recently was a lie, and she didn't want anything to do with God. She didn't even seem to like her new friends anymore. And then she found out her car had been stolen, which caused her to stay home and take care of that business. It certainly had been a pause in her day...almost like God didn't want her heading out the door feeling so grumpy. Had God helped her restart her day by having her car stolen, so she could relax in the warm sun coming through the window, and take a nap? Did God really do this? Had God really stopped her from her normal routine? Was God letting her know He was real? Rebecca thought that was a very strange way of conducting business, if this was God's doing. And then to hear:

"I am the air you breathe."

I have never heard anything like that before, thought Rebecca--not in that way. Is that how God sounds when He talks to us? This was too weird. This was beyond what she understood. And even if she didn't want to, Rebecca was now going to have to talk to Rosie about this. She wanted an explanation. Rebecca didn't think she'd believe all that Rosie would probably tell her, but she needed to talk with someone who might know, and that certainly wasn't Susan. Sue would think she was crazy! "You heard God speak to you?!" She could just hear the skepticism in Sue's voice, if she were to tell her that. And then Sue would tell everyone at the beauty shop, and they would all think Rebecca was crazy, too. No, it would have to be Rosie, and soon. Like today. Like now. There was no time to waste.

Rebecca went back into the house…walking into the living room she looked out the window. Thankfully, Rosie was out front working on her rose bushes. That could make this easier. But Rosie probably thought she was already at work since her car was gone. She better go gently to not shock her from behind. Rebecca glanced over at her Bible…wondering if she should bring it? No, I don't want to. Then this might get into more than I feel like right now. I just want to ask Rosie a few questions.

Rebecca stepped out onto the porch, and she remembered what happened yesterday—a beautiful basket of flowers that greeted her. This morning what "greeted" her was her car missing. What a change of events. Rebecca walked slowly across the street, hoping that Rosie would glance up, but she didn't. She was so involved in tending to her "babies."

"Hi Rosie," Rebecca said almost in a whisper. Rosie looked up, like she was wondering if someone said something, and then she caught sight of Rebecca.

"Good morning. How are you? Are you off work today? I saw your car was gone, and figured it was a work day for you." Rosie wasn't sounding nosey, just factual.

"Well, here's the thing, Rosie. When I was leaving for work this morning, my car was missing. Someone must have stolen it in the night." Rebecca could feel an anger rising up again, so she tried to push it back down.

"Really? That's crazy! In this neighborhood? Hmmmm… I'm sorry to hear it. I hope you'll get it back."

Rebecca replied unhappily, "The police aren't so sure about that. They said the vehicles are normally stripped and sold for parts. Thankfully I have insurance, so it can be replaced. In the meantime, I'll be getting a rental car." It felt good to explain the steps to Rosie, just speaking them out made it all sound a bit more manageable.

"Oh good. I'm glad it will be covered. I'd give you a ride. But you know I don't drive, nor do I have a car. Will you be able to get the rental? Will someone take you there?"

"Oh, yes, it will be fine. I just haven't scheduled it yet. I...I've been...having a strange morning Rosie. Really strange. And...I don't really understand it. I hate to bother you with this, but could we talk for a few minutes?" Rebecca wasn't even sure what she as going to say after that...she was hoping the words would come.

Rosie answered sweetly, "Rebecca, I always have time for you. Yes, let's sit here on the porch. Would you like some coffee or tea?"

"No thanks." Her answer had a short, unfriendly sound, and Rebecca knew it.

They both walked toward the porch, and Rebecca could feel her heart start to pound. She wasn't even sure why. After taking their seats in a couple of Rosie's rockers, they rocked for a short while before speaking. She could tell Rosie was waiting on her, and Rebecca wasn't sure how to start. Then she came right out with it:

"Rosie, have you ever heard God talk to you?" She immediately wanted to withdraw her question. It sounded so *out there*!

Rosie didn't react at first...she continued to rock, and then started humming again, a new tune that Rebecca didn't know. Rebecca wondered if Rosie was going to sing her answer. But then Rosie spoke, "Well, that's an interesting question. There have been times in my life when it seems I have heard God speak directly to me. I could almost count them on one hand. It was very specific, and I didn't hear it with my ears. Did you?"

"Ummm...no. Not my ears. More like inside of me."

"Yes, that's probably the best way to explain it. But it seems so clear, doesn't it?"

"Yes, it does." said Rebecca.

"Were you searching for answers about something?" Rosie was remembering back on the times she heard God, and they were usually about important events in her life.

"Not really, I guess. Or maybe I was. I have to be honest with you, I was having a very bad morning," Rebecca said this with a bit too much negativity. She tried to reel it back some. "I got up on the wrong side of the bed, I guess you could say. I woke up frustrated, and angry about a lot of things." She didn't want to tell Rosie the full extent of her thoughts. "And then I found out my car was stolen, and that didn't help my morning at all. I was...well, really angry about God, and with God, and just everything to do with God!" There, it was out. Rebecca didn't mean to say it, but it spilled out anyway, and now she was glad.

Rosie turned to her, and gave her a comforting smile. Rebecca wasn't sure what that meant, so she remained quiet. Maybe this wasn't a good idea, coming over here this morning. But Rebecca didn't know how to stop it now. It would seem so abrupt, and she didn't want to be rude.

Rosie began with, "You had a good Easter, didn't you?"

"Yes, very good. Thank you again for your flowers." She didn't know where Rosie was going with this. It seemed off the subject.

"Did you sense that God was starting to become more real in your life, and that you were figuring some things out about Him?" Rosie paused, and waited for her answer.

"Yes, I guess I did. I really enjoyed the pastor's talk. I felt so loved by God when he finished." Rebecca started to remember again how with God, "Love" is a noun. And His love is unconditional.

"And so the whole day seemed to be good? And then in the afternoon we even talked about having Justin's memorial in the garden here, and it seemed perfect to you?" Rebecca wondered why Rosie was asking her all these questions about yesterday. What did that have to do with what she came over here to talk about? But Rebecca answered her...

"Yes. It was one of the best days I've had in a long time." And now just thinking about it was making Rebecca feel better. She wondered why Rosie was doing this? She seemed so kind, and caring, even though she was off subject.

"Rebecca, may I say something, that may seem out of the ordinary?" Rosie wanted to be very careful with where she went next with Rebecca.

"Sure. I guess so." Rebecca had no idea what she as getting at.

"Remember on Easter, how Jesus was talked about? How much God loves us, and is for us. How Jesus died and rose again to give us eternal life? How He is our friend. Well, the opposite side of that is that we have an enemy, too. Remember talking about Satan?

"Uhhh, yeah. I guess so."

"Satan doesn't like us, at all. Satan doesn't love us. He is totally against us."

"Ya, ummm, I don't really think much about Satan other than some guy in a red suit with a pitch fork and pointy ears."

"Yes, that's how a lot of people see him. But the thing is...we don't really see Satan with our eyes, just as we don't see God with our eyes. We can see Satan by his actions, just as we can see God by *His* actions. And as you would probably guess, their actions are completely opposite." Rosie stopped and rocked for a few moments, not wanting to overwhelm Rebecca. She let those thoughts sit with Rebecca, waiting to see if she would say anything. But she didn't. Rosie continued.

"One thing Satan really, truly, absolutely doesn't like are people on this earth who are searching for God. And when those people find God, and start to get too close to God, this really riles the enemy up. Satan knows he is starting to lose the battle in their life." Rosie paused again. Rebecca remained quiet.

"This morning, when you woke up, Rebecca, it sounds like the enemy was waiting for you. Satan was not happy with how you spent your Easter. Satan can't pick on everyone at once, because he is not God. He has limited people on his team, so to speak. I can explain more about that at another time. But this morning, I want you to know where the attacks against you were coming from. Satan and his team were after you, from the sounds of it. Satan was probably casting all sorts of doubts at you, he was trying to get you to view people differently, he wanted you to isolate yourself, and he didn't want you to get anywhere near your Bible. This is how Satan operates. We can think of it like we're in a bad mood, or someone is really irritating us, or we don't want anything more to do with God, any number of things. But thoughts like that are coming from the pit of Hell, not from God above." Rosie knew she was starting to get passionate, and she needed to stay calm. To her, this type of conversation was common, and comfortable. To Rebecca, it was probably new and a bit scary.

"So what you're saying is, yesterday I was getting closer to God. And today, Satan was trying to pull me away from God?" This was the way Rebecca was understanding what Rosie was saying.

"Yes, that's right. And Satan was hoping that you would quickly give up on your new-found faith, and go back to his way of doing things. Satan was trying to convince you that you didn't need God. And then if Satan could get someone to steal your car, that would maybe really convince you that God doesn't have your back, and you can't depend on Him...and here's the proof."

Rebecca spoke up after what seemed like Rosie was reading her mind, "This seems to make sense. But I don't understand how my thoughts could change as the morning moved on? I took a nap, and when I woke up, I seemed to be seeing things in a different way. I was having more thoughts about being appreciative, and then when I went out in the back yard and took a deep breath, God said, 'I am the air you breathe.' And it was so clear, Rosie. I've never experienced anything quite like that."

Rosie explained, "God was getting your attention through the Holy Spirit who lives inside of you. When you said yes to Jesus in your life, God didn't expect you to then just go on and do life in your own strength. The Holy Spirit came to live inside of you, and that's how God can speak to you also—deep inside. The enemy works on us from the outside in. Most times God works from the inside out. Those new thoughts you were having after your nap were help from the Holy Spirit pushing the negative thoughts of the enemy away from you. He was counseling you. And then it seems to me, God sealed it by speaking to you, letting you experience His voice. Not all Christians can say they have heard God in that way. It is very special; that's why I can remember each time I have heard God like that. It doesn't happen often. And we can't make it happen, it just does, in God's timing and in God's way. The Bible says in Psalm 51:10-12, *Create in me a pure heart, O God, and renew a steadfast spirit within me. Do not cast me from your presence or take your Holy Spirit from me. Restore to me the joy of your salvation and grant me a willing spirit, to sustain me.* God paused you in your morning, using what the enemy was trying to harm you with, bad thoughts and a stolen car, and God changed it to good. The Holy Spirit is working in you restoring His joy, helping you focus on what is good, and right, and true. I hope this is making some sense to you?"

"Well, it's a lot to take in, and I will think about it. I still have my doubts, and I still have a stolen car to deal with. But I appreciate you taking the time to sit with me like this. I don't know, Rosie, I just don't know about this whole God thing, but I'm not going to give up yet. Not after this morning. I was ready to chuck it all, and just go to work and get back to the way I used to be. But this has gotten my attention, even though I'm a bit overwhelmed right now. Thank you."

"Is it okay if I pray for you before you go?" Rosie knew that prayer was the only way into Rebecca's heart. Human words are only surface deep. It is truly the Holy Spirit who could help this make sense to Rebecca.

"Sure. That's fine." Although Rebecca didn't see a real need. She really just wanted to get going.

Rosie began, "Father in Heaven, You spoke clearly to Rebecca today. Thank You. Holy Spirit, grant Rebecca a willing spirit to sustain her through these doubts and fears. Help Rebecca to turn to You often, and to not isolate herself in times like this. Help her to doubt the doubts and believe your Truth. Thank You for bringing her over today so we could talk, and pray. Help us to trust You for each day, Jesus. In Your Name we pray. Amen"

"Thanks Rosie. Thanks for being here for me." Rebecca got up to leave, and Rosie gave her a hug that felt so secure. Rebecca had a lot to think about. But at least her anger was gone, and she felt like she could get back with Nelson and Jennifer. After the way the morning started, she didn't know what would have happened between her and them. Maybe it was true, God was returning her joy, and her relationships, too…she hoped so. Yesterday had been such a good day. Rebecca wanted more days like that.

15

Rebecca called Ben and told him she wouldn't be coming in at all today. She wanted to just reflect on her conversation with Rosie, and get the rental car taken care of. Then she'd be ready for work on Tuesday. It wasn't long after Rebecca got home that her phone rang. She was surprised that it was Don!

"Hi." Rebecca answered...not feeling much like talking.

"Hi Bec. You okay?" Don sounded genuinely concerned.

"Yeah. Why?" She didn't want to go into anything with him. Not right now.

"Well, I got a call from the police that the car has been stolen." Don waited...

"They called you? Oh, I guess because we're still both on the registration, huh. Sorry, I didn't think about letting you know. Yeah, it was taken last night. Right out of the driveway. They said it would probably be stripped for parts and sold, so I don't think I'll be getting it back. I'll need to look at getting another car." Rebecca didn't know why she was even talking as much as she was.

"If you need any help, Bec, just let me know. Buying a car is not a lot of fun by yourself. It's good to go with someone, to have another person to bounce things off of."

Rebecca thought about that, and how she and Don bought that car together. He really was good with the sales people at the car lot, since he was in sales. He knew their tactics, and he wasn't intimidated by them. Maybe it would be good, as much as she would prefer not to have him along.

Rebecca said, "Thanks. I'll think about it. Oh, and...ummm....I'm sorry I never got back to you after you came by. I've just got things going on. And now this..." She didn't want to say much more, so she just stopped there. The phone was silent for longer than either one of them was probably comfortable with, and then Don spoke.

"Bec. Uh...I'm sorry that I came by without warning that day. I know it probably made you uncomfortable. Next time I'll call first." Don then thought to himself, if there is a next time. He knew she was not at all happy with him.

"Yeah. That would be good. I'm going through some things, Don, and, well, I just have a lot on my mind." Now Rebecca kind of wanted to talk with Don about those things—he *had* always been a good listener. But she didn't know if it was even appropriate. She wondered what the "rules" in talking with an ex-husband were? Maybe there's a book she could find about it...then again, she could barely seem to find the time to read her Bible, so Rebecca knew she probably wouldn't be reading a book about anything else.

"Divorce is hard, Bec. On both people."

She was surprised that Don said that. But then Don was not usually one to beat around the bush. Although it didn't seem to be very hard on him, from what little she witnessed.

"I guess so," she said. Almost matter of fact.

"And...uhhh...I meant what I said...I miss talking with you. I really don't mean to freak you out with saying that. I guess I just wanted you to know—I think about you, and am glad for the good times we once had." Don knew he was starting to sound sentimental, and Rebecca usually didn't like that. She was never much into expressing emotions, so it would probably be best not to do that now.

"That's nice, Don," Rebecca said, although she wasn't really sure she meant it.

Don was surprised at her answer, so he decided to take it a step further, and see... "Uh, Bec. Tomorrow night I'm having dinner with Roger and Kay. I see them from time to time, and they always ask about you. Would you be at all interested in joining us? We're just gonna have a casual dinner somewhere." Don waited through an even longer period of silence on the phone. He had no idea how Rebecca was going to respond to this.

Rebecca was speechless... Part of her felt good, that he would want her there. Part of her didn't want to go at all. She missed Roger and Kay—the four of them always got along so well. She with Kay, and Don with Roger. Rebecca hadn't seen them in a long time even though Kay reached out to Rebecca more than a few times. Rebecca always shut Kay down, not wanting to talk about what happened. Rebecca's thoughts and emotions were swirling in just the 10 seconds or so it took her to respond. She was playing out different scenarios in her head, and what she would even wear…and then suddenly it all got to be too much.

"No. I don't think so. I don't think that would be a good idea. It would be uncomfortable for all of us." Rebecca was glad she was saying no, although now part of her really wanted to say yes. She hadn't gotten out to have much fun since the divorce, other than seeing Nelson and Jennifer from time to time. She spent too many evenings at home, alone. Rebecca knew she was tiring of it. She even gave some thought to online dating sites. But that scared her. Rebecca heard horror stories from some. But then again, good stories from others.

Don let the phone stay silent for a bit after Rebecca said no. He knew her well, and she usually reacted with a "No" first off to most things. That was just her way, and it was okay. She was a deep thinker, and when stuff was just thrown at her out of the blue, "No" was her way of escaping the tension she felt. Plus, Rebecca liked things to be more her idea than his. That made her feel safe and more in control. Don always tried to be patient with her. It saved him many arguments. Don knew to just give her time. That was why it shocked him when Rebecca suddenly spoke again.

"Don. You know what…I've changed my mind. I will go to dinner with the three of you. Maybe it's time to see Roger and Kay again, and it might be easier with the four of us, rather than just me seeing them by myself sometime." Rebecca's body was shaking, and she didn't know why…she was already second guessing herself. Her thoughts screamed, Ahhh….what am I doing?! But she didn't want to waver on this. She pursed her lips tightly shut, and didn't say another word. She waited for Don to speak.

"Okay. Sounds good. I've gotta get back to work now, I'm on a call in about ten minutes. But I'll let you know the time and place when I find out." Don knew when not to push things. He wanted to get off the phone, and let this settle with her. Then he remembered and said, "Oh, you don't have a car. Did you need me to pick you up?"

"No, I'll have a rental by the end of today. I'll be fine. Let me know where and when, and I'll meet you all there. I gotta go now, too. Thanks for the invite. Bye."

"Bye. I'll be in touch." Don hung up relieved, and pleased.

As the phone went silent, Rebecca sat there for a while, not really knowing what to think. She hadn't seen Don but a few times since the divorce was final. Maybe this was about Roger and Kay? They were always such a fun couple. Roger travelled a lot with his job, and Rebecca and Kay would spend time together. She missed Kay. But it all seemed so complicated with the split. Rebecca thought it was better to just let everything and everyone go, and start over. Maybe it was time to pick up some of the things, and the people, she discarded? What had it benefited her to be so alone, and let Don have all the fun? He seemed to have gone on with his life without her just fine. She wanted back in, so to speak...back into life.

As Rebecca reflected back; she had quite the morning...her bad mood, her stolen car, hearing God speak, and now Don calling about the car and inviting her to dinner. Rebecca sort of shook her head at the strange way things were happening. If God really did have a plan for her life, He must have been enjoying writing it with all these twists and turns. Maybe she *should* read *His* Book...there might be some interesting stuff in there. She would try...soon. Just not right now. She had to get her rental car situation solved. After another fifteen minutes on the phone, the car agency agreed to pick Rebecca up about five. She could have the rental until her car was either returned or a new one was bought. So far, so good.

Jennifer's mom would have arrived by now. After texting Nelson about Rosie okaying them the use of her garden, Rebecca gave Jennifer a call. Jennifer said she and her mom would start getting hold of people. They agreed to meet with Nelson soon to work out some details. Rebecca knew that Nelson would handle the bulk of Justin's service, and Jennifer's mom, too. Rebecca liked her role of just supporting them in what they were doing.

Suddenly, Rebecca felt a bit of joy as the thought of Rosie's garden seemed to fill her with renewed hope. Even if she didn't understand all this God stuff, and even if she didn't speak the same language that her new friends did, they were loving her in a way that she appreciated. Rebecca told herself to hang in there with them, for a time, at least. Give these new friends a chance to share what they knew about God, and then she could decide for herself if He was real or not. Rebecca knew if she didn't, then she wouldn't know what she might be missing. That made Rebecca think about the quote from the other day again. She went back to find it:

"Our doubts are traitors and make us lose the good that we might win, by fearing to attempt."

Yes, she would doubt the doubts and "attempt" to keep on keepin' on with her new friends. And now, maybe even with some old friends. Who knows, maybe one day she could actually call Don a friend again? Wouldn't that be a miracle in itself.

After getting back with her rental car that evening, Rebecca put in one of her favorite movies, made some popcorn, and felt a bit of happiness. What a concept! Life wasn't all that bad, even though the morning had started out seemingly horrible! Maybe what Rosie was explaining to her about Satan was true? Did he really come and attack people's thoughts? It sure seemed real enough to her. Easter Sunday had been great, and then out of nowhere, every thought turned dark. If her car had not been stolen,

Rebecca wondered what would have happened at work that day with the state of mind she would have arrived in? She might have gotten mad at Ben and stormed out if he'd said the littlest thing wrong. And the last thing she needed right now was to be searching for a new job. Rebecca pondered the thought, maybe we don't know a lot of the things we have been saved from, because they never happened? We can see an accident we narrowly missed, but what about a job we didn't lose? An illness we never got? God's timing may be the very thing that spares us from a whole lot of hurt and pain. And yet Rebecca knew she wanted to blame God very quickly when things went wrong in her life. She thought, what if God is in Heaven saying, "Oh, you don't even know all that I saved you from today. I let a few things slip through because those things actually helped you...like a stolen car that kept you from going into work with such a bad attitude."

Hmmmm....interesting, thought Rebecca. More stuff I think I'd like to discuss with Rosie.

16

Rebecca got up on Tuesday morning with no idea how the day would go. She pulled some of the hard-boiled eggs from Easter out of the fridge. Her plan had been to make deviled eggs with them, but she hadn't done it. Now they'd make a good egg-salad sandwich for lunch. When some of the eggs peeled easily, and some didn't, she knew why she didn't make this more often...it could be a hassle. Taste testing it, she decided, hassle or not, it's worth it. Yummm!

The rental car was a small, white vehicle that didn't have the luxury her vehicle had, but it worked. At least it was there in the driveway when she was ready to leave for work. Ben seemed happy to see her. Between Justin last week and a stolen car this week, Ben might have been getting frustrated. Some work had piled up. But Rebecca got through that quickly, and enjoyed her sandwich for lunch. Sitting outside, Rebecca thought about dinner that night. Don sent her a text earlier in the day. They were meeting at a local Mexican restaurant. It was one they all four ate at before, so it would seem like old times...Rebecca hoped. She didn't know how strained the conversation would be, especially since she avoided Kay for so long. Kay was always the forgiving type though, so it shouldn't be bad. And if Rebecca didn't feel like talking to Don, they could let the guys talk as the girls caught up on each other's lives.

Roger and Kay had one grown daughter, Lindsey, who was off at college. Lindsey had been a good girl, but ran into some trouble with her new friends that first year away at school—sewing some wild oats. Rebecca and her friends did that. They all grew out of it in time. Lindsey would, too. Rebecca would try to comfort Kay with her own experience. Rebecca knew other things would be more difficult to talk about, especially with Don right there. And would God be a subject of discussion? Rebecca didn't know what Roger and Kay felt about God, so she didn't know how that would go. In that past, God was never part of their discussion. It would probably be best not to bring up God. There was plenty of time in the future for that if she decided to continue on this new path.

Rebecca hated leaving the warm sunshine, but duty called. The phone kept ringing all afternoon, and Ben seemed a bit haggard. Rebecca guessed Ben deserved to feel that way, he had been covering for her so much. She tried to be as patient as possible when he got irritated. As the day was coming to an end, the butterflies really started inside. Rebecca felt nervous. She wished, now, that she said no to Don. But she was going to do this...by hook or by crook. Their dinner was planned for 7:00. She would stop by Jennifer's on the way home. Nelson was going to meet her there at 5:30 to go over some things. Jennifer had been baking with her mom--she said it was a good way to keep herself busy. They were going to just have desserts and coffee at the service.

Rebecca pulled up out front of Jennifer's, and sat in her car for a few minutes. She needed to get her thoughts together. Between trying to be strong for Jennifer in her grief, wondering just who God was going to be in her life, the car, and meeting Don later, it was all a bit much for her. Rebecca just wanted to find a hole and crawl into it. If only she could. Thankfully, Nelson pulled up behind her and that helped her get out of her own head, and back into what needed to be done.

Nelson walked up beside her, making sure it was Rebecca's car before he tapped on the window. He gave her a big smile when she looked at him. Opening Rebecca's door, Nelson took Rebecca's hand to help her out. Not that she needed it. He was just such a gentleman. Rebecca appreciated being treated like that. This was the first time Rebecca would be meeting Jennifer's mom, Erika. To Rebecca, when Erika answered the door, she looked like an older version of Jennifer—same coloring, same eyes, with just a slightly different smile. This put Rebecca at ease. Erika invited them to come in, and said that Jennifer was resting and she'd go and get her. While Erika was out of the room, Nelson asked Rebecca how she was doing with the car and everything. He reminded her she could call him any time. What he didn't know was that Rebecca hadn't wanted to call him. She wanted to vent, and he was too nice of a guy to do that with her. She was thinking all of this, not saying much.

"You're pretty quiet tonight, Becca. I hope this car thing hasn't upset you too much."

Nelson looked at her as he spoke, and she could feel his concern. This was what she meant; Nelson wasn't angry, he was concerned. Why didn't he get mad?!

Rebecca finally spoke up, "I'm okay. It was upsetting. But I'm calmer about it now. The rental is working out just fine until the car either gets found or not. If not, I'll be car shopping soon." Rebecca tried to not show Nelson her ugly side that erupted in the beginning. But she felt it rising up again. She tried her hardest to keep it tucked inside, and put on a fake smile, even if it was just a small one.

Erika and Jennifer then appeared from the back of the condo, and Nelson and Rebecca both got up to give Jennifer a hug. To Rebecca, Jennifer felt thinner. Grief can take away an appetite, Rebecca thought to herself. She remembered after Bonnie died, food just didn't matter much for a while. Her appetite slowly came back to normal, and she was sure that Jennifer's would, too.

"Thanks for coming by. I know you can't stay long, Rebecca, but I appreciate you taking the time to help us with Justin's memorial." Jennifer sounded so sad, and tired. It made Rebecca ache inside for her.

"Of course, Jennifer. I'm not in that big of a hurry. What can I do for you to prepare for Thursday?"

"Finding the garden setting is so huge! Thank you! It sounds perfect. I so appreciate your neighbor letting us use it. There is some seating? Is that right?

"Yes, there is a bench off to the back, and there is a covered area with some nice outdoor furniture there. There are also a couple of other places for seating—some large rocks that people could sit on. And the lawn area is quite large. Plenty of room for people to stand."

"Would it be possible to put a couple of tables there, for some desserts and coffee?" Erika asked. "We want to keep it simple, but welcoming."

"Oh, of course." Rebecca liked being a part of this discussion. It made her feel useful.

Jennifer couldn't believe she was even able to think about this. She was missing Justin so much. The more time passed without seeing him, the more Jennifer was realized Justin was really gone. They usually talked multiple times a day, and texted...seeing each other at least every day, if not every other. Jennifer felt such a hole inside, and it seemed to be growing larger. Where was her Justin...her funny, quirky guy?... The tears started in, and everyone felt such compassion for her pain.

After a bit, Jennifer was able to speak. "My mom has been such a huge help to me this week. I don't even get my own laundry done lately. Mom has helped with that, and we have been making cookies...well, mostly mom...and freezing them, storing them up for Thursday. Mom also contacted the local coffee place, and reserved enough coffee for everyone. We will have water, too. Is there anything else, mom?"

Erika spoke up, trying to save her daughter from talking much more.

She could see the strain on her young face, and it broke her heart.

"It's all going to work out fine, honey. Nelson will get the tables, and bring them in his truck. I'll make sure they look pretty, with arrangements of cookies and coffee." She turned to look at Nelson and Rebecca and said, "We thought about ordering flowers but then realized there would be no need. With a garden as beautiful as you've described—God's natural decorations will be more than enough."

Rebecca assured them, "Oh yes. When you see Rosie's garden, you will know that any arranged flowers would be overshadowed by what has been growing there naturally. Is it okay with you if Rosie joins us for the memorial?" Rebecca felt she already knew the answer, but she should at least ask.

"Oh. Of course." Erika said, "She is more than welcome!" Erika had never met Rosie, but she knew she was going to love this generous neighbor of Rebecca's.

Nelson then added in, "There is only one thing. My buddy had agreed to come with his sound system and play his guitar and sing. But I just talked to him on the way here and he has a terrible cold. He sounds like he swallowed a frog. We both doubt that he will be recovered enough by Thursday night. Is there anyone that you know Jennifer, or Rebecca, that we could call last minute?"

There was silence for a few moments. Rebecca waited to see if Jennifer had a solution. But Jennifer said nothing so Rebecca spoke up, hoping it was okay... "Uh, actually, if you don't mind it not being a young person, Rosie sings. I have heard her, and she doesn't even need a sound system. She has a strong, clear voice that is so soothing...it seems to blend into the garden setting in the most natural way. I don't know what songs she knows. But Rosie is a strong Christian, and it probably wouldn't be a problem for her to sing a song or two that would be appropriate. I can ask her if you would like me to. If not, no problem."

The words were barely out of Rebecca's mouth, and all were in agreement that she should ask Rosie. This would put Rebecca back in a position of being bold, which seemed to be part of her new life. Getting into these situations where she had to step out of her comfort zone. But that was okay, she could do this—after she got through this dinner with Don...

Everyone seemed satisfied with the plans that were made for Thursday, and they all agreed to meet about four at Rosie's to get things set up. If Rosie was willing to sing, they could possibly choose the music at that time. With everything coming together nicely, Nelson asked if he could pray. Rebecca wasn't surprised. She was starting to get used to this being part of the routine when Christian's met together. Nelson began:

"Father in Heaven, we thank You for Your love and devotion to us in sending Your only Son to this earth to make a way for those who believe to be with You. We thank You for welcoming Justin through Your heavenly gates. As we finish up with some of the details of Justin's life here on earth, be with us, help us, and guide us each step of the way. Our words and actions are inadequate. But with You, we know we will honor Justin in the best possible way. Bring Your peace to Jennifer…a peace that surpasses understanding during times like this. Help Jennifer's heart to heal as time passes. Give her Your Hope each day. In Jesus' name we pray. Amen"

Everyone said, "Amen," and Rebecca joined in with her own, "Amen." She wasn't even sure why prayers ended that way…one day, she would ask. Until then, she would just be with these people who seemed to know.

Rebecca said, "I need to get going now. I'll see you all Thursday night, if not before." She gave everyone a hug, and left in what seemed like a hurry. She hoped it didn't feel that way to the three of them. It might have just seemed it to her because of how nervous she was about what was coming next. Rebecca would be glad when the evening was over. At this point…she was not looking forward to any part of the dinner. She probably wouldn't even be able to eat. But, maybe, just maybe, it would be better than she imagined it to be. She surely hoped so…

17

Rebecca got home from dinner exhausted. It was everything she didn't want it to be, and a lot of things she did. As she dropped into bed Tuesday night, her head was spinning. She was glad it wasn't late, because she had a lot to think about. And even some things to pray about.

At first, it was awkward. Rebecca arrived at the restaurant after everyone else, and she felt put on the spot. They were already at a table, and stood up as she came toward them. She wished she could have turned around and run away. All eyes were on her with nowhere to escape. Don was the first one to greet her with a light, sideways hug that said, "I'm glad you're here, but now what do we do?" Then Kay, with her ever-warm smile, stepped forward.

"Hi Rebecca. It is so good to see you. I've missed you." Kay hugged Rebecca in a way that seemed to back up her words. Rebecca wasn't so sure she hugged her back in quite the same way.

"Hi Kay. I've missed you, too," Rebecca said in the best way she could.

Roger stood still, and didn't know quite what to do. He gave a little wave and a half smile, and then they all sat down. It was easy enough while ordering; it was a good distraction. Rebecca took longer looking at the menu than she needed to. She had been there many times and usually got the same thing, the Ultra Tostada. She decided to order that again, after a lengthy time of decision making. When Rebecca eventually put her menu down, and the waiter came to get their orders, the others were into a conversation she didn't know much about. Some friends had gone camping, and there had been some flooding…blah, blah, blah, blah…was the way she felt. Rebecca just looked at them, and around the restaurant, searching for a way to make an excuse and leave.

Dinner arrived quickly enough, and that was another good distraction.

Now she could focus on eating. Kay tried to start up a conversation a few times, but Rebecca mostly let it fizzle out. Rebecca knew she wasn't being nice, and she needed to change her attitude—so she did something she hadn't done before...she asked God to help her be nice. And to her surprise, it seemed to be working. The next question Kay asked her, Rebecca answered in a friendlier tone, and then she asked Kay a question or two back. That seemed to get the ball rolling, and while the guys were talking between the two of them, she and Kay actually started carrying on a reasonable conversation. It was like they were friends again, with very little time gone by. It felt good, and continued on for a good part of the evening. But then the conversation took a turn that was totally unexpected. It got very difficult, much to Rebecca's shock and horror...Rebecca asked about Lindsey, and how her schooling was going? Rebecca said she heard Lindsey had some difficulty adjusting to college. Rebecca only wanted to be an encouragement with that, not to interfere. From the look on Kay's face, Rebecca wished she'd never mentioned it. Kay suddenly looked so disturbed, and it seemed Rebecca entered into a territory where she was very unwelcomed. Rebecca wanted to crawl into a hole.

"Rebecca, Lindsey isn't in school right now. She had to take some time off." Kay paused, like she didn't know what to say next.

Rebecca thought to herself, "Uh oh. It must have been much worse than my experience. Maybe Lindsey got into drugs or something? Maybe she got pregnant?"

"I'm sorry. I didn't mean to barge into anything." Rebecca felt like crawling under the table.

Kay continued, "You're not. It's okay. It's just that last December, Lindsey was diagnosed with Non-Hodgkin's Lymphoma. She has been going through chemotherapy and radiation." Kay stopped, and looked down at her plate, moving what was left of her food around as time seemed to stand still between them. Rebecca wanted to say something, but this was so unexpected, she didn't know what to do. She wished Nelson were here; he would know what to say. Her mind swirled, what would he say?!! What would he say?!!

All that came out was, "I'm so sorry to hear that, Kay." Rebecca teared up as she looked at Kay, and Kay had tears in her eyes, too. Roger and Don stopped talking, getting wind of where the girls' conversation was going. The silence at the table now was almost unbearable...total discomfort, and sadness.

Don spoke first to break the long silence. "I'm sorry I haven't said anything to you, Bec. I probably should have told you a long time ago. But, well..."

Rebecca looked at Don, and then at Roger. All of a sudden, Roger appeared older to her and his eyes were so sad. This was his daughter. Their only child. How devastating for them...and for Lindsey. She was so young, only 19, her whole life ahead of her. She was always such an active young lady. Rebecca remembered going to a couple of her volleyball games in middle-school. She hadn't known much of Lindsey in her high school years, since the problems with Don, but she assumed Lindsey kept up with her activities.

Roger finally looked fully at Rebecca, for the first time all evening. "We didn't want you to find out this way, Rebecca. We were hoping this would just be a friendly dinner, remembering old times together. But then, we probably weren't being realistic about it. How could it not come up? It is such a huge part of our lives right now. In fact, it is most of our lives right now. Lindsey is home with us, and Kay has taken time off work to get her through the treatments. Lindsey is doing fairly well...some setbacks, but mostly just the normal stuff—which is hard enough in itself. We never understood what chemotherapy consisted of...we have learned a lot. And it is a lot more challenging than any of us expected."

Rebecca could tell that Roger was trying to hold it together, and have it not be too alarming for her. She appreciated the effort he was putting forth. When Roger seemed finished, Rebecca knew she needed to say something, to all of them...it was time. She looked around the table, at each one of them, and began:

"I'm just so...so sorry. I know wonderful things are done in curing cancer these days. But even with that, this is your daughter. You love her so very much. I remember her playing volleyball and being full of energy. Lindsey is such a beautiful person, inside and out. It surely doesn't seem fair." Rebecca paused, but they could tell she wasn't finished yet. "I have been removed from your lives, and that is my fault. I have been consumed in my own...misery, and have been living selfishly. Honestly, this is something I am wanting to change, and now...well, now I can really see that I need to think about others, and what is going on in their lives."

Rebecca looked at Kay, and reached out to take her hand. The tears were many for Kay now, and Rebecca grieved for the health of their daughter, and the life Kay put on hold to fight this.

"Kay, you have tried to reach out to me, even in your own pain, and I haven't been there for you. I was curled up inside myself, and I didn't know...but that's no excuse, I should have been there for you." Kay tried to speak, but Rebecca didn't want her to. Rebecca knew Kay was going to tell her it was okay. And it wasn't. So she squeezed Kay's hand and shook her head side to side just slightly, gently letting Kay know she needed to continue. This was not to make tonight all about her, but to let them know she was tired of it being all about her.

Rebecca continued, "Don and I had our problems. This divorce was not just one-sided. What divorce is? I know that I contributed to it greatly. Don tried, but I gave up on it long before he did. And then when we split, when it was really over, I left not only Don but most everyone we knew. I blamed it on others, on their leaving me. But that wasn't the total truth. Like you Kay, you reached out to me, and I didn't answer you. I'm sorry. I didn't think about being a friend to you, I only thought about myself. I'm working on this, and I hope, after tonight, I can be a better friend to you, and even maybe a friend to Don." She looked over at Don, and he didn't show any expression, other than listening to her. She appreciated that. She didn't want to see pity, or anger, or anything like that. She just hoped he was listening…and he was.

Rebecca swallowed hard, knowing where she was going now would really be hard. "This may sound strange to you, but this seems like a night of vulnerability, so I want to share something with you three… I want to do better. I don't know much about God, but I have started going to church. I have some people in my life now who are helping me see things in a way that I've never seen them before. It isn't easy to change. But from what I know about God, He helps a lot. And I need His help. I hope you don't think I'm crazy even saying these things."

Rebecca knew she was just about done, so she stopped for a moment to collect her thoughts, and see if she had anything left to say. She did… "Please forgive me for being so self-centered. I hope we can renew our friendship. And even with you, Don, maybe we can begin in a new way just being friends. I want to be there for you, Kay, and you Roger, and Lindsey. If there is anything I can do. Even if you just need to talk, Kay."

Rebecca knew she was done now; she felt emptied out, and emotional. She didn't know what to expect. But Rebecca did know they were kind people, and they would be gentle. The waiter walked up just then, asking them if there was anything more they needed? He could tell he interrupted an intense time, so he quietly laid the bill on the table, and walked off.

Don started in slowly, thanking Rebecca for all that she said recognizing how hard that must have been for her. And then Don told her something she didn't expect at all…not after the years they spent together, and the conversations they had about God. "Bec, I can't tell you how encouraged I am to hear the things you shared with us. You know me, and you know where I've come from, and how I've been influenced in my life with those I've known to be religious. But Roger and I have spent a lot of time together since the divorce. I needed a good friend. I was hurting so badly. I've tried many things to try and get rid of the pain. But nothing seemed to help until Roger invited me to his Friday morning men's Bible study group. Roger just started going. He was excited about what they were talking about, and he encouraged me to check it out. I've been going about six months now, and I, too, am seeing things in a way I never have before. I see mistakes I make, and I am wanting to know how I can change. I don't have many answers yet, but I feel like I am on the right track."

Rebecca couldn't have been more surprised at what Don just said. She mostly nodded at him with an expression of understanding. Then she looked over at Roger, and simply said, "Thank you for helping Don." Rebecca was surprised that she cared enough to say that. Things seemed to be shifting in her as they sat there. She and Don barely talked at dinner other than their initial hello…and that wasn't much to speak of. She had been trying to avoid him, and been glad to be able to turn all her attention on Kay during the meal, once she got over initially being rude to Kay. Now, it seemed, they all had more in common than they realized. And it all came out because of sweet Lindsey…their relationships were healing because Lindsey was sick. What a strange turn of events.

The evening ended on a somber note, but one of hope in what was to come with the four of them. The good-byes were not drawn out. There was no, "I'll be in touch soon," said. It was more an understanding that they were friends, and it would play out as it should from this point on. Rebecca found out that Kay attended a women's Bible study on Wednesdays. Kay was the one who had been looking in God's direction first, and she brought Roger along. Rebecca was comforted in the fact that they were all new at this, but were all moving in the same direction. Maybe they could be of some help to each other. Roger and Kay were nice people, and Don didn't seem like the "bad guy" as much anymore. It was interesting that Roger and Kay had been drawn to God even before Lindsey was diagnosed. But from what Rebecca was seeing, it was good timing. She couldn't think of anything worse for a parent to have to go through than cancer in their child. Once again, Rebecca wondered about God's orchestration of things…

After lying awake until about one in the morning thinking about everything over and over again, Rebecca finally drifted off to sleep. It had been a long day. Certainly, one of ups and downs. She would need to call Kay soon. Very soon.

18

Thursday came quickly. Rebecca was getting out of work about three. She felt bad asking for more time off, but Ben didn't seem to hesitate in saying yes. Rebecca wanted to get home, freshen up, and be at Rosie's before anyone else arrived. She already talked to Rosie about singing, and Rosie had been more than happy to help in that way. Rosie also volunteered to bake some cookies. Rosie couldn't have been more gracious about everything—she was willing to do whatever was needed. Rebecca found out that Rosie often sang in her church on Sunday morning. After hearing that, she knew that Rosie would be comfortable singing in this setting.

On the drive home from work, Rebecca was a bit anxious. She didn't know why. Everything seemed in order...what was it that was bothering her? Rebecca ran through things in her mind, but nothing seemed to be the cause of how she felt. Then she thought back to her dinner on Tuesday night. It had been so loaded with emotion. But after she fell asleep that night, she hadn't thought too much about it again. Maybe that was the problem...she *should* have been thinking about it—especially with Lindsey being sick. Maybe God was reminding her that she made a promise to herself to call Kay soon. Is this what God does? Was the anxious feeling God reminding her to do something? Rebecca didn't know...but one thing she *did* know, she would call Kay this weekend. Rebecca wanted to be a better friend, and was determined to do her best at that.

When Rebecca went across the street to Rosie's at 3:30, Rosie was more than ready. Rebecca could even smell the scent of freshly baked cookies when Rosie opened the door. It seemed comforting to be there. Rebecca was glad for Jennifer as she would need all the comfort she could get. Rosie took Rebecca into the garden, and everything looked even more beautiful than she remembered. Obviously, Rosie had been tending to her garden with great care in preparation for today. The fountains were flowing, the birds were singing, and everything was in bloom. It looked like such a cheerful place...if only it wasn't such a sad event. Rosie had placed some chairs out back, and also put up a couple of umbrellas on the lawn.

"Oh Rosie, it looks so beautiful. I hope you haven't worked too hard. I could have come over and helped you with the chairs, and the umbrellas." Rebecca was concerned for Rosie.

"It was no trouble at all. I have gardeners who come to mow the lawns, and they were more than happy to help with the umbrellas and chairs. They have been working for me a long time. Once in a while a lady needs a strong young man to help out, and they do. Plus, they like my cookies, so I share with them whenever I bake." Rosie smiled. It was such a warm, genuine, grandmotherly smile. Rebecca thought the gardeners probably loved helping Rosie. Who wouldn't?

"Well, thank you so much for everything. Nelson, Jennifer, and her mom should be here soon. It is so sweet of you to allow us to use your home. Please let us know if there is anything we can ever do for you." Rebecca wanted to pay Rosie back in some way, but she didn't have a clue what that might be. She would think about it.

Nelson arrived next. They heard the bell ring, and they both met him at the door. He was there with one table, and had two more in the back of his truck. He hauled them in, and wouldn't let them lift a hand to help him. Nelson was dressed in a pair of dark slacks, with an open collared blue shirt, and a sport coat. Rebecca had never seen him dressed like that. He was normally very casual. He obviously had a new haircut, changing it up a bit. It was cut short on one side, with a very distinct part, and a shine to the longer hair that he combed on top and over to the left. Rebecca liked it. It made him look a bit younger, although he didn't look all that old for his age to begin with. He was strikingly handsome. Rebecca wondered why she never noticed him this way before? Maybe she'd always been so absorbed in herself, she never took the time. It was dawning on Rebecca that she may have missed out on many things. She was ready to wake up and smell the roses, so to speak. Why not start in Rosie's garden today?

Nelson carried in the tables and set them up out back. This was the first time he was in Rosie's garden, and he stopped to just take it in. He had never seen so many beautiful colors in one place at the same time. And the lawn was amazingly green and lush. Rebecca had been right, this was perfect! It calmed him a bit, just being there. Nelson needed those few moments. He prayed and asked God for help, but this was bringing back so many memories for him. Nelson felt a bit uneasy because he hadn't told Jennifer and Rebecca about Jill yet. All he could do was hope that when he did, they would understand why he waited. When the dust settled, probably when Jennifer's mom went home, he would sit down with Rebecca and Jennifer and let them know what he had been through. Mainly, he hoped his story would be of some help to Jennifer as she processed her own grief.

Jennifer and her mom arrived by 4:30 and they all took some time to sit in the back yard under the canopy and talk before setting out all the cookies and drinks. They were equally amazed at the beauty of the garden, and thanked Rosie over and over for allowing them to gather there. Rosie sang them a couple of songs that she knew well. She did it in the most natural way. It was hard for them to choose which would be best. Her voice lifted their spirits out of the grief they carried in. They knew she was a gift from God to help them all.

Nelson finally said, "Whatever the Holy Spirit puts on your heart at that moment, Rosie, sing that one." Nelson thought to himself, she could sing the alphabet, and it would be inspiring.

The women then all worked together setting out the cookies and filling the water pitchers, while Nelson went and got the coffee. People started arriving at 6:15, mostly people Justin had worked with, and Jennifer's colleagues, too. It was touching to see so many come, knowing that neither Justin nor Jennifer grew up in the area. They obviously were both very loved. While people were arriving, Nelson asked Rosie if he could go to a quiet place in her house to pray. She knew exactly where to take him. Rosie led Nelson to a room in her home that was set aside for prayer when it wasn't possible for her to be outside. Sometimes Rosie sat by the living room window, but many times she went to her prayer room. Nelson felt right at home when he walked into such a hallowed place. He felt honored that Rosie would share it with him. Rosie shut the door quietly behind her as she left him there. Although Nelson felt nervous and inadequate to speak for, and about Justin, he knew that the Holy Spirit would do the work. All he had to do was go out there, open his mouth, and stay out of God's way. Nelson spent enough time with Justin to know his heart, but still, it was comforting for Nelson to know that the Spirit can speak through us when we don't have the words. It was getting close to time...

Taking in a deep breath, Nelson walked out through the sliding glass door into the garden. There were about 35 people there of varying ages. The temperature was perfect, with just a slight breeze rustling through the trees. It made Nelson think of God's presence. His heart was at peace.

"Ladies and gentleman, shall we get started?" Nelson got everyone's attention without even speaking up that loudly. There was a reverence to the mood already, and it pleased him because of the respect it showed for Justin's life.

Nelson began: "On behalf of Justin, thank you for being here. Justin Weldon Palmer was born on May 21, 1982 in a small town in Florida. He spent his last day on earth here in California, and his first day in eternity in the presence of his Savior, Jesus Christ. Today he is remembered by all of us, and the woman he cared about so deeply, Jennifer Higgins. At the request of Jennifer, I have been asked to talk with you a bit about Justin, his life, his faith, and his eternity. It is my privilege to do so."

Nelson continued on, "Jennifer told me a story of Justin, and a friend of his, who was battling some things in life. She said Justin's friend mentioned a verse in Ephesians 2, and Justin liked it as well. It is a verse that gave his friend hope, and in turn, gave Justin hope. The verse talks about God's great mercy, and how we have been raised from the dead along with Christ, and we are seated with Him in the heavenly realms— all because we are one with Christ Jesus. There is no better place to start this evening than right there…in the Truth that Justin believed and lived. Will you pray with me?"

"Father in Heaven, as we gather here today, as Justin gathers in Heaven with You and all Your holy angels. We long to see the face that Justin sees today…Yours. And we know that with a faith in Your Son, Jesus, one day we will—and we will see Justin again. Thank You for the great Hope we have in that, on this day, when hearts are sad, and missing is hard. Lift our eyes toward Heaven tonight, and help us to accept the mercy You offer us while we still live on this earth. Bring peace to our hearts, and healing. We honor You tonight, Lord, as we honor Justin and the life You gave him. In Your holy name we pray, Jesus. Amen"

Nelson paused…he was not reading notes, although he had written a few things down. He wanted the Holy Spirit to lead this time together. There was no one here "official" except God. And Nelson knew that trusting God to show the way was the best "program" they could follow. It seemed at this point that a song from Rosie would be best…so Nelson waited. And Rosie, following the same Holy Spirit, could sense the call to sing. She started as she did so many times, humming…it seemed the tune would change as she hummed, like she was filing through songs until the right one came forward, and then it did, as Rosie started singing the words. It was a song that none of them heard earlier on, but it was perfect, talking of how when the person gets to where they are going, they don't want those still here to be crying. It talked of the joys of Heaven, and leaving the sweat and tears of earth behind. It built to a crescendo that left no eye without a tear, including Rosie. And as the song ended, there was a hush even in the trees that had rustled in the breeze. What beauty…what peace…what only the Lord above could have sent.

Nelson didn't rush to speak when Rosie finished. It didn't seem there was a need. Some are uncomfortable with silence, but it seemed silence was the best way to remember Justin in that moment. No one moved for a few minutes, and then Nelson's heart filled with words of Hope, especially for those there that might question the *why* of Justin's accident and passing.

"In Jeremiah 17:17, it is written, 'You are my refuge in the day of disaster.' What has happened to Justin looks, feels, and seems like a disaster…a young man, dying in the prime of life. So much ahead of him, nothing all that terrible behind him. What could a loving God be thinking? How can the Lord be our Hope, when He allows such pain and suffering? Justin loved God. Didn't God know that? Why wouldn't God be kinder to Justin? Some say this should not happen to a child of God. But a wise man of God says these tough things in life help us to be more firmly planted in Christ. These things reveal the value of our Hope in Jesus. Now, you may be saying, 'How does that work for Justin, he is gone?' True. Justin is not here to have the value of his Hope revealed, but we are. Justin doesn't need his Hope revealed, he's living in it. But what Justin and God have left us with is the *opportunity* to live out a strong faith in the midst of this storm. To find our own True Hope. One day we may say, 'I would have missed understanding this if not for Justin's *disaster.*'"

Nelson didn't know how that was sitting with everyone, so then God put it on his heart to give them all an example. Nelson said, "As we gather here in this beautiful setting, let's look around. As you do, find a special flower—maybe it's your favorite color, or it reminds you of someone you love…whatever the reason. When you have chosen that flower, go to it and break it off, holding it close to you in remembrance of Justin. There is no hurry, take your time walking about the garden until you find the perfect one." (Nelson had not asked Rosie for permission to do this, since he didn't know about it ahead of time. But he knew in his heart that she would be in full agreement.)

Nelson found his own special flower, and then he watched and waited while each person wandered in the garden, looking for their flower. Once everyone was finished, Nelson continued on: "A garden setting is the perfect place to remember the new life we will have in Heaven when we leave here. This is our Hope in the day of disaster. 1 Corinthians 15:35-40 says, *"But someone will ask, 'How are the dead raised? With what kind of body will they come?' How foolish! What you sow does not come to life unless it dies. When you sow, you do not plant the body that will be, but just a seed, perhaps of wheat or of something else. But God gives it a body as he has determined, and to each kind of seed he gives its own*

115

body...There are heavenly bodies and there are earthly bodies; but the splendor of the heavenly bodies is one kind, and the splendor of the earthly bodies is another."

It was heart-warming to see everyone holding a beautiful part of Rosie's garden in remembrance of Justin. Nelson continued on, "When our bodies die, and are 'planted in the earth,' we can trust that one day we will have a heavenly body. We all gather here today in our earthly body. But what we hold in our hand is closer to the beauty that our heavenly body will have. No, we won't be flowers, we will be fully us, fully recognizable, and we will know one another. We won't be floating on a cloud somewhere. We will be walking the streets of Heaven, enjoying eternity with those we knew here on earth who also knew and believed in Jesus. Justin knew that Jesus was the only way to Heaven. Justin knew he needed to give His heart to the Savior of the world, so that the blood Jesus shed on the Cross could wash his sins away. Justin was not a perfect person. He would have been the first one to tell you that. But Justin knew the perfect Savior, and he would have been the first one to tell you that, also."

Nelson knew he was laying it out, and not everyone would be in agreement, so he said, "Justin would not want us talking about him today, although we will spend time doing that when I am done here. Justin would want us talking about where he is now, and how he got there. Justin would want me to tell you what Jeremiah tells us in the Bible. '...blessed are those who trust in the Lord and have made the Lord their hope and confidence. They are like trees planted along a riverbank, with roots that reach deep into the water. Such trees are not bothered by the heat or worried by long months of drought. Their leaves stay green, and they go right on producing delicious fruit.' Justin is planted in Heaven now, soaking in the Living Water. He is not bothered by anything, anymore."

Nelson finished with, "When you leave here today, please take your flower with you. Put it in a vase when you get home. Don't put any water in the vase. But remember where the flower came from—the garden where it was nurtured with love and watered, just as Justin is being now nurtured, loved, and soaking in the Living Water of Heaven. And as the days pass by, and the flower you picked today starts to die, remember Justin. Remember that, yes, he died, because he was plucked from this earth. But he was merely planted in the ground as a seed, a seed that God promises will grow anew in a heavenly realm. And remember that the next time we see Justin, and Justin sees us, we will all be even more beautiful than the fresh flower we hold in our hand on this day. That is the Hope we live in with Jesus. Justin would want you all to know that...Thank you so much for being here for Justin today. And thank you, Rosie, for sharing your beautiful garden with us as we remember our friend. Please, don't hurry off. Jennifer would love for you to stay a while, have some coffee and cookies, and enjoy a time of sharing with one another why you picked the flower you did, what it means to you, and what Justin meant to you. May God bless you all."

Nelson stood for a moment, as everyone slowly started to move about the garden. Rosie made her way over to Nelson and gave him a hug. Rosie knew words were not needed. She knew Nelson poured his heart out, in honor of Justin, but most especially in honor of Jesus. She was proud of how boldly he proclaimed the Gospel of Christ, and she was pleased her garden had been put to such good use. As Nelson hugged Rosie back, he glanced up to see Rebecca across the lawn...their eyes met and she nodded to him. Nelson wondered what she thought about all that the Holy Spirit had him say, but Rebecca's nod let him know she was fine.

Jennifer came up when Rosie walked away, and she just cried on Nelson's chest. She uttered the words, "Thank you...Justin would be pleased." Her heart was touched beyond what she could say in that moment. Jennifer wanted to tell Nelson that she had been struggling with God's goodness, and her hope had been wavering. She would in time. For now, all Jennifer wanted to do was cling to what the Holy Spirit spoke through Nelson, using it to help her on the path of healing.

Many stayed until about nine. But then they knew it was time to go. Rosie was sitting and visiting with a few people. Everyone was aware that this was her home, and they didn't want to overstay their welcome. Rosie gained the respect of all who were there. They were so touched by her song. Rosie told them she hoped they would carry its message in their heart. Rosie knew these young people needed Jesus to see them through all that life would bring them.

After everyone left and they sent Jennifer and her mom on their way, Rebecca and Nelson helped clean up. As Rebecca worked side-by-side with Nelson, it made her long to have a partner in her life again—someone who would help her through the good times and the bad. She thought that person would be Don. It scared her to think about growing old alone. Rebecca's thoughts were many as they finished up together and said good-night to Rosie.

Nelson walked Rebecca back across the street, saying good-night at the door. Giving Rebecca a hug, they promised to see one another soon. Rebecca watched through the window as Nelson went back to his truck and drove off. What a godly man, she thought. That's the type of man I need in my new life.

19

Rebecca hadn't looked at her phone all evening while at Rosie's. When she got home she saw there was a message from a number she didn't recognize. When she listened to the voicemail, it was the police saying her car had been found, and sure enough, it had been stripped. There was no salvaging it. Rebecca knew what she would be doing on Saturday. The rental only lasted so long, and she didn't want to waste any time getting started in finding a new car. The news was not what she wanted to hear. But after an evening like they had, it paled in comparison to what they experienced at Justin's memorial service. Rebecca was so pleased with how it all went, although she didn't expect anything different. With Nelson handling so much of it, and Rosie's hospitality, what else would it be but good. Now, to decide what kind of car she would be getting. Rebecca felt it was time for a change. The car she had was one she and Don decided on together. Now, she would be deciding alone. But, she would see if Don could go with her. It was a big decision to make, and she wasn't so sure about dealing with the sales person by herself. She would call Don in the morning.

Friday at work wasn't busy. Throughout the day, Rebecca thought about what Nelson talked about on Thursday night. She had done as he suggested, and put her flower in a vase, with no water. Rebecca chose a burgundy snapdragon because it reminded her of her childhood. She couldn't remember where she saw them growing when she was younger, but she thought they were intriguing. When Rebecca talked with Rosie about why she chose that flower, Rosie told her that there are many thoughts associated with the Snapdragon. The one Rosie liked best was that it was associated with strength, dignity, and unique beauty. Yes, Rebecca would hate to see it die. But she also wanted to remember that it must, just as we must, to one day live eternally in Heaven with a new beauty that God would give us. Rebecca wondered how Nelson knew so much about the Bible...but then, she did know...he read it. She really wanted to get started doing that more.

Rebecca called Don on Friday and told him about the car. He wasn't surprised, and he said he didn't mind at all going with her to look. Don suggested getting a previously owned one. Rebecca sort of agreed, but she would wait and see. The plan was to go for coffee first, and then visit a few car dealerships. When Don showed up on Saturday morning, Rebecca decided to do something that surprised even her...she invited Don in for coffee. It felt strange to sit with him again in what used to be their kitchen. Rebecca's hands were shaking as she pulled out a mug from the cupboard and poured him a cup. She knew just what he liked in it, a bit of sugar, and a lot of creamer.

"I don't have creamer. Is milk okay?" Rebecca didn't use creamer, and this was unexpected.

"Sure. That would be fine." Don wasn't about to make any waves.

"How was work this week?" Rebecca knew she sounded strained, but she was trying. It had been so long since she asked him such an ordinary question.

"Good. Not too busy. Just busy enough."

"Same here. I have been taking some time off because of Justin's passing and all, but it will get more back to normal now." Rebecca didn't know what else to say after that...and they both sort of stared into their coffee cups for a bit.

Don broke the silence..."What kind of car are you thinking of, Bec?"

There was that familiar tone again...Rebecca would have to get used to it if she was going to do this car-hunting thing with Don.

She answered, "I don't know for sure. Something a bit smaller, and sportier, I guess. You know how I like the sporty cars."

"Yeah. You do." Don knew she was a Mustang girl. She had already owned one, and would probably want another one. Don said, "We could start at the Ford dealership." They exchanged a knowing smile.

Rebecca appreciated that Don was trying to pay attention to what *she* wanted. He had always been pretty good at it, but she could tell he was really trying to be on his best behavior. It was sort of like a first date, with the nerves, and not knowing what to say next. Rebecca didn't know if she liked this situation, or not...and if she didn't need help buying a car, she might put an end to being with Don today sooner rather than later.

Don noticed Rebecca was a bit lost in her thoughts. "What do you think?"

"Yeah. That sounds good. Let's start there. After chatting some about car choices, Rebecca said, "Let me get these cups to the sink, and I'll gather my things. Would you mind driving? I never know where to park on those car lots. It makes me nervous."

"Sure. My car is a bit messy, so if you don't mind that, I can drive."

"No problem. Be right back." Rebecca went upstairs for a few minutes, leaving Don some time to look around from where he was sitting at the table. Not much had changed. Of course, their pictures were gone, and replaced with other ones, or none at all. The furniture was still in the same place, so it seemed the house had been frozen in time. He wondered what the upstairs was like, and assumed it was probably the same also. Rebecca didn't make changes quickly, even when she wanted to.

Rebecca reappeared downstairs, and said, "Let's go, then."

"Okay. Sure."

As Rebecca and Don went from car lot to car lot, they kept coming back to talking about the first lot they visited that day—the Ford place…yes, the Mustang. Rebecca saw a blue one she liked, and it seemed she couldn't focus on much else after that. She tried to be patient and consider other options, but she knew what she liked, and didn't vary far from it. They ended up back with the Mustang about four, and made a deal. It was a used car, but in great shape. As Rebecca got in to drive it home, it warmed Don's heart to see the big smile on her face. He had not seen her that happy in so very long. He was glad to have been able to share this experience with her, and hoped he had been some help. They talked about having dinner. But then Rebecca said she was tired, and would prefer to go home for the evening. Don didn't push it. If they were to be friends in the future, he knew he had to go slowly. Don was learning in Bible study about the Fruit of the Spirit, and patience was on the list. He hadn't had as much patience in the past as he would have liked, so he prayed about that as Rebecca drove off.

"Lord, I need Your help. I want to be the man You want me to be. To everyone, not just my ex-wife. Help me to hear You more, and to listen, and to obey."

Praying was still very new to Don. But Roger and he talked about it, and were encouraging each other in that way. Don so appreciated Roger through the divorce. Even though Don was very skeptical when Roger first invited him to join him in the Bible study, he trusted Roger, so he went. Don figured if he didn't like it, he at least had given it a try. Don did like it, and continued to go. Now he was looking for a church. He visited Roger and Kay's church, but it wasn't really where he felt comfortable.

Rebecca drove home, as happy as a lark that day! With every turn she made, she could feel the car grip the road in a way her old car never did. She felt lower to the ground, which she liked, and the pick-up the car had was exhilarating. She truly felt like she made the right decision. Maybe getting my car stolen was a very good thing, Rebecca thought to herself, otherwise I would have driven the last car for another five years, at least. Yes. This is good. And fun. And I am thankful. Now, I have one last thing to do today, and that is to give Kay a call. I'm glad I set the reminder in my phone so I didn't forget.

Parking her new car in the driveway, she got out and glanced across the street. Rosie wasn't out front, but she would want to talk with her soon. She hadn't seen Rosie since Thursday. Rebecca was hoping they hadn't worn her out. But then again, Rosie knew how to take care of herself. Rebecca would check on her no later than tomorrow though. And maybe she could bring Rosie dinner or something.

Going inside and putting her stuff on the counter in the kitchen, Rebecca noticed the two coffee mugs still in the sink from morning. Oh…that's right. There were two of us here. Rebecca sat down for a moment to collect her thoughts about Don. Her mind ran in many different directions, and she wasn't sure which ones were right. She realized that she liked Don, as a man. She always had. And in the past, she loved him very much. But when the walls started going up between them, especially on her side, she felt very distant from him. She lived in one world, and he in another. Rebecca wondered, with God now in both of their lives, could the walls come down? Could we be friends again? She didn't know, and she didn't know if she even wanted to.

Rebecca's thoughts were interrupted by a knock on the door. "I wonder who that could be?" she said out loud as she walked to the door. She looked through the peep hole and could see Nelson's face smiling back at her. She quickly opened the door, and saw he had dinner in hand.

"Hi Becca! I hope it's okay. I was close by, and I was hungry for pizza. Thought I'd pick one up, and then I wondered if you'd eaten yet?" Suddenly Nelson felt like he overstepped Rebecca's boundaries. She looked tired, and she always stayed so private. He did feel he knew her better now, though, having gone through what they had with Jennifer.

"Uhhh…sure, Nelson. Umm…come on in. I haven't eaten yet. Sorry, I'm just a bit distracted. I don't mean to be rude." Rebecca's mind was in so many other places, Nelson was the last one she expected to see. Although she really didn't mind him being there, and was thankful for his thoughtfulness.

Nelson replied, "Okay, thanks. I won't stay long. I see a new car in your driveway. Looks awesome! I love Mustangs. Is that yours?"

"Yes. I bought it today, with some help from my ex-husband, Don. He is in sales, so I felt more comfortable car shopping with him." Rebecca suddenly felt like she was cheating on Nelson for some strange reason.

She knew she didn't owe Nelson an explanation, so she let it drop from there.

"Oh, that's good you had help. I'm not good at dealing with car people. I'm much more of a techie guy. Break a computer, I'm your man. Cars? Not so much." Nelson was his cheerful self, and Rebecca's unease quickly dissolved. "What will you do with the rental?" Nelson asked.

"I'll call the rental agency tomorrow, and get it returned. I'm kinda glad to have had the other one stolen." Rebecca paused... "Is it bad to say that?" She didn't want Nelson to think she was not a good person.

"Not at all! I like to see God work in mysterious ways." Nelson smiled as he said it.

Then the two of them went into the kitchen and ate their pizza, talking about many things. It gave them a chance to talk about Thursday also, and Rebecca pointed out that she had put her Snapdragon in a vase, without water, as Nelson suggested.

"You know, Becca, I didn't know that was going to be part of Justin's memorial. The Holy Spirit works in amazing ways. I prayed hard before speaking that night, and I knew that I didn't have to worry—I could just follow God's leading. When God put it on my heart to ask everyone to pick a flower, I knew that I was hearing from Him. It was such an amazing sight to see everyone walking around the garden on a mission from God! And I truly hope that the words God gave me that night were taken to heart. We have such a wonderful eternity waiting for us in Heaven. I think about Justin being there, already enjoying that time with Jesus, and I'm actually a bit jealous. I know that might sound strange. But everything we still go through here, Justin no longer has to deal with. Justin is at perfect peace, and he knows perfect love. Love here on earth falls so short of God's love in Heaven. Life here is tainted by sin, and decay. One day, we will see what Justin sees, and experience what he is experiencing, and we will be so pleased we chose Jesus."

Rebecca loved listening to Nelson. The God-talk, as she described it, rolled off his tongue as naturally as if he were making out a grocery list, or talking about a baseball game. Rebecca wanted to one day be at ease with God like Nelson was. Although that seemed so very far away. But she was determined to keep trying. Then a thought came to her...

"Nelson, would you do me a favor? Would you come into the living room with me, and help me open my Bible? I know this might sound crazy. But I fear it for some reason. It's like there is something stopping me, and maybe I need the courage you have." Rebecca wondered what Nelson was thinking, but he answered her without a pause.

"Sure, Becca, let's do that right now." Nelson took her hand, and led her into the living room. They sat down on the couch together. Nelson sat a respectable distance from her, but still close enough that it seemed very personal.

Nelson looked at the Bible on the coffee table, and he thought of picking it up himself. Then he heard the Holy Spirit say, "Let her pick it up." Nelson gently said, "Go ahead and get your Bible, Becca, and we can find a good place to start reading."

Rebecca seemed hesitant, but then she reached out for it. It felt good to have it in her hands again. She remembered back to when God made the sun reflect off the silver pages. Rebecca was hesitant to open it, in fear of looking like she didn't know what she was doing. But truth be told, she didn't, and Nelson already knew that. She could be herself with him. Rebecca turned to look at Nelson as he started to explain some things.

"The Bible has the Old Testament in the front, and the New Testament in the back. The Old was written before Jesus came to earth. The New is about Jesus' birth, and everything that happened while He was here, after He rose from the dead, and all that will happen in the future. The New Testament is a good place to start when we are new believers. And many begin with the book of John." Nelson gingerly helped Rebecca find the book of John.

"Now, you might want to just take it slowly, and read through the first three chapters of John. It will give you a better understanding of Jesus as God. It also talks about Him being the Word, Creator, Life, and Light. You don't have to read it all at once. Read just a little bit at a time. And after reading a little, you can ask God what it means. Are you okay with this so far?" Nelson didn't want to overwhelm Rebecca.

"Uh, yeah. I think so. Can we read just a little and practice together?"

"Sure. Do you want to start, Becca? Just read like one through three." Nelson pointed and said, "See those little numbers there, those are the verses. So when you start to read this, you are reading, John one, one through three. That's how it's said."

"Okay, I'll start with one. 'In the beginning the Word already existed. He was with God, and he was God. He was in the beginning with God. He created everything there is. Nothing exists that he didn't make.'" Rebecca stopped. Although it sort of felt silly to just read such a little bit, it already seemed like a lot to understand. But Nelson again put her right at ease. He was always so positive.

"That was good, Becca. Now we can just simply ask God, 'What does this mean? Lord, can You help us understand Your Word?' Then we wait a bit, and just relax, and we look at the words again, and maybe read it over slowly, sentence by sentence. May I?"

"Sure." Rebecca was happy to let Nelson take over the reading.

"*In the beginning...*, this is when the foundation of the world was formed," Nelson explained. "*The Word*, meaning Jesus, the Son of God, was already *with God*, and *He was God*. That might seem confusing because we think of Jesus being born two thousand years ago. Which He was, but Jesus already existed in Heaven before He was born on earth. He was there with His Father. Jesus came to earth, from Heaven, to save us."

Rebecca asked, "So, were we in Heaven before we came to earth, too? I have heard that we were, and even that we are reincarnated when we die."

Nelson replied, "No, we weren't. Only the Son of God, Jesus, was in Heaven first. And we aren't reincarnated. We are born only once, and die only once. We were created in our mother's womb, and even though it says in Scripture that God knew us before we were ever born, this means that God has no limits of time and space. He sees everything past, present, and future. In fact, when the Bible talks in Revelation about the end of this world, and the world to come, God is writing about what He has already seen played out. Our Father in Heaven knows how it all ends, and we can, too, when we trust and believe His Word. But I don't want to get too heavy for you here...sorry. I just get excited to tell it all." Nelson had to keep himself on track, so as not to overwhelm Rebecca. She was so willing, he didn't want to push her away with too much information.

Rebecca and Nelson looked over these three verses for a time, and continued to talk about each piece, and it seemed to be a help. Rebecca was seeing that it was not to be feared. The Bible was to help her learn more about God, and life in general. Rebecca was so thankful to have Nelson's knowledge to draw from. She realized this was going to be a slow journey, from what Nelson was saying. But she was determined.

When it was time to say good-night about 8:30, they knew they both enjoyed a special time together. And even though Rebecca had not given Kay a call yet, she figured God was pleased with her. Tomorrow she would surely call Kay. For tonight, she would live in the comfort of having opened the Bible up together with Nelson, and feeling a great peace from having done so.

Life was changing for Rebecca...and she knew it. AND, she was looking forward to driving her new car to church in the morning! Rebecca smiled as she climbed the stairs to bed thinking, I want all that God is willing to give to me. Oh. That makes me sound so selfish. Rebecca reminded herself that she needed to give herself to God, too.

20

Rebecca had an easier time waking up on Sunday morning. She knew it was the excitement of driving her new car. When she went out the front door and saw it sitting there, she was pleased. It was such a fun car to drive. Rebecca was leaving earlier for church so she could go the long way. And after church, she planned on taking a drive...maybe even over to the coast. She wanted to get some fish-n-chips, and sit by the water's edge for a bit. It was going to be a warm day, so the weather on the coast would be perfect.

Rebecca parked far out in the parking lot at church, not wanting to get a nick the very first day. It wasn't half as crowded as Easter Sunday, and she was glad. Walking in, she took a bulletin, and made her way to her seat. She wanted to continue sitting in the center, more toward the front. It was important to feel a part of the people there, and not isolate herself in the back, like she was tempted to do. The sermon rang true to her that morning, as the pastor spoke about listening to God, and obeying Him. He used an illustration about a man who had been told by God to go pray for another man who was blind. And the first man didn't want to, because the man he was going to pray for was dangerous to the Christians. Rebecca couldn't remember their names. The pastor pointed out how the one man argued about doing what he was asked to do by saying, "But Lord..." And then it said, "But the Lord said, 'Go and do what I say.'" The pastor talked about being, *But Lord* people. He encouraged all of them to say, "Yes Lord, your servant is listening." Rebecca wondered how anyone could argue when they actually heard God talking to them like that? And was curious what God's voice sounded like? She heard God say to her, "I am the air you breathe," but that was in her head somehow. This story seemed very different. Rebecca made a note of where it was in the Bible, Acts 9, so she could read more about it later. Rebecca brought her Bible to church. Maybe she would sit by the ocean and read that part when she got there.

Church ended, and Rebecca got up with the rest of the crowd, making her way into the lobby. She wished she knew these people. She knew just saying hi to them during the greeting time wasn't going to do it. She would need to find a better way. Maybe she would join one of the groups they talked about, or a Bible study like Roger and Don were doing together. Rebecca stopped at the information counter to ask, but the lady behind the counter was already talking to someone else. Rebecca didn't want to wait...she wanted to get going in her new car.

As Rebecca walked toward the parking lot, she thought she heard someone call her name. But no one knew her, so they must be calling someone else with the same name. Then she heard it again, "Rebecca!" She turned to see Don walking toward her, and her heart jumped in her chest as she thought, what is he doing here? I never told him what church I was going to. Rebecca slowed down, and let him catch up with her.

"Hi Bec! I didn't expect to see you here. Is this the church you normally go to?" Don asked in a way that made her believe he really didn't know.

"Uhhh, yeah...this is where I've been the last few weeks. Have you been here before?" She felt like running away from him, but she tried so hard to stand still and be calm.

"This is my first time. I have been trying out churches in the area, and I found this one on-line. Thought I'd visit it this morning. I liked it." Don didn't want her to think he was invading her territory though.

"It's good." Rebecca knew she was answering him in a not-so friendly way.

Don responded, "I liked what he said this morning. I'm so new at this, sometimes I get lost in what is being said. But I was able to follow the story he talked about."

Trying to be a bit friendlier, Rebecca said, "I was, too. I made a note of where it was in Acts, so I can read it again later. I'm headed to the coast right now, so that might be a good place to do that." The minute the words were out of Rebecca's mouth, she wished she hadn't said them. She really didn't want to share her plans with Don like that. It wasn't any of his business.

"That sounds nice. I hope you enjoy your time. I know we used to like to go to that seafood place in Half Moon Bay and get fish-n-chips. I wonder if it's still there? I haven't been in that area for a long time." Now Don was the one regretting his words. He knew it sounded like he was looking for an invitation. He wasn't, although he wouldn't have minded if she invited him. A day with Bec would be okay, and a ride in the new car would be fun, too.

"Yeah, I wonder, too." There was a long pause between them, neither of them knowing what to say at that point.

Don broke the silence. "Well, it was great seeing you here. I don't know if this is the church I will stay at, but I did enjoy it. I don't want to make you uncomfortable though, if I do attend here..." Don's voice trailed off.

"Nah, that's fine. It's a big church. It's open to you as well as me." Rebecca thought about going to the second service if Don did start going to the first like this morning. But she would see how it played out. "Uh, and thank you again for helping me yesterday. I do like the car...very much."

"You're welcome. See ya later. Have a great day!"

"Okay, yeah....later." Rebecca suddenly seemed distracted as Don turned to walk off. When he glanced back he noticed that Rebecca was still standing there. She hadn't moved. Don wondered if he should have waited? Had he been rude? Don looked again at Rebecca when he was almost to his car, and she was still there. She had a strange look on her face, and he hoped she was okay. Don thought maybe he should go back over and ask her, but he didn't want to bug her. He got into his car, and sat there a bit longer, waiting to see what she would do. Rebecca eventually turned to walk to her car. But then stopped again. What is she doing? Don pondered. Hmmm...I can't just drive off not knowing. I'll wait a bit longer.

Rebecca started walking toward her car again. Don figured she was fine then, so he started his engine, and looked to pull out. He saw Rebecca walking toward the church, or was she headed toward his car? He wasn't sure... He drove slowly, keeping her in view. Then it seemed, that yes, she was headed toward his car, so Don pulled into an empty spot and waited for her.

When she approached, Don asked, "Is everything okay, Bec? You seem undecided about something." Don had no idea what she as doing, and this was not like her.

Rebecca looked like she was struggling as she said, "Don, I need to say something, and it's going to sound very strange."

"Okay, Bec, whatever it is, don't worry about it. I'll listen." Don was getting concerned.

"I'll just say it Don...I think...I'm not one hundred percent sure, but I *think* I heard God speak to me just before you walked off."

Don waited. Rebecca seemed very puzzled, so he asked her, "What do you think you heard?"

"Well, it's hard, because I feel uncomfortable with saying this. Both that I heard God speak, and also what He said. What I heard was, 'Take Don with you.' And I have to be honest with you, I'm not feeling so good about that. Sorry." Rebecca needed him to know this was not her idea.

"Bec, you don't have to invite me. That's fine, really." Don was sincere, and Rebecca knew it.

"I know I don't. I know you don't expect me to. But when I think about what the pastor talked about this morning, I know I want to start my life with God by saying 'Yes' to Him. I don't want to be a, *But Lord* person. I was hoping God would start out easy, asking me to do things like call Kay. I can say, 'Yes Lord' to that."

"I know what you mean, Bec. I wondered what I might be asked to do that would make me want to say, *But Lord.*"

"So what I want to do today, Don, is drive off in my car, by myself, and enjoy the day alone. But it seems what God is asking me to do is to take you with me." Everything in Rebecca was rebelling against this. She wanted to scream! And she was, inside her head.

Don replied, "I don't know what to do. I know you don't really want me to go with you, so I should say, 'No thank you.' And that would probably be the best thing in both our minds. Then again, what if I am supposed to go with you today, and I say 'No.' Am I then saying, *But Lord*? I don't want to do that either. I'm new at this, too. I wish we had some sort of expert Christian with us right now to settle this."

They both looked around the parking lot, wondering who that might be. Other than going in and talking to the pastor, it looked like this was going to be up to them.

Rebecca said, "Don, let's just do this. If we do it, maybe we will know what we would have missed if we had said, *But Lord.* Why don't you just follow me to my house, and we can leave your car there." Rebecca talked quickly, like if she didn't get the words out, they would be stuck inside her forever.

Don agreed, "Okay. I'm with you. If this is crazy, then we will be crazy together."

When they got to Rebecca's house, Don walked over to the Mustang and got in. At the last minute, Rebecca said, "I'm going to run into the house and get a couple bottles of water. I'll be right back." When Rebecca came out, she locked the front door, and walked up to the car, but she hesitated. Something didn't seem right to her. Maybe it was because she hadn't seen the familiar white car pick Rosie up for church that morning. Had she just missed it because she left early? Maybe she just felt uneasy because Don was sitting in her car.

Rebecca said, "Don, if you don't mind, I'm going to run across the street for just a minute. I want to check on Rosie." Don knew Rosie from the years he lived there. He hadn't seen her in a long time. Don was surprised at Rebecca's concern for Rosie, knowing that Rebecca had usually kept her distance from the neighbors. But then he remembered Rebecca talking about Justin's service, so maybe this had something to do with that.

When Rebecca got to Rosie's porch, she rang her bell, but no one answered. She thought maybe Rosie hadn't gotten home from church yet. Wanting to make sure, Rebecca rang the bell again. Then Rebecca heard something from inside. It sort of sounded like an animal, but Rebecca knew Rosie didn't have a dog or a cat. She rang the bell again, and Rebecca heard what could be Rosie calling out. Rebecca's heart started beating faster. She tried the door. It was locked. Rebecca called out, "ROSIE? ARE YOU OKAY?!" She heard the faint call again, and then she knew there was something terribly wrong. Running back across the street, she quickly told Don there might be a problem and to come with her! He could see the panic in her eyes. They both ran back across the street together. While Rebecca tried calling Rosie on her cell phone, Don went around to check the other doors on the house to see if he could get in. Rosie wasn't answering her phone. Rebecca suddenly heard Don calling her from the back of the house. Don was standing at the sliding glass door when she got to him. From there, they could both see through the window that Rosie was lying on the floor in the fireplace room. When she caught sight of them, they could see the relief on her face. She didn't look to be in pain but she obviously couldn't move. Rosie waved to them, but the position she was in kept her from being able to call out in a loud voice. They yelled to her through the sliding-glass door, "WE WILL CALL 911. Hold on Rosie! Help will be here soon!"

Rosie made a motion like using a key. They couldn't quite understand what she was saying. She put her hands together like forming a ball, or a rock, and pointed to the right. Maybe there was a rock there, with a key under it. Don went over to look, and sure enough, after a short search, he found the key. They were soon inside. Rosie said she wasn't in too much pain, she just couldn't move. She said she tripped on the rug that morning and wasn't able to get up. She didn't know if anything was broken, or what the problem was. Rebecca asked her about her ride to church, why they hadn't discovered her this morning? Rosie said she told her friend yesterday that she wasn't going to church this morning. She had a cold the last two days, and felt it was better to rest. "But not on the floor!" Rosie laughed when she said that!

Rebecca stayed with Rosie, not wanting to move her until medical help arrived. She got her a pillow for her head and sat with her. Don went to the front door to wait for the police. It wasn't long and they could hear the sirens approaching. They all felt relief. Rosie would soon be tended to.

Don let the paramedics in, and they were so kind to Rosie. They asked her a lot of questions, and took her blood pressure, and felt her for broken bones. Everything seemed to check out okay. But they needed to get her to the hospital just to make sure. Rosie didn't really want to go, but she agreed that a few x-rays might be in order. They gently moved Rosie onto a stretcher and took her out the door, leaving Don and Rebecca standing there together. Rebecca let Rosie know that she would lock up the house, and then come to the hospital to see how she was doing. Rosie gave her a thumb's up and blew a kiss as they wheeled her out. Rosie had such a calmness about her in a tough situation. Rebecca was so glad she hadn't had to lay there any longer than she did.

Don and Rebecca went back across the street. They knew that their trip to the coast was not to be, but they also knew that God was teaching them something very important. When God speaks, no matter how quiet, or if we want to do it or not, the answer should never be, *But Lord*. What if it *had been* today? What if Rebecca continued to walk to her car in the church parking lot, and not listened to God's voice. Rebecca would have headed straight to the coast, and who knows when she would have checked on Rosie. What if Rebecca had come home tired, and put off seeing Rosie for another day? Rebecca suddenly realized, God wasn't asking her to go to the coast with Don. God was just telling her to take Don *with* her. God knew Rosie needed help, and by her inviting Don along, they would need to go by the house to drop off his car. God could see ahead of them, and God could see Rosie's need. All they could see was what *they* didn't want to do. But because of the pastor's sermon that morning, they were better prepared to listen and obey. They were learning…and this lesson, they learned together.

As Rebecca said good-bye to Don and prepared to go see Rosie at the hospital, she said, "Don, this God stuff isn't easy. But it sure makes sense. Thank you for being willing to do what we were being asked to do today. I'm so glad Rosie didn't lay on that floor any longer than she did."

Don answered thoughtfully, "You're right. We are so new at this. I hope you don't mind, but I'd really like to go to your church again. After today, I know that God is speaking through the pastor there, and that helps me to trust that it is a good place to be. I can go to a different service than you. I promise I won't be in your way."

"That's fine, Don. We will work it out. I know what you mean. If he's teaching the right stuff, and we can learn to follow God better by his teaching, it is a good place to be. You are welcome there. Maybe we can even sit together sometimes. I don't mind." Rebecca was pleased that she actually meant what she was saying.

"Thank you. I'll be in touch. Let me know if you need anything concerning Rosie."

"I will. Thanks again. Bye, Don."

"Bye."

Don left, shaking his head at how the day was turning out. He looked forward to sharing this whole experience with his men's Bible study group. Don hadn't seen God work like some of the other men had. Many of them had been Christians a long time. But Don knew they would appreciate hearing about what happened today. Yes, Don definitely wanted to attend *Forever His Church* again.

21

The drive to the hospital was not the trip Rebecca expected to make on Sunday afternoon. But she was happy to be there for Rosie. Especially after all Rosie had done for them. When Rebecca got to the ER, she was directed to where Rosie was. She found her lying in the bed, being taken care of by a nurse. The nurse looked up as Rebecca walked in, finished what she had been doing, and then left the two of them alone. Rosie said she had seen a doctor, and x-rays had been taken. They were just waiting for the results.

"How are you feeling? Do you have a lot of pain?" Rebecca asked Rosie.

"No, not really. Just mostly sore I think. I'm sorry for inconveniencing you like this. I'm sure you had other things to be doing today."

Rebecca quickly replied, "It's really okay. I'm just glad we discovered you before much time passed. What happened?"

"Well, I have been resting the last few days because of my cold..."

"Oh, I was wondering why I hadn't seen you out front."

"Yes, it's not a bad cold. But I know if I rest, I will get over it more quickly. By today I was feeling better, so I was doing a few things around the house. I tripped over the edge of the rug and landed right on my hip. You hear so much about people breaking their hip, I was so hoping I wasn't one of them...I'm not that old." Rosie laughed. "But after I fell, I had trouble moving. I couldn't get up. I wished I had my phone with me, but it was in the kitchen. I could hear it ringing from time to time."

"Yes, I called it, too, when you didn't answer the front door."

Rosie went on, "There was only one thing I could do at that point, and that was to pray. I asked God to please bring someone by to help me. It reminded me of the verse in Acts nine about Saul praying. He had been struck blind..."

Rebecca couldn't help but stop Rosie before she finished. "I'm sorry to interrupt you, but can I just say something? This morning in church the pastor was talking about that man, Saul. And how the other man came over to pray for him to help him get his eyesight back." Rebecca was excited to know exactly what Rosie was talking about! She felt like she finally knew something that was in the Bible.

"Yes, Rebecca. That's the story. And it says that when God asked Ananias to go see Saul, and to lay hands on him to have his sight restored, God told Ananias that Saul was praying to Him right then. That always touches me when I read that because we sometimes wonder if God hears our prayers. And God, Himself, said that He knew Saul was talking to Him right then."

"And, Rosie, you're not going to believe this. It was that very part in the Bible that brought Don and me to you today!"

"What do you mean?" Rosie wasn't sure what Rebecca was saying.

"Well, I was leaving church, and I was headed straight to the coast. I got a new car, by the way."

"Oh, what is it?"

"It's a blue Mustang. Parked right outside!" Rebecca said with a smile on her face.

"Nice! Congratulations!" Rosie was truly happy for her.

"So, what happened was, as I was leaving church, I ran into Don. I'm sure you must have been a little surprised to see him show up at your house with me." Rebecca waited, she wanted to know what Rosie would say to that.

"A little, yes." Rosie stayed out of Rebecca's business.

Rebecca continued, "Anyway, leaving church, I ran into Don. It was his first time there. I told him I was driving to the coast, and I was going to read more in Acts 9 to go along with what we learned that morning. The pastor said we aren't supposed to argue when God asks us to do something. We shouldn't be *But Lord* people, like the guy was in that story. I hadn't planned on asking Don to go with me...not at all. But after Don and I spoke, I thought I heard God whisper to me, 'Take Don with you.' I didn't want to, and I tried to ignore it. I tried to get to my car and just leave. But something wouldn't let me. So I went back over and told Don what happened. That's how we ended up at your house. We stopped by my house to drop off Don's car, and I told him I wanted to just check on you before we left. I hadn't seen you out front like I normally do."

"Rebecca, that is the best story! Thank you for telling me. It helps me to see the Holy Spirit working in all of our lives. He guides us on the right paths. I was praying, and God was answering by whispering to you.

What's interesting is, God didn't tell you I fell. But God put you where you needed to be to help me. I am so thankful! Thank you for listening to God, and for being His rescuer. Many times, we are God's hands and feet on this earth. It's not that God can't do it without us, but He likes to use us to accomplish a lot of His work."

Just as Rosie finished talking, the doctor came in.

"Nothing is broken Ms. Daniels. I'm thinking that your hip probably popped out of the socket when you fell, which is extremely painful. But then it reinserted itself. It will be sore, and a bit weak for a period of time. Please be careful on it. You will know when the strength returns enough to resume your normal activities. Until then, don't push it. Is there anything else I can help you with today?" The doctor was very kind.

"Nothing else. Thank you! I appreciate your care. Everyone has been wonderful. Can I go home now?"

"Yes. Do you have a ride?" the doctor said, looking at Rebecca.

Rebecca quickly offered, "Of course, I can give you a ride home…if you don't mind riding in a Mustang! You can share my new car with me!"

"That would be fun, Rebecca. Thank you."

The doctor let Rosie know, "I'll send someone around with a wheelchair to take you out." And to Rebecca he instructed, "You can get your car and pull it right up to the ER doors."

"Thank you. I'll go do that now. I'll see you in a few minutes, Rosie."

"Okay. See you outside." Rosie was thrilled beyond words that she didn't have broken bones. As hard as it would be to take it easy for a few days, because she wanted to get back to her garden, she knew that she would need to cooperate. She wasn't getting any younger these days. Sixty-six wasn't old, but she realized she was creeping up there.

The ride home with Rosie was such a relief, knowing nothing was broken. Rebecca got Rosie into the house and comfortable in her chair, promising to check back with her before the end of the day. Then Rebecca knew what she needed to do next…call Kay.

After getting in the house, Rebecca poured herself a glass of iced tea before sitting down. It had been an eventful day. First seeing Don at church, then expecting to go to the coast but finding Rosie instead. Rebecca didn't know how the call with Kay would go. She had butterflies wondering, would it be a normal chat? Lindsey was sick. Would Rebecca be able to handle it? There was only one way to find out, and the time had come.

The phone was ringing…"Hello."

"Hi Kay. This is Rebecca. I hope this is an okay time to call." Rebecca could hear her own voice shaking a bit.

"Hi. Yes, this is a good time. Thank you for calling. Lindsey is resting.

She had treatment on Friday, and it is starting to hit her now."

Rebecca replied, "I see. I have to say, I'm not very familiar with chemotherapy. We hear about it all the time. But I guess we really don't know what it is until we go through it. Can you help me understand it?"

"Sure…I can. It's pretty straight forward. Lindsey mostly has appointments at the oncology clinic as an out-patient. I take her, because even though she can drive, it's better to let her rest. They hook her up intravenously to a bag of the chemo meds that slowly drips. They have put a port into her chest for the IV, so they don't have to look for a vein each time. That's very helpful. The treatment can take a few hours. It's not painful. The clinic has a lot of cancer patients there, going through the same type of treatments, different meds, for different cancers. We really get to know the staff because we see them so often. Lindsey's chart is growing quite thick by now. After Lindsey gets her treatment, we usually head home and she feels okay. But then when the chemo meds start to take effect, it can make her very sick. They have good anti-nausea medications to give her. They help a lot. Lindsey has lost most of her hair, and she hates that, especially being a girl. She has been doing well, but it is rough going. She is so tired, and her immunities have to be watched. If she gets around colds or flus, or most anything, it can be very dangerous for her. She's being a trouper. I don't think I could handle it as well as she is."

Kay felt like she poured a lot out at once. She hoped she hadn't overwhelmed Rebecca. Especially since she was nice enough to call. Kay knew their "everyday language" changed since Lindsey got sick. She likened it to speaking "Christian-ese" to those who don't walk with Jesus yet. A lot of terminology surrounding an illness becomes common place. But to those who aren't dealing with cancer, it can seem foreign.

Rebecca replied, "Poor Lindsey. I'm sorry she's having to go through this. And you and Roger, too. You are such good parents. I know your hearts must hurt for Lindsey."

"Yes, it's not what anyone wants for their child. Roger has even asked God, 'Please God, give it to me. Not my child.' But Roger also accepts that God has a plan in all things, even when we don't understand it. Because honestly, Rebecca, we don't understand this. Lindsey is such a good girl. She hasn't given us many problems, just the typical stuff of childhood. She was on her way to a good education. Her life came to an abrupt halt because of this stupid cancer. Why our daughter? But, then, I'm sorry for saying that. Please forgive me…I wouldn't want this to happen to anyone's child."

Rebecca was quick to say, "Please, don't apologize. I don't have children, Kay, but I know this is so hard for you. I'm glad we can talk about it."

"Me too! Thank you for calling. Not many want to hear about such difficult things. Thanks for letting me vent to you. I hope I haven't scared you off from calling again. Sometimes it's just a particularly trying day, and it starts to get to me. To watch Lindsey resting here, I'm relieved. I know when she is sleeping that she isn't feeling the horrible effects of chemo. It's like the only break she gets."

"I want to be here for you, Kay. I'm sorry I haven't been." Rebecca truly meant it.

"It's okay. I know you were going through a lot with your divorce. They say divorce is death without the casseroles. I didn't bring you a casserole. I should have." Kay actually chuckled a little at that, although it might not have been appropriate.

Kay continued..."Rebecca, when Lindsey was diagnosed, it didn't seem real. Other people get cancer. Other families. Not ours. And when we first went to the hospital and I saw the pictures on the walls of cancer patients, I couldn't comprehend it. It seemed we must be there for something else. But it's our daughter this time...our reality. It sunk in a while ago—and now we are living in it, fully. And it is hard. I miss my job. But I wouldn't want to be anywhere else, but with Lindsey. We don't know the outcome of this. This type of cancer has a good survival rate. She was only at Stage 2. But we won't even know if she is cancer free for five years after she is done with treatment. That is a long time to wait to see if your child will live or die. And even then..."

Rebecca was so glad to be listening to Kay. Obviously, a lot had been pent up in her, and maybe she couldn't even share some of this with Roger. Rebecca didn't know, but maybe they had different struggles in this situation. Kay was such a strong person. Rebecca never knew her to complain much, and not that Rebecca thought of this as complaining. Kay was just telling it how it was.

"Kay, I am so glad you have shared this with me today. I had no idea, and now that I know, I want to help you. Please call me anytime, and I will check back with you, too. If you need anything, or even need me to take Lindsey to the clinic sometime, I can do that. My boss is very flexible. Please don't hesitate to call me."

"Thank you, Rebecca. I will keep that in mind. I hope things are going well with you. I know the divorce was very hard for both you and Don."

Rebecca replied, "It was. But Don and I seem to be mending our relationship some. We may even be able to be friends in the future. Time will tell. I saw Don at my church today, which is a story for another time that I'd like to tell you about."

"I would love to hear it when you're ready. Time and God tell a lot. We are learning that through Lindsey. Hang in there, we'll talk soon."

"Okay, bye for now."

"Bye."

Rebecca sat sipping her tea as the sun dropped behind the hills outside. Her heart was sad about Lindsey, but she had a hint of joy, too. All this day held, showed the hardships of life, and also that God hears our prayers. God answered Rosie's call for help. Rebecca hoped that God would also answer Roger and Kay's cry for help for their daughter. Only time and God would tell, from what Kay said. They would all wait and see.

Rebecca gave Rosie a call before turning in for the night. Rosie was already in bed, reading. They agreed that Rebecca would pick up some dinner tomorrow night. Rebecca looked forward to that time with Rosie. There was a lot she would like to talk with Rosie about.

22

Picking up some barbecue and a salad, Rebecca went right to Rosie's house after work. When she talked to Rosie earlier, Rosie said she had been resting most of the day. She had some soreness, and weakness, so she didn't want to push it. Rebecca was glad to be able to help Rosie. She knew Rosie would have been there for her any time, day or night.

After they ate, Rebecca tidied up the kitchen, and then helped Rosie to the back garden. She knew Rosie loved to be out of doors, and probably hadn't ventured even that far today. The flowers smelled so good, and the birds were singing.

After getting settled, Rebecca asked Rosie, "Can I make a request?"

"Sure, what it is?" Rosie had no idea. She was curious what was on Rebecca's mind.

"Would you sing a song while we sit out here? I love to hear you sing." Rebecca looked at Rosie, wondering if she made her feel uncomfortable. She knew it was okay when Rosie started her familiar humming, and then began to sing a song that Rebecca actually knew.

On a hill, far away, stood old rugged cross.
The emblem of suffering and shame.
How I love that old cross, where the dearest and best
For a world of lost sinners was slain.
So I'll cherish the old rugged cross
Till my trophies at last I lay down
I will cling to the old rugged cross
And exchange it some day for a crown...
...Then He'll call me some day, to my Home far away,
Where His glory forever I'll share...

When Rosie finished, Rebecca had tears in her eyes. The song took her back to times with her grandma. She knew that song from an old record that her grandma had. As a child, Rebecca would be fascinated with how the needle would play a tune from grooves on a piece of vinyl.

Rebecca quietly whispered, "Thank you," when Rosie finished. They sat for a time, just watching the birds land on the feeder, and fly away. They enjoyed the fresh new blossoms that were plentiful. It seemed that neither one of them wanted to interrupt the peace that surrounded them.

Rebecca eventually stepped into the stillness with a question. "Rosie, why can't life always be this peaceful? Why do things have to be so hard sometimes...or a lot of the time? I just want to live in this moment forever."

Rosie knew exactly what Rebecca was talking about. Rosie, too, wanted to stay in moments like this. But Rosie had seen too many moments in her lifetime that didn't resemble this, and she knew it was in those times that she came to appreciate this peace.

Rosie spoke gently to Rebecca, "When we have no peace, it feels horrible. Sadly, a lot of the world lives without true peace most of the time. When Jesus left, after He died and rose again, He said a wonderful thing that's recorded in the book of John, *"Peace I leave with you; my peace I give to you. I do not give to you as the world gives. Do not let your hearts be troubled and do not be afraid."*

"But Rosie, so much of the time I am troubled and afraid. I wish I weren't." Rebecca longed for more of what Rosie seemed to have.

"I know Rebecca. I believe every human being on this earth struggles with those things. Which is probably why Jesus talked about peace in some of His last words to us. Jesus knew how it is here on earth. And He wanted to give us what money can't buy...a peace from Heaven above. I truly believe Jesus is so looking forward to having us in Heaven with Him. Then we won't have the hard times we experience now. Moments like this will last for all of eternity."

"Rosie, have you had a lot of hard times in your life? I'm starting to see things differently. But it is also making it confusing for me. As I start to believe in God, and His goodness, then I struggle more with the bad things that happen. Why did Justin have to die? Why does my friend's daughter have to battle cancer? Why can't God just stop these things from happening? God has the power to do that, doesn't He?"

Rosie calmly answered, "I know...those are the tough questions. We wonder why God doesn't do something? Let me get my Bible here. God has answers that we don't have, and if we read on in John, I think it says something that could help both of us understand." Rosie reached for the

Bible she had sitting by her chair, and she turned directly to John. It was obvious to Rebecca that Rosie knew her Bible well.

"In John 14, where I just was quoting about Jesus leaving us with a peace, but not the peace the world gives, Jesus talks about the prince of this world here in verse 30. Do you know who the prince of this world is?" Rosie didn't mean to put Rebecca on the spot...she was hoping Rebecca would be comfortable talking about this.

"No, I really don't. Isn't Jesus a Prince?" Rebecca felt very inadequate, but she also knew Rosie would be kind.

"Yes, Jesus is the Prince of Peace. But our enemy, Satan, is the prince of this world. And because of that, this world can be very dark, and scary, and hurtful. Satan is not our friend. He is out to harm us, especially when we love Jesus. God protects us from many things that we aren't even aware of. But still, we live in a fallen world. This means, the enemy prowls around looking for someone to devour. That is basically his job, if you want to think of it like that. This is what we have to deal with since the time of Adam and Eve in the Garden of Eden—now talk about a perfect Garden!" Rosie's face lit up when she said that. She stopped a moment to look around at the beauty of her own garden.

Then Rosie continued on, "In the beginning, God created a perfect world. But it wasn't enough for man, so to speak. Man didn't stay within the boundaries God set for Adam and Eve. They ate from the Tree of Knowledge in the Garden—the one tree God told them not to eat from. When they did that, they were exposed to good and evil. Now, there was another tree in the garden, and that was the Tree of Life. God didn't want Adam and Eve to then eat from that tree, after being exposed to the evil, because they would have lived forever on this earth—God made them leave the Garden, and one day die. We think of death as a bad thing. But actually, we can think of it as a *gift* from God. Death is our escape route out of here...out of pain and suffering. When we die while believing in Jesus' saving Grace, we are released from the evil in this world. We go to a place where evil doesn't exist. We are no longer exposed to it. That's the place that Jesus longs for us to be, with Him, and away from all this garbage here. Is this making sense, Rebecca?"

"Yes. Yes, please continue." Rebecca longed to hear more about all of this.

Rosie went on, "Our Father has the answer to all the pain and suffering we go through. The answer is His Son, Jesus. Jesus came to earth, and defeated death by dying on the Cross, and rising again. In doing so, Jesus took away any need to fear death. Jesus' blood washes us clean from what happened in that original Garden. Jesus prepares us for going Home to Heaven. When we know we are headed to a wonderful place without suffering, we can better endure life's hardships. We can look at this world as a place we are just passing through. Think of our homes here as just pitching a tent. Think of the place that Jesus has gone to prepare for us as our real Home."

Rosie looked at Rebecca, hoping she was not overwhelmed. "Do you have any questions about this so far?"

Rebecca furrowed her brow and looked right at Rosie. She said, "Rosie, I just hate the bad things, like what happened to Justin, my friend Bonnie, and so many others. Can you help me better understand what God is doing? It seems so mean at times."

Rosie understood meanness, and she knew it didn't come from God, but from the devil himself. Rosie stopped talking for a bit, and got lost in her own thoughts. She had her own dark seasons, and she thought back even to her parents' trouble in just being married. She knew her parents' faith grew stronger through their struggles as a mixed-race couple. So many were against them and didn't understand their love. Only the love of God overrode the hate they felt from others. Rosie's parents trusted in the God who loved them, and who saw them both as His children. Rosie knew God used for good what others meant for harm. Her parents shared their faith and trust in Jesus with her when she was a young girl.

Rosie then focused back on Rebecca and continued, "When people get sick here and die, or die in accidents, or however they depart this earth, we see that as a tragedy. And it is, for those of us left behind. It is so sad and hard for us. But I once heard it said that it's like a boat sailing off into the sunset. We see it disappear past the horizon. But others see it arriving on the other side. That's the way it is for those who go to Heaven when they leave here. We have to say good bye to them, as their friends and relatives. But their friends and relatives who are already in Heaven are rejoicing at their arrival. Rebecca, what we see as bad, God sees in a very different way. And the suffering that happens with all of this death and dying stuff, the very stuff that Satan wants to use to harm us and make us question God, and even turn our back on God, God uses it for good. These things change lives by affecting us so deeply, that a decision has to be made. We come to a place where we have to decide, am I for God or against Him? This may seem unkind, but it is only the enemy, Satan, who is unkind. In God's kindness, He doesn't want us floating through life not making a decision. Because not making a decision to believe in what Jesus died to give us, is actually making a decision. God wants us to wake up from our slumber. Many are sleeping through life, just going about their business, making a non-decision for Jesus. But that is actually making a decision *against* Jesus. God doesn't want us leaving here not thinking about this. Things happen in our lives so we *will* think about where we will spend eternity...while there is still time. Our Father wants us to know His Son, Jesus, and all He gave us when He died and rose again. Once our life on earth ends, it will be too late. Our decision, or non-decision, will affect all of our eternity. And our Father wants our eternity to be spent in Heaven with Him."

Rebecca sat back, and tried to take in all that Rosie was saying. "Rosie, where does your confidence in all this come from? I seem to have too many questions, and not enough answers." Rebecca let out a long sigh...

"I have questions every day, Rebecca. That's why I keep my Bible close at hand. In here (Rosie held up her Bible), I find the answers. This is God's Instruction Manual for us. Sometimes I have to search for the answers, but they are here. The more I am familiar with God's Word, the more I trust in it. We never arrive at a finish line on this earth. We are always learning, and growing. It's all a process. But it is quite the adventure. The closer we get to God, the more exciting that adventure becomes. We start to see things the world misses—God's daily miracles. That helps to build confidence, too."

"Do you think God saves us from bad things happening, things we don't even realize?" Rebecca had been pondering this question for a while.

"Rebecca, there will come a time on this earth when the Holy Spirit will be taken out of the way. It talks about this in 2 Thessalonians. This will happen during the end times. People are mistaken if they think that God isn't involved in all of our lives. He is. Even with those who don't believe in Him. God saves us all from so much simply because of His presence here on earth. Right now, the Holy Spirit holds back the lawless one in this world. The lawless one is Satan. We can't even know all that God saves us from. Sadly, we complain a lot about the stuff that is allowed, forgetting to give thanks about so many things. We never know how much God is actually working to help us."

"I guess you're right. I forget to be thankful for a lot of things. I am quick to complain about things that don't go my way. And God did use Bonnie's death to get my attention. That's probably why I went to church in the first place. God was waking me up from my slumber, wasn't He?"

"Yes, probably so. One day you may be thankful for the pain you have been through." Rosie knew this was stretching Rebecca.

"But Rosie, I am fearful about some of the things you are talking about."

Rosie wanted to help to reassure Rebecca. "As Christians, the Bible says we are to wait for Jesus' return with eager anticipation. It will be a happy day! We can look forward with great Hope. When all is said and done, God will restore this earth. In Revelation 21:3, it says that God will once again dwell with His people on this earth. The garden we sit here looking at today is tainted with sin in this fallen world. As beautiful as it is, it's not as amazing as Heaven will be. One day we will see gardens in their full glory. We are assured that Satan loses because God has already won the battle through Jesus. We are just waiting to see it come to fruition! We can read the end of the story in Revelation and be at peace. The victory is ours! We need not fear."

"Rosie, I truly appreciate all that you are sharing with me. I will probably need you to repeat it to me many times for it to sink in. I'm grateful for your knowledge about all of this. I do need to get going now. Is there anything I can do for you before I leave?"

"If you wouldn't mind helping me out of my chair, that would be wonderful." Rosie smiled as she said it. She knew she would be stiff when she tried to get up, and a helping hand would go a long way.

"Of course." Rebecca stood, and helped Rosie to her feet. She led Rosie through the sliding-glass door, and closed it behind them. Rosie felt a little shaky on her feet, so Rebecca asked Rosie if she could help walk her to her bedroom. Rosie agreed it might be a good idea. As she led Rosie down the hallway, it reminded Rebecca of being with her grandma. It was a sweet remembrance. She helped Rosie locate her nightclothes, and turned back the bed for her. Rosie said she was able to change, so Rebecca just laid the things on the bed. She gave Rosie a gentle hug, and said, "Good night."

"Good night, my dear. Thank you for your kindness."

Rebecca let herself out, locking the door on her way. As she walked back to her house, Rebecca thought about all the years that this wonderful woman lived across the street from her. Rebecca knew she had shut out so much of God's goodness in the past, including Rosie. It was time to open her heart to what God had to offer. Rebecca was determined to fight against the temptation to resist God, and see where He would lead her from here.

23

It wasn't too long and Rebecca saw Rosie back outside tending to her garden again. She checked on Rosie daily, making sure everything was okay. Many times, they would sit and talk about things concerning God, and life in general. Rosie was so full of wisdom. Rebecca was finding out that Rosie lived through many trying times, and many joy-filled times. They were truly getting to know one another.

Rebecca's life seemed to be on a new path, and she was liking it. Her world was opening up again after the divorce. Rebecca knew she had been shut down, not only inside herself, but to everyone around her. Although she thought the divorce was what she wanted, the wound of being separated from Don still cut deep—it was a lonely time. Rebecca was seeing now that the divorce, and Bonnie's death, may have been the very things she needed to get in touch with God. Like Rosie told her, God brings things into our lives that help us think about Him. Rebecca had been trying her best to read her Bible almost every day. She didn't always get to it, but she was making progress. After finishing John, she moved on to Acts and other places that Rosie suggested. Rebecca was learning many things and some pieces were starting to come together.

Jennifer was hanging in there. She was sad much of the time, but she had gone back to work when her mom left. They had an interesting evening with Nelson after Erika went home. Nelson said he wanted to tell them something. They were hoping he wasn't moving away, or sick. But that wasn't it at all. When they got together at Jennifer's one night for dinner, Nelson told them about Jill. At first, they were shocked, and a bit confused. Why hadn't he said something before? But Nelson lovingly explained that when Justin died, he wanted to tell them, but it didn't seem like the right time. He didn't want to distract from what Jennifer was going through, her own grief, by sharing his grief. What Nelson did tell them ended up encouraging Jennifer a great deal. She could see that Nelson had come through something very similar, and had gone on with his life. The thing that concerned her though, was that he never found someone else. Nelson assured her that she would be okay—that if she wanted to marry, God would provide what was best for her in that situation. Nelson said he wasn't in any hurry to meet someone after Jill died. He had been devoting himself to growing in his relationship with Jesus even more, instead of looking for outward comfort too early on. In that growth, he was finding a great satisfaction in being able to serve God as a single man. It was a season that lasted longer than he thought it would, but he was okay with that. He shared with them in the Bible where it talks about how an unmarried person can spend time doing God's work because his interests aren't as divided with earthly responsibilities. Nelson said he was not ruling out marriage for the rest of his life. But for now, however long it lasted, he wanted to focus on Jesus. Nelson told them he sometimes gets lonely, but he works through those times by being in the Word and prayer...and of course good times with friends and family. Jennifer and Rebecca didn't quite understand his thinking, but they wanted to support Nelson. He was always so good to the two of them.

Rebecca had taken a few trips in her new Mustang, and she was enjoying it immensely. She even invited Don to go with her one day after church. Don was attending church weekly, and sometimes they would sit together. Not every time, and Rebecca liked that. She didn't want the people in church thinking they were a couple when they weren't. She was getting to know those that sat around her during first service, and that was good. Kay invited her to her Bible study, but Rebecca couldn't go since it was on a Wednesday morning when she was at work. She was thankful to have Rosie...Rebecca felt like she had the best Bible study around when she was one on one with Rosie.

The after-church car trip with Don had gone pretty well. They drove over to the coast, since it seemed they "missed out" on that adventure. Even though they both knew God had other plans for them that day. The day they did make it to the coast turned out to be a nice time together. At first Rebecca was nervous, just having Don in the car with her. They tried to chat like old times, but it seemed awkward. Then when they tried just listening to music, that was awkward, too. Songs they used to listen to together came on the radio every so often, and it seemed too familiar, and yet not. What does one do with an ex-spouse on an excursion? They were trying to find out. They stopped in for fish-n-chips at the place they remembered, and the conversation seemed to lighten up from that point. Maybe they had just been too hungry after church to be super friendly?

They talked about the house, how it was holding up, and what needed repairs. Don said he would be happy to come by and help with the faucet in the bathroom, and he did that a few days later. They asked about each other's health, and Rebecca told Don all about Justin's accident. He only heard about it briefly before. Don was sad to hear what Jennifer was going through, although Don had never met her. He was glad Rebecca was making friends, and especially that she was spending time with Rosie. They talked about attending church, and the things they knew and didn't know about God. Both seemed very willing to stay on that path until things became clearer. All in all, life was moving along for Rebecca, and she was pleased.

Around the middle of August, on a Saturday, Rebecca got a call from Kay. They had been talking, and rebuilding their friendship through the months although Kay kept very busy with Lindsey, and that was understandable. When Rebecca heard Kay's voice on the phone this time, she knew that there was a problem.

Kay said, "Rebecca, I was wondering if you could come over. There's something I need to talk with you about." Rebecca tried to read into her voice what the problem could be, but she wasn't able to tell. Was Lindsey struggling? Was there an accident? What could it be? But Rebecca didn't want to ask on the phone, since Kay wanted them to speak in person.

"Sure, Kay, I can come over in about an hour. Does that work for you?" Rebecca was trying to be the calm one this time.

"Yes. Yes. That should work fine."

"Okay. I'll see you soon. Is there anything I can bring you?" Rebecca was hoping Kay just needed a favor.

"No. Nothing. Just come when you can."

"Okay. I'll be over soon."

"Thank you."

The phone went silent. Rebecca finished what she was doing at home, getting ready to head over to Kay's. Rebecca was nervous. Their friendship was going well, but she felt sick in the pit of her stomach for some reason. She wondered if she had done something to upset Kay? Had Roger? What could it be? Rebecca sat on her couch for a few moments, gathering her thoughts. She saw her Bible sitting there. Reaching for it was much easier than it was in the past. Turning to a place in Philippians she had been reading—it reminded her not to worry about anything, but pray about everything. Yes, that's what I need to do. PRAY!

Father, I need Your help right now. I don't know what is going on with Kay. I hope it's nothing big, and maybe she just needs a shoulder to cry on about Lindsey. I'm not an expert at these kinds of things. I am new at being of help to people who are struggling. Please be with me today, as I talk to

Kay. You have the answers. I don't. You have the wisdom. I don't. I need You. In Jesus' name. Amen

Kay met Rebecca at the door, and ushered her into the family room. Rebecca noticed that no one else was home. She wondered where Roger and Lindsey were, but Kay soon answered that question.

"This is a good time, Rebecca, Roger took Lindsey out for a bite to eat. They spend time together on Saturday, one on one." Kay didn't sound happy for some reason. Rebecca wondered if it was hard for her to have Lindsey out of her sight.

"Well, that's nice." It was all Rebecca knew to say in the moment.

Kay looked around the room, and fidgeted with her fingers a bit before speaking. "Uh, Rebecca. I want you to know that I really have tried to stay neutral with you and Don. I never want to interfere in what's going on with the two of you."

Rebecca was shocked to hear Don's name brought up. What could this be? Her mind started swirling in many different directions at once. Was Don sick? Had he found someone else? Before Kay could even speak again, Rebecca had him married with three children and living in Timbuctoo. For some reason, that bothered her. Rebecca spoke almost without pause, although it seemed like ten minutes passed in her mind. "Yes, Kay. You have been a good friend to both of us."

"I'm not supposed to be telling you this. Roger would be mad at me for interfering, and Don would be none too happy either. Don swore me to secrecy, that's why I haven't said anything up to this point. I know you have been seeing each other from time to time at church, and sometimes even outside of church. Otherwise, I wouldn't even be telling you this."

"What is it, Kay? Although I'm not sure it is my business anyway, concerning Don. I certainly don't tell him everything I am doing."

"Don was laid off from his job a while back. He is really struggling, financially, and he had to move out of his apartment yesterday. He has been doing his best to make his payments to you with what money he does have so you can continue to stay in your home. But he can't afford both his apartment and the house until he finds another job. He has a job opportunity that could come through in a couple of months. But until then, he's really in a bind…and he doesn't want you to know. He doesn't want you to worry about your home." Kay stopped to see what Rebecca's reaction would be. It was hard to tell, and Rebecca didn't say anything for a few moments. Then she spoke.

"I didn't know," was all Rebecca seemed to be able to say. Her heart went out to Don. He was always such a good provider, and money was never anything they worried about. In the divorce, Don had been generous. He wanted her to keep the house, and she was thankful for that. She knew it was too big for one person, but she wasn't ready to move at that time. She wanted the comfort of a place she knew, and he afforded her that. Maybe it was time to sell it? But that would take time. And she wasn't sure she even wanted to.

Kay added, "I know you weren't aware. Don is very good at not letting on when things are bothering him. We didn't even know for a few weeks that he lost his job. He was hoping to find a new one before he had to share the news. But times are harder now. Finding a sales position that pays more than commission is not easy to come by. The job he had was so good for many years. But they are selling the company, and moving a lot of new people in, and a lot of the old employees out. It is sad for those that have been there for a while."

"Thank you for letting me know. I don't know what to do." Rebecca paused to think... "It will be hard because I'm not supposed to know this, and I don't want to get you in trouble with Don, and even Roger. But I appreciate you telling me. I'll need some time to consider this, and see what I can come up with. I can make the payments myself for a while until Don gets a new job. But then, what if that takes longer than he expects? And even then, he'll know I know when I tell him to stop paying me so he can have a place to live. Arrggghhh....this is frustrating. I want to help. But if I help, he will be upset with you for telling me. I don't want him sleeping in his car somewhere."

"Yes, we would have him here, Rebecca, but with Lindsey, it makes it difficult right now. We have to consider her health." Kay looked worried.

Rebecca said, "Oh, I know you do. And Don would never want to put Lindsey at risk. With him being out with the public all day, he would bring in too many germs." Rebecca was always careful when she visited Kay to make sure she wasn't sick, and with washing her hands, etc... Don would be careful. But would it be careful enough? They couldn't take that chance. The less people in Roger and Kay's home, the better.

Just as they were finishing up, Roger and Lindsey walked in. Lindsey looked worn and tired, much too tired for a young person. Her hair was starting to grow back some, but she still kept a hat on most of the time. Rebecca greeted them, but then quickly left. She didn't want Roger to know that she knew anything. He was already looking at her in a strange way...probably because she looked worried. Everybody was worried! What was up with that? Rebecca wondered as Christians why they worried when they weren't supposed to? Would that ever end? From what Rosie was saying, the Bible talks a lot about not fearing, and the reason it does is because we *fear*! But there is a lot to fear it seems. Now this...Rebecca would need to talk with Rosie, and soon.

24

Rebecca pulled into her driveway, and breathed a sigh of relief when she saw Rosie out front. She was hoping Rosie would be there. Rebecca practically jumped out of her car, and walked briskly across the street. Rosie had seen her pull in with her bright new Mustang, and she smiled and waved. Rebecca was so thankful that Rosie always seemed ready and willing to be there for her. Rebecca wished she could say the same. She mostly went to Rosie with struggles she was having. Rebecca was realizing she should be more aware of what Rosie might be going through. Rebecca didn't want to take advantage of Rosie's open-heartedness.

"Hi Rosie!" Rebecca called out as she crossed the street.

"Hi Rebecca! How are you this sunny Saturday?" Rosie could tell by the way she hurried over, and the look on her face, this could be serious.

"I'm upset, Rosie. Sorry to barge over here like this. Mind if we talk some?"

"Sure, let's sit here on the porch. I'm ready to rest for a bit anyway." The day was warming up, and Rosie didn't want to get overheated.

"Rosie, let me go in and get you a glass of water. Would that be okay? You sit, and I'll serve you."

"That would be lovely. In fact, there is some lemonade in the fridge. How about you get us both a glass of that?"

"For sure. I'll be right back." Rebecca knew her way around Rosie's house well by now. Knowing where the glasses were made Rebecca feel comfortable and glad. She and Rosie had now spent many hours, both inside and out, talking about life, God, and everything in between. They were all treasured times together.

Rebecca reappeared on the front porch, and handed Rosie her glass. The ice clinked as Rosie took it, and she laughed! "Oh, how I love that sound after working in the yard under the hot sun. It makes my mouth water to know refreshment is soon on its way… What can I help you with, Rebecca? You seem very concerned."

"I am, Rosie. Very. I just found out something I'm not supposed to know. And now that I know, I don't know what I'm supposed to do about it." Rebecca said the words so fast she wondered if Rosie would even understand what she said. But she did.

"Oh. Sorry to hear that. On both sides. When we know what we shouldn't, it can get troublesome."

Rebecca continued, "It's not like it needs to be a big secret. It's not like that. It's just that it concerns Don and me. My friend Kay told me something, and Don doesn't want me to know. Kay told me that Don moved out of his apartment yesterday because he lost his job. And the hard part is, he's doing it because he's trying his best to keep me in this house. He's homeless now, while I'm living in luxury, so to speak."

"Oh. Wow! This IS a toughie…tough to hear and tough to know how to proceed…especially when you're not supposed to know."

"Yes. That's what I say. I mean, I appreciate Kay telling me, and putting her neck out there. Her husband is not going to be happy with her either. Both Kay and Roger have been very good about not interfering in what's going on with Don and me. But this time Kay felt she needed to say something."

"I agree. She did. But that was a hard call on her part."

"Yes, it was. She didn't feel good about it." Rebecca said. "And, they can't take Don into their home right now because of their daughter being sick." Suddenly, it hit Rebecca, a thought out of nowhere, and a thought she wished had never come into her head… Uh oh…no. No. That wouldn't work. No! Rebecca was battling with thoughts she didn't want, and she certainly didn't want to say anything out loud to Rosie about them. What if Rosie thought it was a good idea? That would hold her accountable to something she DIDN'T want to do. She would stay quiet, and just see where this conversation led.

"I understand. Cancer is serious business." Rosie noticed that Rebecca was struggling with something. She could read her pretty well by now. But Rosie didn't want to push. She knew that all in God's timing, their conversation would be what it should be. Rosie didn't want to play Holy Spirit, Jr.

Both Rosie and Rebecca went on rocking, and sipping their lemonade. Rosie could tell Rebecca was stalling as they swatted at a few flies, and talked about how fast the lawn seems to grow in the summer. Rebecca had since hired Rosie's gardeners since she hadn't been happy with her own. Rebecca said they were doing a much better job. After talking about all that, Rebecca eventually got around to the business at hand.

"Thanks for letting me share this with you, about Don. I know you have your own things to be concerned with in life. You're always so welcoming to me. What would you do if this were your situation, Rosie?"

There it was…a question. A question needed to be asked before Rosie knew she had permission to speak about a solution. But even then, she needed to ask a few questions of Rebecca…to get her thinking on her own. Rosie learned that no one wants to be told what to do, for the most part. When the idea comes from within, and especially when it is Holy Spirit driven, Rosie knew things were much more apt to proceed in the right direction.

"Rebecca, the first thing to always do, in any situation, is ask God. Why don't we do that right now? Do you mind if I pray?"

"That's fine with me. I hope God has the answers." Rebecca truly did. Maybe God could come up with something better than what she was thinking.

"Dear Father in Heaven. Jesus has gone to prepare a place for us in Heaven when we leave here. But for now, we are still here. And Don, bless his heart, is out of a job. You know that, Lord, and You know when his next job will begin. We pray it will be soon. He is a good man, and a good worker, and whoever gets him will be blessed. Until that time, Don and Rebecca have a situation here. Don can no longer make the payments on two places, and Rebecca can hold out for a time on her own. But Don needs a place to live. Can you please help him find one that he can afford until he begins work again? Show Don, and Rebecca, what would be best. They don't want to lose their home. But if they must, we know that You will take care of that situation, too. You blessed them with their house, and You have a plan for it in the future. Give Rebecca, through Your Holy Spirit, the wisdom needed to help Don. Don doesn't want to be a burden, and he wants to provide. We trust that You will give the answers needed. In Jesus' name. Amen"

Rebecca's heart was pounding out of her chest, and she didn't like it. She knew the answer before Rosie started praying, but then when Rosie was praying, she felt so convicted she needed to say it out loud…as much as she didn't want to. Rebecca thought she better just blurt it out before it got stuffed down deeper, and it made it harder on her.

"ROSIE!"

"Uh yes?" Rosie was taken back a bit with the forcefulness with which Rebecca spoke after the prayer.

"…I have to ask Don if he would like to move back into the house for the time being. I don't want to. It goes against everything inside of me, it seems, except maybe the Holy Spirit you keep teaching me about. It's almost like I can't NOT say this out loud to you. And I don't want to. I don't want to say it. I don't want to do it. I don't want to! But there! It's out!"

Rebecca sat back in her chair, and rocked quickly, sighing deeply, not really wanting to hear what Rosie would say next. She didn't want Rosie to agree with this. She wanted Rosie to talk her out of it, to tell her that couldn't possibly be what God wanted her to do. She had a slight glimmer of hope until Rosie spoke.

"Rebecca, wow…wow… That's hard. Thank you for saying it out loud. If this truly is what God wants, then saying it out loud will weaken the enemy's forces against it. Of course our enemy doesn't want us to welcome people into our home, and especially our ex-husband. The enemy likes families split apart. He likes dissension. He likes anger. And what you are talking about here is going against what Satan has accomplished so far, splitting you and Don up and making you enemies with one another. You moved past that barrier by becoming friends again. And to open your home to Don in his time of need…well, that would really anger the enemy. That is the last thing Satan wants you to do. He doesn't want you to show love to anyone, let alone your ex-husband. It shouts to the world that God can accomplish amazing things in our life, and that Jesus can heal relationships that seemed beyond repair."

"Rosie, do I want to anger the enemy? That sounds scary?" Rebecca wasn't so sure she wanted to step into that hornet's nest.

"When I say you're angering the enemy, I mean that there is a spiritual battle going on. The Bible says we don't fight against flesh and blood, but against spiritual forces in an unseen world. It's not that you're going to notice a whole lot of difference, but the enemy will. Satan will notice that you're not listening to his lies, and instead you are listening to the Holy Spirit within you. The battle will rage in a place that we can't visably see…it will be the angels against the demons. Satan will probably try to bombard you with more lies. But even in that, we can take authority over those thoughts with the power of the Holy Spirit within. Let me go get my Bible, okay? I want to read something to you?"

"Sure!" Rebecca watched Rosie get up and go into the house. It gave her some time to think about all that was going on. Would she really ask Don to move in for a time? Now that she said it to Rosie, would she have to do it? And how would she go about it? God was going to have to help her because when she brought it up to Don, the secret would be known that Kay let the cat out of the bag. Don could be very angry…but then again, he could be very relieved. Rebecca hoped the second would be true.

Rosie came back to her chair, and sat down. She turned toward the end of her Bible in Ephesians and read to Rebecca about the armor of God.

Rebecca remembered talking about this before with Rosie. But this time, it became personal as Rosie read:

"Be strong with the Lord's mighty power. Put on all of God's armor so that you will be able to stand firm against all strategies and tricks of the Devil. For we are not fighting against people made of flesh and blood, but against the evil rulers and authorities of the unseen world, against those mighty powers of darkness who rule this world, and against wicked spirits in the heavenly realms."

When Rosie finished reading this, she went on to explain, "We are to use every piece of God's armor, the sturdy belt of Truth, the shoes of peace, the shield of faith, the helmet of salvation, the breastplate of righteousness, and the sword of the Spirit. Now as we have talked about, these aren't actual physical shoes and swords and shields. They are only seen in the spiritual realm. As you pray, stay in the Word, as you are doing. By talking with other believers, listening to sermons, building your relationship with Jesus through quiet times with Him, you will be putting on the armor. When times like this come, and the enemy is not happy with the loving decisions we make, we are protected from falling prey to his schemes. We can stand firm. Oh, how I wish we could actually see this battle with our eyes. We would believe it so much more. For now, all we can do is trust, and continue to remain faithful to God."

Rebecca asked, "So, Rosie, my making a decision to care for Don in this way, even though I don't want to, will be a good thing in God's eyes? He won't see it as sin that I have my ex-husband living back in the house with me?" Rebecca wondered about this. She knew she shouldn't be living with a man she isn't married to, according to God's Word.

"Of course not, Rebecca. God is not asking you to take Don into your bedroom while he is there—nothing even close to that. God would only be asking you to make your guest room available to Don. That is a very different thing."

"Okay. That seems easier. For some reason, I thought it might be the whole shebang, and maybe that's why it scared me even more to think about this as a possibility." Rebecca was relieved. At least part of her fears were removed. Now, how to broach this subject with Don?

"Rosie, how will I even talk to Don about this? I'll probably see him at church tomorrow. I know I can invite him to sit with me. But maybe church is not a good place to bring it up. Although I'd feel protected!" Rebecca laughed, and then got serious again. "I don't want to wait too long. I know Don is probably staying in a hotel right now, and that will add up quickly. He can't afford it."

Rosie said, "Let's pray again. It seems you have gotten some answers, so we will continue to let God lead your way through this. What God has begun, let's let Him finish...Father, if this is truly from You—that Rebecca should speak with Don about staying in her home while he searches for a job—please make a way for them to have a conversation about this, possibly tomorrow. Help them to communicate clearly, both understanding that this is not a commitment to be married again, but only a way to help one another in a time of need. Soften Don's heart to hear that Rebecca knows of his situation. Help him to be okay with it, and to know that she only wants to help him. Help Don have a forgiving heart toward Kay in all of this, too. Thank you, Jesus. In Your Name we pray. Amen."

Rebecca took a deep breath in and blew it out slowly. "Well Rosie, looks like God is showing me what I need to do. I will have to trust that He will help me do this—both talking to Don about it, and if he accepts the offer, living with him for a short time. Maybe it will be good to have a man around again..." Rebecca shocked herself when she heard those words come out of her mouth.

"I will be praying for you each day, you and Don. I know that God will provide the help you need if this is His will." Rosie nodded toward Rebecca, letting her know it would be okay.

"Thank you, Rosie. I don't know what I would do without you."

Rebecca got up, gave Rosie a hug, and walked much more slowly back across the street. Entering the house, she looked around. Could it be possible that she and Don would be living here again, together, for a time? It seemed very possible now. And Don didn't even have a clue yet. He was probably staying in some hotel nearby, wondering why God wasn't providing for him...first his job, now his apartment...poor Don. He didn't deserve this. Rebecca's heart was warming to the idea already. That surprised her. She thought, God truly changes hearts and minds, even when we don't really want Him to. God was teaching Rebecca to bring things into the light, and let God decide what is best. That was new to her. Rebecca wanted to be done hiding things in the dark and letting the enemy rule her life. Sometimes it seemed easier to keep things hidden. But she was finding in the long run, it probably wasn't. Another step on her long journey with God seemed to be beginning.

25

Rebecca got up early for church. She knew this was going to be a big day, or a hard day, or some kind of day...she wasn't even sure yet. She hoped Don would be at church, and she could sit with him. But what if he wasn't there? What if he was with someone else? How would she get to talk with him about talking after? Too many thoughts. Why does the mind go in so many different directions at once? Rosie taught her to pray, always, and even though she didn't feel like it, Rebecca prayed, and asked God for help, once again. She wondered how she ever made it through anything before when she wasn't praying? She was barely making it through things now with prayer, or so it seemed.

The church parking lot was mostly empty when she arrived, so she waited in her car for a bit to see if Don would arrive. He usually came early. He was normally inside by the time she arrived. Sure enough, she saw his car pull in, and she saw that he was glancing over at her. Don probably wondered what she was doing there so early? He gave her a wave as he walked toward the church. She wished she'd gotten out earlier and been standing by the door. This didn't seem to be going the way she would want it to, already. But she knew she needed to calm down. Rosie said we have to be like a branch and stay attached to the Vine, Jesus—let God flow through us instead of doing things on our own. Rebecca prayed again and got out of her car.

Don was already seated inside. Rebecca went over to him and asked if it was okay if they sat together today. Normally, when she spotted Don, she would sort of wave him over to a seat by her if she wanted to sit together. She could tell Don wondered what was up. But he didn't say anything. The service wasn't starting for another ten minutes. Rebecca couldn't bring herself to say much of anything until the music was just about to start. Then she practically blurted out, "Don, how about we have lunch today after church!?" Don really knew something was up now…she was sitting with him, and asking him to have lunch. He wondered if she was going to ask him for extra money that month. Don knew he couldn't give it to her, although he would like to.

"Sure, Bec, we can do that." The music began, and their conversation ended.

The sermon that morning was probably a good one, but Rebecca didn't hear much—her mind wandered in too many directions to comprehend what the pastor was saying. She was SO nervous, although she was here to help Don. The problem was, would he want her help? And just how mad was he going to be? Rebecca knew she was going to have to go slow, and really listen to what God would have her say to Don. She needed to get her head screwed on straight or this thing was going to turn into a catastrophe.

When church was over, Don asked if she would like to ride in his car to breakfast. Rebecca was fine with that, so they took off to the local pancake house. They chatted about church at breakfast. Don seemed to pick up on some good stuff from the morning. He was telling her how Paul and Barnabas parted ways over a disagreement, and it surprised him. Two mighty men of God, arguing? But the pastor said when they split up, it only spread the Gospel further. The Holy Spirit then directed Paul and Silas where to go. Don was talking about what it might sound like to hear directions from God when Rebecca interrupted him.

"Don, have you ever heard the voice of God?"

"No. I don't think so." Don didn't know what Rebecca was getting at. He remembered the day Rebecca heard God speak to her in the parking lot at church, and they had been able to help Rosie. "Are you hearing something now?" Don put his ear up into the air, jokingly, but Rebecca didn't laugh. She seemed dead serious.

"Don, be serious."

Wow, that was a line Don heard many times in their marriage. He can't say as he liked it, but he wanted to go easy today. Maybe this was different. Maybe this *was* serious, and he needed to be paying attention when God was wanting to be heard.

"Okay, Bec, I'm sorry. I know that you have heard God, and that He had a good reason for it. Maybe that's the same way Paul and Silas heard the Holy Spirit?"

"I don't know…maybe. Maybe they heard an audible voice. I just know that my life has changed since I am learning more about God, and I want to make sure that I am doing what He wants me to do. Sometimes, that means doing things I don't want to do, or should I say, would rather not.

Similar to that day with Rosie." Rebecca still didn't know quite how to broach the subject, although it seemed God was leading her in that direction.

"Yeah, I know what you mean," Don said. "I don't exactly hear God's voice in the way that you did. But I sense God directing me in different ways...like to be kinder, to listen more, to trust, when it is hard." Don liked talking with Rebecca about God. It was something they never had in their relationship.

Rebecca said, "Rosie has been teaching me a lot about listening to God. She seems to know all this so well. I am envious of her at times. But then, she has been at it for a lot more years, that's for sure. I feel like I'm just getting started, and have so far to go."

"Me, too, Bec. When I go to Bible study with Roger, some of those guys know the Bible so well. I'm intimidated, and think I shouldn't speak up. But they encourage me to talk. They are a great group of guys. They have been such a big help to me."

"Kay wanted me to join her group, but I can't. It's on Wednesday mornings while I'm at work. Kay and I have been spending a lot more time together lately. Isn't it interesting how all of us now are learning about God? Who would have thought years ago that we would be where we are today?"

"Really. You're right. We were all so busy just living our lives, we didn't have much time for God. But with our divorce...oh sorry. I hope you don't mind if I talk a bit about what we went through..." Don thought he might have opened up a can of worms there.

"No. That's fine, Don. We might as well get it out into the open." Rebecca really didn't want to. But then again, they probably should.

"I didn't really want a divorce, Bec. But you knew that. Right?" Don sort of scrunched up his face, hoping he hadn't stepped too far right off the bat.

"I know. I know I was the one in the bigger hurry there. I just seemed to be making you so miserable. Maybe I was wanting it as much for you as for me?"

"Maybe. But I wasn't all that miserable. I just wished we could have talked more without arguing, I guess. Maybe we could have resolved some things before it dissolved our marriage."

Rebecca remained silent for a few moments, thinking about what Don just said. And then she knew, it was time... "Don. I need to talk to you about something today. You probably knew that when I came to sit with you, and when I asked you to lunch. I might as well not beat around the bush. Perhaps if we had been forthright in our marriage, it could have survived, like you said. Now, I don't want you to be angry, at me, or anyone else. I say this to help, not to make you feel bad." Don was looking at Rebecca with wide eyes, wondering what was coming next. But, he wanted to welcome it. What if they really could start to communicate better?

"Okay, Bec. Go ahead. I'm really going to try and be open to what you have to say. Let's start here and now, doing things differently."

Rebecca knew this was it. But still the words were stuck in her throat...she was having a hard time being bold. She took a sip of her coffee, hoping it would help to loosen up her lips. She hoped this wouldn't cause a scene.

"I know about your job, Don." Rebecca stopped right there. She knew there must have been a better way to begin. She wanted to pause before it got worse.

Don just looked at her. He didn't say a word. He couldn't. He didn't want to...so he picked at his food, drank his coffee, and took a bite of his pancake before he spoke. "Oh, really? How did you find out?" Don sounded agitated. He hated being unemployed. It made him feel worthless.

"That's not what's important here. What's important is that I care about you..." Rebecca could feel the Holy Spirit start to take over in a way she never had before. "I care about what is happening to you, even though we are divorced. You have always been generous with me. You have been kind when I wasn't. I am learning to appreciate things about you that I never noticed before. I was too consumed with my own wants, and not seeing what you might need. But I can't do that anymore. I can't be that person anymore. I don't want to be...not to anyone. I'm hoping that God is changing me, like Rosie talks about. But I don't know, because it's slow going. I only see little changes now and then. But this is one of those times when I know God is working, because He wants me to help you Don, even if I don't want to. And I don't mean for that to sound harsh. I'm just trying to be truthful with you. What I mean is, it's not that I don't want to help you. But I believe God is asking me to help you in a way that is uncomfortable for me. I know I need to listen, just like with what happened to Rosie when we were able to help her. What if I hadn't listened on that day? I hate to think." Rebecca needed to stop, and take in what Don was thinking about what she was saying. She felt like she maybe said way too much.

"Bec, I appreciate your honesty. I get what you're saying. My walk with God, as they call it, is slow going, too. I feel like I fail in so many ways but the guys keep telling me it's okay. They tell me how Jesus died for our failures, and He loves us anyway. I try to believe that."

Rebecca agreed, "Me, too. It's hard though, isn't it?"

"It sure is." Don was in agreement with Rebecca, and she seemed to be in agreement with him. It felt good after all the turbulent water that had passed under their bridge.

Rebecca knew it was time... "What I want to ask you, I would like you to give thought to... I have been grateful you allowed me to keep the house. I know that was big, on your part. My lawyer didn't think I would get the house in the divorce. He said, 'No way. It will need to be sold.' But you weren't like that. You worked it out so I could stay, and that has been a big help to me. Now I would like to be a big help to you, and ask you...if you...would like to stay at the house until you find work?" There, it was out...and Rebecca waited to see how it was received. Don sat still, looking at her, like there was no one else in the place. She waited, and he said nothing.

"Don, I hope I have not overstepped here."

Don remained quiet for a few moments longer before he spoke.

"I don't really know what to say. I never thought I'd move back into our home, and I don't mean it that way, of course. It is your home now. But right now, because of my present circumstances, I can only feel relieved to hear your offer. I had to move out of my apartment because of the job situation. I am staying in a hotel, hoping to get a job ASAP so I can sign a new lease somewhere. But the job market is tough. I was feeling at a loss, and honestly, it has been stretching my faith. It seems since I've known God, things get harder, not easier, and I don't understand that. I try to do things right, and things go wrong. It seems out of balance to me. I'm not giving up on God, but I have been tempted." Rebecca could see that Don was getting emotional, which he rarely did. She knew it was not because of wanting sympathy, but because he was truly touched by what she offered him.

Rebecca felt she could speak again. "This is not easy for either one of us. I want you to know that. I like you Don—you have always been a decent guy. Maybe we can be friends. But I was concerned what this would mean, so I talked to Rosie about it. I don't want you to get the wrong idea with this. And also, I didn't know if us living together would be a sin, since we aren't married anymore. Rosie told me it was fine, that with you sleeping in the guest room, we are not sinning. She said I am just being loving in a way that God would want me to." Rebecca hoped that all came out right.

"I totally understand, and I will be very respectful of you should I move in with you again. The guest room would be welcomed, especially over a hotel. Let me take some time to think about this, and I will let you know. Okay? But no matter what, I want you to know how much this means to me. I'm glad that God has been rebuilding our relationship to the point that we can even consider this option."

Rebecca and Don finished their breakfast talking about lighter subjects, and then Don drove Rebecca back to the church to get her car. They said a cheerful good-bye, and to Rebecca it seemed Don was truly feeling relief. Rebecca was relieved also. She knew that God had to be a part of their conversation. Otherwise it wouldn't have gone so smoothly. It hadn't been like that between them for a long time. This time, they had been able to talk about difficult things without arguing. God was working miracles Rebecca never thought were possible. Now she would wait and see if Don would soon be moving in. She didn't know how she would handle that. But she knew God would be there to help her…and Rosie would help her, too.

26

Monday came and went. Tuesday came and went. Wednesday came and went...and still no word from Don. Rebecca wondered if he had gotten angry after they talked. She surely hoped not. Not hearing from him was worrying her. It was hard to concentrate at work. It was hard at home, thinking Don might show up at any minute. Rebecca was surprised she hadn't even gotten a text from him. She would give Kay a call if she hadn't heard from Don by Friday night. Rebecca was thankful to have dinner plans with Nelson and Jennifer tonight. That would keep her occupied some. It had been a couple weeks since the three of them had been together. Rebecca missed her friends.

Nelson swung by to pick Rebecca up about 6:30, and they headed over to get Jennifer. They were going out for a good steak dinner. Jennifer looked happy as she came bouncing out of her place toward the car—happier than Rebecca had seen her in a while. After Jennifer got in the car, they found out why. Jennifer received a promotion at work, and it was a good one. It was going to require a great deal of travel, and she was pleased about that. Jennifer liked the thought of going wherever the company would send her. Nelson and Rebecca were so happy for her. They knew Jennifer needed a boost in her life. Things seemed to drag since Justin's accident. They had been concerned, thinking that Jennifer might be falling into a depression.

The restaurant wasn't busy, being a Thursday, so they got a nice booth with lots of privacy. After dinner had been served, they chatted about trivial things. Then the subject of Justin came up. Jennifer told them she was remembering a time when they took a ride on Justin's motorcycle. It was such a beautiful day. They rode up into the Sierras, and met with another couple also riding their motorcycle. They enjoyed a delicious dinner in a steak house in Sonora. Nelson and Rebecca could see Jennifer start to drift away in her emotions…it was becoming difficult again…her smiles were disappearing.

After giving her some time, Rebecca gently asked, "How have you been, Jennifer? I haven't walked in your shoes like Nelson has. I've been concerned about you." Rebecca was surprised that she took the lead this time. She would usually follow Nelson into difficult discussions.

"It's hard…very hard. I would think my heart wouldn't hurt so much by now. But it actually hurts more. I think I was in a fog for the first few months. I really couldn't comprehend that Justin was gone. It seemed more like he was out of town. But as I come up on the five-month mark, the reality is all too real. My mind is starting to catch up with the pain in my heart, and it's awful! It's an actual physical ache that I feel in my chest. I've heard that many grieving people go to the hospital thinking they are having a heart attack. But it's a broken heart. I don't know how long I will feel like this. Will my heart always ache?"

Nelson knew he needed to say something. But he wanted to proceed carefully. "I agree with you about grief. It is a physical ache in the heart. All our lives, we hear about broken hearts. But when we feel the actual physical pain of that, it comes as a surprise. My heart hurt for a long while. I have heard that all grief is different, so I can't tell you how long it will last for you. I do want to let you know that my heart doesn't hurt anymore, Jennifer. I want to give you hope with that. It hurt much longer than I would have liked it to. But it doesn't now. Are you able to talk with anyone about your grief?"

Jennifer answered, "I have joined a grief group at my church. There are about eight of us who get together once a week and share what's going on. It is founded on prayer and Scripture. I'm glad about that. And I have finished the book my mom recommended about Heaven. That helped, too. I didn't know the Bible spoke so much about Heaven. I wish the pastors talked about Heaven more. They are always telling us how to get there, but not so much on what to expect when we arrive. After reading that book, I have a better idea. Can I share a few things with you?"

"Sure, that would be great! What better topic to cover than Heaven!" Nelson wanted to hear all she had to say. He hadn't studied much about it.

"I'd love to know more!" Rebecca exclaimed.

"I jotted down some notes. Do you mind if I read some stuff to you?" Jennifer was digging in her purse. She knew she wouldn't be able to remember specifics, and she loved some of the things she learned.

"We are willing and able to listen," Nelson said with warm smile.

"Here they are. I found my notes. I won't go on too long. But this is cool. The book talks about recognizing Moses and Elijah on the mount of

Transfiguration. And if we can recognize people we have never met, how much more will we recognize family and friends? I'm so excited to know that I will know Justin when I see him in Heaven. And, we will be one big family in Heaven. How special that is for those who feel alone without family on this earth. That is backed up by scripture when Jesus said, 'My mother and brothers are those who hear God's Word and put it into practice,' That's in Luke 8:19-21. Also, all babies go to Heaven. In 2 Samuel, David said this about his infant son, 'I will go to him, but he will not return to me.' People wonder about children, and this proves that God doesn't wonder, He has a plan for them. The book says we have an inheritance waiting for us in Heaven because in Daniel 12:13, it says 'You will rise to receive your allotted inheritance.' It makes me wonder what that will be like? I know I'm not getting a big inheritance down here on earth." Jennifer chuckled at that. She then asked if she should go on...if she was boring them? Both Rebecca and Nelson urged her to tell them more.

"Let me see..." Jennifer said, looking at her notes.

The waiter came to pick up their plates, and he asked them if they wanted dessert. They ordered something, just so they could stretch the evening out a bit longer. They were all enjoying their time together.

Jennifer read, "We are going to have resurrected bodies like Jesus did. That means we will have our five senses. Jesus cooked and ate fish, so He must have smelled and tasted it, too. He obviously saw it, and heard it crackling on the fire. And, we will have a feast in Heaven. In Isaiah 25:6, it is said our Father will prepare for us the finest foods. I can't wait for that! Even better than our steak tonight...and this dessert!"

The waiter had served them a piece of cheesecake with strawberry sauce, and a brownie with ice cream. They were sharing it, since they were already full. As they enjoyed it, Jennifer continued...

"There will be no more sin. Romans 6:23 says, 'the wages of sin is death.' If there is no more death, there must be no more sin. How awesome that we won't have the Tempter there to mess with our lives anymore. Maybe we won't even have to count calories," Jennifer said, as she took a big bite of cheesecake. "And get this! We will rest! Doesn't that sound good after an exhausting day at work? Revelation 14:13 says, 'they will rest from their labor, for their deeds will follow them.' We also won't all live together in one big room, dorm style! From what it says in John 14:2, there are many rooms. Jesus is preparing a place for us. I sure like to have my alone time, so I look forward to that, too! The psalmist says you turn my wailing into dancing. Dancing will be a part of Heaven. How fun! Well, I could go on, but I think you get the idea. There is a lot to look forward to in Heaven. And reading this book has really helped. It does help me to grieve in a healthier way. The Bible says we are not to grieve as those who have no hope. I have great Hope now, so that is how I want to grieve."

Nelson spoke up first. "I really appreciate all that you shared with us. Would it be possible for me to borrow that book from you? I think I have had some misconceptions about Heaven, and that makes certain things hard to live with on this earth. I think it's time that I know the full Truth of what the Bible has to say. And you are right, I wished this was taught more on Sunday mornings. Jill has been gone a long time, and it would have been a good idea for me to look into some of these things years ago. We get fooled into thinking that Hollywood movies about Heaven are correct. But think about it. Are they written by Christians who know their Bible well? I would say, for the most part, not. Many of them are probably writing the script with their own misconceptions. I'm glad there are more and more movies coming out that are Biblically based."

Rebecca wanted to agree. But before she could speak, Jennifer said, "Thank you, Nelson. I agree, and I would be happy to loan you the book. And then we could have even more discussions about Heaven. If no one is going to teach it, we can take it upon ourselves to investigate Heaven."

Rebecca added in, "Being with the two of you tonight has really been an encouragement to me. Thank you for your friendship, and for your faith. You have helped me learn so much. Without you, and Rosie, I don't know what I would have done. I know this has been an extremely hard time for you, Jennifer, but God is using it in so many ways. I know if you could change it, and have Justin still here with you, that is what you would want. But Justin would be proud of you and how you have continued on in your life, and in your faith."

Jennifer looked at Rebecca with tears in her eyes. "Thank you," was all she could say.

Rebecca took a deep breath, and said, "As you know, I am single right now, too. My divorce was final a couple of years ago. At that time, I was bitter and angry about a lot of things. Then my good friend, Bonnie, died. I believe that was sort of like a final straw. I had to find hope somewhere, so I went to church. I didn't know when I met Nelson in the parking lot that cold rainy night, or when I met you at Nelson's 40th birthday party, that we would all be sitting here today talking about Heaven. I didn't even know you were Christians at that time. I'm so glad that God saw fit to bring us all together like He did. I have needed this. I also want to tell you my life could be changing a bit. I recently heard that my ex-husband, Don, is out of work, and out of a place to live. I have invited him to stay with me until he is employed again...merely as friends. He will be staying in the guest room. I have not heard back from him yet about his answer. He said he was going to think about it. It is probably very hard for him to do this also. This may seem shocking, but I am doing it because of God. It is not an easy decision for me to make. But I feel God wanting me to be as generous to Don as he has always been to me. I tell you this because I'm hoping you will support me in this decision, and pray for me. This could be very challenging. I'm not sure how I will be with it. But I am trying, and I hesitate to say that, because when I do, Rosie is always quick to tell me it is God doing it through us, and we are to rely on His strength. That is something I am still learning to do."

Jennifer was the first to speak, "We are here for you, Rebecca, through thick or thin. And of course, we will support you and pray for you." Nelson was quick to follow with the same support. Rebecca was finding that this is what good friends do, and especially good Christian friends. Being there, even if they don't understand all the ins and outs. When God's will is being done, all are in agreement. It seemed it had been that way when Rebecca and Don talked. She again wondered why she hadn't heard from Don.

The evening ended with just a few crumbs of cheesecake left on the plate. No one could eat another bite of anything, and they were ready to call it a night. Everyone had work in the morning. As they walked out of the restaurant, it felt good to be together. Rebecca knew she had been blessed with these friendships, and that was not a word she used often. She wondered if she was starting to talk like a Christian? Maybe it was rubbing off on her. She knew that was not a bad thing, but a very good thing.

27

It was now Friday. As Rebecca ate her breakfast before work, she was really getting concerned about Don. She wondered if she should call him, instead of talking to Kay. It was probably best to keep Kay out of this as much as possible. Just as Rebecca went to reach for her phone, a text message came through. It was from Don. What timing, she thought. Then, as she read the message, she was both relieved and frustrated.

"Hi Bec. Sorry I haven't gotten back to you sooner," it said...she waited, as the three dots made their way through the small bubble on the screen, wondering what he was going to say next. She was glad they were both using iPhones so she could see when he was writing to her.

The text continued, "I wanted to think and pray a couple of days about your offer. But I know it has been a week now. I didn't mean to keep you waiting," three dots again. Rebecca thought to herself, well, you're keeping me waiting now! But she didn't text anything back. She had no idea what he was going to say.

Don wrote, "I had a job interview, and was hoping I would have good news before I got ahold of you. Unfortunately, I haven't heard anything back, as yet,"...three dots... "Then on Wednesday morning, I woke up with vertigo. The room was spinning out of control. This is the first morning I can even lift my head. On Wednesday I couldn't even open my eyes,"...three dots.... Rebecca knew Don got vertigo from time to time. It frustrated her that he hadn't even asked her for help. She was relieved it wasn't anything worse. She wondered, what has he been doing, lying flat on his back in the hotel room, alone?

Don continued texting, "Today I'm better. I can walk around. Still taking it easy. Hopefully, by tomorrow it will be gone."

The dots stopped. Was Don waiting for her to reply? Rebecca knew she

171

had to get over being frustrated before she wrote back. She didn't like that he hadn't even let her know why she was waiting. But then, she knew Don well enough to know that he wouldn't have wanted to bother her. Rebecca prayed, please, Father, help me be patient here. I don't want to get into an argument before this even happens, if it is going to happen. I don't want to go back to my old ways of reacting. How would You have me respond to Don?

Rebecca then punched in the letters, "I'm glad you're feeling better." That was all she texted at the moment. She wondered why she was so agitated. Then she realized...she had been waiting each day to hear whether *her* life was going to change. Rebecca hadn't realized how it affected her until she heard from Don just now. She had been angry that he had been taking so long. Thankfully she prayed before texting back, because her flesh wanted to respond with, what the heck? I offer you a room, and you don't have the decency to at least let me know?! But she hadn't done that, and she saw that as progress. Lord, help me. I'm still angry. I need You.

"Thank you," was Don's reply. She knew he probably knew she was agitated. Rebecca decided she wasn't going to play into the devil's hands this time. She was going to battle this with prayer as Rosie had been teaching her to do. She told her flesh it was just going to have to wait, while the Holy Spirit in her took control of her texting fingers.

Rebecca wrote, "Is there anything I can help you with?" Whoa, Rebecca knew that had to come from the Holy Spirit. All she wanted to do was shut down the phone and get to work. She was finding this interesting...

"I appreciate your offer,"...three dots...

Rebecca's flesh responded in her head, Oh, here we go. Don being Don—not accepting help from anyone.

Don's response continued, "I have been living on snacks in the room, which is fine. I wasn't all that hungry, and I can order in some food today. But would it be possible for you to drop off a couple bottles of water on your way to work? They are so expensive to buy them from the fridge here in the room."

Rebecca was shocked! Don was asking her to help him! Really? As much as her flesh didn't really want to, Rebecca was also pleased that he was asking for help. Maybe Don was praying on the other end, too?

Rebecca wrote back, "Yes. I can do that. Where are you staying?"

"It's right on your way to work. The Summer Inn. Room 225."

"Okay, I'll be by soon. Take it easy."

"Thanks, Bec. Much appreciated."

Don still hadn't answered her about the offer to live at the house. But at least she knew he was alive and breathing at this point. She would hear about their living arrangement all in God's timing. Rosie said we humans are always in such a hurry—we don't give God time to work in our lives. Rebecca certainly wanted this to be a God thing, if they were to live together again.

Rebecca found Room 225, and knocked on the door. Don answered, looking pale, and a bit wobbly. She had seen him where he couldn't even turn his head in bed. He told her the room really spins. She never had vertigo. Rebecca took the water in and put it in the refrigerator for him, handing Don a bottle as she did. He quickly took a seat in the chair. She could tell this had been a bad episode. Poor guy.

"I hope this will be enough. I brought you four bottles. It was all I had at home. I will stop by the store after work and get some more."

Don quickly said, "I didn't mean to take all your water!"

She could tell it bothered him. "No, that's fine. Obviously, I'm the one more able to get extra water right now. It's not a problem at all."

Rebecca was so thankful now that she hadn't been mean. Don was in no shape to be messed with. She was pleased the Holy Spirit helped her. It felt good to be nice.

Don said in a weak tone, "Thanks. I'm going to rest here for the remainder of the day."

"Sounds like a good idea."

Don added, "I'm hoping by tomorrow I will be able to get out and about again. I have more job hunting to do. I might have a good offer in San Antonio coming in."

Rebecca was surprised that a wave of disappointment ran through her when Don mentioned San Antonio. Would he be moving away? She never really considered that. Rebecca didn't realize that she liked having Don close by. She knew if an emergency should arise, with the house, or whatever, he would be there. What if he moved away?

"Oh. San Antonio," was all Rebecca could say about that. Walking toward the door, Rebecca said, "Well, I need to get to work. Ben will be waiting for me. I hope you feel better soon. I'll check back with you later." Rebecca gave him a small wave. The thought of giving him a hug didn't seem right. Don waved back, and smiled as best he could. His eyes didn't look right, and she figured he would be going to bed soon after she left.

After the door closed, Don thanked God for Rebecca. He had always loved her, and it had hurt him so much to see their marriage be destroyed—to lose the life they had together. He envisioned them being together until they were old and gray. Don wanted children so badly—he knew he had put that need in front of the needs of his wife. As they tried through the years to conceive, even going so far as to involve doctors and whatever help they could get, it wore their marriage to a frazzle. Rebecca wanted children, too, in the beginning. But he knew she could see his disappointment each time another month would go by without a baby on the way. Rebecca's love for him started to die in the process. She wanted Don to love her with or without a child. And he did…but just not enough. That had been a big mistake on his part. He hadn't been trusting God in that decision. Don knew he had a better knowledge about God now. He was beginning to understand that if God wanted them to have a child, God would have provided that for them. They had the best doctors money could buy, and still it didn't happen. God must have been saying "No" for a reason—even if they couldn't understand it. Don felt like he let his marriage fail in the midst of it all. Now he didn't have a child, or a wife. It made Don sad, and he would give anything to make that right somehow. Even if God didn't restore their marriage, maybe they could be friends and find healing in that. Don went back to sleep, thinking about all of this, and praying that God would mold him into a man like David in the Bible…one who has a big heart for God.

28

Rebecca called Don a couple of times during the day. He only answered once, and told her he was resting. She didn't want to bother him. When work ended, Rebecca went by the grocery store and picked up more water. She got some food from the Deli section to take to Don. They had some pre-cooked chickens which were hot, so she got that, and some potato salad. Rebecca noticed the disposable utensils there, too, so she got those and napkins. Then she spotted the chocolate cake! She bought one of those for herself. After she dropped dinner off for Don, maybe that would be her dinner? She liked that idea!

When Rebecca knocked on Don's door, he answered and looked much better. He had some color back in his face, and he smiled upon seeing her. He said he was sorry for not answering her calls during the day, but his phone was on silent much of the time. Sleeping seemed to help him get over the vertigo faster, and he wanted it GONE. Don invited Rebecca in, expecting water, but smelling chicken. It made his mouth water after living on crackers and cheese. A good hot meal was welcomed. He thought about ordering something during the day, but didn't seem to care all that much about eating until he smelled the chicken.

"Come on in, Bec. It's so nice of you to check on me, and to bring water." Don didn't want to ask about the chicken. What if it was for her and she just hadn't wanted to leave it in the car? Then he would have felt bad.

Rebecca immediately responded, "I brought you some chicken, too. And potato salad. I hope that's okay?"

"Okay? That sounds perfect!! I haven't had a hot meal for a few days." Don regretted saying that the minute the words were out of his mouth. He didn't want Rebecca feeling sorry for him, or thinking he was complaining. Don quickly added, "I haven't been much up for eating. But tonight, for the first time, I am."

"Well, that's good. Because there is plenty of chicken here to last you a couple of days, and salad, too. I also bought some chocolate cake for my dinner! I didn't want to leave it in the heat of the car." Rebecca laughed, as did Don. He knew her sweet tooth. Rebecca joked with him, "I don't plan on leaving that with you."

Don wasn't surprised. But then he had an idea. "Why don't you stay and have some chicken with me, Bec? I would love the company."

Rebecca hadn't even given any thought to staying, but the chicken was starting to smell good to her. She didn't answer right away. Don wasn't surprised...he knew he had thrown that to her out of the blue. He didn't want her to feel any pressure.

After a few minutes, Rebeca said, "That might be a good thing. I was just going to have the cake. And as much as that appeals to me, maybe I should eat some protein first, and not be such a big kid." Immediately, Rebecca regretted saying it. She didn't like talking about children with Don, at all. Not even in jesting. She took a deep breath, and turned away to gather her thoughts. She knew they needed to get past this big *elephant* in the room, especially if they were going to live together for a time, although she didn't even know his answer, as yet.

Turning back to Don, Rebecca sheepishly said, "Don, I'm sorry. I'm very uncomfortable mentioning kids around you in any form, even when it's a joke about myself. You probably know that. I think one day soon, we should sit down and talk, and clear the air about some things. Especially if you are wanting a room at the house for a time. I don't want to be walking on eggs shells with each other."

"Bec, I agree. Let's do that. Oh, and I have been praying and thinking about your offer, and I would like to take you up on it, if that is still okay with you. I thought maybe this job in San Antonio might have an answer for me sooner, rather than later. But they haven't even let out a peep yet. And this hotel is adding up. So if it's okay with you, I'd like to stay with you for a while."

"The offer is still open to you." Rebecca didn't know what more to say at that point, so she focused on the chicken dinner. "I brought some plastic utensils from the store, and some napkins. How about I set us up right over here, and we can both eat. Then I'll get on home. And, I'll share some of my chocolate cake with you when we're done, if you'd like." Don just smiled at her. He knew she was being extremely generous, in her own way.

As they sat and ate dinner together, the conversation seemed easy enough. Don was still weak and a bit wobbly, so Rebecca didn't want to stay too long. They talked about how they would work out the living arrangements, and when Don would be ready to move in. They agreed that Sunday was probably a good day. Rebecca would get some things out of the guest room on Saturday and ready it for him. Don told her how much he appreciated what she was doing. The subject of children didn't come up again. They both seemed to understand that needed to be saved for another time.

When dinner was done, and two-thirds of the chocolate cake had been eaten, Rebecca put the remaining food in the fridge, and packed up the cake to go home—she knew she might want it for a late-night snack. Don seemed strengthened by the food, and Rebecca was pleased to see that. Don was laughing by the time dinner was over. He also shared with her how hard job hunting was. The positions out there were few, and the competition stiff. He knew he would keep trying until he found something. Rebecca got ready to leave. Just before walking out the door, Don gave her a hug. Rebecca didn't know that she welcomed it, but she could sense she needed to relax some and trust Don. He had always been a gentleman, and he didn't mean anything more by it than gratitude. When you fill a man's stomach, it does touch his heart, she thought to herself.

Rebecca walked out to her new blue Mustang sitting in the parking lot. It always made her smile when she saw it, knowing that was *her* car. No matter if the trip was short or long, it was a fun ride. Rebecca thought back to how her car had been stolen, and how it seemed like such a terrible thing…such a hassle, and yet in the end it brought her so much pleasure. Could God really take what was bad and have it turn out good? It seemed so. When Rebecca got in, she noticed she had a new text message on her phone. It was from Rosie. She wanted her to come by tomorrow. Rosie had been missing her. How sweet, thought Rebecca. She loved having Rosie for a friend. She always looked forward to their visits.

Rebecca stopped for gas on the drive home, and then the rest of the way she thought about the dinner with Don. Don seemed calm, and when she listened to him, she could tell he changed. She wondered if God was changing how they communicated with one another. Rebecca also noticed that keeping her heart open to God, she was more open to other people, including Don. She didn't feel so defensive and ready to strike at a moment's notice. Rebecca knew she had always been so protective of her privacy. She hadn't wanted people to see inside of her. What if they didn't like what they saw? But the Bible kept telling her how much she was loved. And how much God wanted to help her in so many ways. Some of that was starting to sink in, even if just slightly. Rebecca was still figuring out how all that worked. Reading her Bible was a help, although she was taking it slowly—sometimes just reading a line or two, and then asking God to help her understand it.

After getting ready for bed, Rebecca wanted to go back to the place in the Bible she had just been reading the day before. With a glass of iced tea, and her piece of chocolate cake at her bedside, she found it in Romans 7. Even though the words seemed twisted around, they made such sense to her. Rebecca could relate to them. Rebecca wanted to know who had written Romans. She googled it and it said Paul was the author—the man who was blinded on the road by Jesus' light. Paul had been called Saul. She was getting to know the names of people a bit more, and that felt good. Paul was talking in Romans 7 about knowing he was rotten as far as his old sinful nature, and he wasn't able to make himself do what was right. When he tries to not do wrong, he does it anyway. And when he wants to do what is right, he does what is wrong. To Rebecca, it sounded like her everyday battle. Paul talked about having a war with his mind. Rebecca wondered how it was possible that this man, who she never met, and who lived thousands of years ago, experienced the same exact struggles that she did? Paul called himself a miserable person. She felt that way much of the time, too. But then Paul asked who would save him from that life? And he had written, "Thank God! The answer is in Jesus Christ our Lord." Rebecca thought, oh good! At least there is an answer!

Rebecca felt guilty so much of the time—for the things she thought, even if she didn't do them. But as she read on, she liked how Romans 8 talked about there being no condemnation now for those who belong to Jesus. She didn't want to live feeling guilty and condemned anymore. She said yes to Jesus, and was trying to learn a new way. Rosie had been telling her how it really has so much to do with the Holy Spirit. That the Holy Spirit lives inside of us, and He will be in control more and more when we give Him the permission…even over our thoughts. Rebecca wanted that. Maybe she could talk to Rosie more about that tomorrow? Her brain was getting tired, and the chocolate cake was calling to her.

As Rebecca ate the last of her cake, her heart was grateful, even though there were many questions, and many things she still struggled with. Then she thought about Paul, and she didn't feel so alone. Rebecca thought about how Paul wrote down all his secrets. He was totally exposed to the world. Paul was a help to her. He struggled, too. It seemed that she would make some progress, and then slip back again. But there it was again…the condemnation. Rebecca didn't want to live in that horrible feeling anymore. Rosie said that conviction was different than condemnation. Those two words weren't clear in her mind yet. She hoped one day she would get them straight. Rosie said conviction is from God, and condemnation is from the Devil. It was hard to not mix the two up when the enemy was lying to her about who she was.

As Rebecca drifted off to sleep, she thought back to texting with Don that morning. It felt like progress. She hadn't been mean to Don. She hadn't been short with him, even though she wanted to be. She stopped long enough to say the right thing, and look how it turned out—they had a nice dinner together, and discussed when he would be moving in. Instead of arguing that morning, and blowing the whole thing out of the water...what would that have accomplished? She had no idea why Don wasn't getting back to her. The battle in her mind told her all kinds of lies. But the truth was, he had been praying, and then he hadn't been feeling well. Don wasn't keeping her waiting to be mean, he was doing the best he could do at the time. Rebecca hoped to be more patient with people.

Rebecca remembered back to what a friend once told her, "Whenever I have a slow driver in front of me, and I get frustrated with them, I tell myself that maybe they have a cake on the seat, and they are driving slowly because of it." This came from a personal story. It had been her friend's third birthday and her mom had a cake on the backseat of the car. It was decorated with a doll in the middle. Her mom stopped too quickly and the cake slipped off the seat onto the floor. They had to repair it when she got home. Her friend would say, "It's a silly story. But it helps me be a more patient driver."

Rebecca knew Rosie said even patience comes from the Holy Spirit. Always with the Holy Spirit...Rebecca was tired. Enough for tonight!

Lord, help me sleep. Thank You, Jesus. Amen.

29

Saturday felt good. Rebecca could relax in her pj's the entire morning, with nowhere she had to be until she wanted to. She did need to get the guestroom ready...which reminded her, this may be one of the last mornings in a while that she would be home alone. How would it be to hear Don moseying about in the morning again? Rebecca sure hoped she would be able to handle it okay. So far, so good, with the way they were communicating. Time would tell.

The morning turned out to be a bit overcast, which was never the best as far as Rebecca was concerned. For her, the more sunshine the better. But it did afford for a longer time being cozy under a blanket, which she liked. As Rebecca curled up on the couch, she decided to just sit for a bit, and pray. She was getting in the habit of picking up her Bible and reading when she sat down, and it was surprising her how easy it was becoming. She remembered back to the day when God literally had to shine His "light" onto the silver pages so she would notice it. God had become a bit subtler in His ways lately. Rebecca was hoping that was because she was getting to know God better, and He didn't need to work so hard at getting her attention.

While sitting in the stillness, and praying...Rebecca pictured her Father in Heaven, sitting on His Throne. She couldn't see His face, but He seemed very large. She saw Jesus, again not His face, sitting at the Father's right hand. That's the way the Bible described them. She wondered about the Holy Spirit...where was He? But she figured she couldn't picture Him in Heaven since He lived inside each believer. Remembering Jesus' history in the New Testament, and how He was on this earth for 33 years, she thought about the hard job Jesus had to do while He was here—so many abandoned Jesus, and Judas betrayed Him with a kiss—how that must have hurt. Jesus' job seemed hard. But as she thought about the Holy Spirit's job, it seemed even harder to her. The Holy Spirit lives inside of each sinful human being that has said yes to Jesus. Each day, the Holy Spirit is with us, going through all the ups and downs and struggles we go through. He wants to be heard by us, but we shut Him out so much of the time. How patient the Holy Spirit must be, to not abandon us even though we are not very considerate of Him. To Rebecca, it seemed the Holy Spirit's relief would come when we die and arrive in Heaven. But that still left Him here on earth inside of millions of believers. Rebecca thought of the Father, the Son, and the Holy Spirit—she didn't know if all her thoughts were correct. But it was interesting to take some time thinking about God.

As Rebecca rested on the couch, she thought more about *rest*. She grabbed her Bible now to see if she could find the verse that talks about rest. Sometimes Rebecca could see something she read, pictured on the left side of the page, or at the top, or the bottom, whichever it was. But she had a hard time locating that verse again if she hadn't marked it. Rebecca learned that if she could remember just a few words of the verse, she could do a search online, and usually locate it. She wondered how it must have been before all these advances in technology? She remembered her grandma having a Bible. It had tabs sticking out of the side of it. It fascinated her when she was younger. Rebecca had never seen a book like that. Now she figured they must have been labels with John, Acts, Romans, etc... Rebecca suddenly wished that she had her grandma's old Bible. It would be a treasure to her.

When Rebecca googled, "enter into rest," sure enough, Hebrews 4:11 came up. She was so thankful to have this help. It talked about God resting from all His work on the seventh day. Thinking about the Holy Spirit again, maybe when He gets to rest from all His work on the *final day*...or maybe she was just having crazy thoughts as she sat by herself this morning?

It was time to check out the guestroom. Rebecca climbed the stairs, turning left instead of right. Her room was down the hall on the right, and she was glad the guest room was down the opposite way. There was an office in between, another bedroom, and a bathroom that Don would use. She was thinking she would let him have the office as a sitting room, too, so he could be on the computer job hunting, and maybe watch his own TV in there. Sitting in the living room together at night might not be good for the two of them. A little space would probably be welcomed.

The guest room was a nice size with a queen bed. She pulled the sheets off to wash them, and made sure the closet was cleaned out. She had been storing some things in there, but it wasn't a whole lot. She checked the hanger supply, and put a wastebasket in the room. Then Rebecca looked to see that there were towels in the bathroom. It has been a while since she'd had a guest. Everything appeared to be set...just needing to put the sheets back on when they were done.

It seemed time to check in with Rosie and see what she was up to. Rebecca knew she was expected. Rosie asked if she'd come by, but they hadn't set a time. It was about one before Rebecca showed up at Rosie's, and Rosie was working in her garden out back. Rebecca went through the side gate when Rosie didn't answer the front door. Rebecca had done that before. She was always careful not to startle Rosie, calling out to her as she walked around the side of the house.

"Rosie...are you back here?"

Rosie looked up and smiled from her garden kneeler as Rebecca approached. Rosie called out, "Hi neighbor! I'm just about done for the day. Your timing is good! This sun is getting too hot for me since that morning fog burned off. I used as much of its cover as I could to get some weeding done."

Rebecca noticed how the hot summer sun faded some of the beauty of the spring flowers, but it still looked like a showcase yard. She responded with, "Hi there! Good to see you, Rosie! Can I give you a hand up?"

"That would be lovely! I think my back and knees have had it, even with the bit of cushioning on this bench. I'm sure glad they put handles on here for the times I am alone. It helps." Rosie smiled, knowing she was showing her age, but still feeling young inside.

After helping Rosie up, the two ladies walked toward the canopy area, and took a seat. Rosie already put out a pitcher of cool water that she had been using, and a couple of glasses...obviously waiting for Rebecca's visit.

Rosie said, "Oh, I have some cookies in the house that I made yesterday. Would you like some?"

"Sure, you know me. Always a sweet tooth. I'll go in and get us some." Rebecca popped up and headed into the house before Rosie had a chance. She didn't want Rosie waiting on her.

Behind her she heard Rosie say, "Sitting down feels so good!"

When Rebecca returned, she found Rosie gazing off into the yard, lost in thought. It seemed to Rebecca that she shouldn't disturb her. Rebecca sat down quietly and waited to see what Rosie might be thinking. It wasn't too long and Rosie started to speak softly... "Rebecca. I have lived in this house many, many years now. I think it's 32 years. I have seen many neighbors come and go, and I want you to know how thankful I am to have you across the street. I remember the day you and Don moved in. You were newlyweds then, if I remember right?"

"Yes. We were. Not married long at all." Rebecca hadn't thought about that for a while.

Rosie continued, slowly. She seemed to be contemplating something. "I know we didn't talk much before. But I have so enjoyed getting to know you more these last months. You bring me great joy. Do you know that?"

Rebecca was taken by surprise. She didn't know quite what to say. Rosie was always very sweet, but she didn't talk about her feelings a lot. Rebecca wondered why today? Rosie still seemed allusive in a way, so Rebecca just said, "Thank you. I like getting to know you, too."

Rosie continued... "I really coveted your company today, Rebecca. May I tell you why?"

"Sure. What is it Rosie?" Rebecca had no idea where this was going, but she was intrigued.

"You and I have talked about many things, and you have told me a lot about yourself through these last months. And I have told you things about my life, too. But there is something I have never discussed with you. I don't share it with many people. But God has put it on my heart to talk with you about a season in my life that was very hard for me. I think God wants you to know that He loves you deeply, and that we were brought together as friends for a good reason."

Rebecca was getting more and more curious as to the direction this conversation was going. She remained quiet, hoping that Rosie would soon let her know.

"Back in 1976, when I was a much younger woman in my twenties, I lived in an apartment not too far from here. I had a roommate, and her name was Hannah. Hannah and I had a lot of fun together. She was about five years younger than me. We were two single women, although Hannah was dating a man, and they were very serious. I dreaded the day she would come home and tell me they were engaged. I didn't want our time together as roommates to end. But, that day did come, and Hannah was thrilled. I had no choice but to be happy for her, and I was. Her fiancé, Teddy, was a fine man. They had a beautiful wedding, and I was one of her bridesmaids. They were so happy, and it wasn't long before she announced she was pregnant. It wasn't a planned baby. But they were so much in love, they were happy to have this new little one join them in their lives together."

After a few sips of water, Rosie continued, "When Hannah was eight months pregnant, she went into an early labor. The doctors thought they could stop the contractions, but they weren't able to. Hannah delivered a sweet baby boy named Noah. Back in those days, we didn't have cell phones, so I waited at home until Teddy called to tell me the good news. When Teddy called, he was crying. I didn't know at first if they were tears of joy, or of sorrow. But I was soon to find out. Teddy told me that Noah was a perfect little baby with a head full of dark curls…but sadly, Hannah didn't survive his birth. She had complications during delivery. The doctors tried their best to stop the bleeding, but they weren't successful. Teddy gained a son on that day, but Noah lost his mom. I wept so many tears after hanging up the phone. I cried throughout the night, and for a long time after. Hannah and I were like sisters, and I planned on being there to be an aunt to her child."

Rebecca didn't want to move. Her heart went out to Rosie as she listened to this godly woman tell her story.

"Today is Noah's 40st birthday, and also the day my best friend went Home to Heaven. There isn't a year that goes by that I don't stop on this day and think of Hannah. Oh, how I wish you could have known her. But I also want to say, as I have gotten to know you these last few months, I appreciate what God has done. Even all these years later, He brought you into my life as my friend. God is ever faithful. I knew it was time to tell you about Hannah. And to let you know, I feel like a part of my heart that was lost with Hannah, has been found because I get to share days with you right now. What a great blessing you are. I am grateful for this season we have together."

Rebecca remained quiet…she didn't want to rush Rosie in her thoughts, and she also wanted to have some time to absorb what Rosie was saying. Rebecca knew that Rosie had faced some hardships in her life, but she didn't realize that they both had a best friend in Heaven. All the times that she told Rosie about Bonnie, she knew now that Rosie really understood her pain and missing. Rebecca also sensed a joy in Rosie—joy at having had Hannah as her friend, and in remembering her each year on this day—and also, in their being friends now. That pleased and surprised Rebecca. Rebecca hadn't really thought about Rosie being blessed by her—Rebecca always thought she was the blessed one, having Rosie to talk to. Rosie was always so helpful. It made Rebecca feel good to know that in some ways, she was also a help to Rosie. When Rebecca finally spoke, her heart was full of love for this woman who she once barely knew, but had now become so close to.

"Rosie. Thank you for telling me about Hannah. I know that you miss your friend in many of the same ways that I miss mine. God did bring us together for a reason, didn't He? I'm just sorry that I waited so long to be open to you. I was so closed down for so many of the years that I lived across the street from you…even while I was still in my marriage. You were so gracious to welcome me when I was ready. You never rushed me. You are a dear, sweet woman, and I am grateful for you. Can I ask you, does Noah live nearby? Were you able to be with him as he grew up?"

Rosie answered now with a bit more sadness in her voice, "No, I wasn't. Teddy decided soon after his birth to move to the east coast so his parents could help with Noah. He turned into a fine young man. He has visited me through the years, and I see Hannah's smile in him." Rosie wiped away a tear that slipped down her cheek, and she turned to smile at Rebecca saying, "In all things, God provides."

The two women sat for a while, watching the birds, and chatting about this and that. Rebecca let Rosie know of Don's plans. Then Rebecca said she needed to get back home. She knew she still had sheets to put on the bed before Don arrived tomorrow. Before she left, she gave Rosie a long hug, and told her she loved her. She'd never done that before. Rosie returned the sentiment. It was an afternoon that neither one of them would forget.

As Rebecca crossed the street toward home, she thought to herself, You never know what has happened in someone's life until you spend time with them. Rebecca was so glad she and Rosie had this time. Rebecca didn't know how long she would be able to stay in her home, depending on finances with Don's situation. Rebecca wanted to cherish every moment with Rosie, until they all moved on to a new season in life. Rebecca was seeing, God was good.

30

Walking out of church on Sunday morning, Rebecca felt good. Better than she had in a long time. She didn't know if it was what the pastor talked about, the music that inspired her, maybe the conversation she had with Rosie...or all of the above? It felt good to feel good. Rebecca wanted more of that. Life seemed filled with such dread a few months back. How was it possible that it could change that quickly, after so long? She wanted to give God the credit. But Rebecca wasn't sure what to think—she just knew she wanted more of whatever it was that was helping her.

Don hadn't gone to church. He texted her earlier that morning to let her know that he was still a bit dizzy, and he was putting all his energy into packing up his things and checking out of the hotel at eleven, as required. He said he would get the sermon on his computer, since it was online. Rebecca had done that a few times, too. It sure was convenient, and it was tempting sometimes to not actually go to church. But Rebecca tried her best to be there on Sunday.

As Rebecca walked to her car, thoughts about the sermon kept coming to her. The pastor talked about Paul again. She was seeing that Paul was everywhere in the Bible. And he seemed to always be struggling. In this story, Paul was up on some sort of charges in a courtroom setting. It was somewhere in Acts, Rebecca couldn't remember. She really needed to start taking a few notes, it would help her when she got home to find these things again. A guy named Festus shouted at Paul. She could remember the name Festus because of watching reruns of an old western on TV. There was a character in that show with the same name. Rebecca always thought of it as a rather funny name...maybe because he was kind of a funny character. This character in the story in the Bible wasn't funny. He seemed mean, and when he shouted at Paul, he said that Paul was insane and that all Paul's studying had made him crazy. Paul told him that he wasn't insane, that he was speaking the sober truth. Then Paul said something to the king, and the king fired back at Paul, too—something about Paul trying to make him a Christian so quickly. Rebecca could feel the king's "pain." Before she became a Christian, when others who were Christians would talk to her, she felt pressured. Like the king did, they seemed to expect her to change on the spot. Not all of them, but a couple who talked with her. Rebecca started to think back then on Nelson, and even Jennifer. They had never been like that. In fact, she wasn't even sure what they believed until Justin died. They always loved her right where she was. And if the subject of God came up, or they prayed before a meal, they never made her feel uncomfortable about it.

The pastor ended the sermon with Paul saying he was praying for the king and everyone else who was there. She could tell that Paul wanted them all to know God like he did, and he wasn't worried about what it cost him. Rebecca wanted that kind of faith, and the kind of faith that Nelson and Jennifer had. A bold faith, but not a brash one. A caring faith, full of love. Rebecca saw that in Rosie, too. Yes…it was a good morning.

Rebecca stopped at the store on the way home. She wanted to make sure she had a few things in the house that she knew Don liked. He always wanted his bananas in the morning, and she got his favorite cereal. She hoped he still ate like that. Rebecca never liked cereal, even as a kid, so she didn't keep any in the house. Rebecca got some regular coffee, too, since she mostly drank decaf. On her way through the checkout, she spotted a magazine about sports. It had Don's favorite team featured on the cover. She wondered, did God put that in my sight so I would pick it up for Don? Rebecca wasn't sure, but she didn't want to resist the Holy Spirit if He was a part of this, so Rebecca bought the magazine with the rest of her groceries. She saw a text come through on her phone while she was in line. Rebecca looked at it quickly. It was Don. He wanted to know when it would be a good time for him to get there. When she got back to her car, she sent Don a text.

"I'm just leaving the grocery store. I should be home soon. So anytime."

Don texted back, "Sounds good. Thanks much!"

Rebecca drove home with almost an excited feeling inside. She was a little taken back by it. It was like she was having a friend stay over, and it seemed like it was going to be fun. Then Rebecca wondered if it would be? She hoped it wasn't going to be more of the same from the past—two people just co-existing in the same house, barely speaking to each other, and when they did, their words had an edge to them. So far, when she had been with Don, they were kinder to each other than in the past. She hoped it wasn't because they were both on their good behavior in public. She knew if that were true, it wouldn't last long. Rebecca said a quick prayer, and headed home, hoping for the best.

After putting the groceries away, and setting the sports magazine on the coffee table next to her Bible, Rebecca sat down for a moment, expecting Don at any minute. She thought about the man she married many years ago. Don had changed. But then, so had she. Of course, there was some physical aging. But what about who they were on the inside? When they first met, and went on their first date, it wasn't love at first sight for them. They had a nice time. But they weren't sure "this is it," so to speak. Don waited about two weeks to ask her out again, and she accepted. This time they had gone to downtown Pleasanton. They started early enough that the sun was still up. They strolled up and down the sidewalk looking in the windows, and talking about where they might want to eat. Don took her down a side street she had never been on before, and he "spoiled her appetite" before dinner by buying her an ice cream at the drive through dairy. She laughed and told him how she loved dessert before her meal. Don said it wasn't normally his style, but he was open to change. They laughed a lot that night as they enjoyed dinner later at an Italian place. They both had a glass of wine with their meal, but she noticed that Don stopped at one. Rebecca appreciated that about him, especially since he would be driving her home. After that, their dates were more frequent. She introduced him to her parents about six months into their relationship, and that had gone well. They weren't youngsters, so by the time a year had gone by, they were talking marriage. They had fallen in love. Preferring a small wedding, just a few friends gathered with them at a local winery in Livermore. Their honeymoon consisted of a long weekend away in Carmel, and all seemed to be well for the first few years.

Rebecca's thoughts were interrupted by a knock on the door. Opening the door, Don stood there with a couple of suitcases, his laptop bag, and a bouquet of flowers in his hands. It caught her off guard. If not for the suitcases, it almost felt like he was there to pick her up for a date. Don reached out and handed her the flowers. Rebecca took them, almost not wanting to meet his eyes. But she did and said, "Hi. How are you? Come on in."

Don replied, "I'm doing much better, thanks." After setting his laptop bag on the chair inside the door, Don went back out to get his suitcases. Once everything was inside, he wasn't sure what to do next...

Rebecca wasn't so sure either. "Thanks for the flowers," seemed appropriate.

"You're welcome. I didn't want to come empty handed." Don could tell their conversation was strained. He didn't want to sound too forward, so he waited to see what Rebecca would do. He knew where the guestroom was. But it didn't seem right to go up the stairs without an invitation.

"Come on into the kitchen. I'll put these in some water. Speaking of which, would you like some water? Did you have enough to hold you over at the hotel?" Her voice trailed off as she turned to go through the hallway into the kitchen.

"Yes. I did thanks. But I could go for some now. Want me to get it?" Don didn't want Rebecca to think she needed to wait on him. She was doing him such a big favor by letting him be there.

"Sure. Help yourself."

Don got some water and sat down at the table. He was still dizzy, but he didn't want to let on. He knew he was almost through the vertigo, and he didn't want to seem like a burden on his first day there. Don watched as Rebecca made her way around the kitchen. It certainly took him back to their days together. She found the familiar vase that came with flowers he sent her years ago. While filling it with water, and cutting the ends off the stems, they chatted lightly. When the flowers were done, Rebecca sat down at the table.

"Don, how do you think this should look? I have a few ideas, but I want to make it comfortable for you. I have set you up in the guest room, and I thought you could use the office as you look for jobs. With the TV in there, it could also be your room in the evenings instead of us trying to figure out what to watch together downstairs. Not that we can't do that sometimes. I may be jumping ahead…crossing too many bridges, but…" Rebecca thought she sounded too bossy.

"That all sounds fine. I have to tell you, after staying in the hotel for just a week, being in a home again is going to be most welcome. However we work this, I'm fine. I know you have to work, and I'm going to be in and out."

Rebecca remembered that she had an extra key. The one that Don gave her when he left. She got up to get it out of the drawer. "Here," was all she said as she handed it to him. He knew it was his key, but neither one of them said anything about it.

Don broke the tension by asking, "Would it be okay if I took my bags upstairs and got settled in a bit?"

"Of course. Do you need any help?"

Don responded with, "I got it. You go ahead and do your thing. Don't worry about me."

Rebecca watched him as he went for his bags. She had a feeling that once they got past their awkwardness, this was going to be okay. Maybe they were just finished with wanting to argue about everything. And maybe God had done enough work in both of them to be of help. This would certainly be a test of that…married or not, living with someone can be challenging.

While Don was upstairs, Rebecca could hear him rustling about, hanging things in the closet, and even whistling a little. As he kept busy doing all that, Rebecca decided to give Kay a call. She wanted to update her on what was going on, and also see how Lindsey was doing. Rebecca settled in on the back porch and made the call.

"Hi Rebecca. How are you?" Kay sounded like she was forcing her cheerfulness. Rebecca knew Kay well enough to know when her voice was tired.

"I'm fine. How are you today, Kay? You sound tired. How are things going?" Rebecca could hear the emotion in Kay's voice when she spoke again.

"Things are tough here. We took Lindsey over to the ER today. She was going through a bad spell and we didn't want to wait for the clinic to open tomorrow. They admitted her for some testing. It could be an infection, and with her immunities being so low, we have to be very careful. Roger is with her now. I just ran home for a few things that she needed."

"I'm so sorry to hear that. Is there anything I can do for you? How is Lindsey feeling?" Rebecca's heart sank to hear the sadness in Kay's voice, although she knew this happened a few times before with Lindsey. It was part of the process with chemo.

"Please pray. Lindsey needs to get through this without it taking her down too far. She is so weak."

Rebecca said, "Of course. Would you like me to take you back to the hospital? I can drive you over there?"

Kay thought for a moment, and then she said, "You know what? If you could meet me at the hospital and give Roger a ride home while I stay with Lindsey, that will give me a car at the hospital."

"Sure. Should I leave right now?" Rebecca was glad she called. She didn't know Lindsey hadn't been feeling well.

"Yes. I'm leaving in just a few minutes." Kay sounded stressed and in a hurry to get back there.

"Okay. I'll see you soon."

"Okay, thanks Rebecca. Bye."

It felt strange, but Rebecca knew she needed to let Don know she was leaving. It had been years since she checked in with anyone. Making her way up the stairs, Rebecca knocked lightly on Don's door. "Come in," Don said, while hanging the last of his clothes in the closet.

"Thanks for the hangers in here. I didn't bring any of my own." Don seemed at ease.

Rebecca said, "No problem. And, uh…hey, I just gave Kay a call and it turns out Lindsey is sick with an infection and they admitted her to the hospital. I'm going to meet Kay at the hospital so I can bring Roger back home. That way Kay will have a car there."

Don immediately responded, "Do you want me to go with you? Can I be of help?"

"No. It's fine. You go ahead and get finished here. I'll probably pick up something to eat on the way home. Would you like something? Should I get us a pizza?"

Don looked at Rebecca, and nodded. "That sounds great. Thanks."

"Okay. See you later."

"Sure," Don said to Rebecca's back, as she turned to leave. He could tell she was in a big hurry. His heart went out to Roger and Kay. Please, Lord, help them all, Don prayed silently. He didn't know if it helped, but praying was something he could do in the moment.

After settling in, Don went back downstairs to the living room, and sat on the couch. When he looked at the coffee table and saw both the Bible and the Sports magazine, he couldn't help but smile. His wife…or he should say, his ex-wife, was not the same person as when he moved out in the divorce. Never would he have imagined seeing a Bible sitting there. And seeing a magazine that he knew Rebecca bought for him, really touched his heart. She didn't like sports, and it was a new issue.

Don didn't know why God orchestrated his life in such a way that he would be living here with Rebecca again. If he had been asked six months ago if this was even possible, Don would have answered without a doubt, NO! But here he was. Don wanted to watch what God was doing, and do his best to listen, and follow. So far, the results of that were good. God had a path for his life, and he wanted to be on it. From what Don learned in the Bible, divorce was not God's path. But God was showing Don that even with the mistakes he and Rebecca made, restoration in a relationship was possible. They were becoming friends…that was healing enough in itself. Don couldn't help but close his eyes and pray…

Father in Heaven. You see me sitting here right now. You knew this would happen when we had no idea this was even possible. You have helped us come through something so painful, and I want to trust You for the rest of my life. I don't know what it will look like. I don't know if You have a job for me in San Antonio? I don't know how long I will need this guest room. But thank You for taking care of me during this time. Bless Rebecca, and help her to know that I want to be a friend to her. Thank You Jesus. Amen.

Don dozed off, and it felt good. He could relax is this moment, and trust God for the ones to come.

31

Don woke up to a knock at the door. Was it Rebecca with her hands full of pizza? Don sort of jumped up, and that was a mistake. The dizziness returned and almost sent him back to the couch. Let's try that again, he thought to himself...more slowly this time.

When Don opened the door, smiling at Rebecca, he came face to face with a man he didn't know. They both looked a bit shocked. Don's first thought was, this is who the sports magazine is for. Don's heart sank a bit.

"Uh, Hi. I'm Nelson. A friend of Rebecca's."

"I'm Don. Her ex-husband. Bec's not home right now." Don felt good being able to use a familiar name with her. He felt like he was staking his territory even before he knew if he needed to. Don heard about Nelson some, but Rebecca had been pretty quiet about it all. Don certainly didn't expect Nelson to be dropping by today.

"Oh. Nice to meet you, Don. Becca has mentioned you might be needing a place to stay."

"Becca?" thought Don. "Really? He calls her Becca?" Then Don said out loud, "Yes. I'm living here right now." Don made it sound like it had been a long time already, when it had only been a few hours. He felt like they were dueling it out, and they didn't even know if they needed to.

Both men stood in silence for a moment looking at each other, not knowing what to do until Nelson spoke again. "That's great."

Great? thought Don. He thinks it's great that I am living here? Maybe this isn't what I think it is at all. Maybe that's why Bec hasn't said more about Nelson? Wouldn't she have at least mentioned if they were dating? Don's demeanor quickly changed, and he said, "Would you like to come in?"

"Oh, I don't know. I just stopped by to say Hi, and since Becca's not here, I don't want to bother you." Nelson wasn't sure how welcomed he would be by Rebecca's ex. Nelson didn't know what Rebecca told Don about their friendship.

"No bother. Come on in. Bec shouldn't be too long, and I wouldn't mind a little company,"

"Okay then."

The two men walked into the living room, and Don offered Nelson something to drink. He declined, so they sat down to talk. Nelson noticed the magazine, and that started their conversation about baseball, and how the season was going, and how many games they had been to, etc… You would have thought they were old friends by the time Rebecca returned.

Rebecca was quite surprised that there were not one, but two men, occupying her house while she was gone. At first, she was none too pleased. It felt like her home had been invaded, and she was already regretting this whole situation with Don. Coming in with pizza, Rebecca glanced at the two men and then headed to the kitchen barely saying a word. She knew she already had an attitude, and she was going to have to quickly adjust it quickly, or damage control would be needed. Rebecca could tell whatever they were talking about had come to an abrupt halt. There was only silence from the living room, and the noise of her rustling around in the kitchen. Rebecca knew she was taking longer than was needed to set a pizza down. But time was what she needed before she spoke.

After what seemed like too long, Rebecca walked back into the living room and tried to be cordial. "Hi. What's happening here?" Her voice had more of an edge to it than she wanted it to.

They both spoke at once, and then Nelson backed off, letting Don go ahead… "I heard a knock at the door and thought it was you. Turns out it was your friend, Nelson, here. We've been getting to know one another. Hope you don't mind."

"Mind? Why should I mind?" But she did. She didn't really know if she liked the idea of the two of them getting friendly. Nelson was her friend. Don had plenty of friends. He needed to keep his "hands" off Nelson. She didn't have enough friends to go around.

Nelson then spoke up. "Sorry to barge in, Becca. Don was kind enough to invite me in when I got here. I thought maybe you would be free for a burger or something. But it looks like you already have plans. I should head out."

Rebecca was starting to get a hold of herself, and she said, "I'll be right back." She went into the kitchen to take a few deep breaths. She thought about what Rosie would do, so she offered up a quick prayer for some patience, and to be loving. When she went back into the living room, Don and Nelson were still being quiet. She figured they were both waiting to see how to proceed.

Rebecca started in, "Look, I've got plenty of pizza for all of us. Want to stay and have some Nelson? Don and I can't possibly eat it all." Rebecca was trying to sound as cheerful as possible.

"Well, I don't know." Nelson could tell she wasn't all that pleased. "I could just head out and get something on the way home."

"No need. Eat with us." Rebecca knew it didn't sound welcoming, but it was the best she could do.

Don spoke up, "It's fine with me. Stay and eat, Nelson."

Nelson knew it would probably cause more harm than good to leave. He could tell Rebecca was working on being the person she felt God was calling her to be, and he wanted to encourage her in that way.

"Okay then, I'll stay. Thanks, Becca."

The three of them sat around the kitchen table, sharing the pizza and in the end, Rebecca couldn't have asked for a nicer afternoon. They talked about their lives, and she filled them in on how Lindsey was doing. It even seemed that with Nelson there, it eased the whole situation with Don and her being comfortable in the same house again. Don was very open with Nelson about his job hunting, and Nelson even agreed to be on the lookout for him. By the time the day ended, they were practically planning the next time they would share a pizza. No one was more surprised than Rebecca.

On that first night back in the house together, Rebecca laid in her bed wondering what was happening in her life? Things were changing, and for the better…although her heart hurt for Kay and Roger. The visit to the hospital to drop off Kay and get Roger touched her heart deeply. She had seen Lindsey for a while in her room as she was sleeping. Roger was sitting by her bedside when she and Kay arrived. Roger's head was in his hands, and he seemed to be praying. He looked up when they came in, and Rebecca could tell he had been crying. How difficult it must be for a father to watch his child hurting, and not be able to help. The doctor came in right after their arrival with the report, and it turned out that Lindsey did have an infection, and she needed to be on IV antibiotics for a time. The doctor was encouraging, saying that most likely it would do the trick. Rebecca watched as Kay and Roger listened to the doctor. She never witnessed parents dealing with this situation before, and she didn't know how they did it. Their child's life was hanging in the balance, and they had to stay strong in the midst of it all. Rebecca didn't think she would be able to…and she was glad in that moment that she and Don never had children. She heard that having a child was like having a piece of your heart walking around outside of your body. She had no idea what that would even feel like, and watching this scene, she didn't want to know.

In the hospital room, Rebecca stayed quiet, not wanting to interfere with what was happening. Her eyes fell on Lindsey, while Roger and Kay talked with the doctor. Lindsey looked as pale as the white pillowcase she was lying on. She didn't have her hat on. The full effect of the cancer was there—she had gotten so thin. This was not the same girl Rebecca watched playing volleyball. Rebecca wondered how this doctor viewed her? Did he see her as only a sick person? Did he know she was a vibrant young woman before all this? Then Rebecca remembered a story her friend Sue told her about one of her clients at the salon. The client had a young boy with cancer. He was home with his family one Christmas, lying on the couch, bald. The tree was up, and the stockings were hung, so to speak. One of the nurses from the clinic stopped in to drop something off to the family, and when she walked into the home the mom heard the nurse say, "This is so sad." The mom realized in that moment that the nurse did not picture them as a family who lived a normal life outside of the clinic. She only knew the boy as a patient in the clinic, not the child who felt the full effects of chemo days and weeks after it had been administered. The mom wasn't mad. But it was eye opening to her. This was her child. And yes, it was sad because they were a real family. But the mom also understood that if the nurse felt the full weight of it all, she probably would not have been able to do her job every day in the clinic, and the mom was grateful for the job that the nurse did.

Rebecca's attention had been suddenly brought back by Roger's touch on her arm. "Are you ready to go? I really appreciate you giving me a ride home so Kay can have the car here."

Rebecca responded, "Oh sure Roger, no problem. I'm happy to help." Using the word happy in that room hadn't seemed appropriate, and Rebecca wanted to be sure she didn't say anything that would hurt Roger even more. Roger didn't seem affected by her words as he simply said, "Thank you."

What a day it had been. From having Don move in, to seeing Lindsey at the hospital, and then finishing off the day eating pizza with Don and Nelson. Yes, life was taking some strange turns, but Rebecca didn't want to go back. She wanted to move forward on this path, and see what was around the next bend.

Rebecca wanted to read a bit of her Bible before falling asleep. But she had forgotten it downstairs and she didn't want to go and get it. She was thankful that she uploaded a Bible app on her iPad that usually sat by her bed. Rebecca grabbed it and clicked it open. The last thing she had been reading was in John 9 about boy who had been born blind. It said, *As Jesus was walking along, he saw a man who had been blind from birth. "Rabbi," his disciples asked him, "why was this man born blind? Was it because of his own sins or his parents' sins?"*

"It was not because of his sins or his parents' sins," Jesus answered.
"This happened so the power of God could be seen in him."

Rebecca couldn't help but think of Lindsey's illness as she read this again. Had Lindsey sinned? Had Roger or Kay sinned? It seemed that wasn't the reason for her being sick from what the Bible said. That comforted Rebecca, and it also reminded her to pray for Lindsey. Please, Father, help Lindsey to get through this infection. Help the antibiotics to do their job. Please help Roger and Kay to stay strong through this. Thank You Jesus. Amen.

Rebecca put her iPad on her nightstand and turned to shut off the light. Yes, it had been quite the day. And it was comforting to finish it knowing that what was happening to Lindsey wasn't anyone's fault. Rebecca hoped to see Lindsey healed like the man that had been born blind. Rebecca wanted to see that kind of power from God up close and personal…if those kinds of things still happened.

32

It had been a few weeks since Don moved in with Rebecca when the call came from San Antonio. It was now early September and the weather was still warm in the Bay Area. They were sitting out back having a salad.

"Bec, I heard from the job in San Antonio today. After months of searching for a job, I'm excited that someone has called me back to talk further."

"Oh really? Wow! I kind of thought that job was past being a possibility." Rebecca wasn't sure what she felt about this news. Things had been going well for the two of them in the house. They had their daily routines, and it seemed comfortable enough. Once in a while, the kitchen was a bit crowded with the two of them trying to go to the same place at the same time, but that was small potatoes. Don settled into the guestroom, and he spent most evenings in the office, on the computer or watching his shows. Rebecca was usually downstairs, or across the street visiting with Rosie. Don and Rebecca spent some time together, but tried to give each other a lot of space. Rosie told Rebecca she was happy to see that she and Don were getting along so well. Rosie said she had seen most couples not even able to talk after a divorce. Rebecca certainly understood that. Rebecca hadn't wanted to talk with Don in the past either.

Don continued to inform Rebecca about the job…"Me, too. I thought maybe they filled the position. But I guess these things always take more time than we want them to. I'm excited at seeing what they have to offer if this interview goes well. It's in a couple days."

"When would the job be starting if they hire you?" Rebecca wondered, almost hoping it wouldn't be too soon.

"I don't really know. The job posting just says they are interviewing until the job is filled. It seems they have been looking for someone for quite some time. It's a little different position than I am used to. It is kitchen cabinetry, and the sales person has to learn a lot about all of that. But they are willing to train. I know sales, but I will have some things to learn, which is fine with me." Don was willing to do almost anything at this point. He didn't want to impose on Rebecca past his welcome.

"Sounds interesting. Commission only? Or salary, too?" Rebecca did hope the best for Don.

"It starts with both, but moves into commission after six months of building up clientele."

"Okay, well, let me know if you need a ride to the airport or anything." Rebecca wasn't even sure she could do that for him, being that she was working during the week, but she wanted to offer Don something."

"Oh, don't worry about that. I'll get a car. That's pretty easy to do these days."

"Yes. I guess it is."

The rest of the evening, they chatted about different things, and actually seemed to be avoiding the whole topic of Don possibly moving to Texas. When he left two days later for the interview, the house seemed different to Rebecca. She wasn't sure she liked the quiet when she got home from work that first evening without Don being there. After wandering around the house, and trying to find something to do, she decided to go on over to Rosie's. Maybe a good talk with her friend would help.

Rosie answered the door with the phone to her ear. "I need to go, Scott. Rebecca is here. I'll talk with you soon."

Rebecca knew that Scott was an old friend of Rosie's who lost his wife some years back. They talked about him a few times. She knew he needed a listening ear as he processed his grief.

Turning her full attention on Rebecca then, Rosie said, "Hi! How are you this evening? Did Don get off to Texas okay?" Rosie knew he was going. Rosie knew most everything about Rebecca's life these days. They were in frequent contact.

"Yes. He left this morning. I'm not sure how long he'll be gone. The house is kind of quiet without him." Rebecca didn't know if she even wanted to be saying that. "I'm sorry. I didn't mean to interrupt your conversation with Scott."

"No. It's not a problem. We were just about done anyway. I know what you mean about Don," Rosie agreed. "Having someone in the house is nice. Scott and I miss that companionship."

"I know it's hard. I'm so sorry... Don and I are adjusting well to this. It's not like when we were married...we're okay being friends. We give each other the space to do our own thing. But we also eat together sometimes, and we enjoy talking over our day."

"That's good to hear. We never know what God has planned when He places people in our lives. We have to watch and see God's purpose in all things." Rosie wasn't sure it was yet time to talk about this with Rebecca— the specific things the Bible has to say about marriage and divorce. But maybe it was? Rosie knew she would need to go carefully…and listen to the Holy Spirit's direction.

"Do you think that God brought Don back into the house for a reason, Rosie?" Rebecca was almost afraid to ask the question.

Rosie didn't answer right away…she wanted to see if this was the open door to speak. Rosie had been waiting and watching from across the street. She, too, was interested to see what God was doing. What was His purpose in all of this? Rosie understood she couldn't know the mind of God. But she did know His Word, and Rosie thought there would probably come a time to share these things with Rebecca.

"God does everything for a reason," Rosie said. "He is involved in all the intimate details of our lives. Some think He's too busy for trivial stuff, that He is only concerned with the big stuff. But God knows every hair on our head. He knows when a sparrow falls from the sky. There is a sweet song about that…mind if I sing a bit of it?"

It had been a while since Rebecca heard Rosie sing, and she always welcomed those times. "Of course not! I LOVE to hear you sing!"

Rosie started her familiar humming and then sang a song that Rebecca had never heard before. It was so beautiful when Rosie began with these words…

Why should I feel discouraged, why should the shadows come,
Why should my heart be lonely, and long for heav'n and home,
When Jesus is my portion? My constant Friend is He:
His eye is on the sparrow, and I know He watches me;
His eye is on the sparrow, and I know He watches me.
I sing because I'm happy, I sing because I'm free,
For His eye is on the sparrow, and I know He watches me.

When Rosie was finished, Rebecca couldn't help but applaud. She hoped that Rosie didn't mind, but it so touched Rebecca's heart. And it made her feel good to know that God was watching, and that He cared that much.

"Rosie, are you happy most of the time?"

"Happy? That's a good question. I learned a bit about the difference between happiness and joy many years ago. I always wanted to be happy. But there were times when I wasn't, of course. I learned that happiness is the result of our circumstances. And as I heard one lady speak on that many years ago, about our circumstances, it was good. She said that she had been asked how she was doing? And when she answered, 'Fine, under the circumstances.' She was then asked, 'What are you doing under there?' I realized upon hearing that that I didn't want to live under my circumstances either, because circumstances come and go. But then there is joy. And the Bible talks about joy. Like the joy of the Lord being our strength. Or even the verse about this being the day the Lord has made, I will rejoice and be glad in it. I learned that rejoicing could be constant when we know that Jesus is truly our Friend, even though happiness is usually fleeting. Daily, I strive to live in the joy the Lord gives, and I don't yearn for the happiness as much these days. Although I do enjoy being happy, too." Rosie gave Rebecca a big grin.

Rebecca couldn't help but smile back, saying, "I never thought about there being a difference between joy and happiness, but what you said makes sense. Thanks, Rosie." Rebecca loved Rosie's wisdom, although Rosie always gave credit to God for any wisdom she had.

"Rosie, what do you think about Don and me? I get confused sometimes." Rebecca was surprised she was pursuing this with Rosie.

"What do you mean 'confused'?" Rosie wanted to make sure what Rebecca was asking.

"Well, I like Don. I always have. Even when I wanted to divorce him, it made me sad. I think, though, that my anger at him overshadowed how I really felt about him. I was so hurt that he wanted a baby so badly, and I couldn't give him one. I knew he wasn't blaming me. But it felt like it, so I wanted to blame him back for something. We were both tested, and I was the cause of not getting pregnant. Maybe it would have been easier if it had been his problem, so to speak. He was always kind. But I could see the pain in his eyes. I know I've told you some of this before…kids were so important to him. It seemed like his life wouldn't be complete without them. For me, I could go either way. I think he sort of resented that, too. I don't know for sure. We have discussed all of this, but I think we need to discuss it even more. I guess I'm saying all of this to say, if it hadn't been for the lack of children, I think our marriage could have made it. And here we are, now in our forties, and it's too late for children for me. I mean, he could find someone younger and still have a child, if he wanted to. So, what do we do about *us* now? Do I even think about maybe repairing our marriage since it seems we can get along better? Or do I leave it alone, and let him find someone younger so he can still maybe have children? And now with this job in San Antonio—maybe that's where he is supposed to be? Maybe his new wife is waiting for him there? I just don't know…" Rebecca's voice trailed off…she had so many different thoughts running through her head, she wasn't even sure if she was making sense.

Rosie seemed to get it. She began to talk with Rebecca, gently saying, "You have many good questions. I can see where the confusion comes in. One thing we always have to remember, Rebecca, is that God is not a God of confusion, but of peace. I think that's in 1 Corinthians 14, or thereabouts. Whenever I am confused about something, I try to take a step back and see it from God's perspective. The enemy, Satan, wants us to drown in our thoughts and run around like a chicken with our head cut off…that is not of God. God says, sit with Me. Talk with Me. There is no rush. I have a perfect plan for you."

"But Rosie, how do we do that? How do we know what God's perfect plan is for our lives?" Rebecca knew she didn't fully understand how to be in that place of peace that Rosie was talking about. She always seemed to get caught up in her own thinking.

"Well, let's take this down to the basics. If we're talking about marriage here, and divorce, we go to God's Word and see what *He* has to say about it. Get His perspective. Would you like me to find a few verses that speak to your situation?" Rosie wanted to make sure that Rebecca's heart was ready.

"Sure."

"Okay, I'm going to pray, and then we will read a bit together." Rosie knew without prayer, things would be much more difficult.

"God ahead," Rebecca said, bowing her head.

Rosie began, "Father, thank You for this time together. Thank You that Your Word speaks Truth into our lives and breaks through the confusion of the enemy. We can trust You. And even when we want to resist what You are telling us, we can know that if we keep our focus on You, You will make things clearer to us. Help our will to be Your will. In Jesus' name. Amen."

Rebecca responded with an, "Amen."

Rosie picked up her Bible, and flipped through the pages. She seemed to be looking for something specific. Rebecca was glad about that. Getting right to the point might stop her head from spinning.

Then Rosie spoke up, "Here it is. A lot of it is in 1 Corinthians 7. If we go down to 7:39, it says that a wife is bound to her husband as long as he lives. Of course, if he dies, she is free to marry anyone she wishes. And I know this is hard, but if we go to Mark 10, it says that if a woman divorces her husband and marries another, she is committing adultery."

Rosie paused, looking at Rebecca. She knew this needed to be taken slowly. Rebecca seemed to be okay and listening, so Rosie continued. "It says that the exception to this is if there is adultery in the marriage—then you are free to divorce and marry again. This sounds kind of crazy in this day and age, Rebecca, when divorce is so common. And of course, if there is danger involved in the marriage with abuse, I can't believe that God would ask for that to continue."

Rebecca interjected, "But Rosie, what if a woman is divorced, like I am, without adultery being a part of it? Without abuse? And then what if she remarries before she knows this, or really believes this? What is she supposed to do then? Divorce her present husband and go back to her first husband?"

Rosie sort of chuckled. She wasn't making fun of Rebecca. But Rosie knew this was a place that many find themselves, and the enemy likes to torture our minds about that. "Here's the thing, Rebecca, wherever we are when we find God to be our all in all, is right where He will accept us and love us. He is asking us to seek His forgiveness where it is needed, receive that forgiveness, and then start living for Him right here, right now. We are to seek His will with all our heart...with our present spouse."

"That makes sense," Rebecca said, relieved. "But what does the Bible say about the position I am in. I haven't remarried, and neither has Don. And there is no adultery. What do *we* do?"

Rosie knew there was a verse about that, and she had been waiting to share it with Rebecca. It would be difficult to hear. She wanted Rebecca to be ready to receive it. She trusted she was... "In 1 Corinthians, there is a verse about a situation like you and Don have. It says in 7:10-11 that a wife must not leave her husband. But if she does leave him, she is to remain single or else be reconciled to him."

"Whoa! WAIT! Really? It says that in the Bible? I didn't know it was that specific! I don't know, Rosie, that's pretty harsh. I mean, not really like harsh, but...well, in my face, I guess. For the most part, I left Don. Even before the marriage was over, I left him emotionally. He really ended up having no choice. He knew it was what I wanted, or he thought he knew. I didn't even really know. I was miserable, and I was making him miserable, and divorce seemed to be our only option."

"Rebecca, many things in your life have changed since you and Don divorced. From what I understand, neither one of you was a Christian at that time. You couldn't be expected to live like a Christian when you weren't. But if either of you *had been* a believer, God would have wanted that person to stay in the marriage to help the unbeliever learn about the love of Jesus. The Bible does say, though, that if an unbelieving spouse wants to leave a marriage, the believer can let them go. Is this making sense to you?"

"Yes, I think so. It's a lot to take in. But I think I am following you," Rebecca said this with her face slightly crunched, like she was really trying to absorb it all.

"Rebecca, now that you and Don are both believers, you can choose to start to live your lives in a new way—in a way that pleases God. As Christians, our daily prayer should be, 'Lord, thy will, not mine.'"

"Rosie, I don't know that I'm liking this. I'm realizing this goes a lot deeper than just how I *feel,* and how Don feels. This is about what God's Word has to say about all of this. A person really has to believe that the Word of God is true, otherwise, who would follow it? This could definitely change the discussion I would have with Don in the future about where we go from here. But I don't see that happening yet. I'm not so sure that I'd want to be married to Don again, or that he is even considering that a possibility. I'm not even sure that I believe the Bible 100 percent. I like parts of it; they seem helpful. But this...all this stuff about marriage..."

"I know, Rebecca. This all takes time to pray about and process. God is not in a hurry." Rosie wanted Rebecca to know that God was kind and caring.

"Thank you, Rosie. In our new walk with God, who knows. Who knows... Wow. You always show me the way we're supposed to live, through God's Word. Even when I am resistant to it, I appreciate you lovingly talking me through it."

"You're welcome, Rebecca. Thank you for being willing to listen. Sharing God's Word with others is not always an easy job. In fact, many times it can be challenging. The world, meaning those outside the family of God, reject most of what God's Word has to say. And even as believers, it takes time to want, to want what God has to say in here. That's a funny way of saying it. I can't say as I want all that is in this Bible. But I choose to obey it. I have to take *my* desires and nail them to the Cross, and that is painful. But in the end, I know that God wants these things for us because it's what's best for us while we live in this world."

"I'm not sure what to do now, Rosie...but I will pray. I need to go on home now. You know I will be back with more questions." Rebecca got up and gave Rosie a big hug. "I appreciate you so much."

"It's good to see you, Rebecca. Let me know if you need anything while Don is gone."

"I will. Thanks. I'll let myself out."

"Okay, bye."

"Bye."

Rebecca made the familiar trek across the street toward home. Rosie always left her with a lot to think about. Rebecca did notice that her head wasn't spinning like it had been on the way over. But it was concentrating on the verses Rosie shared with her. She wanted to spend some time in 1 Corinthians 7, where Rosie had been reading. It seemed to have a lot to say about marriage, and that's where she needed to be while Don was gone. She didn't know what Don's news would be when he returned. But even if he was accepting the job in San Antonio, they needed to talk about this. Rebecca was now glad that Don wouldn't be in the house when she got back. It would give her time to process it all. God knew she needed that.

33

Having been gone for four days, Don only called once—that was to let Rebecca know the interview was going well. They were showing him what the job would entail. He and Rebecca hadn't talked long—Don did say he wanted to do some looking around over the weekend to see what the housing situation was there, and he would probably be back on Monday.

Jennifer was back in town. With so much traveling with her new job; Rebecca barely saw her of late. Jennifer wanted to have Rebecca and Nelson over for a barbeque on Saturday. It would be nice to be together again. Rebecca stopped at the store on the way over to pick up some chips and dip. She paid with cash, which she didn't normally do. As Rebecca left the store, it seemed that someone was trying to get her attention. She turned back to see that the next person behind her in line was walking toward her with cash in her hand. Rebecca dropped some money, and she was amazed at the honesty of the person returning it. When Rebecca got to the parking lot, she noticed a sticker on the window of a car. It said, "Jesus Saves." Rebecca laughed to herself. "Yes, You do Jesus. Thank you." It felt like a personal message to encourage her that day.

Arriving at Jennifer's, Rebecca found Nelson already warming up the grill. Jennifer was making a salad, so Rebecca opened up the chips and stirred together some onion soup mix with sour cream. It was an easy dip, but always a crowd pleaser.

As the women worked together in the kitchen, Rebecca asked Jennifer, "How are things? How's the new job going?"

"It's good. It keeps me busy. Maybe too busy. But maybe that's what I need right now. I don't know…" Jennifer appeared happy, but her voice didn't match her demeanor.

"Is busy good, or do you get extremely tired?" Rebecca didn't know what worked best with a close, difficult grief. Bonnie had been a good friend, but not someone Rebecca saw daily.

"I get tired. And when I get tired, I get sad. My heart still aches. I wish it didn't. I think I should be through this by now, but maybe not. I finished the grief group. I'm wondering if I should go to another one? I seem to be stuck in the sadness."

"Maybe. Do the groups go on all the time?" Rebecca didn't know how that worked. She never attended one.

"They do, but at different places. They are good. But I think I need to spend more time in the Bible, too. I haven't been doing that as much with this new job. I feel it. I miss it. I have a hard time holding onto Hope when I don't read about it. It seems the world sucks the Hope out of me. The news is usually bad around the world. I sometimes wonder what any of us are doing here…"

"I know what you mean. I was in the grocery store just now, and I was so surprised at the kindness of the people there. I lost some money, and they returned it to me. Why should we be surprised at something like that? Shouldn't that just be the norm?"

Jennifer nodded, "Yes. You would think so. But I was watching some videos on line about a set-up to steal a bike. I was shocked at those who would come into the camera range, and see the bike sitting there, and just jump on it and try to ride away. They rigged it so they couldn't. But still…why would a person just steal a bike like that?"

"It beats me. Makes me even more grateful that my cash was returned today."

Nelson walked back in, "The grill is just about ready for the burgers."

"They are in the fridge," Jennifer told him. "I already made them into patties, so it should be easy. Sorry this is such a simple dinner tonight."

Both Nelson and Rebecca immediately said, "It's fine! It's just good to be together."

Nelson snacked on some chips and dip. Then went out the door, saying, "I'll let you know when these are just about done."

"Okay. We're pretty much set in here." Jennifer was glad to be with friends again. Traveling with strangers got lonely. She wanted to be around people who knew her.

When it came time to eat, the conversation flowed well. Nelson was sharing a bit more about what happened with Jill, and how his life had been since then. Jennifer was glad to have the two of them to talk to about Justin. She filled them in on Justin's family, the little she knew, and how her life was going. Jennifer said she still was not dating, and had no desire to, as yet. Rebecca was taking it all in, and feeling good to have these friends she could trust with such personal issues.

When the conversation seemed to die down some, Rebecca wanted to let them know about Don. She said, "Don is in San Antonio on a job interview. He has been gone almost a week. It sounds like things are going well. And he is looking at housing there."

Nelson said, "Wow, that sounds promising!"

Jennifer added, "It sure does! Are you glad that you could soon have your house back? I mean, without a permanent guest? Or is that going okay?"

"Actually, it is going very well, and I wanted to talk with you both about a conversation I had with Rosie, and get your feedback on it. Is that okay?"

They both said, "Sure,"

Rebecca continued, "Well, after Don left for San Antonio, I went over to Rosie's. I wanted to clear up a few things that were spinning around in my head. Honestly, I'm not sure how I feel about Don living with me, or should I say, even that we are able to be friends. It all seems strange, and yet, right. If you know what I mean?"

"Uh huh," said Nelson. "You know, I have to tell you, I enjoyed getting to know Don a bit when I stopped in that day. It was the first time I met him, and he is nice guy."

"Yes. He is." Rebecca agreed. "Here's the thing. Rosie knows the Bible a lot better than I do. I really had no idea what it says about divorce, and remarriage, and all of that. She showed me a few things, and I have been spending some time reading about it. And I don't know what to think, or what to do. I mean, do we just do what the Bible says, not paying attention to how we feel about it? Is that what God is asking us to do?"

Nelson was quizzical, "I'm not sure what you mean?"

"What I mean is, the Bible is pretty darn clear about marriage. But do we follow it like a road map? Or do we make our own decisions? And even if I wanted to follow it, it does take two people. Maybe Don has no interest in what it says about our situation."

"Well, that's true, it does take two," Jennifer added in. "What exactly are you thinking? Or what does it say? I'm not well versed on it all."

"It says that adultery is a reason for divorce. But as far as with my situation, when there is no adultery involved, if I leave my husband, I should stay single or go back together with him. Otherwise, if I re-marry, I am committing adultery with my new husband."

"Wow! Really? Where is that?" Jennifer asked.

"It's in 1 Corinthians 7. Believe me, I know, because I've been reading it and other things for days." Rebecca almost sounded exasperated.

Nelson knew he needed to say something, but he wanted to go easy. He knew that in this group he probably had the best knowledge of this part of the Word because of studying it when deciding to remain single after Jill died.

"That is a powerful piece of Scripture. What do you think about it, Rebecca?" Nelson wanted her to feel at ease talking to them about it.

"I don't really know what to think. I have always lived my life doing what I felt like doing, not what God said I should be doing. I mean, I have had a couple of instances where God has intervened in my life since becoming a Christian...like with Rosie when she fell that time. But this is way beyond that. This is messing with my whole future, if you know what I mean?"

Nelson said, "I do. I do."

Rebecca continued, "Don has no idea what I have been studying while he has been gone this week. And I don't know how I'm going to talk to him about all this when he returns. What if he does get the job in San Antonio? What then? Am I supposed to marry him and move there? And what if he doesn't get the job, and he stays here? Do we get married? Right now, I don't think I want to get married to him at all. Will God be mad at me if I don't? And this is just my side of it all...wait until Don enters into this discussion!"

Rebecca put it all out there. She had gotten worked up telling them what had been rolling around in her head...with no idea how her friends were going to react.

"Those are good questions, Rebecca," Nelson said. "Very good. I can't say as I have the answers for what you're supposed to do, but it's good to talk about it all. I've studied that part of Scripture. It's in verse 7:32 that it talks about an unmarried man being able to spend his time doing the Lord's work. That's a hard calling, but it's one that I wanted to embrace for a season and see how it went."

Rebecca commented, "You seem to do very well with it, Nelson."

"I guess so. I do get lonely at times. This world pulls us in so many directions. God's direction can get lost in the busyness of it all. I want to honor God, and even more so because the enemy would have me turn against God in the sorrow and missing of Jill. I wanted to take as long as necessary to heal and focus on God in all of it."

Jennifer started to cry, and it was more than just a few tears. Rebecca and Nelson didn't know what to think. Had they said something wrong? They waited to see if Jennifer needed to talk, or what? Nelson put his hand out and rubbed her back a bit, trying to comfort her in her grief. When Jennifer was able to speak, she started through her sobs... "I...uh, I need to talk to you both about something." The sobs came harder now. "I'm sorry. Let me breathe here for a minute."

Jennifer stopped for a bit, and then continued on, "I...there is something that has been eating away at me, and I want to confess it to you both. When you talk about honoring God, Nelson, I feel that I haven't done that. That Justin and I didn't do that. And I feel to blame for Justin's death because of it."

"We are here to listen. You take your time. There's no rush." Nelson truly meant that, and he knew that Rebecca agreed because he could see her out of the corner of his eye nodding her head."

"Justin and I were not honoring God in our relationship. Even though we both loved God, we were sleeping together. We didn't want it to be that way in the beginning, but that's where we ended up. And I agonize over our decision now. Maybe God took Justin because we were sinning. Maybe if we waited I would still have Justin here with me. I would give anything to go back and do it differently. But I can't now, and it hurts so much!!" Jennifer's sobs started again.

Nelson spoke first… "The flesh is a powerful thing. Don't we all know that?! Even Jesus knew when He walked this earth how hard it was. He had to battle Satan with, 'It is written…'"

"What exactly does that mean?" Rebecca needed more.

"It means that when Jesus was in the desert, being tempted by Satan, He felt the same pulls. And even He knew the power of God's Word. And Jesus used it! As should we! We cannot battle Satan on our own. Jesus didn't, and we shouldn't attempt to either. The flesh pulls us in so many ways. And the Bible says, 'the spirit is willing, but the flesh is weak.' That seems opposite of what I just said, but that means the flesh is so willing to bend to the ways of this world and all the darkness it contains. The flesh pulls HARD! I have been in battles where it seemed like I could almost feel the claws of the enemy gripping me…wanting me to go his way! It can bring me to tears! But by drawing upon our inner strength, the Holy Spirit, we can have victory. Jesus was victorious! He promises us the same."

"But how do we do that, Nelson?" Rebecca wasn't sure she understood.

Nelson answered, "Prayer is the only way. And reading the Truth until the lies are drummed out of our head! I speak from experience."

"Experience?" Jennifer slowly stopped her sobbing, and was able to join in a bit more.

"Yes. Experience. I can't tell you how much I have been tempted during this time of singleness and even when I was with Jill. Jennifer, I want to say to you, what you and Justin did, in sinning, was not the cause of his death. Please know that. Jill and I resisted that temptation, and still, she is in Heaven along with Justin. So, don't let the enemy torture you with that. Seek God's forgiveness, it is there for you through Jesus, and let it rest at the Savior's feet. Jesus doesn't want you to get stuck in your sadness because of decisions you made in the past. Jesus wants you to get to know Him more through all of this, and honor Him anew each day. Jesus died on the Cross for you to be forgiven. Your sin is not so great that His blood cannot cover it."

"Oh Nelson, thank you for saying that. I am going to try to remember that when these thoughts torture me, as they have been. Your story with Jill encourages me. I want to be at peace about this. It's just so hard."

Rebecca still had questions. "But Nelson, what about now? Here we sit, on this day, each of us with our own struggles. You live a celibate life, by choice, to honor God. Jennifer seeks forgiveness to honor what Jesus died to give us. What do I do? You're both living in a finished section of your story. It seems like mine is still being written, and I don't know how it turns out. I don't know how I want it to turn out. And Don isn't even aware that he is part of this story."

They all sort of chuckled at that statement. It felt good to add a little lightheartedness to their discussion.

Nelson said, "I want to read you something. I'll be right back." Nelson went and got his Bible out of his truck, and when he returned, Rebecca and Jennifer were waiting to hear what he was going to share.

Nelson opened his Bible, and said, "In Romans 3:20 it says, '...*the more we know God's law, the clearer it becomes that we aren't obeying it.*' The three of us sit here today different people than we were last year, or even a few months ago. Each day we live, when we focus on God, we learn more about who He is, and what He wants for our lives. The closer we get to God, and I know this sounds crazy, but the farther away we know we are in complete obedience to His commands. Our encouragement about all this is in verse 21 that starts with, *'But now God has shown us a different way of being right in his sight—not by obeying the law but by the way promised in the Scriptures long ago. We are made right in God's sight when we trust in Jesus Christ to take away our sins.'* When we know better, we can do better. But we also know more and more how much we need the blood of Jesus. It's the only way to be right in God's sight."

Nelson went on, "When Jill and I were together, we had to work hard as a couple to keep from sinning in our relationship. But did that mean we weren't sinners? Of course not. In Romans 3:12 it says, *'All have turned away from God; all have gone wrong. No one does good, not even one.'* We may not have sinned in the way that you and Justin did, Jennifer, but we had our own sins going on. It takes time to identify some of our sins, because some are so deeply hidden, like pride, hate, and unforgiveness are big ones. The enemy can hide those inside of us calling them 'deserved' feelings. Are you following me with this?"

Jennifer said, "Yes."

Rebecca was not so quick to answer. She had more questions. "I'm still confused as to what I'm supposed to do. I get that we all sin, every day. But what about future sin...like say I decide I don't want to go back with Don. Am I forgiven for that? I mean, I guess I could choose to remain single, too. That would be a choice. Like with you, Nelson."

Nelson answered, "There is no sin that Jesus' blood can't cover, except the sin of unbelief. Because, obviously, if we don't believe He is our Savior, we aren't covered by His death and resurrection. But here's the thing...daily, we have to die to ourselves. And I mean, daily. That takes practice, because our flesh will rise up and say, 'I WANT MY WAY!'"

"No kidding," Jennifer added in.

"So, to get specific, Rebecca, with you and Don, you know what the Bible says. You have read it. You are studying it, and praying about it. But your flesh is still screaming, 'NO.' God understands that. It is a battle of the wills...God's will, and yours. It will be that way until Jesus comes back. When we don't want to do what the Bible tells us to do, we are in a very hard place. There is a verse that has helped me in that. It is found in Psalm 37:4." Nelson turned there and read, "'*Take delight in the Lord, and he will give you your heart's desires.*' I didn't understand this verse for a long time. I thought if I delighted in the Lord, I would get what I wanted. God helped me see it in another way. When I delight myself in Him, the desires of my heart change to His desires, and then I desire them, too."

"What?" Rebecca really wasn't getting this. "If we delight ourselves in God. Meaning what? Spend time with Him in prayer and reading the Bible, getting to know Him, and His ways, *falling in love* with Him? Is that right? We fall in love *with God*? Then it changes our heart? It changes what we want to what God wants, and in the end, it *is* what we want?"

"Yes! You got it exactly!" Nelson was pleased that she had been able to speak it out so clearly.

"Whoa. That's crazy!" Rebecca wasn't so sure she was buying it, even though she said it.

"Here's what I know," Nelson finished up with, "What I want, isn't what's best for me. Only my Father in Heaven knows what is best for me. I wanted Jill. If God had asked me, I would have stated that without question. But life here on earth is very short, and eternity is forever and ever, and ever. God has a plan, and He is working it out for the good of all. I want to be a willing participant in that plan. I want to trust God with all of it, even when I hate it! And I hate living without Jill. But, my heart has been changed as I live each day without her. And it has been changed for the better because I keep giving my heart to God. I say, 'Thy will be done'—even when it's different than my will. And it works. It's crazy, it seems backward, but it changes something in our hearts that words really can't convey. It is a life of obedience—similar to what Paul lived, only I would never want to compare my life to his. Paul was such a great man of God. But in that obedience, there is a joy that the world cannot offer us. The world doesn't even understand it. Most Christians don't understand it."

Rebecca was starting to get tired, so she said, "It is getting late, and I do need to get going. But you have given me so much more to think about. I'm so resistant to this. Right now, I want what I want. It seems best to me. And I know that it doesn't just involve me. Don would have to be on board also. I have no clue where he is at with all of this. If I could ask, though, would you both pray for me. I do want to be in God's will. At least I think I do. I just wish that meant a decision about a job, or a car, or a move…not a marriage."

Nelson and Jennifer both agreed to pray for Rebecca, and each other. And as the evening ended and they said their good-byes, there had grown an even stronger bond between the three of them. Rebecca never experienced conversations like these with her other friends, except for Rosie. And deep in her heart, she longed to go here, to these depths, with Don, also. Maybe that's what would change her heart? This was running through her mind when she left Jennifer's. Time and God would tell. It seemed like she had a lot of work to do with God. Rebecca wondered if she was even willing…

34

Don was not due to return home until sometime on Monday night. Rebecca was so thankful for having had a week to think about all that she learned. Even on Sunday, the pastor was preaching out of Romans 7, and it talked once again about marriage. Rebecca was listening. Sometimes it seemed like God designed the sermons just for her. God was making things as clear as possible, even though that didn't help with the decision. It was still hard.

When Rebecca got up for work Tuesday morning, Don was still asleep. She guessed he'd come in very late since she hadn't heard him. She tried to be quiet getting ready, and left at her normal time. Rebecca had butterflies in her stomach. It felt like her whole life changed in just the week that Don had been gone. She wondered if Don was even coming home to the same woman? Rebecca didn't have any idea what their conversation would be like when she returned home that evening. Should she even address all this with Don yet? Maybe he would be exhausted from his trip, and it wouldn't be a good time. Rebecca was so new at hearing the Holy Spirit; she hoped that she wouldn't mess it up.

Work was busy in a normal sort of way. Rebecca's boss, Ben, had quite a bit of work to do, and he appreciated her help with it. When lunchtime came, Rebecca decided to sit outside again. The fall season was coming, and soon it would be turning colder. There wouldn't be as many days to soak up the warm sunshine. It had been a good summer...an interesting one, with Don. When Rebecca returned to her desk, she saw that there was a bouquet of flowers sitting there. She wondered who they were for? Many times, flowers were delivered for different people in the office. She always enjoyed being the one to carry them to the person they were meant for. There was rarely a time that it didn't bring a smile to their face and ohhhs and ahhhs from those who saw it happening. Why was it that flowers always made a person feel so special?

Rebecca took a look at the envelope before sitting down. She wanted to get them delivered right away. Then she noticed it had her name on it. Why would she be getting flowers? It wasn't even close to her birthday. Rebecca went around and sat down at her desk. Opening the card, it simply said, "Can we have dinner together tonight? Don."

"UH OH!" Rebecca said, loud enough for Ben to hear her.

"Did you call me, Rebecca?" Ben almost shouted back.

"Uh. No. Sorry. I was just talking to myself." Rebecca gave a big loud sigh. What could this mean? So many thoughts swirled through her head the rest of the day. Rebecca didn't get back to Don right away, although she knew he was probably waiting for her answer. Then again, he wouldn't know when the flowers arrived, unless they had been on some sort of tracking system from the florist shop. She didn't even know if they did that? But it would be a good idea. Rebecca always wondered when she sent flowers if they arrived or not. Finally, about four, she sent Don a text.

"We can do dinner. Want me to pick up a pizza?" Rebecca really didn't feel like a pizza, but it was always an easy choice.

Don immediately texted back, "No need to get a pizza. I'll take care of it." He had obviously been waiting for her answer.

"OK," was all Rebecca wanted to say.

The last hour of the day seemed to drag. Rebecca was so focused on what was to come, she had no interest in what was going on at work anymore. Her heart felt sort of sick. Had Don gotten the job? Was he moving? He would be expecting her to be all happy for him, and congratulate him...which she would do. Or at least give it her best effort. Then again, if that were true, then he would be moving away and maybe it would let her off the hook with what she needed to talk with him about? If Don had no interest in their marriage, and the job was his first priority, then God couldn't expect her to drag him back into a relationship with her. She would surely be released from her obligations then...although she didn't truly believe that. Rebecca knew better by now. If it were just about the distance, God's Word probably couldn't be ignored. Rebecca was going to have to approach this in a way she never had before. She almost wished Rosie was having dinner with them for moral support.

When Rebecca arrived home, Don was waiting for her in the living room. She expected him to be upstairs in the office. But then again, she guessed he really didn't need to be looking for a job anymore. Rebecca was dreading this whole scenario. Her discomfort level was off the charts.

Don got up and gave her a quick hug and, "Hello." She noticed he wasn't exactly dressed for 'pizza'. With slacks and a button up shirt, they must be going out. The offer must be very good in San Antonio, and they were celebrating. She was starting to feel a little happy for him. It's never nice to be short on money and he probably wanted to treat her to something better than a pizza.

"Hi Don. Uhh, are we going out? Or did you just get home?"

"We are going out. If that's okay? We have reservations at 6:30. Can you be ready in about 45 minutes?" Don was hoping she wasn't too tired from her day. This wasn't going to be an easy conversation.

"That should be okay. I'll do a few things and get changed. How was your trip?" Rebecca knew there wouldn't be much time for his answer as she turned to go upstairs. But it seemed appropriate to throw the question out there.

"It was fine. I'll tell you more at dinner. I don't want to hold you up right now," Don said to her back as she walked away.

"Okay. Sounds good. I'll get ready."

Forty-five minutes later, Rebecca came down wearing a summer dress and sandals. She had let her hair down, which is how Don liked it. It revealed the slight waves that framed her slender face. He wondered if she had done that for him? His mind was working so fast he didn't know what to think at this point.

As they walked out the door, Don told her he would drive. Rebecca was fine with that since he hadn't mentioned where they were even going. She knew the restaurant wouldn't be far since they left at 6:15 for a 6:30 reservation. It was somewhere close by. When they pulled into the parking lot, Rebecca was a bit taken aback. The restaurant where they ate on their first date was in this parking lot, along with a few other places. It was a little too close to home, comfort-wise. Why would Don choose here? He knew this restaurant had special meaning to both of them. Rebecca always avoided this place since their divorce. It brought back too many memories that she would rather not think about anymore.

"Uh. Are we going where I think we're going?" Rebecca asked Don, a bit miffed.

"Yes. I hope you don't mind." Don knew she did. But he was hoping she wouldn't get too mad before they even got inside.

"Well, it wouldn't be my choice." Rebecca swallowed the unease she felt, and tried to act like it would be okay. She wondered why Don would want to celebrate his new job here? It felt like a slap in the face. But Don wasn't normally like that, so maybe she was thinking about it in the wrong way. Rebecca prayed, and asked the Holy Spirit to take over since her flesh was not wanting to cooperate. Rosie taught her about that, and sometimes it worked well. Other times, her flesh seemed to rule—tonight Rebecca felt a peace come over her, and she was thankful.

They were led to a table with a "Reserved" sign on it, and the waiter offered them something to drink. Both ordered water with lemon. In the past, it would have been wine, but things were changing in both of them. For Rebecca, she knew she wanted to be totally clear-headed for what was about to come. They chatted some while deciding on what to eat. The menu had a few changes to it, but they both ended up ordering their favorite meal from the past. They laughed when they realized that. It felt good to share an inside joke with each other. Rebecca missed that part of marriage…where one person could say something, and the other person could finish it. It was funny to them, but no one else understood. Sometimes it would be something simple like, "Did I eat that onion already?" from an old comedy routine. It would cause them both to laugh.

While they waited for dinner to come, Don ordered an appetizer. That made it easier than just sitting there staring at the walls, or each other. Don hadn't yet mentioned the job, and Rebecca really didn't want to bring it up. She figured Don would get to it when he was ready.

Dinner arrived, and Don did something they hadn't done together before. He asked Rebecca if he could pray before their meal. Rebecca was astonished, and pleased. She said, "Sure."

"Father, thank You for today, for this meal, and for having time together. We appreciate all You do in our lives. In Jesus' name. Amen."

Rebecca added in her own, "Amen."

Don then began to go where Rebecca didn't want to go…to the job.

"Bec. I wanted to bring you here tonight to tell you about San Antonio. But maybe you already figured that out? A nice meal can help a conversation go more smoothly, and I know you love the food here."

Rebecca answered almost too quietly, "I do. I haven't been here in a long time."

"Things went very well with the job interview. I haven't heard the official word as yet. These things take so much longer than we want them to. They are interviewing only a handful of people, and not rushing. They are wanting to make sure that it will be a good fit. But by all indications, I think they will be contacting me. Of course, I won't give up looking into other opportunities should they arise, because I don't want to put all my eggs in one basket."

"That makes sense," Rebecca calmly answered. She was pleased to hear that no official offer had come yet…or was she?

Don continued, "I also took a look at the housing situation while I was there. I found a couple of things that would probably work. That was encouraging. It seems like all doors would be open once the call comes through. What do you think about it?"

There it was, the question that Rebecca didn't want to answer. "Uh, what do I think about it? Well, I'm happy for you. I know how hard it is to be out of work. It never feels good." That was about all she wanted to say. Rebecca didn't know what door God was opening…the one for Don to be able to move far away, or the one for her to be able to move into the discussion about their marriage? Rebecca's heart was beating faster than she would have liked for it to, and it was making it hard for her to eat. Rebecca pushed the food around her plate until Don spoke again.

"Yes, it is hard. I especially don't like to imposition you, Bec. You have been so kind in giving me a place to stay through this time."

Rebecca quickly said, "It's really been okay, Don. I think we've been doing well together, don't you?"

"Oh. Yes! I do too. I'm glad that you see it the same. And taking you to dinner is a small thank you for all of that you have done, too." Don felt relief, because he knew that what was coming next might cause a commotion.

"Well, you're welcome." Rebecca took in a deep breath. This was getting hard. Something was stirring in her soul, and she wasn't sure what it was. She kind of just wanted the dinner to be over and to get home to the safety of her room. Alone seemed good right now.

"Bec. I need to talk to you about something…something that happened while I was in San Antonio."

All Rebecca could say was, "Oh." It sounded cold-hearted when the word came out. What was stirring in her soul suddenly quit, and she could feel her heart start to break. She sensed this conversation was over before it ever got started. Why would Don bring her here? This suddenly seemed cruel…but she didn't fully know why.

Don heard the tone, and he knew he needed to get to the point before Bec walked out on him. He knew her well enough to know that long drawn out speeches weren't good.

"Here's the thing. While I was away, I was meeting a lot of people at the new company. I was wined and dined. It's a very generous company. All they were offering me seemed very good."

"Okay," was about all Rebecca could add.

"Yes. It was all good, except one thing…" Don paused for longer than seemed necessary.

"What was that?" Rebecca didn't even know if she cared now.

"They offered me everything I wanted, except…" Don didn't know if he should say it.

"Except what!?" Rebecca was practically exacerbated at this point.

"Except…you. The job didn't offer me you."

Their eyes locked, and Don knew he needed to explain himself further before he lost Rebecca here. He could tell she was stunned.

Don quickly continued, "When I was in San Antonio, I realized I missed you, Bec. I missed being here in the house with you. I missed the hope that I think I have buried deep in my heart that maybe someday...we could, uh, maybe even start to date again. Hence, tonight. I wanted to take you on a date. I wanted to take a chance and see if going to our favorite place together could possibly be the start of something new...or should I say, old, but in a better way than we did it before. I know I made so many mistakes. I know I could have done better. And when I was away, I thought of all the ways that I would like to do it better...if you would be willing to give me a chance."

This was not at all what Rebecca was expecting. And now Don sat there, looking vulnerable, and sincere, and she had no words... Rebecca had been fully prepared to hear Don say that he'd not only gotten the job in San Antonio, but that he even met someone while he was there. He was moving into a new home, a new job, and a new relationship. Rebecca felt like she could cry, and she wasn't even sure why. Was she happy? Confused? Overwhelmed? All of the above? Rebecca just sat there, not even knowing which direction to look...

Don waited. He knew he shocked Rebecca, and he didn't want to rush her. Don was glad he had gotten the words out, although he wasn't sure they were the right ones. Suddenly he couldn't even remember what he said. Don knew that he had to do this...to take this chance. It weighed so heavy on him while he was away. It built in intensity each day, and that was why he only called Rebecca once. Don hadn't wanted to let Rebecca know the struggle he was having at being away from her—it confused even him. Don never stopped loving Rebecca, but he stopped liking her for a time. He had been mad that she didn't share in his desire for children. He wanted to try harder each time it failed. Rebecca wanted to try less. And even though adoption was an option, they got to a point where that wouldn't have even been healthy for them. Their relationship was in no shape for parenting by then. It seemed best that they just call it quits. But since this job loss, and their living together, Don was seeing Rebecca in a new light. He saw her heart softening toward life in general, and even toward him. Her friends changed, too. Don really liked Nelson. Rebecca's demeanor around home was even different than Don remembered it being. And Don knew he wasn't the same either. God was changing his heart in this whole process. With the job loss and the financial struggles, it was causing him to go to God more. And through Roger, and his Bible study group's encouragement, he was learning a new way to handle life, and even relationships. The group kept saying that God was a Restorer of all things. Don began to wonder if that could mean he and Rebecca? Would she ever want that? Would he? Being in San Antonio had shown him some things. Distance made his heart grow fonder. He wondered what the distance had done to her.

Rebecca eventually interrupted his thoughts, "Uh, wow! You surprised me there." It wasn't very poetic the way she said it. It wasn't encouraging...she just didn't know what else to say.

"Yes. I know. I didn't know how best to tell you what was in my heart. I hope that I wasn't too blunt. I've never been great with words." Don's head hung down a bit...not feeling sorry for himself—he was just wanting something he didn't know if he could ever have again.

"I think you did okay. I just don't quite know how to answer you at this point." Rebecca didn't even know how she was going to share with Don all that she, too, had been going through while he was processing his own things in San Antonio. All she knew was that tonight her side of it should wait. This was enough for one evening. Rebecca needed some time.

Rebecca tried to handle this with care. She didn't want Don to feel bad. "What do you say we let all this sit for now? I appreciate what you have said. It is very sweet. Let me think about this...uh...because I...uh, have some things I'd like to talk with you about, too. But I'd rather do that at another time, and in private, if you don't mind?"

Don just said, "Sure." He had no idea where Rebecca would go with this. He was surprised she seemed to accept it with a bit of openness. He was thankful for that.

The drive home together was pleasant enough. Don felt relieved to have at least voiced his feelings. And Rebecca knew it opened a door for her to talk with Don about her own week. Don had been bold. She wanted to be bold, also. They obviously needed to talk about their future together...if there was to be one. For now, they would let it rest where they were.

35

Rest was not to be. Kay called Rebecca early Wednesday morning at work—Lindsey was back in the hospital with a *high* fever. Kay was asking for prayer. It seems that the infection never completely cleared...in fact, it had gotten worse. They were trying different antibiotics. But Lindsey's immunities were so low, she had nothing to fight it with on her own. Rebecca left work and met Kay at the hospital. Ben had no problem with her leaving. Roger was there, too. He called Don, unbeknownst to Rebecca. The four of them gathered next to Lindsey's bedside. Never would they have thought they would be in this situation, not only with Lindsey, but with each other in prayer.

Lindsey stirred a bit in the bed, and Kay attended to her as Don and Rebecca stepped out of the room with Roger. Roger filled them in on what was going on.

"The doctors said she can fight this. We know she can. She is a strong young woman. She has seen many battles before." Roger was hope-filled.

"What can we do, Roger?" Don asked, wondering if the doctor was being fully truthful with Roger—of course the doctor would want to give them hope.

Roger answered back, "Pray. Pray. Pray. I don't understand the power of prayer completely. But when the doctors do all they can do, and we pray with all our heart, I do know we are doing everything possible. I called our men's group, too. If you know of anyone else that will pray, please let them know."

Rebecca was quick to say, "I want to go and call my neighbor, Rosie, right now. She is a powerful person when it comes to praying."

"Okay. Thank you," Roger said in a tone of relief.

Rebecca turned to go, and then she turned back. Rebecca didn't quite know what she was doing, but she felt she needed to ask Roger something.

"Roger, it just came to me. What would you think of having Rosie come to the hospital to pray for Lindsey? Would you and Kay, and Lindsey, be comfortable with that? She is an amazing woman. She has seen so much of life, and she knows God so well."

Roger immediately answered, "That would be very good. I know Kay would be in agreement with that, too. She said you have talked with her a lot about Rosie."

"I have. She knows Rosie through me," Rebecca answered.

"Okay, go ahead and give her a call," Roger said.

And Don added in, "If she can come, and if you want me to go and get her, I will."

"Thanks. I'll let you know."

As Rebecca walked off to make the phone call, she saw Roger and Don go back into Lindsey's room. Rebecca's heart was so sad for this whole situation. This was Roger and Kay's only daughter…only child. How could God be doing this to them? Hadn't they all seen enough sadness already in their lives? When would it end?

In talking with Rosie, Rosie said she was more than willing to come to the hospital. Rebecca let Don know, and he went to pick her up. Rebecca took Kay down to the cafeteria to get her something to eat, while Roger stayed with Lindsey. Kay was a bundle of tears the minute she left Lindsey's bedside. She held it together when she was with her, but this was tearing Kay apart piece by piece. Rebecca had no words…she tried her best to soothe Kay. Kay ate quickly, what little she could, and then wanted to get back to Lindsey's room.

It wasn't but about an hour, and Rosie came in with Don. She was her usual Rosie self, confident, not fearing, Bible in hand. They all seemed to part the way as this bronze-skinned, white halo-haired woman of God made her way to Lindsey's bedside. There was a peace that entered into the room with Rosie. It was like she was designed for this type of mission.

Rosie walked right up to Lindsey and took her hand. With her other hand, Rosie laid the Bible on the bed and stroked Lindsey's head with such a calmness it seemed like the breath of God was showering down upon Lindsey. Lindsey had mostly been sleeping, waking only for a sip of water from time to time. When Rosie bent to whisper to her, they could hear Rosie say, "Oh child, you're burning up with fever. No need to worry…Jesus can take care of you just fine."

Lindsey seemed to be trying to open her eyes. Rosie smiled, and it seemed to give everyone in the room a new-found confidence in the power of God. Rosie then spoke out loud, so that all could hear her.

"Lindsey, do you know how much God loves you? He is watching over you at this very moment, and He has sent his angels to care for you like it says in Psalm 91. God's angels serve us here on earth." Lindsey actually curled her lips up just a bit at that.

Rosie spoke then ever so gently to Lindsey, like Lindsey could hear every word she said. "There are many ways that God heals a person, Lindsey. We always trust that God heals in His timing and in His way. Our Father always wants us to ask Him—that's why I love to pray for all kinds of healing. Today, together, we are going to pray for God to heal you. You have some infection that He can heal, and also your cancer is not a problem for our great God. We are going to trust God to answer our prayers in the way He deems best. I don't want you to fear in any way. You can just relax and let us pray over you."

Lindsey's lips seemed to indicate an actual smile this time. Her eyes would open and close as Rosie talked. It seemed Lindsey really could hear everything that was going on.

Rosie spoke directly to her, "Are you ready to receive healing today, Lindsey?"

Almost before the words were out of Rosie's mouth, Lindsey gave a small but definite nod. It surprised everyone in the room. Kay let out a gasp, and Roger wrapped his arms around his wife, as they drew close to Rosie on one side of Lindsey's bed. Don and Rebecca walked to the opposite side. Rosie asked all of them to reach out their hands toward Lindsey, and Rosie began to pray:

"Father in Heaven. Lindsey is sick. You know her so well. You know every cell in her young body. You can see where she needs healing. Jesus. You have given us the authority in Your Word to pray with boldness and strength..." Rosie picked up her Bible and read, "In Matthew 10:1 it says, 'Jesus called his twelve disciples together and gave them authority to cast out evil spirits and to heal every kind of disease and illness.' We are going to believe God for this authority today, Lindsey, because in John 14:12 it says, 'I tell you the truth, anyone who believes in me will do the same works I have done, and even greater works, because I am going to be with the Father.' Jesus, by Your authority, we COMMAND this fever to be GONE. We tell all the infection to go now in Jesus' powerful name. We take authority over this illness in Your name, Jesus. Romans 16:20 declares, 'The God of peace will soon crush Satan under your feet.' Satan, you are crushed today, and we tell you to go NOW, in Jesus name!"

Rosie stopped praying, and waited a bit. Then she began to whisper in a language that none of them could understand. Lindsey was moving around slightly in the bed as Rosie began to pray out loud again, "Infection, be GONE, in Jesus' name. There is NO PLACE for you here in this child of God."

Lindsey started to open her eyes more, and was turning her head from side to side. Her mouth opened, and she started breathing out in short puffs, almost like panting. Rosie seemed encouraged by this, although the rest of them had no idea what this meant.

Rosie continued, "We thank You Jesus for all that You are already doing in Lindsey. It's in Your powerful name that we pray, just as You instructed us to do over 2,000 years ago. We thank You, Jesus!"

Lindsey's eyes were open now, and she was looking up at her parents. She appeared a bit puzzled, trying to speak. It seemed she couldn't at first. But then Lindsey faintly uttered, "I feel better."

Kay reached out to touch her forehead, and then Kay quickly turned to Roger and said, "Her head is cool. The fever is gone!"

Roger reached over to feel Lindsey's head, and he agreed. "It does feel cooler." They both looked at Rosie, astounded. "Does healing happen that quickly, Rosie?" Roger asked.

Rosie said, "It can. Thank You, Jesus."

The rest of them chimed in with giving thanks. This may have been something that Rosie experienced before, but the four of them, Roger, Kay, Don, and Rebecca stood astonished as this was taking place. They watched Lindsey being strengthened in front of their very eyes.

Lindsey spoke again, with a bit more strength this time, saying, "I feel lighter."

"Thank YOU, JESUS!!" Rosie's excitement was building now, too. But she wasn't rushing through her prayers. They could tell she was patient in waiting upon God. There were times where they would all just be quiet and still, waiting to see what Rosie would do next. And most importantly, what God would do next.

"Lindsey," Rosie sweetly asked, "do you know that Jesus can save you from all this pain and suffering? Do you know that Jesus' death and resurrection is our greatest Hope?"

Lindsey looked directly at Rosie then, and she said quietly but with a determination, "I believe in Jesus as my Savior and Lord." They were all astounded. Lindsey had been too weak to even open her eyes and now she was able to speak a full sentence.

Rosie turned to talk to Kay and Roger about what was happening, and she told them that she really believed Lindsey's infection was gone. The fever going down was a definite sign of change in Lindsey's body. She wanted to now pray specifically for her cancer, if that was okay with them? They quickly responded, "Yes, please do!"

Rosie prayed, "Jesus, thank You for taking the infection away. We trust the power of Your name. Now we tell this cancer to GO NOW, in Your Name, Jesus! Any cells that are not healthy, we pray for renewed health and vitality to them. Any spirit of sickness that is here, GO NOW in Jesus' name. Any lymph nodes that need to be healed, we command it be done in Jesus' name! Any organs that have suffered from this cancer, we pray for restoration."

Rosie asked Lindsey, "Do you have pain anywhere?" Lindsey pointed to her stomach, and said she felt pain there and really all over her body. Rosie prayed again, "Lord, in Your name, we tell this pain to GO NOW! All pain must leave! From the top of Lindsey's head to the tip of her toes, and any extra pain in the stomach area BE GONE!" Rosie seemed to take such command over the infection and the pain—she talked like it had to listen to her.

"How are you feeling now, Lindsey?" Rosie kept a close watch on what God was doing.

"I feel better. I don't hurt like I did. Just some pain."

Rosie again said, "Thank You, Jesus. We give You all the praise and glory for healing Lindsey today! We tell any remaining pain to GO!" They noticed that Rosie never neglected to give thanks to God each step of the way.

There were so many prayers being said in the room, it brought some of the nurses in to see what was happening. They stood just inside the door, not wanting to interfere with the scene they saw before them. They had tears in their eyes as they saw Lindsey, the young woman who was practically comatose a bit ago, lifting her head and looking around the room—taking in deep breaths, and then breathing out, "Thank You, Jesus!" over and over. There was no mistaking that there was a something amazing going on!

Rebecca heard one nurse turn to another one and say, "This room is filled with so much love."

Roger slowly went to his knees, lifting his hands toward Heaven, giving thanks. Kay stood with her hand on Roger's shoulder, bowing her head and shaking it back and forth, praising God!

Rosie continued to pray small prayers over Lindsey as she was gaining strength. Kay gave Lindsey some sips of water, and then Lindsey asked for her bed to be adjusted so she could sit up straighter. Lindsey was still weak, but Rosie told them to give her time. Rosie said that even in the Bible it talks about the person being given something to eat to regain their strength after being healed. Rosie knew that they all witnessed a miracle with Lindsey today. She told everyone present that this was the work of Jesus, and not her, and that the "Kingdom of God was near them today." It seemed important to Rosie that everyone understood that.

The doctor was soon called, and he came in wondering what was going on. Dr. Endur had been Lindsey's doctor from the beginning of her cancer diagnosis in December. Roger and Kay knew him well by now. He walked right over to Lindsey's bed, and she looked up at her doctor in recognition. Lindsey smiled, and said, "Dr. Endur. Jesus healed me today! I feel much better!" Lindsey's eyes were brimming with tears. Dr. Endur asked Lindsey if he could examine her, and she agreed. He didn't have all the tests necessary for a complete diagnosis, but when he finished, Dr. Endur turned to Roger and Kay and said, "I have been a Christian for many years. But I have to say, today my faith has taken on new dimensions. Lindsey's fever is gone. The tenderness in her stomach seems better."

Dr. Endur said, "Lindsey, are you hungry?" She was able to answer, "Yes. I'd like a cheeseburger with fries." Dr. Endur laughed and turned to the nurses, instructing them to fulfill Lindsey's request. One of them left immediately to get her some food.

As all eyes were on Lindsey, Rosie stepped off to the side of the hospital room. Nobody really noticed, but Rebecca looked over to see what Rosie was doing. Rosie had her Bible open and was hugging it to her chest. Looking up, Rosie kept repeating, "Thank You, Lord Jesus." It was like Rosie was so connected with Heaven that she brought Heaven into that room.

Dr. Endur told Roger and Kay that they would monitor Lindsey and complete some tests to see where she was at with her cancer. And if there was no sign of further infection, and Lindsey continued gaining strength each day, he would be discharging her. Roger and Kay could scarcely believe what they were hearing. But when they looked over at Lindsey, they knew it was true.

It took time for the room to clear out, for good-byes to be said and hugs to be exchanged. When Don and Rebecca walked Rosie out of the room after saying good-bye, they all had great hopes that the tests would be good. Rosie didn't say much on the ride home with Rebecca. Rebecca could tell Rosie was deep in prayer, still, even though she wasn't speaking out loud. Don followed behind them.

Rebecca stopped in front of Rosie's house, not even wanting her to have to walk across the street. Rebecca got out, opened Rosie's car door, and walked her up to her front door, making sure she got in safely. Rosie turned to Rebecca as she stood inside, and she said only one thing, "To God be the glory." Rebecca knew Rosie didn't want any thanks given to her. But Rebecca had to say, "Thank you, Rosie. Our faith grew today because you shared the strength of your faith in Jesus with all of us." Rosie just smiled, and gave a small wave good-bye as she shut the door.

Don was out of his car when Rebecca pulled into the driveway. They couldn't help but just hug each other, and then they walked into the house…changed people. They had no idea where they would go from here.

But they both knew they would never go back to who they were before. It had been a day like no other.

36

After a miraculous night, it would seem all of life changed. But it didn't. Rebecca went back to work on Thursday morning, Don continued looking for a job while he waited to hear from San Antonio, and Rosie tended to her garden across the street. All seemed normal, until Kay called about a week later. She was crying again. They knew Lindsey had been released from the hospital two days after Rosie prayed over her, and tests had been done to see where her cancer was at. Now Kay was calling...

"Rebecca!!" Kay almost shouted through the phone.

"Yes?" Rebecca didn't know how to respond to Kay's emotional outburst.

"Dr. Endur just called. He said that in all the tests they did on Lindsey, there is no sign of cancer anywhere in her body! Anywhere! And Lindsey is feeling better and stronger every day!" Kay was really crying now, and Rebecca knew it was a happy, relieved cry! Rebecca started to cry, also.

"Oh, Kay! That is soooo good! Sooo amazing!"

"I know! Rebecca, I have heard about the power of prayer. But I have never seen its results so up close and personal."

"Me either! Wow!" Rebecca thought back to how she said she wanted to experience something like this, and now she was...they all were!

Kay said, "I have a lot of people to call. But Roger and I wanted you and Don to be some of the first to know. Having you there with us that night meant the world to us. And that you called Rosie to pray...how can I thank you enough?!"

"Well, you know what Rosie would say about that—all the thanks go to Jesus. Rosie wouldn't want us to credit her with any of this." Rebecca could already hear Rosie voicing those words.

"Oh, I know! But we will be forever indebted to Rosie for her part in this. I'll talk with you soon! Please let Don know, and of course, Rosie!"

"I will. Right now!" Rebecca knew her next stop would be across the street after she spoke to Don.

As Kay was hanging up, Rebecca heard her say, "God is good! Talk to you soon."

Rebecca quickly went upstairs to Don's office...it was strange that she was saying that now—*Don's office*. She knocked rapidly on the door, not wanting to wait a minute to tell him. Don said, "Come on in!"

Opening the door, Rebecca burst out with, "Don! Kay just called! Lindsey has no sign of cancer left in her body! All the tests came back good!"

Don jumped up, and came over to give Rebecca a big hug. She hugged him tightly back! Even though they still hadn't had the heart-to-heart about the details of their dinner conversation, their relationship was more relaxed. Watching God work to heal Lindsey made God so real to them. They even started to read the Bible together. It seemed whatever they read, God spoke to them in a more profound way than before—especially Scriptures on healing.

Rebecca said, "I'm going across the street to tell Rosie. Would you like to go with me?"

"I sure would. Thanks for asking me. I haven't as yet been able to really connect with Rosie after that day. I know that you and she have great conversations about God. I look forward to getting to know Rosie in that way more."

"She's awesome, Don. I hope you can."

Don and Rebecca practically ran down the stairs and out the front door. Rosie was, thankfully, on her front porch, having just finished up some gardening. She saw them coming, with smiles on their faces. Rosie already knew, not only in her spirit, but in the faces of her neighbors, that Lindsey was well. When Don and Rebecca walked onto her porch, Rosie was already giving her thanks to God.

Rebecca called out, "Rosie! Lindsey's tests came back good! No sign of cancer! The prayers worked, Rosie! They worked!"

Rosie smiled. She shut her eyes and nodded. With a look of peace and gratitude on her face she said, "Our sweet Lord. Oh, how He loves us. Lindsey will be fine. She will be fine. We praise You, Jesus!" Then she looked at Don and Rebecca and said, "Come and sit with me a while. It's been quite the wait to hear this good news. I have been praying each day for that precious child."

Don and Rebecca took a seat on Rosie's porch, and the three of them sat their rocking away with happiness. After a time, Don spoke up. "Rosie, I want to thank you."

"For Lindsey? That was God's doing, Don. All God."

"Yes. I'm coming to understand that more. But what's also on my heart is to thank you for all that you have poured into Bec. She talks about you, and how you have taught her so many things about God. I am new at this Christianity thing, too, so I know how valuable it is to have people who will help in the process of learning who Jesus is. Roger has been a help to me, and the men's group I go to is a big help."

Rosie listened. She was never too quick to speak. Rosie wanted to make sure that Don was done before she said anything. When he seemed to be, Rosie said, "Well, Don. You are right. We need to have people around us who help us in our walk with Jesus each day. The world pulls at us, in so many different directions. We need to be there for each other for encouragement. That is what Rebecca and I have been doing these past months. And she has blessed me in so many ways. When I see what God is doing in Rebecca, and the peace she is starting to live in, my heart is full of joy."

Don responded sincerely, "I've seen it. It makes me happy, too."

Don turned and addressed Rebecca. "Bec, I hope you don't mind if I say some things to Rosie?"

Rebecca nodded in affirmation, "Yeah, sure." But she was wondering where Don was going with this?

Don faced Rosie again, and continued on. "Rosie, Bec is not just the woman I was once in love with so many years ago, she is even more than that now. She is a woman of God that I enjoy being around like never before—especially since returning from San Antonio. Bec is comforting. She has changed in ways that maybe I am only able to see because I believe God is changing me, too. I heard somewhere, about difficult situations, that 'God worked it out, but He had to work it out of *me* first.' I believe that to be true. Since allowing Jesus to be my Savior, God has been working things out of me that needed to go, while He was working out the details of my life. And I know that God continues to work in my heart each day."

Don paused. He looked at Rebecca to see if she was okay with what he was saying to Rosie. Rebecca seemed to be fine, which Don felt gave him license to dive in even deeper.

"I'm sure Bec has shared our struggles with you, Rosie. And I appreciate how you have been there for her. I wasn't a terrible husband. Would you say that is true, Bec?" Rebecca nodded in agreement again. Don continued, "But I could have been so much better. If we had God properly positioned in our lives during our marriage, I believe we would have never needed to divorce. Even with all that we were going through, we could have worked it out. We could have gotten through the disappointments and the hurts with God's help. The pastor at church talked about God being our *first* love, and how that will help us to love others. I know now that is what keeps a marriage secure. We can't do it in our own strength. Keeping our eyes on Jesus helps us not to focus on what we think is lacking in our mate. I know now, if I had been looking to God when we were married, I could have trusted more in God's plan for our lives. And if that plan meant that we were not to have our own children, I know that God could have satisfied that desire in me in a different way—one of God's choosing. But instead, I allowed that longing to turn into anger, and I took that out anger on Bec when it was not her fault. I am truly sorry for that."

Rosie and Rebecca were patiently listening to Don. Rebecca wiped away some tears. They all could sense that the Holy Spirit was there with them on the porch.

Don continued. "I don't know where I'm going with all this. But I sense God wanting me to share it with not only Bec, but you, too, Rosie, because my heart is full of gratitude for your help. Without God in our lives, we would not be here with you today, Rosie. We wouldn't have been at Lindsey's bedside with Roger and Kay. I would have been off somewhere else, doing my own thing, having never moved back in with Bec because she would have still been angry with me for the way I treated our marriage. But because of God, we have experienced things we never would have expected. And Bec and I both know that our lives will never, should never, be the same again."

Don waited a bit before continuing. It seemed the Holy Spirit was speaking things to him that he needed to process. "What's coming to me now is that I believe God is having me tell you all of this to say, if God can heal cancer in a young woman, I know, without a doubt, that He can heal the 'cancer' that destroyed our marriage. I believe that is exactly what Jesus has been doing these past months. And I know...wow...uh...this is going to sound crazy...umm...and it is not AT ALL what I expected this day to hold." Don was stammering a bit, seemingly shocked at the words that were coming to him... "But I truly sense that the Holy Spirit is prompting me to say something right here, right now, with you as our witness, Rosie."

At that, Don got up from his chair and knelt in front of Rebecca. And before Rebecca even had time to think about it, Don took her hand saying, "Bec. I love you. I have always loved you. But the love I have for you now is different. It is a love that I know comes from our Father above. Because of God's unfailing love, I know I can trust what I am about to ask you... If you will consent to be my wife again, nothing would make me happier. I'm not even asking you to give me an answer today, because no one is more surprised than I am that God has me on bended knee before you right now...so please take your time. There is no pressure here. But I want you to know, and I believe God wants you to know, that I love you with all my heart. And if you will give me a chance to be your husband again, I will dedicate myself to God first, and then to you; letting it be God's love that will sustain us the rest of our days together on this earth."

There was silence all around, until Rosie started humming. Maybe she wanted to give Rebecca more time to answer, maybe God was prompting Rosie to help ease what could be a "No" answer with a song. But then, Rosie stopped humming. No song came from her. She got quiet, and she looked over at Rebecca. Rosie could tell God was working in Rebecca's heart, and silence was needed.

With Don still on bended knee, Rebecca looked at Don and spoke with a calmness that surprised even her.

"Don. What I have experienced since I said, 'Yes' to Jesus has been nothing short of miraculous. My heart has changed in ways I never thought possible. The anger I once felt, not only toward you, but toward most everyone, has melted into forgiveness. I know that can only be the work of Jesus. Rosie has taught me so many things about how God works in our lives, and I have to tell you, in the beginning, I was not buying it. It seemed a bunch of hocus pocus. But over time, and with good friends like Rosie, Nelson, and Jennifer, I have seen God in action. I have seen how God's love works. I have seen how broken the world is without a Savior—how broken my life was without Jesus."

Don was listening, not knowing what to expect. Rosie was watching the two of them, praying for God's will in their lives.

Rebecca went on, "While you were in San Antonio, God was working many changes in my heart, changes that I have yet to share with you. I learned what the Bible has to say about divorce, and marriage, and a lot of other stuff. It was hard to hear and hard to read. I wasn't sure I wanted anything to do with it...actually, I was pretty sure I didn't want anything to do with it. It felt like I was being pressured into doing something against my will just because it was God's will. I didn't like that. But I have continued to pray about it, and ask God's help in wanting His will above my own—that is definitely new to me. And up until this very moment, I didn't think it was working. I didn't think God was hearing my prayers for help, even though we were getting along better, especially since you returned from your trip. But getting back together with you still seemed out of the question. I have to admit, I'm inspired by what I witnessed with Lindsey. I can't help but think how God used that as part of His plan to show us His amazing healing power and love. We saw it! How cool is that?"

Don smiled and said, "Yeah! I'm with you! That was a life changer for me."

Rebecca continued on, "But now, Don...I think...no, I *know*, what God is doing here is not only *His will* for my life, but what *I want* for my life, too. Nelson told me that when we delight ourselves in God, He will give us our heart's desires. I feel that change in me. I sense God answering my prayers even as we speak. I know now with God as my *first love,* He is filling me with a love for you that I have never experienced before. It is intense, and it is real. More real than the first time we said, 'I do.' I know that I will still have struggles along the way. There will probably be times when I will wonder what it is I've done? But from what I have learned so far about God, I can trust that God will help those parts of my heart continue to heal. When I am not wanting to be in line with His will, I will trust that God will help me through those doubts and fears." Then Rebecca gave a chuckle, which lightened the intense mood between them, as she said, "And the parts that I struggle with, I know I can run over here to Rosie and she will open up the Bible, and she will set me straight!" They all laughed at that.

Don stood up, and taking Rebecca's hand, he lifted her out of the chair to face him. She was smiling with a joy that helped Don know, this was no accident today. This was okay. This had been perfectly planned out by their loving God.

"Bec, after hearing what you have been saying, I feel free to fully ask you then on this day, will you marry me...again?"

Rebecca paused just a moment or two and then said the words she never thought she would say, "I will be happy to be your wife...again."

Rosie couldn't help but applaud what she just witnessed! What a glorious day it was! Rosie then began to sing the song God placed on her heart. Don and Rebecca sat back down in their chairs rocking to the music that filled their souls. As they sat there holding hands on Rosie's porch—their hearts were full, happy, and amazed. Rosie's song helped to speak what they couldn't possibly find the words to express.

Amazing grace, how sweet the sound, that saved a wretch like me.
I once was lost, but now I'm found. Was blind but now I see.
'Twas grace that taught my heart to fear. And grace my fears relieved.
How precious did that grace appear, the hour I first believed.
Through many dangers, toils, and snares. We have already come.
'Twas grace that brought us safe thus far, and grace will lead us home.
When we've been there 10,000 years, bright shining as the sun.
We've no less days to sing God's praise, than when we first begun.

Don and Rebecca looked at each other as Rebecca cheerfully said, "We have a wedding to plan!"

Rosie smiled and said, "I know the perfect garden setting!"

37

Late in October on a warm fall evening, Pastor Matt from Don and Rebecca's church officiated their wedding. They gathered with a few friends among the remaining flowers in Rosie's garden. Roger stood next to Don, Kay stood next to Rebecca, and Rosie's voice lifted above it all in praise for all that God had done.

Pastor Matt said that everyone in attendance was witnessing the miracle of God's healing power. He spoke out of Ephesians 5, beginning with, "Husbands are to love their wives with the same love Christ showed to the church." Pastor Matt said, "A man is actually loving himself when he loves his wife, and a wife is loving her husband when she respects him."

Don and Rebecca carefully listened to their pastor speak words of truth into their marriage as he said, "Revelation 2 includes a letter written to the church in Ephesus. Don and Rebecca wanted me to read it to you today, even though it doesn't seem very 'wedding-like.' It is important to them as a reminder about not just working *at* life together, but focusing on God *in* life together. The letter says, *'I know all the things you do. I have seen your hard work and your patient endurance. I know you don't tolerate evil people. You have examined the claims of those who say they are apostles but are not. You have discovered they are liars. You have patiently suffered for me without quitting. But I have this complaint against you. You don't love me or each other as you did at first. Look how far you have fallen! Turn back to me and do the works you did at first....Anyone with ears to hear must listen to the Spirit and understand what he is saying to the churches. To everyone who is victorious I will give fruit from the tree of life in the paradise of God.'"*

Pastor Matt continued, "Today is the day to remember where love originates. It is most poignant here in this beautiful garden setting because the Lord created Adam and placed him in the Garden of Eden. Then He said it was not good for man to be alone, so he was given Eve. But love suffered because man took his eyes off God. That still affects us to this day. Ever since then, our Father in Heaven has yearned for all of us to turn back to Him. When Jesus was asked about the most important commandment, His answer was, *You must love the Lord your God with all your heart, all your soul, all your mind, and all your strength.' The second is equally important: 'Love your neighbor as yourself.' No other commandment is greater than these.* Don and Rebecca have taken these words to heart. They know this is what has brought them to this day. They know with God's love as their first priority, their love for each other will be strengthened. Their friend, Nelson, is now going to read a passage of Scripture they have chosen."

Nelson walked forward, giving a nod and a smile to both Don and Rebecca. He read out of Ephesians 5, *"Follow God's example in everything you do, because you are his dear children. Live a life filled with love for others, following the example of Christ, who loved you and gave himself as a sacrifice to take away your sins. And God was pleased, because that sacrifice was like sweet perfume to him."* The sweet perfume this evening in Rosie's garden is a reminder to all of us. Breathe it in for a moment. Don and Rebecca would like us all to take a look around and see that the Lord is good."

As Nelson took his seat next to Jennifer, Pastor Matt continued sharing about God's plans for marriage.

"God has worked amazing miracles in Don and Rebecca's life through their obedience. Some may say obedience is the way to Heaven. But as we read in Ephesians 2:9, *'Salvation is not a reward for the good things we have done, so none of us can boast about it.'* Don and Rebecca are not here today trying to earn their way to Heaven by obedience. Their obedience is because they are so grateful for the gift of eternal life through Jesus Christ which they have already received. Through learning about Jesus' death and resurrection, they know that all their past mistakes have been washed away by the blood of Christ. What Don and Rebecca desire today is to honor Jesus' name, and the love He showed to mankind, by renewing their relationship as husband and wife. They have written some words for each other that they would like to share.

Don turned toward Rebecca taking both her hands in his.

"Bec. Wow! You are beautiful. I see God's beauty in your eyes. It's something this world does not contain. You are more lovely than the most beautiful blossom here in this garden. God planted His seed of faith in you, and I have seen it take root and grow into something that can only be Heaven sent. I am so blessed to be able to once again share this life with you. I promise you on this day, in front of these witnesses, to love you with a love that is greater than what I have to give. I will daily go to Jesus, and ask His help in being the man that I should be. I will ask for God's guidance, and I will follow it as best I can. And when we find that to be lacking, I will be open to talking with you about it, praying with you about it, and growing together in our faith and walk with Jesus. I promise to continue to grow through reading my Bible and prayer. I promise to keep men around me who will hold me accountable, and to gather with other believers as often as we can. I will use all that God gives me to be the man of God He desires me to be, so I can be the husband you need for me to be. With the Holy Spirit's strength in me, you can trust that I will have your best interest at heart, and I will love you as Christ loves His Body, the Church. Thank you for trusting me with your love."

Don then placed a new wedding ring on Rebecca, and kissed it, sealing it with his love.

Rebecca spoke next. Looking up at Don, holding onto both of his hands, she said, "Don, this is the day that the Lord has made. I am rejoicing and am glad in it. Thank you for not giving up on me. Thank you for loving me with the love that God has placed in your heart for me. I long to be the woman of God that the Bible talks about. I see in you the desire to follow God, too, and that gives me great confidence in exchanging these vows with you today. I never thought when I gave my heart to Jesus, that He would give me a heart that would be able to love again the way that I love you today. I didn't know what to expect, but I know now that it was beyond what I could have comprehended. You have been patient, and kind. I appreciate you. Many will not understand what has happened here, how a man and woman can divorce and then love one another again. We wouldn't have understood it either. But now we are living it, and as time goes on, I hope many will witness God's amazing healing power and love, and be encouraged by it. I know, with God as my first love, my love for you will grow even deeper and truer as we grow old together. I give you this ring as a symbol of God's redeeming love."

Rebecca placed the ring on Don's finger from their first wedding, and kissed it.

After their vows were exchanged, the guests enjoyed the wedding festivities while Don and Rebecca took some time to walk over into the corner of Rosie's garden. They sat on the little white bench there, wanting to soak in all that was happening. It was a clear night with just a gentle breeze…the peace of God surrounded them.

From across the yard, they could see Rosie smiling and chatting with Jennifer. Don and Rebecca talked of how Rosie had been such a powerful force in their lives. They knew Rosie set an example they would follow on how to live for Jesus each day. And though it was hard for Jennifer to spend time again in this garden, after having Justin's service here in the spring, she told them she wouldn't have missed this celebration for anything. They could see God was healing her shattered heart. It would take time. But one day perhaps, God would bring someone new into Jennifer's life.

Over on the other side of the patio, Lindsey was standing with her parents talking with Nelson. They could only imagine from the look on Nelson's face, what that conversation held. Nelson knew about the prayers for Lindsey's healing. But now he was witnessing how well she was doing...her hair was short, and cute, and her strength was coming back day by day. She had a bounce in her step again. Rebecca knew this was touching Nelson deeply after the heartache he had been through with Jill's passing. Today was a day to rejoice in so many ways, and they could tell Nelson was embracing it all. He was such a good, godly man.

This was the first time, too, that Lindsey had seen Rosie since she prayed for her. When Lindsey first arrived at Rosie's house, they greeted each other like they had always known one another. Of course, Rosie offered Lindsey a cookie. Rosie never took these healings for granted. She knew that God answered prayers in many different ways. Rosie saw many go Home to Heaven after praying for them. But that never stopped her from praying. Seeing how well Lindsey was doing reminded Rosie why.

Don held onto Rebecca's hand as they sat and talked. In lifting Rebecca's hand a bit, the setting sun sparkled off the single diamond Don had chosen to signify not only his love for Rebecca, but their love for God. Don was familiar with Isaiah 61:3. After going through hard times, God will give *a crown of beauty instead of ashes* and *festive praise instead of despair*. Don inscribed this new ring with just three words, "Beauty from Ashes." Don's heart swelled with thankfulness for all that God had done. And even though the job in San Antonio passed on hiring him, Don knew that the right job would come in God's timing—and wherever it was, he now knew it *would include* Rebecca. Don turned and gave Rebecca a gentle kiss on the cheek, and she leaned her head onto his shoulder. Sitting there, their conversation grew quiet. Just being together in that moment was enough.

To someone looking on, this might have seemed like the perfect ending to a fairy-tale. But after all they had been through to get to this day, Don and Rebecca knew it was only the beginning of a real-life lived out with Jesus Christ.

A LITTLE BACK STORY
ABOUT THIS BOOK FROM THE AUTHOR.

It seemed God put it on my heart to write a book of fiction. I was surprised, since I hadn't read fiction in years. I waited a few days, and then the story started to come to me. I wrote the first few paragraphs in my phone. When I told my friend, Lynn, what I was doing, she responded like I expected. She said, "You don't even read fiction." After sharing those first paragraphs with her, she said, "Keep writing." After reading it to my husband, he said the same thing.

I visited FILOLI the day I started writing this book. It's a garden estate near where I live. Coming out of the ballroom at the estate, there was a picture on the wall. It said, "Rosie in the garden." I don't even remember what the picture looked like. I just remember thinking, that's a good title for the book. I had no idea who Rosie would even be.

Now I had the title of the book, and two characters. Rebecca, who I knew very little about except that she attended church and said "yes" to Jesus in the first few paragraphs I'd written. And Rosie, who I knew nothing about other than her name would be on the cover. Each chapter came after a time of prayer. The words would pour out of my fingers onto the keyboard almost like a waterfall! I would watch the story unfold almost as if I were reading it. If Rosie was thinking something, it would be revealed as I wrote it. When Rebecca walked out her front door and noticed something, I would "see" it at the same time she did. I never knew fiction writing could be so much fun!

This book was written in a little less than two months. After seven months, it was available for readers—God's number of completion. A second book, *Rosie on the plane,* took three months to write, while this book was being worked on. The second book is actually a prequel to the first. The third book, *Rosie at the lake,* is being written as I type this. I didn't know there would be multiple Rosie books, or that they would focus on Mentorship, Discipleship, and Fellowship. It's been God's plan, not mine, since chapter one. Perhaps I've merely been His "pen" in this project, letting the ink of His Holy Spirit flow freely. My only desire along the way, was that this work of fiction would tell the whole Truth of the Gospel of Jesus Christ.

Everything I have lived through, heard about, and people I have known, get all stirred together into a big pot of writing "stew" and come out as the characters and situations in these books. I guess this is how it's done. Who knew? To my friends and family, if you think you see yourself as a character in this book, it could be you! Hey, I'm in here, too. But remember, it will only be a small *part of you* because no one character is all one person. So, enjoy the parts you like about yourself, and tell yourself that the parts you don't like must be someone else! I hope you have as much fun reading this as I had writing it!

For the cover, God provided in such an amazing way. I was visiting my friend Lynn's Bible study group in Oakdale. It was held at Sara's home. When I saw Sara's backyard, I knew I needed to take some pictures of it. She graciously agreed to that request. The yard was beautifully landscaped. But there weren't many flowers in the hot summer heat of the San Joaquin Valley of California. We toured around the yard, and I saw some red roses lying on a rock. I took many shots of that, and one worked perfectly for the story here. God impressed it upon me that there be a diagonal design on the cover. The rock you see provided that. God is amazing! Also, hidden in the rock a dove can be seen. Thank you, René, for spotting that. Notice the large rose of "Rosie" in the light, and the not-yet bloomed rose of "Rebecca" moving from the darkness into the light. To add to all this, Sara told me that her first name was really Rosemary...she had been called Rosie as a child. The cover picture was actually taken in Rosie's garden!

ACKNOWLEDGMENTS
GIVING THANKS

All praise and glory go to the Father in Heaven, the Son at His right hand, and the Holy Spirit who dwells in all those who have given their lives to Christ Jesus.

Thank you, Jim, for over 40 years of love and support. With Jesus, we are a cord of three strands that cannot be easily broken. You make these books possible with your techie expertise.

Connie Fulmer Dixon, you encouraged me to keep writing. I never thought it would be fiction. But here we are! You continue to help with the edits, and I appreciate you so much!! In your busy life of servitude, you make time for this, too. I thank you with all my heart!

Jim, Lynn, Bob, and Paul, you read through this before it was a printed book. Thanks for your encouragement when fiction is so new to me. This has been fun! Thanks for joining me on the journey!

Karen, Jeanette, Lynn, and Sandra, thank you for taking the time to proof read all or parts of this. You've helped iron out leftover wrinkles.

My brother Keith, thank you for thinking of Rosie at work. Your "donation" provided what was needed for the Mentorship picture page.

ABOUT THE AUTHOR
diane.dcshorepublishing.com

Diane C. Shore lives in San Ramon, CA with her husband Jim of more than 40 years. They are enjoying these years together after raising three sons, and now being the grandparents of six. Writing and sharing stories about God is Diane's passion. God continues to lead her and show her new ways of how He expresses His love toward us each day. Whether it is sitting one-on-one with someone, or speaking to a group, Diane is excited to boldly proclaim the Good News of Jesus Christ and how He works in our daily lives.

WATCH FOR ROSIE II — COMING SOON!

OTHER BOOKS BY DIANE C. SHORE

ISBN: 978-0990523161

ISBN: 978-0990523130

A true story of what Jesus can do with a broken heart.

*It*STARTED *in the*DARK

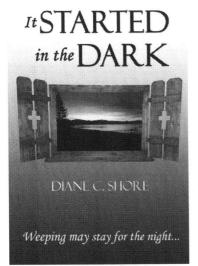

ISBN: 978-0990523109

A true story of what Jesus can do with a broken heart.

*It*ENDED *in the*LIGHT

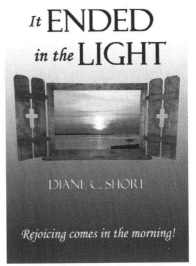

ISBN: 978-0990523147

Made in the USA
San Bernardino, CA
10 December 2017